Praise for Ernessa T. Carter's *32 Candles*

"From page one, [Carter] delivers the goods. . . . *32 Candles* is sure to resonate for those who thought themselves unworthy of true love . . . but were pleasantly surprised."

—Examiner.com

"I loved *32 Candles*. It's ridiculously good. It's my favorite fiction debut of the year. . . . *32 Candles* is sad, funny, smart, and entertaining, basically everything a great book should be."

—ColorOnline.com

"The author creates a heroine that is multifaceted, quirky, humorous and above all, endearing. . . . *32 Candles* [is] a laugh-out-loud read that's never disheartening or too depressing. . . . Hang on for the ride."

—*The Afro-American Newspapers*

"[Davie's] need for sweet revenge adds a welcome dark edge."

—*Publishers Weekly*

"A debut tragicomic romance. . . . Potent and well rendered."

—*Kirkus Reviews*

"First-time novelist Ernessa T. Carter has created a quirky and likable character in Davidia Davie Jones."

—*Network Journal*

" 'My gawd, this was a good book.' Those were the first words out of my mouth when I finished this 335-page read. . . . This is an easy five out of five stars and one of my top five favorite fiction novels I've ever read in my entire adulthood."

—AssociatedContent.com

# 32 CANDLES

# 32 CANDLES

### ERNESSA T. CARTER

Amistad
*An Imprint of* HarperCollins*Publishers*

HarperCollins books may be purchased for educational, business, or sales promotional use. For information please write: Special Markets Department, HarperCollins Publishers, 10 East 53rd Street, New York, NY 10022.

A hardcover edition of this book was first published in 2010 by Amistad, an imprint of HarperCollins Publishers.

FIRST AMISTAD PAPERBACK EDITION PUBLISHED 2011.

*Designed by Lisa Stokes*

The Library of Congress has cataloged the hardcover edition as follows:

Carter, Ernessa T.
    32 candles : a novel / Ernessa T. Carter.
        p.   cm.
    Summary: "The deftly wry, deeply romantic story of Davie Jones—an 'ugly duckling' from small-town Mississippi with a voice like Tina Turner, who escapes to Los Angeles to try to make it big, and risks losing her soul along the way to finding her fairy tale ending"—Provided by publisher.
    ISBN 978-0-06-195784-0 (hardback)
    1. Women singers—Fiction. 2. Los Angeles (Calif.)—Fiction. I. Title. II. Title: Thirty-two candles.
    PS3603.A777A615   2010
    813'.6—dc22                                                          2009047503

ISBN 978-0-06-195785-7 (pbk.)

11 12 13 14 15   OV/RRD   10 9 8 7 6 5 4 3 2

*To my dearest mother. Wish you were here.*

# CONTENTS

PART I
THEN

# ONE

SO YOU'VE PROBABLY HEARD OF THIS thing by now. It's called life. And it's hard. Even when it looks easy, it's hard. That's pretty much everybody's situation, and it was mine, too.

And on top of the usual business of life, I was ugly. I knew this because I lived in Glass, a little town in western Mississippi, where people aren't ever afraid to tell you how they feel—especially if they're women. In fact, it's impossible for a Southern black woman not to state a thing as she sees it. So they would often come up and say what they were thinking on the subject of my looks, while I was out with Cora, whose beauty offended them.

Cora had caramel-tinted skin—not light enough to be called yellow, not dark enough to be called plain. She was just right, with a heart-shaped face and large brown eyes that kept the title of ugly far from her door.

And there was another thing about Cora that offended the women in our town. She had a lot of friends. A lot of male friends, but not one female friend. That's really why folks hated her.

She was the kind of woman that men met at Westons, the one bar in Glass. She went there near about every night, and some of the time she didn't come home. But a lot of the time she came stumbling in the door, reeking of alcohol, with a guy right behind her.

These were the guys she called her friends if she called them anything at all. And she didn't care if they had a wife or a girlfriend, she'd still bring them home to the one-bedroom shack that she inherited from her mother. She wouldn't even shush them as they walked past her daughter (me), sleeping on the couch in the front room. And she'd show them a good time. From what I could hear, sex with Cora was fun and exciting and *real loud*.

Cora's men were often appreciative of her friendship. I always waited till they had left to get up and use the toilet. And when I walked past her bedroom, sometimes the lights would still be on and I'd see wrinkled money on the nightstand. Or sometimes there'd be a bill that needed paying and Cora would ask one of her friends real pretty if he could take care of it. And I'd watch as he stuck it in his pocket.

I'd guess about seventy percent of the friends that Cora brought home came back for more. I'd also guess that by the time this story begins in the spring of 1984, she had slept with at least half of the husbands and boyfriends in town.

And that's why black Southern ladies, who wouldn't deign to walk on the same side of the street as her most days, would go out of their way to come over to us in Greeley's Mini-Mart and say things like, "Oh dear, when you planning on putting a comb through this child's head?"

Or, "She sure is dark, ain't she? You'd lose that child in too much night."

Or, "Why, she didn't inherit none of your looks, did she? Maybe she got that face from her daddy." A beat. "Whoever that is."

And Cora would smile, mean as a snake, and say, "She named after him."

Which of course didn't tell them nothing, since my name was Davidia, and there were at least a dozen Davids in town. Cora never said, but I always suspected she'd done that on purpose.

I had serious doubts that she actually knew who my daddy was. I wouldn't be surprised if she had just decided on the name that would hurt the most people. I think she liked the idea of wives and girlfriends, lying awake at night, wondering, *Is that his child? Is that dark, nappy-haired thing his child?*

And in their eyes, this made me even uglier. It made me so hideous that they could justify going up to Cora and calling me ugly straight to her face, as if I wasn't standing right there.

I always wanted to tell them not to bother, that insults against me slid off Cora's back like the hot water of the quick five-minute showers she took after her men left.

Cora didn't like me. Sometimes I thought she might have even hated me. But I knew for sure she didn't like me.

It wasn't the hitting. All Southern black mamas hit. It's in their nature, like it's in a jaguar's nature to attack on sight anything that ain't a jaguar.

But the only time Cora ever touched me was to hit me. That's how I knew she didn't like me.

So when those women would come over to us in the mini-mart, I'd look at them, thinking, *Don't you see you can't hurt her through me? She's not even holding my hand for God's sake.*

Still, I never said anything when they called me ugly. I wasn't much of a talker. This is actually an understatement. I should say that I never ever talked unless I absolutely had to—and sometimes not even then.

MY GRANDMAMA TOOK care of me until I was five. Then she died and Cora moved in. It actually took me a while to figure out that this woman was my mother. I had never met her before and my grandmama had only referred to her in passing as a poor lost soul who still hadn't found her way to Jesus.

I'm still not sure when I put two and two together, but by the time I was six I had figured out who she was, how alcohol smelled, and what sex sounded like through a couple of thin walls.

Also, I had figured out how to amuse myself after Cora went out for the evening. And the night that I stopped talking was like many of the ones that had come before it.

As soon as the door clicked behind Cora, I went to get two towels out of the linen closet. These towels were my Tina Turner hair and my Tina Turner dress.

I took off all my clothes and wrapped one towel around me. Then I secured the other one to my head, using a shoelace from one of my Payless ProWing sneakers, like one of them Indian headbands.

Hair in place, I got some lipstick out of Cora's makeup tray and put it on my lips. I made dark red circles on my cheeks and smeared it on my eyelids, too. This was my Tina Turner face.

Then I dug Cora's red high heels out from behind the radiator, where I had been hiding them all summer. These were the magic shoes that made my entire Tina Turner transformation complete.


CORA DIDN'T REALLY believe in buying me anything beyond what was strictly necessary for my ongoing survival. But a week before that night, one of her friends had given me a black Barbie with yellow wood glue in its hair.

"We can't get the glue out," he said, and that was all. He handed it to me and walked to the back of the house with Cora.

I ran my finger along the smooth yellow stripes that bound her strands of hair together and made her unwanted by some other black girl.

"Your name is Gloria. You can be my backup singer," I said to her.

Gloria and I were both outcasts, which is probably why we worked so well together.

The night I stopped talking, my black Barbie introduced me to the imaginary forms of the other twenty kids in my kindergarten class.

"Presenting Davidia Jones!"

I imagined the crowd clapping, while I loaded Cora's Ike and Tina Turner *Workin' Together* album onto the record player.

Then I sang the entire side two for them, word for word, from "Funkier Than a Mosquita's Tweeter" to "Let It Be." By the time I got to the end, my classmates were on their feet and clapping.

"Sang another one! Sang another one, Monkey Night!" Everybody was cheering and crying and jumping up and down like they were at a Michael Jackson concert.

In real life, Monkey Night is what the other kids in kindergarten called me. Mississippi may have had some of the lowest standardized test scores in the nation, but I'll tell you this right now: The kids at my school excelled in creative cruelty. They nicknamed me Monkey Night within three weeks of making my acquaintance, because I was "ugly like a monkey and black as night."

I was going to reset the needle on Cora's record player for an encore, but Gloria stirred in my hand. "No," she said, her falsetto voice shrill with anger. "Not unless you stop calling her Monkey Night! Her name is Davidia!"

The imaginary faces of the kids in the audience filled with remorse.

Perry Pointer, who was always putting gum on my seat and kicking me real hard in the shins, was the first to speak. "I'm sorry, Davidia," he said. "Please be my friend."

He brought a candy bar out of his pocket. "I'll give you a PayDay if you be my friend."

"No," Gloria said for me. "She don't want to be your friend, Perry Pointer. You don't deserve no friends."

Perry started to cry, but Gloria ignored him and said to the other kindergartners, "The *rest of you* can be Davidia's friend, if you stop calling her names and talking about her. If you do that, she'll be your friend and sing you more songs."

Everybody cheered, including Tanisha Harris, who was the most popular girl in kindergarten because she always wore cool beads at the ends of her cornrows, which her mama changed out every day to match her dresses.

That night, she was wearing blue beads and a blue sequined dress. I always took the time to plot out exactly what Tanisha would wear in these imaginary scenarios, because she was usually the one that led the crowd in chanting my name.

"Davidia! Davidia!" she shouted. And the rest of the kids joined her, getting louder and louder until I put back on the Tina Turner record and started singing and dancing to "Proud Mary"—my encore song.

"*Big River keep on rolling . . . Proud Mary keep on—*"

"What the fuck you doing?" came Cora's voice from behind me.

I was worried even before I saw her face, because I didn't smell the alcohol on her. Cora's general hatred for everyone and everything only seemed to burn hotter when she hadn't had a taste of something. But I was a little braver back then, so I did turn around.

My eyes searched for and found the reason for her return. There was a green and white packet of cigarettes in her hand. Only Cora would come all the way back from the bar to get her cigarettes, the particular Virginia Slims she liked, because of their ad campaign slogan, "You've come a long way, baby!"

How she managed to figure these liberated ads had anything to do with her, I do not know. But she was faithful to them, would even drive back from the edge of town to make sure she had them, since no self-respecting Glass man would ever smoke Virginia Slims, and no self-respecting Glass woman would ever talk to her, much less allow her to bum a cigarette.

"What the fuck you doing?" She took a step toward me. Loomed. "What the fuck you doing?"

"I'm Tina Turner," I said, before my mouth could catch up to my good sense.

She backhanded me, sending my Tina Turner hair flying off my head. Then she beat me. Beat me until both of us were exhausted and I lay on the floor burning all over and naked except for the red high heels. There were tears coming out of my eyes. I knew, because I could feel them on my hot face. But they didn't feel like they were coming from me exactly. They felt like my body's physical reaction to the situation, like sweating in the summer. I knew the tears weren't coming out of my heart, because all I felt was anger at myself.

I stared at my Tina Turner dress crumpled on the floor. Away from the magic of my body, it had morphed back into a towel. If only I were bigger, if only I were faster—

"I better stop before I break something," Cora said. I had no idea whether she meant break some part of herself or me. She snatched the shoes off my feet. "Don't let me catch you in my shoes again, you hear me, heifer?"

I heard her.

"You sounded like a goddamn saw, carrying on like that." The click of her cigarette lighter came from above me. She lit her Virginia Slim and took a drag.

That's when I decided to stop singing and, while I was at it, to stop talking. At that moment, it seemed like it was probably in my best interest.

THE THING ABOUT being really dark is that you don't bruise. I went to school the next day, and nobody noticed anything different, except that I had stopped talking all of a sudden.

Miss Karen, my kindergarten teacher, told me to my stone-silent face that I was just going through a phase. But a few months later, she started withholding toys and other things from me unless I said thank you. Out loud. I guessed she had let go of that "phase" theory.

Quitting toys cold turkey was like most things, I discovered: hard to be without at first, but after a while you got used to it.

With enough time and patience you can get used to anything. Believe that.

THOSE WERE DARK days, which is why I remain grateful for the discovery of Molly Ringwald movies, two years after I lost Tina Turner.

There was one particularly sad friend of Cora's named Elmer. He worked with her on the assembly line at the Farrell Fine Hair factory, and either he was in true love with her or a straight fool for lost causes, because he seemed to adore my mother.

It wasn't her fault. She didn't encourage his love and made it real clear that he wasn't her only friend. But still . . .

One night he showed up with a box-sized bulge in his left pocket. Even at eight, I recognized it as one of those boxes that jewelry came in. That's what living with Cora had taught me.

"I got something for your mama," he said when I answered the door.

I opened the door wider and looked back at Cora, who was watching a rerun of *Good Times* in her big easy chair.

"I got something for you," he said to her when he got inside the living room.

Cora's eyes lowered to his left pocket. "What you got, baby? Is it in your pants?" She was the queen of saying nasty things in a sweet voice, and Elmer deflated a little. I supposed it was hard for any man to have his jewelry box reduced to a hard-on.

"I got to talk with you about it, first," he said. He pulled a five-dollar bill out of his pocket and handed it to me. "You wanna go into town? See the dollar show on me. And get you some popcorn, too."

I looked at Cora. Sometimes she let me have presents. Sometimes she didn't. And five dollars was a lot of money to give to an eight-year-old.

"She don't need five dollars," she said to Elmer. "Come back with four," she said to me.

I nodded and walked out.

"She still not talking?" I heard Elmer ask her behind me.

"I guess not," Cora said. And then the door closed on that conversation.


THE DOLLAR THEATER in Glass wasn't picky. They pretty much played whatever all the other dollar theaters in the chain were playing, especially if there weren't any black movies available. It was August 1984, and everybody must've been playing *Sixteen Candles*, because that's what was showing at the one movie theater in Glass.

I gave the old black man at the box office window my folded five-dollar.

bill, and he gave me back four wrinkled ones. Then I went into the theater and watched a white movie that didn't have a single black girl in it and loved it. The first time I saw it, I loved it. And as the credits rolled against the backdrop of Molly Ringwald kissing the most popular boy in school over a birthday cake, I cried, because before then, I had not known that unpopular girls could make good.

In fact, I thought, maybe you, Davidia Jones, might one day have the same kind of ending. A Molly Ringwald Ending. Maybe that will happen for you in high school, just like it happened for Molly Ringwald. Yes, maybe a boy, a boy just like Jake Ryan, will come along and transform you from Monkey Night into the luckiest girl in school, because he sees you for what you really are. Special in a good way.

I floated home on long dirt roads and found the house dark when I got to our cement front steps. Elmer's car was parked outside, so I supposed that he and Cora had already had their gift conversation and moved into her bedroom.

But I was wrong. Elmer was still in the house, sitting hunched over in the easy chair when I walked in.

He looked up at me, his eyes red like mine from crying. "Your mama gone to the bar."

My eyes went to the jewelry box that was now in his hand and not on Cora's vanity, as I had expected. At the time, I thought it strange that Cora would turn down jewelry. It would take me years of mainstream movies before I realized that the velvet box had actually housed an engagement ring, the one kind of diamond that Cora's nature prevented her from accepting.

"She don't love me. She don't care if you got a daddy or not," he said. "She don't think about nobody but herself."

More shocking than finding him sitting alone in the dark living room was the realization that this was actually news to him. I was glad that I had already decided to stop talking by then, because I did not have any words for somebody that blind.

But I also didn't have anything else to do, so I sat down on the couch and waited with him. About an hour later, he got up and left, silent as a ghost. And I never saw him again.

I'm still not sure why that scene wasn't enough to kill my newfound sense of romance. I thought about it often during my first year in Los Angeles, and I wondered why it didn't occur to me then that if I kept on down this road of impossible hope, one day that would be me walking out of Cora's house a shell of a human being. Just like Elmer.

# TWO

THE FIRST TIME I SAW HIM, I loved him. Just like I loved *Sixteen Candles* from day one. I spotted him across the street, and I loved him. As he walked toward me, skin the color of sunshine, smile whiter than snow, I loved him.

It was 1991, I was fifteen, and I didn't know his name.

But I knew my mama had lied.

Two years beforehand, she had sneered into her brandy-laced morning coffee and said, "All them people on TV and in the movies falling in love. Now these movies got women in real life losing they mind, talking about, 'I want me some big love.'

"But there ain't no such thing. Believe me, I done slept with too many mens talking about, 'I loves my wife. I loves that girl I go around town with. I got BIG love for them.' Fuck them bitches, I'm telling you, there ain't no such thing."

However, I didn't believe a word of it as I watched this boy walk toward me. Gooseflesh appeared on my dark arms and every nerve in my body rose up like antennas finding their station. And even as my brain turned to static, I recognized these things for what they were. Big Love.

He was tall: six-one, maybe six-two. He had brown eyes that were soft enough to be appealing and a buttery face that was hard enough not to be too pretty. He was wiry with muscle, but not the regular, descended-from-slaves, black boy muscle. He had the kind of body that comes from machines and weights, from actually working out.

That's not what made me love him in an instant, though. I loved him because I could see all the beauty that he carried inside of him. It was practically pouring out of him and spilling onto the sidewalk as he came up to me, awesomely turned out in jeans and a short-sleeved polo.

"Excuse me, do you know where Greeley's Mini-Mart is?"

He had a Southern accent, but he wasn't from around here. I knew this because I had laid eyes on everyone in Glass, and I had never seen him before. I also knew this because his accent was smooth, polished, like he ran all his words under the faucet for a couple of seconds before letting them fall out of his mouth.

I could barely hear his question over the static in my head. It was so loud, and I was at a loss as to how to function now that this vision had walked into my life.

I wondered if this was how Molly Ringwald felt when she met Andrew McCarthy in *Pretty in Pink*.

The first thing I thought to say was "I used to sing Tina Turner at the kindergarten concerts I threw in my head."

The second thing I thought to say was "Everybody calls me Monkey Night."

And the third thing I thought to say was "Cora lied. I believe in Big Love now, because I am in love with you."

In the end, though, I didn't say anything. I pointed across the street, keeping my eyes just beyond his shoulder.

He turned around and chuckled. "Right behind me. Aw, man."

He looked back to me with an embarrassed smile. But it wasn't really embarrassment. Even then I could tell that he was one of those boys who only pretended to be ashamed of himself. I could tell that just from the way he ended our conversation with a "Thank you very much."

I didn't answer. I couldn't answer. I couldn't even smile.

I just watched him walk back into the sunshine. I wondered if that was where he had been born, where he came from. The sun.

No, our first conversation did not go as well as I would've hoped, but I could already feel it. The grabbing hold, the transformation that was now starting to take place just because I had met him. He was my Jake Ryan. And more importantly, he was my Molly Ringwald Ending.

EVERYBODY AT SCHOOL was talking about him the next day. That's how I found out that the boy I was dreaming of was named James C. Farrell.

"His great-grandmama started Farrell Fine Hair—I ain't lying," I heard one girl say to her boyfriend as I put my books away.

"He got two fine-ass sisters," a basketball player said to his buddy, while not paying attention in math class.

The three Farrell siblings, according to hallway and classroom gossip, were the main heirs of the vast Farrell Fine Hair fortune. Their father, who was the president of one of the oldest black hair companies in the United States, had moved his family from Houston, Texas. And now he was working out of the Farrell Fine Hair offices in Columbus, Mississippi, and sending his kids to Robert C. Glass High School.

No one could quite figure out why he had decided to do this. Sure, the main factory was in Glass, but even the floor managers there didn't make their kids go to the local public school. It was like planting silk trees in a cotton field.

"Coach talking about making him quarterback, even though he ain't never been played with us before," Corey Mays, a large football player, said to Dante Hubbard, another football player; they were both in the lunch line behind me.

"Man, that's fucked up," said Dante.

"Well, you know, he from Texas. They for real about playin' that shit out there. And it not like we exactly threatening up state with Pointer."

Perry Pointer was now the most popular guy in school: cute, athletic, dumb, and mean as shit, so of course he was king of Glass High. But from the sound of it, he was about to get his throne straight snatched from him.

And that only made me love James more.

THAT AFTERNOON I saw the Farrell sisters for the first time.

I was walking down the cement steps when they came out the school's main entrance. They strutted like Charlie's Angels, in acid-washed jean skirts and baggy, off-the-shoulder, neon-colored sweatshirts that somehow managed to hug their bodies in all the right places. They even wore heels—and mind you, this was at a time when teenagers never wore heels outside of prom.

Every head turned as they glided past in a cloud of designer clothes and expensive perfume. Even mine. Because seriously, I had never seen anything like them outside of a magazine ad.

I could not help but stare.

Not that they noticed. They walked with straight-ahead eyes and thrown-back shoulders, seemingly unaware of us pie-eyed regular folk. It wasn't a manner I recognized back then, but now that I live in Los Angeles, I realize that the Farrell sisters moved like women who were used to lots and lots of attention. Like celebrities.

They were spectacularly gorgeous, though not necessarily in the same way.

The taller sister had the glowing skin and open face of a Disney princess. You almost expected a bluebird to land on her bare shoulder. But the other sister was chilling to look at, with sandy brown hair and gray eyes so cold, they made Alaska look like a warm destination. I guessed that this was the one named Veronica.

Earlier in the bathroom, I had heard Tanisha Harris, who was now the head cheerleader, say to her friend, "Tammy—that's the younger one. She real nice. She want to try out for the team. But the older one—Veronica—think she too good for that shit. You should see that bitch. She think she all that."

After my first glimpse of Veronica, I would have to accuse the head cheerleader of being wrong. Veronica didn't think she was all that, she knew. Knew in the way that only the very beautiful and the very rich can.

Up until that point, I had trained myself out of wishing for things. I thought that I had learned down to my very bones that I would never be pretty or rich or even liked. And I had accepted it, because at least I was smart, and at least I had books and Molly Ringwald movies to keep me busy.

But now, I stood there with my matted 'fro and my oversized thrift store dress and my shoes that were run down at the heels. I watched those beautiful girls jump into Veronica's red convertible, like they were the Sweet Valley High twins, and I wished. I wished I could be like them. Easy and breezy like a cover girl, with the wind blowing in my naturally straight hair.

I BEGAN TO stalk James the next week. Of course, it didn't start off as stalking. It almost never does. It was more like a research project at first.

The school newspaper did a page three article, entitled "New Kid on the Field," with a pretty complete background on the school's new quarterback, and I clipped it.

The *Glass High Call* informed me that James had been on the honor roll at his old high school. Also, Notre Dame, USC, and just about every college in Texas had sent him letters of interest—but he hoped to attend and play for Princeton. He'd probably get his wish, since he'd scored 1450 on his SAT his junior year—being next in line for the presidency of Farrell Fine Hair probably didn't hurt, either.

According to the article, James didn't have a girlfriend back home in Texas, but the reporter hinted that a certain TH (the same initials as the head cheerleader) already had her eye on him.

I cut the article out and placed it reverent-like between the pages of my hardback edition of *The Color Purple*. It was my favorite book and home to Celie, the black character I identified with most in the world, because she was ugly and got treated ugly but still found her way to a happy ending. Sort of like Molly Ringwald. And exactly like me. Eventually. I hoped.

So I clipped that article and put it in my book. Then I started stealing looks, which was not as easy as it may sound. I was a sophomore and James was a senior, and we didn't have any classes together.

On account of that, getting my daily fill of James required me to first nail down his schedule. For a full week, I carried my entire class load of books around in my backpack, so that I could stand down the hall from his locker and follow him to his classes. If my fellow classmates hadn't already taken to ignoring my silent presence, my stuffed-to-the-gills backpack might have drawn stares or, even worse, questions. But luckily they had grown disinterested in me over the years and had ceased believing that I could get any stranger. It lent me a certain invisibility, which I used to my advantage in tailing James that first week.

He had three classes in the same hallways as me.

So every day in chemistry, at 11:05 A.M., I raised my hand. From the very first time I did this, Mrs. Penn could tell that this meant I needed a bathroom pass. All the teachers at Glass High knew/were warned that I didn't ever speak, so this would be the only reason for me to raise my hand. Within a month, it became so clockwork that Mrs. Penn would hand me the pass without breaking from her lecture.

I would then walk down the hallway and crouch outside the door to college biology and look in on James.

He usually sat slumped back in his seat, taking notes while the teacher talked.

I would stare at him for three minutes, which I timed on my green plastic watch. Then I'd walk back to class, because I didn't want to spend so long away that Mrs. Penn started suspecting that I was doing something other than using the bathroom and stopped giving me passes.

I would have done this during gym and advanced algebra, too. But unfortunately his calculus teacher kept the door closed with the window shade pulled down, so that was no good. And a bathroom pass during gym only meant that you could go back into the locker room to do your business.

So 11:05 cued my best three minutes of the day, the time I looked forward to the most.

When I sat alone at lunch, I thought about the next day's three minutes. When I fell asleep at night, watching *Sixteen Candles* or *Pretty in Pink* or whatever Molly Ringwald movie I had chosen for my bedtime story, I also thought about those three minutes.

And when I woke up in the middle of the night because of Cora's dramatic moans—she always laid it on real thick for the new guys, like this was the best sex of her life—I'd just lie there, listening to her performance and thinking about James.

Then I'd fall back to sleep with a smile on my face.

THE REASON THAT James and his sisters had been transferred from their nice private school in Texas to our real less academically stellar public school in Mississippi became apparent about two months into the semester when signs on wooden sticks started popping up like flowers all over town, just a few months after our local congressman died unexpectedly of a heart attack.

They said: "FARRELL III," in large white letters, "JAMES C." above that in smaller white cursive, then "U.S. REPRESENTATIVE '91" in red letters across the bottom.

At first it was just the signs in yards. Then they started appearing in store windows, then regular people's windows, then the next thing I knew, it seemed like the town was fair to wallpapered with them.

I liked that they all said "James C. Farrell," even if it wasn't my James. I took to brushing them with my fingers whenever I saw them hung up on a gate. Without exception they were all cool to the touch, even though the summer heat had yet to let up and the air was still hot and sticky.

"That's why he put them kids of his in this monkey house," I heard a lunch lady say to another lunch lady while I was waiting in line with my red Free Lunch ticket in hand. "It don't matter if he a Farrell. People ain't going to vote for him if his kids ain't in school just like the rest us kids."

My James, I had figured out from the signs, was a IV. I wondered if when we got married, I would have to take the IV along with his last name.

Davidia Farrell the Fourth.

I liked that. It was a name with history and resonance. And it occurred to me that after I married James and we moved away from Glass, the new people I met would never be able to tell—unless I chose to let them know, which I wouldn't—that I came from nothing and that I used to be nothing. James would change my life in that way.

I SHOULD SAY that stalking James wasn't all about sneaking looks and clipping articles. Sometimes I found things through no intention of my own. I guess it's what other people might have called luck.

Not having a steady source of money, I'd fallen into the habit of hanging back a little after the end-of-class bell rang. You'd be surprised what kind of stuff kids left behind. I picked up change just about every day, and once in a while somebody would leave a bill. Sometimes I'd find whole wallets, but that's not as lucky as it sounds, because it's a lot harder to steal money when you know who it belongs to. I much preferred the orphaned bills, which came without guilt. Usually, if it was a whole wallet, I would just turn it in to the principal's office.

One day after chemistry class, I found something better than money. A Polaroid. A two-shot of James and another guy, who he had in a friendly headlock. They were both laughing—not just smiling for the camera.

I recognized the other guy as Corey Mays, the football player who I'd heard talking about James replacing Perry Pointer as the team's quarterback.

He and James had become best and instant friends of the sort that only football can make, and they could often be seen walking the halls of Glass High, side by side but not equal.

Corey wasn't as smart as James—he was in chemistry with me, a sophomore, even though he was a senior. And of course, James had a lot more money. Corey's mother bought his polo shirts from the mall during the Dillard's one-day sale—and only because Corey had asked her for them within a week of making James's acquaintance.

James bought all his clothes in New York from stores that bore the same names as the labels on the inside of his jeans and collars. He never wore the same thing twice in a week, and he never wore anything with a designer name plastered all over it. His clothes were so expensive, they were completely simple. Flat-front Calvin Klein khakis with polos or T-shirts that stretched just enough across his chest to let you know he had muscles. His sunglasses had "Ray-Ban" stenciled in tasteful cursive on the handles and were perfectly suited to his face.

After football practice, he would jump into his forest green Saab. "His daddy gave him that car. It's only three years old," I heard Tanisha Harris say to another cheerleader during gym.

James was too cool to insist on a brand-new, showy convertible like his sisters. But even his hand-me-down vehicle reeked of expensive habits and expectations that Corey, in his seventeen-year-old dented Volkswagen Rabbit, which he had inherited from his tired, single mother, would never know.

I liked Corey. He had chosen me for his partner in chemistry by taking the empty seat next to me and saying, "You smart. You going to be my partner." Real simple.

He didn't seem to mind that I didn't speak. And even better, he spoke to me about a steady stream of sports teams and people I didn't know, but that was okay. I liked his voice and the real emotion that ran through it when he talked about Ozzie Smith or the '87 Lakers lineup or the pass his boy James had thrown at the last game. He must have really understood me, because he never expected answers and he never asked me questions. Also, he never offered to help me with any of our assignments.

"I'm gonna stay out your way," he said during that first week. And he was true to his word. He'd stare off into space or tell me about last night's football game while I poured and calculated.

He was like a radio that knew instinctively when to turn on and off while I worked. Plus, he always clapped me on the back and said, "Yeah, boy!" or "Yeah, that's how we do it!" when the teacher passed us back our papers with red A's on the fronts—which made him the only person outside of my mother who ever touched me. So I liked him. But unlike most girls my age, I knew the difference between affection and love, because I didn't love him. Not like I loved James.

Besides, Corey was for real in love with Veronica Farrell. He followed her around like a homeless dog, even though she had a reputation for only dating college boys, and even then, only college boys with some change in their pockets.

But Corey had plans for getting rich that Veronica's disinterest only encouraged. All these scouts out here looking at James, well, there were also scouts looking at him, he told me. "They can only be one quarterback, but they got all type of room for running backs," he told me. "Especially if you real consistent-like. Colleges like that. Flashy don't cut it if you cain't get that ball down the field."

And Corey made sure the ball got down the field. He was James's fiercest ally: He never showboated, and he did his job.

While James liked football and seemed to take it as seriously as any young man of talent raised in Texas should, everybody knew that after college that was it. According to Corey, "James already been said it don't matter if the NFL come knocking on his door. He supposed to take over Farrell Fine Hair, so his daddy can retire."

It made me feel sorry for James. When I made it to eighteen, everything would be different. Because of my good grades, I would go to college on a scholarship. I would start talking again, and then I would go on to be anything I wanted. My life would be mine. Finally.

But James's life would belong to somebody else. He had probably always known exactly how it was supposed to turn out, and that was kind of sad.

It was a Monday when Corey dropped the Polaroid. It fell out of his open backpack while he was pretending to fight with another football player. High school boys were an enigma to me. They fought when they disliked each other, and they pretended to fight when they were good friends. I had never seen two boys hug at my school. And I wondered if this was just a phase or if it was always like this. Did boys who liked each other go on play-fighting forever?

Anyway, Corey and his friend were play-shoving each other, and that's why Corey didn't notice the picture fall out of his backpack and onto the floor underneath our lab table. I saw it from my chair. Saw who was in it immediately, even though it was halfway under the chemistry table. Still I didn't dare pick it up.

Maybe I could have pretended that I was picking it up to give it back to Corey, if anyone caught me. But then I'd have to give back the only non-newspaper-generated picture that I had ever seen of James.

So I waited. And I prayed that Corey wouldn't look under the table and see his dropped picture.

I faked more interest than usual in his sports analysis during class. I turned my face to him and pasted on what I hoped was an open expression.

Finally the end-of-class bell rang and Corey left, his backpack still hanging open. This happened often with Corey. Usually I tapped him on the shoulder and pointed to the open backpack.

Today I let him walk out of there, dropping pencils and other backpack paraphernalia like an unwitting Hansel.

As soon as he cleared the door I ducked underneath the desk and picked up the Polaroid.

"Hey, Monkey Night!" I looked up. Corey was standing in the doorway.

"Did you see a Polaroid back there of me and James? I think it fell out my backpack."

I stood up and shook my head, quickly stuffing the picture in the back of my jeans.

He came farther into the room. His eyes searched the floor as he picked up all the pencils he had dropped.

"What was you doing under the table?"

I bent back down and came up with a pen that he had dropped and handed it to him.

I had learned that in a mute existence, an action often took the place of an answer.

In this case, an action took the place of a bold-faced lie.

*I was picking up your pen, Corey. See? Here you go.*

He smiled at me. "Thanks! Tell me if you see that picture."

I took the picture out again when he left. I could imagine the person behind the camera saying, "Hey, over here."

And instead of James putting his arm around Corey's shoulders, he took him by surprise with a playful headlock. Everybody laughs and the camera flashes. Even Corey, though if any other guy had put him in a headlock like this, it would be an act of humiliation, an affront to his manhood.

But not with James. This was a picture that Corey kept and apparently liked enough to come back for when he realized he had lost it.

And now I had stolen it.

I let my eyes sink deep into the sunshine of James's smile and marveled over his effect on people.

# THREE

THAT DAY AFTER SCHOOL, I OPENED my locker and took ten one-dollar bills out of the spaghetti sauce jar where I kept all my found money. On my way home, I detoured down Main Street and walked into Greeley's Mini-Mart.

In those days, Walgreens had yet to find its way to Glass, and Greeley's was where you went when you didn't have the time to run to four different places for everything you needed. The selection was small and a little overpriced, but usually it did in a pinch.

And it especially did if you were Cora, because Mr. Greeley, the owner, was a friend. They had met in the bar about a week or two after his wife, Hattie Mae Greeley, passed from a stroke, and he had been coming round to the house on the second Tuesday of every month ever since. He had confessed to Cora that second Tuesdays had historical significance. After their children had grown and moved out, Hattie Mae had moved into another room and informed him that he could only visit her on the second Tuesday of every month.

This was on account of Mrs. Greeley having an appointment at the Perfect Cut on the second Wednesday of every month, so if Mr. Greeley messed up her perm with all his moving and sweating on top of her, she didn't mind so much.

Cora told me this on one of the rare nights that she had come home drunk but without a man. Somehow, this always put her in the storytelling mood. And I suppose I was easy to talk to, seeing as how I never said anything back.

Cora told me Mr. Greeley had broken down crying after the first time they did the do, then thanked her for helping him remember his dead wife.

I'm sure that Cora had comforted him, took him in her arms and whispered words in his ear that made his tears taste like brown sugar. The secret of Cora's many friendships was that she was always nice. The first time.

But in the retelling of the story, she had snorted and said, "Lord know if he really wanted to remember that witch, he should have chose himself a ugly woman to lay down with."

Still, if we came into Greeley's when not too many people were there to see, Cora could count on a significant discount. She'd give me the list and exchange sweet talk with Mr. Greeley while I worked my way down the narrow aisles, picking up soap and detergent and all the other necessaries that Cora didn't like to think about until she absolutely had to.

The day after I stole the Polaroid, I walked past all the essential aisles, making my way to the fifth aisle where the books, office supplies, wrapping paper, and stationery were sold.

I stopped in front of two large scrapbooks. One had holographic rainbows on it and the other was a simple, elegant brown.

This was bad, because while one reflected how James made me feel on the inside, the other reflected who James actually was.

I must have been there, trying to make that decision, a long time, because Mr. Greeley came and stood over me with his saggy jowl and rheumy eyes. "You buying it or casing it, girl?"

I picked up the rainbow scrapbook and handed it to him.

As I followed Mr. Greeley back to the cash register, I imagined myself handing the scrapbook to James in the hallway right before prom.

"What's this?" he'd ask.

And I'd cock my head to the side, all of a sudden shy, although it had been bold to offer him the scrapbook in the first place. "It's a scrapbook. I got it because the rainbows made me think of . . ."

I'd trail off and look away, too embarrassed to say it.

But he'd make me. Maybe he'd touch my shoulder, or try to catch my eye.

"Made you think of what?" he'd ask. Firm but gentle.

And I'd finally meet his eyes and answer, "You."

Then the music would start up and we'd kiss.

"You know you ain't going to get no discount on this, right?" Mr. Greeley said. "That's just for your mama."

The image of James and me quickly subsided as I offered Mr. Greeley the ten one-dollar bills.

He looked at it over his reading glasses.

"Actually, that's going to be ten-fifty. You got tax on top of that nine-ninety-nine."

I stared at him.

"You don't got fifty cents?" He moved around, annoyed, like he was thinking of not giving it to me.

I wondered how Cora could bear to have this horrible old man on top of her. At that moment, I did not blame his dead wife for barring him from her bedroom, and I did not blame Cora for thinking he was full of shit.

I put the bills on the counter. I hoped this action translated into *Do you want this ten dollars or not, old man?*

Though I suspected he was reading it as *I'm trash and came in here trying to get one over on you, because you're having relations with my mother every second Tuesday of the month.*

Either way, he took the money. But he grumbled as he put it in the register without ringing up the sale. "Next time you come around here without your mama, make sure you figure out the tax."

I took the scrapbook and walked out of there. Angry at him for making such a show of it, and scared of what I had been prepared to do.

Growing up, I had learned to hold on to my pride in little ways. If I didn't talk, then I didn't get beat or made fun of as much. On the other hand, there was power in not talking, because people didn't like it when you didn't talk, and it was a certain kind of aggression, when you knew people didn't like a thing, but you did it anyway.

And of course, finding cash like I did wasn't exactly honorable, but on the other hand, I always had a little of my own money to spend. I had *Pretty in Pink, Breakfast Club, Say Anything,* and *Some Kind of Wonderful* on VHS. And those were all tapes that I had bought with my own money, without having to ask Cora for anything—not that she would have given it to me if I had.

But the best pride holder I had learned by far was the Not Wanting of Things, which made life a whole lot easier.

Because who cared if no one ever paid you attention if you didn't want it in the first place?

And who cared if Cora had me going to school in hand-me-downs—I didn't want clothes.

I didn't want a fancy house, I didn't want to be popular or even liked. I didn't want anything.

Except James.

And when Mr. Greeley had hesitated like maybe he wasn't going to let me have this scrapbook, a thought had flashed through my head: *Maybe I could find fifty cents on the floor.*

I knew better than anyone that people were always dropping things. If I dug around for it under the counter, I'd probably find enough pennies, or maybe even some nickels or dimes.

I could see myself on my hands and knees searching for that fifty cents while Mr. Greeley watched me with a sour look on his face.

And it scared me. Not the thought of doing it, but knowing that I would do it. For James.

It felt to be about one hundred degrees as I walked out of the air-conditioned store into the Mississippi sun. But I was cold all the way home.


THAT NIGHT, I listened to the game on the radio while I transferred all the articles from between the pages of *The Color Purple* to my new scrapbook.

I used a glue stick and pasted in the articles, two to a page. Though if the article had a picture of James, it got its own page.

I saved the first page for last and stapled the Polaroid to that one. Then I used a faded green marker from my junior high days to draw a heart around the whole thing.

I stared at the picture.

I wondered if the house that James lived in was as nice as the one in *Sixteen Candles*. I knew that they had moved into the old Glass Plantation house. I had never seen it, since like most plantation houses, it was located in such a way that you didn't just pass by it during your daily routine.

The house was about four or five miles from where I lived, down a long dirt road that led to the Glass House and nothing else but the Glass House. Corey had been invited by James a few times to hang out, and he described their house to me in a series of monologues. He told me that the family didn't swim in a pool but a whole lake that sat a little ways behind the house. He said that they had their own live-in maid to keep the place clean, because the house had six bedrooms and a kitchen that was bigger than Corey and his mom's entire apartment. James and Corey had eaten in the kitchen the times that Corey had gone over, and the maid had served them after-school snacks, which had just about blown Corey's mind. From what I could tell, he had never been invited to stay for dinner, because he had never described the dining room. But I assumed that it was just as grand as the rest of the house.

And the dining room was where I imagined James and me kissing for the first time, just like Molly Ringwald and Jake Ryan in *Sixteen Candles*. We'd be sitting on top of a large glass table in that dining room, a birthday cake between us. He'd thank me for coming, and I'd thank him for inviting me, and then we'd both lean forward for The Kiss. The Kiss that would mark my final transformation from Monkey Night into the girl who got a Molly Ringwald Ending. I couldn't wait.

AT AROUND MIDNIGHT, I woke up to the sound of Cora screaming. "Oh, fuck me, baby. Fuck me real good. Oh God, baby. I cannot believe this."

New friend.

I turned on my back and stared at the ceiling. I would have to wait for them to finish, so that I could get back to sleep.

I hadn't heard them come in, but I could smell someone's cologne on the air. A strange but nice scent in our musky house.

Then there was a break in Cora's screaming and I heard something else in the night. A car idling outside the house.

Uh-oh. This had happened a few times. An angry wife or girlfriend finally got sick of her man not coming home at night and would show up on Cora's doorstep.

But it almost never happened with her new friends.

Someone must have followed him here.

And that someone was now sitting out there in her car, maybe thinking about loading a gun.

Cora had almost gotten stabbed by a girlfriend once, and I had often thought that it was just a matter of time before somebody showed up here with a gun.

I sat up on the couch and peeked out the window. If I could see that the woman had a knife, I would run and hide in the basement. If I could see she had a gun, though, I would have to call 911 before she came in here and started shooting people.

But when I looked out the window, what I ended up seeing was Veronica and Tammy Farrell's convertible. It was idling out on the street in front of our house, but no one was in the driver's seat.

I looked around and eventually my eyes found Veronica Farrell, standing on the cracked path that led to our house. She was standing perfectly still, like a tree. And she was staring at our door with such a look of hatred in her eyes.

A Saab was parked behind my mother's car, a larger, newer, nicer version of the one that James drove.

My mother screamed out in the bedroom again.

I wondered where in the hell a woman like my mother would run across a man like Mr. Farrell. I had once seen an austere photo of James's father in our local newspaper, and he didn't seem like the type that hung out in bars.

But then I remembered . . .

Before James C. Farrell the Third started his congressional campaign, he was the head of Farrell Fine Hair. And Cora worked on the assembly line at Farrell Fine Hair. Had they run into each other while he was touring the factory? On the way to the bathroom maybe? Had their eyes connected in the hallway?

But I stopped wondering after Cora's and James the Third's origin story when I looked back to the sidewalk and saw Veronica Farrell staring straight at me. She lowered her right hand, and I thought for a second that maybe she really did have a gun.

Maybe she was going to shoot me and my mama and her daddy for lowering himself enough to come into this place. But then she turned and walked back to her car.

The engine revved as she turned the key in the ignition. She looked like a beautiful robot as she drove off into the moonlight without a backward glance. That I could see.

## FOUR

I COULD NOT FALL BACK TO sleep after that.

It was only a few months into the school year, and Veronica had already developed a reputation for being very, very mean. In fact, she flat-out scared people. Case in point: As much trash as Tanisha Harris had talked behind her back on that first day, she had never gone on to say anything to Veronica's face. Also, Veronica didn't get messed with for being high yellow. I had seen girls darker than her get shouted down with calls of "light-skinned bitch" at Glass. But there was just something about the older Farrell girl that froze everything that came into her vicinity. The normal insults would get stuck in the throats of even the most ornery kids at our school, which was impressive, because Mississippi kids are pretty bold.

I told myself that what had just happened didn't matter, and that Veronica Farrell probably hadn't seen me. For the first time in my life, I prayed that what the kids and the Southern ladies said about me was true: You could lose me in too much night.

Because then she definitely wouldn't have seen me. Wouldn't know that I was the daughter of the woman who had cast a spell on her father.

But she had looked straight at me. And her father would be back. I could tell from the way he carefully left the house, tiptoeing so as not to disturb me.

He was going to be a repeat. The one-offs always rushed out of there, like running away could erase its happening.


I GOT UP early the next morning, got my books out of my locker, and arrived at my class about twenty minutes before I had to be there.

I opened my Spanish book and studied, though I knew this to be a use-less endeavor. The teacher had announced the first day of class that fifty percent of our Spanish grade would be based on oral performance. Still, Spanish was a requirement. And though I had thought about requesting a transfer to special education classes, I already knew that I didn't quite have the grades or a low enough mark on the mental health questionnaire—I had filled one out at the school's insistence halfway through my first silent year of high school.

While working on exercises in my Spanish workbook, I focused on going to see James during chemistry. I tried not to think about the fact that I had four classes with Veronica: honors English, advanced algebra, health, and worst of all, gym.

I tried to believe that Veronica had not seen me and did not know that I belonged to Cora Jones.


MY NEXT CLASS was English. And to my relief, Veronica didn't say any-thing to me. She didn't even look at me as she passed by my desk.

But then came our algebra class, where we got our test papers back.

It was our first test of the year, and according to Mr. Wolder, only three of us got A's and only one of us got an A+.

From my desk in the back of the classroom, I saw Veronica smile over her shoulder at her friend Elise, who sat right behind her.

Elise was pretty and light-skinned, and her parents were solidly mid-dle class. But she wasn't as beautiful or as light as Veronica. And when her parents died, she would not be set for life like Veronica. But just like Corey, Elise was almost slovenly grateful to be friends with a Farrell.

However, unlike James with Corey, I never felt that Veronica actually took Elise seriously as a friend. It was more like Elise was a less pretty stand-in for Tammy Farrell—a substitute to laugh at and hang on every catty word that came out of Veronica's mouth until she could meet up with her little sister for lunch.

My heart sank when I saw Veronica smile at Elise, because it wasn't a regular smile. It was smug. And not smug like I got an A, but smug like I got the A+.

At that moment I saw two things clearly:

1. I was sure of every single answer I had written down for that test because I had more time to study than most due to me not having a social life and me being determined to escape to college as soon as I graduated from this hellhole called high school. My test was perfect.
2. Veronica was not the kind of girl who liked coming in second place. Once the announcement was made, she'd definitely turn around and look at me. Really look at me. Just like she had looked straight at me the night before. But now it was daytime, and she was a smart girl. She'd figure it out. . . .

I raised my hand for a bathroom pass.

Mr. Wolder laughed and said, "Not yet, Davidia. Let me announce these A's first."

My disappointment must have been evident on my face, because he laughed again. "Oh, don't look like that. Look it here, you got the A+. Good job, Davidia."

He held out three pages stapled together, with a huge A+ written on the top in red marker. I could feel Veronica's eyes on me, knew they were narrowed into icy slits.

I didn't take the paper. It was too cold to lift my arm away from the warmth of my body, but Mr. Wolder put the test down on my desk anyway.

"Davidia Jones got the A+, but Veronica Farrell got the next highest grade, a 95. Good job, Veronica."

He went on to the third person's name, but I couldn't hear it, couldn't listen. Dread was now a taste in my mouth, like silver filling up my throat.

Veronica leaned over to whisper to Elise.

"Who's that?" I could read the question coming off her lips.

Elise looked over her shoulder at me, then turned back around to answer.

I couldn't see her lips, but I knew her answer. "That's Davidia Jones. But everybody call her Monkey Night."

And then an almost comical expression of faux recognition came over Veronica's face. "Oh, Monkey Night," she repeated, just loud enough for me and a few others to hear. "I thought I smelled something ugly in here."

All the students in my row fell out laughing.

But Mr. Wolder didn't look up from passing out his papers. He must not have heard Veronica, or maybe he didn't want to hear her. There was only so much a teacher could do, and when someone like me walked in, an ugly girl who didn't talk, a lot of teachers wrote me off. You can't save a child who won't talk to you. You can't defend someone who will always be made fun of no matter what they did. And they didn't get paid enough, and they were tired. I got that, and fully blamed Cora for this situation.

In fact, at that moment I hated her for putting me in this position. Just when I had almost succeeded at becoming invisible, she had to go and make friends with the father of the meanest girl in school..

I had seen Veronica with James in the hallways. All smiles for him. The hardness of her gaze softening whenever she was in his presence. She loved her brother, and she probably loved her father. And she wasn't the sort of girl who let things like this go.

Goddamn Cora.

I raised my hand for the bathroom pass again. Godfuckingdamn her.

———

HERE'S THE STRANGE thing about peace: For a teenager it is unrecognizable. Until you lose it. Knowing peace, appreciating peace is truly an adult art—one that I had not mastered before I came to know Veronica.

In some ways, I took her subsequent abuse to be a punishment for not being truly grateful that most of the kids had ignored me before Veronica, that the constant whispers about me had died a tired, overused death. I had even had the nerve to resent that most of my fellow high schoolers still called me Monkey Night, that is when they called me anything at all.

What I hadn't realized was that God had done right by me before that day, and I kicked myself for never bothering to thank Him for my first anonymous year of high school. Because by Tuesday, I had come to think of my school as a field of mines. My one goal in every class I had with Veronica was to concentrate above the whispered insults.

On Wednesday, one boy, in a fit of trying to impress her, put a monkey squeeze toy in my seat. I sat on it, and the class started laughing almost before they heard the loud squeak.

Veronica was beautiful when she laughed. The sound was as soft and precise as her accent: ta-ha-ha-ha. As if those four syllables were all that she allotted for each laugh.

It was basketball week in gym class, and by Thursday I had learned to play a new type of defense—the kind where I stayed as far away from Veronica as I could possibly get on a standard-sized court. That only worked about half the time, though. Invariably she would pop up behind me. Like a vampire. Then she'd body check me so hard as she ran past me, that I fell.

"Watch out!" she would yell as she dribbled away, so the gym teacher would think it was me being clumsy and not Veronica out to get me.

She and Tammy would make monkey sounds whenever I passed by them in the hallway. Tammy scratched her head and her tummy while making the sounds, putting as much enthusiasm into making fun of me as she did into her cheerleading. But Veronica just stood there with a sly smirk on her face and one hand cupped around the side of her mouth as she made the sounds.

By Friday, Veronica had made something old new again, and everybody was doing the same things that they used to do to me in elementary school.

I'm fairly sure that's the day I started out-and-out hating Veronica's guts.

I did not blame my strangeness for my new position, and this was because, against all odds, I was not one of those teenagers who believe that everything bad that happens to her is her own fault.

No, I had read the books. I had seen the movies. And I knew.

Cora was a really bad mother. And Veronica was a fucking bitch.

STILL, I DIDN'T think she had told James or Tammy about Cora and their father.

James still walked down the hallway as carefree as ever. I didn't think he could fake being that relaxed if he knew what his father was up to—at least not that effectively.

And Tamara seemed to have more fun than malicious intent when she helped her sister make fun of me. She never did it when she was by herself. In fact, she averted her eyes whenever she walked past me, which suggested shame.

Neither Farrell sister ever acted a fool around James.

This only made me love him more, because as bad as things got during the rest of the day, James was above the fray. Whenever I was near him, I was safe.

ON SATURDAY, Mr. Farrell showed up at our house with flowers, Hennessy, and a ten-dollar bill for me.

"So what movie you going to see?" he asked, smiling down at me like it was my idea to get out of the house. Cora must have told him that I usually went to the dollar show when her friends made early evening house calls.

I shrugged.

"She don't talk," Cora said.

She was sitting at a black plastic table that had come with the house, built into the living/dining room wall. The top of it was designed to look like marble. But it didn't really look like anything but plastic pretending to be marble.

"You don't talk?" He said this in the same tone of voice somebody might use to say, "You've been to China?" Chummy, like me being a Southern female who didn't talk made me interesting, as opposed to a complete freak.

I shook my head.

"She ain't mute or nothing. She just don't talk, cuz she don't want to."

Cora relayed all this for informational purposes only. She had been explaining this situation to newbies for over ten years now, and she was beyond bored with the whole thing.

He reached out and squeezed my hand. "Well, you keep gathering them thoughts till you got something good to say, hear?"

Mr. Farrell was very nice. Very charming. I would have smiled and squeezed his hand back, except that I hated him, because I really did not understand why he was here with Cora when he had a perfectly beautiful family at home.

I took the ten dollars and a library book and left. When I got outside, I noticed that Mr. Farrell's Saab wasn't parked in our driveway. Apparently Mr. Farrell had decided that it was better not to advertise his affair to the entire neighborhood. Still, I wondered how he had gotten here. I couldn't see him walking all the way from his house on the far outskirts of town.

That gave me an idea about what to do with all the spare time I suddenly had to fill now that Cora was not going to the bar that night. I walked down dark country roads, untamed by streetlamps. Taking a page from that Harriet Tubman biography that I had read, I followed the North Star through the woods until I emerged from the glen in back of Farrell Manor—that's what they had renamed it: Farrell Manor. They had even taken the Glass Plantation sign down and replaced it with one that had "Farrell Manor" written in gold cursive letters against a green background.

The house was large and white, with columns and everything, as if it was trying to do its best *Gone with the Wind* impersonation. And I imagined that if and when I ever saw an actual human being on the large porch they would be dwarfed by the house's enormity. I won't go too far into the detail of the house, because I don't remember it as well as I used to. But even by Hollywood standards, it was enormous. I believed Corey's stories about all its bedrooms and the live-in maid as soon as I laid eyes on it. And when I walked around the perimeter, I saw that the Farrells had also put in a tennis court, which was such a foreign thing in a town like Glass that it felt a little like staring at a spaceship.

Light peeked out from every heavily curtained window. I wondered what they were doing up there. Was Veronica inside, or had she followed her father to our house again?

No, I decided, she hadn't. I hadn't seen her car outside our house, and really, what reason did she have to follow Mr. Farrell that night?

She knew where he was.


AFTER ABOUT A month, I got used to being Monkey Night again, and I gave up any illusions that the treatment would stop.

I've noticed in life that regular folks seem to really like people who hold them in cold disdain. I think this explains the popularity of a lot of people who I don't think should necessarily be popular, like Martha Stewart and most of the English aristocracy.

From Veronica's first day at Glass, she had made it clear that she hated the school and that she found the students in it to be small town, provincial, and boring. And the other students loved her for it.

Mainly because she was right, I think. The great majority of Glass was provincial and boring—it hadn't really changed much since the fifties when Farrell Fine Hair had built their second factory outside of Texas in our town. Plus, Veronica gave them something to aspire to, and even better, something they could never achieve. Much like nirvana, and a life without sin, nobody outside of Veronica's immediate family would ever achieve actually being liked by Veronica.

So this meant that everybody at school, save James and me, expended a lot of energy trying to get Veronica to like them.


THE THING THAT pissed me off most about Veronica's treatment of me was all the extra attention I was getting, which resulted in me having to give up James.

Everybody looking at me meant that I couldn't look at James without somebody figuring out that I liked him. Which would turn an already bad situation into a nightmare, since we weren't quite at the Great Transformation point yet.

So no more chemistry class breaks. No more shadowing him in the hallways. No more waiting for him to finish practice, just so I could watch as he walked from the field to his car.

Basically no more stalking.

I think I would have been okay with the rest, if it hadn't been for not being able to see James on a regular basis. But factoring that in, the Dark Days returned.

# FIVE

I WAS TIRED WHEN I WOKE up, tired when I went to bed. I walked around all day with my eyes on my shoes. It reminded me of how I had felt for those two years after I had stopped talking but before I had discovered Molly Ringwald movies. Truth be told, I was dying without James.

He didn't have the same lunch period as me, and our schedules weren't such that we necessarily had to be passing each other in the hallway. So if the fortunes weren't with me, I could go days without seeing him. I was missing him in a way I can only describe as something terrible. Like a piece of my heart was missing, and I knew where it was, but I couldn't go to it, because of certain situations. . . . Yes, Something Terrible.

But then one night, while watching *Pretty in Pink* at bedtime, it occurred to me that this Veronica situation might be a good thing. Something bad always happened to Molly Ringwald before she got her perfect kiss. In *Pretty in Pink*, Andrew McCarthy dumped her right before prom. In *The Breakfast Club*, she got in that horrible fight with Judd Nelson. And in *Sixteen Candles*, she not only missed Jake Ryan's call but was also humiliated when her panties were held up on display for a bathroom full of freshmen geeks—just like I was being humiliated now.

Maybe this was God's way of telling me that it was time for me to make my Big Move. I had to sew together my own prom dress or transform Ally Sheedy from goth to pretty, or help my horrible sister get married. But what was I, Davidia Jones, supposed to do in order to get the guy I liked to finally notice me?

Well, I knew that first I had to get him to see me in a different light. Like when Molly Ringwald talked to Andrew McCarthy at the record store, and he realized she was pretty cool. I had to get James alone. But how?

I thought and thought on it for a whole week, then the answer came to me like a lightning bolt during one of Corey Mays's litanies. I could go to one of James's football games. I didn't know what I'd do once I got there, or how I'd get him alone, but it would be a start.

So the first Friday of November, I spent two of my dollars to get into the Glass vs. Roosevelt game, and I found a spot underneath the bleachers. I laid a blanket down over the one patch of grass that had managed to grow in all that darkness and opened John Grisham's *A Time to Kill*. It was a thriller that I had just picked up at the library because the back of the book said it was set in Mississippi. That it was also engaging had taken me by pleasant surprise.

In fact, it was almost hard for me to put the book down when the announcer yelled out, "Presenting the Robert C. Glass High School Tigers!" and then started calling the players' names.

As the quarterback, James's name was the last to be called. When he ran across the field in his yellow and black uniform, everybody stood up and cheered even louder. Their rhythmic stomping sent metallic shudders through the bleachers over my head.

I put down the John Grisham novel then and closed my eyes. I imagined walking up to James and talking to him, telling him everything that had been on my mind since I had first laid eyes on him.

It was a good fantasy, but it was interrupted by the harsh shrill of the referees' whistles.

I opened my eyes and saw that there was now a pile of players on the field. That's why the referees were blowing their whistles; they were also gesturing for the players on top to start unpiling.

As the players removed themselves, I could see James curled around the ball like a fetus around its thumb.

I did not quite understand what was going on, but I guessed he'd done good because the crowd started cheering even louder than when he first came out.

The two teams got back in formation, and James threw a pass. But it didn't quite reach the player he was aiming at.

On the sidelines, Tammy and the other cheerleaders did a "That's okay" cheer.

Then he threw another pass that didn't quite make it. I heard murmurs above me about how it seemed like he was favoring his throwing arm.

The crowd got quiet.

Now James was on the sidelines, talking with the coach. The coach said something, and James started shaking his head.

Then the coach pointed at the bench, but James folded his arms and shook his head again.

A general gasp went up from the crowd. You see, in the South, football is like the army. You don't question orders, you just do whatever the coach tells you to. So James refusing to sit down was a big deal. Unheard of. Like a black child suddenly saying in an English accent to its mama, "No, madam, I will not retrieve a switch so that you may beat me with it. I believe your request to be not only abusive, but also *absurd*."

And say that did happen. Of course country logic would say that the mama must now beat her child even worse than she first intended, so that they would never have to have that kind of conversation again.

The coach must have been fully conversant in country mama logic, because he was pointing off the field and yelling with such enunciation that I could almost hear the words coming off his lips.

"I don't know how they do it in Texas, son, but in Mississip', players don't be talking back to their coach. Get out of here."

For the first time in my history of stalking James, I saw a truly alarmed look pass over his face. "But Coach—" I could see him start to say.

"I said, get!"

James was totally still for second, just blinking at the coach.

Was this the first time he had ever gotten in real trouble for something he'd said or done? Maybe so, I thought.

Then the alarm passed, and he took off his helmet and threw it—yes, threw it! By the time it hit the water table, jostling the little paper cups of Gatorade, he was stomping off the field followed by a chorus of boos.

I was confused, as I would continue to be confused at sporting events for the rest of my life, because I didn't know whether the crowd was booing for or against him.

THE AWFUL THING about James getting kicked out of the game was that he felt bad, and I didn't ever want James to feel bad. But the really good thing about James getting kicked out of the game was that it meant I could follow him to the locker room without too many people noticing.

So I trailed him at a distance back to the school. On the way, I spotted a yellow flower growing in the weeds and picked it.

A few minutes later, I was standing outside the boys' locker room door. I could hear the sound of metal rattling. He must have been kicking the lockers. Then it was silent for a long time.

I cracked the door open. James was sitting on a long bench with his head in his hands, the bottom of his palms covering his eyes.

Maybe he was crying, I don't know. I wanted to go to him, give him some words of comfort.

But of course, I just let the door close. I took out a piece of notebook paper and wrote down what I would've said to him if I could bring myself to speak: "You'll never fall so hard that you'll never get up"—corny, I know, but I was in high school. A platitude was the best I could do.

After I wrote that, I stuck the yellow flower behind my ear and waited. I was too scared to go in, and too hopeful to just go away. So I just waited for him to come out.

It didn't take long. Guys like James, eighties heroes like James, never spent too much time feeling sorry for themselves.

About fifteen minutes after I finished writing my note, the door to the locker room swung open with a creak, and James emerged, freshly showered and dressed in a striped polo and jeans. He smelled great. He wasn't wearing any cologne, it was just the pink gym shower soap. But he still smelled good. The static filled my head immediately.

He stopped in front of me, and I could read the "Hi" on his lips.

I held out the note.

"Is this for me?" I think he asked.

I nodded.

His fingers grazed mine as he took the piece of paper from me. And as soon as he touched me, the static stopped. It was like a radio got thrown in my bathwater and my nerves short-circuited, leaving nothing but quiet.

"I like your flower," he said.

I smiled my thanks.

His eyes skimmed over the words once. Then twice. Then he smiled. At me.

I was fixed to faint. But I kept on my feet, because you can't get a Molly Ringwald Ending if you're stone-cold passed out on the ground. That ain't romantic.

"Thank you," he said. "This makes me feel a whole lot better. And you know what? I'm going to keep this note, and I'm going to look at it the next time something like this happens."

It was the perfect thing to say, but I was not surprised. James seemed like the kind of person who always knew the perfect thing to say. In every way, he was the opposite of me.

"What's your name?" he said next. Another perfect question.

I had thought that as soon as he talked to me the words I had held back all these years would come spilling out. But when I opened my mouth, my throat felt as dry and empty as always and nothing came out.

Then I heard the clicking of heels, coming down the hallway. I knew it was Veronica even before I saw her. A teacher at our school would never wear heels that were high enough to click. And who else but Veronica would wear them to a football game?

I didn't turn around. Just stood there. Still as a wood dove. Hoping that I would blend into the linoleum floors and beige metal lockers.

"Ronnie," said James, waving her over. "Come meet . . ." He waited for me to give him my name.

Veronica came to stand next to James, her head cocked to the side, her eyes unreadable. "Davidia," she finished for him. "We already know each other. We have four classes together."

Then she actually smiled at me. I very nearly dropped dead of shock. "Hi," she said. "What are you doing here?"

"She somehow managed to cheer me up," James said. He winked at me. "Thanks."

He pocketed the note.

And Veronica seemed to regard me with new eyes. "Do you have any paper?" she asked me.

I handed her my notebook, still not quite believing what all was happening. That James was speaking to me, and Veronica was suddenly being nice.

She wrote in large but elegant and slanted cursive. "Veronica Farrell" and then a phone number.

"Here's my number," she said. "I appreciate you cheering up my big brother. Call me if you want."

She handed the notebook back to me and said to James, "We should get going."

James gave me another smile and walked away with Veronica, who looked over her shoulder and waved before they turned the corner. She actually waved. At me.

I didn't realize I had stopped breathing until they disappeared around the corner and air filled my tight lungs.

It was already happening, I realized. James was already transforming me into a person worth noticing, a person that the most popular girl in school would give her number to—a number I wouldn't be able to use because I didn't talk, but still. If this was what happened the second time I met James, what would happen the third? Would he ask me on a date? Would we go to the movies? Would he kiss me like Andrew McCarthy kissed Molly Ringwald after their first date in *Pretty in Pink*?

I could not wait to see.

THE NEXT MONDAY, Veronica's participation in the hallway monkey calls stopped. She didn't speak to me again directly like she had with James there, but she stopped saying nasty things about me in a polite tone of voice within my earshot. Also, she ceased letting it register on her face when my paper came back with a higher grade than hers.

In fact, after two weeks, nobody was bothering me anymore. Not even Perry, who was still riding high on the victory that the team had managed to snag with him stepping in as substitute quarterback after James had been thrown out of the game. It was like I was invisible again, and this time I knew enough to appreciate it. Best of all, I could resume stalking James, without having to worry about Veronica and her sister coming after me for it.

I had already thought my heart chock full of love for James, but there must've been some room left, because over the next two weeks, something else came to reside there.

It sent me floating through the halls, unable to see time as anything but filler between James sightings.

Back then, I thought it was a new, shiny layer of love that I had never known before. But having lived for seventeen more years, now I recognize it for what it really was: hope.

Because if he could recognize the beauty of my hastily written note enough to smile at me and keep it, then maybe he would recognize the beauty of me, even though I failed to wear mine on the outside like his sisters—or the head cheerleader. I saw him with her sometimes, had heard they were dating now.

But I didn't care. Jake Ryan had also dated a pretty girl before meeting The One in *Sixteen Candles*. And as sure as I continued to breathe, I knew that James would eventually be mine.

RIGHT AROUND THE time that Veronica and her minions stopped terrorizing me, Cora turned on the news, and it said that Mr. Farrell was now our district's U.S. representative.

The Saturday after he got elected, Mr. Farrell—no, Congressman Farrell—showed up at the house with a bottle of champagne. While Cora was in the kitchen opening it, he handed me a hundred-dollar bill instead of the usual ten.

My mouth dropped open when I saw Benjamin Franklin on the front, then I smiled up at him in happy disbelief.

He grinned back at me. "Now where have you been hiding that beautiful smile all this time?"

Of course I didn't answer that.

Then he winked at me and whispered, "Our little secret."

Now this is where it got kind of strange, because it felt like he was paying me not to tell anybody about him and Cora, which was funny on a few different levels, since:

1. I didn't talk.
2. Who would I tell? I didn't have any friends. And most of all,
3. Veronica already knew all about it. So his secret was out.

It made me wonder how much he was paying Cora to keep quiet about their affair. It had to be a lot if he was throwing hundred-dollar bills at a kid like no big deal. And Cora's lifestyle was not luxurious, so she had to be sitting on a wad of cash. Maybe it was even in the house someplace.

I didn't let my thoughts go too far down that road, though, because if Cora suspected I was even thinking about trying to find her stash of money, she would beat me within an inch of my life. Again.

Still, it gave me pause to think that we were both hoarders when it came to money. It made me wonder if we had more in common. Actually, it made me hope that we had more in common. Because if my mama could keep a man—a congressman like Mr. Farrell—coming back every Saturday even after he got elected, then maybe I could get and keep his son.

Mr. Farrell, however, did not show up the next Saturday. I guess the hundred dollars and the champagne had been his way of saying good-bye.

Cora did not seem surprised. She got dressed and went down to the bar like she used to before Congressman Farrell started coming around. That night she brought home a small, fat man who reeked of menthol-flavored smoke, the complete opposite of the congressman.

Cora liked rich and handsome men just as much as the next woman, but she almost seemed relieved to be rid of Mr. Farrell. And for weeks after that, every friend she brought home was the kind that favored jeans, T-shirts, and tennis shoes.

# SIX

THE MONTHS FLEW BY, AND THOUGH I vigilantly stalked James, it took until March 1992 for him and Tanisha Harris to break up. I overheard in the girls' bathroom that he broke up with her after she tried to convince him to turn down his early acceptance from Princeton and apply to colleges in Mississippi, so that they could stay close to each other after he graduated.

The very same day I heard that story, I walked myself into the school library during lunch and began researching colleges near Princeton. Overall, my grades were excellent, but with the steady C's I kept getting in Spanish on account of not talking, I didn't think I had much chance of getting into Princeton, especially since I'd need a full scholarship. However, Rider University, a nearby and much lower-tiered college in Lawrenceville, New Jersey—that I could probably swing.

By Molly Ringwald Ending rules, it was James's turn to make a Big Move, so I was forced to wait him out. But I also wanted to prepare myself for our future together, so I spent a lot of time keeping up my non-Spanish grades, and doing all sorts of research. I started taking practice PSATs in order to get into Rider. I watched and rewatched my Molly Ringwald movies so that I'd know what to do and say when James finally came for me. And I stuck to a steady diet of romance novels, about women who thought they were ugly but then it turned out they had been beautiful all along, they just didn't realize it until they met the man of their dreams.

IN APRIL, the Farrell siblings decided to throw a party. Tra-la-la. Everybody was talking about it. I didn't know every last detail, but this is what I had gleaned from overheard conversations:

1. The Farrell parents would be out of town, on account of Congressman Farrell having to go to Washington, D.C., to do his job.
2. Everybody who came to the party would have to be invited by James, Tammy, or Veronica. And I heard Veronica tell Elise in algebra, "We're not having any plus-ones."
3. The invitations—yes, actual invitations—would be going out on Friday, which meant no one would know that they were invited to the party of the year until the day it was actually going to happen.

I should take a moment here to explain a few things about my school. Maybe you've noticed that I haven't mentioned any white kids so far. That's because, in the entire thousand-plus population of Glass High, there were only two.

See, Glass was a very small county that had been founded by a group of ex-slaves turned sharecroppers. And these founders weren't proud, black people with whip scars on their backs and tales of what it had been like on the dirt roads going north before they got caught. These were the black people who hadn't run. The ones who had stood by with stoic faces when their babies were sold off to neighboring plantations.

They were the black folks who had stayed on at the Glass Plantation, even after Emancipation, for lack of anywhere else to go.

They were slaves, and then they were barely paid workers for the same people who used to own them. Then they became sharecroppers when the Glass family sold the plantation and its acres to some other rich people.

They worked for those rich people and the rich people after them. And when Farrell Fine Hair bought most of the unused farmland in Glass and built a factory on it, they worked for them.

Most of the foremen and white-collar workers at the factory sent their kids to the private Catholic school in the next town over, Wills—which was referred to by most Glass residents as The White People.

As in "I'm fixin' to go to The White People to see about this job." Or "He up there at The White People College." Or "We got a game with The White People tomorrow." Which meant "I'm going to Wills to interview for a job" and "He's attending school at Wills Community College" and "We're playing Wills High in the football game tomorrow." There were black people who lived in Wills and even played on their sports teams. And Glass often played games against schools that actually had all-white teams. Still, this strange nickname had stuck for some reason.

Glass was its own municipality, and we had come to like not having to deal with white people much. We didn't beg them to let us drink at their fountains in the sixties, and even though it was the nineties now, we still weren't asking to go to their schools.

So you need to understand that having the Farrell family at our school was the equivalent of throwing Japanese koi in a lake with a bunch of catfish: All we could do was look up at them in wonder.

Back then, they seemed like such magical beings. Like God had decided to send these people to us from another world. And every time one of them talked to you, it was an Event in Your Life.

Years later, I'm continuously surprised that despite her presence in my life, Veronica Farrell only ever talked to me directly once in high school. During the Note Incident.

And I remember every single word she said.

———

THE FRIDAY THAT the party was supposed to go down, Veronica's lackey, Elise, spread the word that all those who were invited would have invitations in their lockers by the end of the school day. I didn't have to eavesdrop to get this information, because everybody was talking about it.

The guys were cooler about it than the girls, who kept asking for bathroom passes so that they could check their lockers during class. But even the boys seemed to hurry into the hall right after the end-of-class bells rang. And they, too, were checking their lockers first thing first.

By the time sixth period was about to roll around, Principal Simmons had announced over the speaker system that no more bathroom passes would be issued for the remainder of the school day, so students should make sure to use the bathroom before class.

Expectations were at a fever pitch. Even the boys weren't acting so cool about it anymore. During health, my last class of the day, a few of them were talking about how "that wouldn't even be right" if Farrell didn't invite no dudes.

The suspense was killing them.

And as soon as the bell rang, feet hit the floor, running. Miss Patrick was cut off from giving out an assignment for the weekend, and most of the kids were out the classroom door before the last bell had even finished ringing.

The popular kids (like Elise and Corey and the head cheerleader) also rushed, not only because they were caught up in the excitement of the day, but also, I suspected, because they knew what a fine picture they would make as they opened up their invites in front of lesser beings.

I, however, hung back. I had a feeling in the back of my heart that there maybe was an invitation in my locker, that this would be the Big Move I had been waiting for from James. But I was scared to trust this feeling too much, because I wasn't sure if it was my usual good intuition or just wishful thinking. As much as I had hoped and prayed over this matter since the Farrells had announced their party, there was still a chance that my locker would be empty when I got to it. And unlike all the other kids, I didn't see any reason to rush toward possible disappointment.

A kind of numbness overtook me as I moved through the halls. I watched the other students jumping up and down with joy while waving their invitations in the air. Or staring with dejected faces into empty lockers and an even emptier Friday night. By the time I got to my locker, my used-to-be-good intuition had reversed its thinking, and I decided that the only reason I was opening my locker was to throw in the books I wouldn't need to do my weekend homework.

Which was why I let out a gasp of surprise when I saw the manila invitation lying on top of the books in my locker.

# SEVEN

MY FIRST THOUGHT WAS THAT JAMES had finally come through. My second, crushing thought was that somebody else's invitation might have been dropped into my locker by mistake.

So I put my books down on the floor and picked up the envelope . . .

. . . only to find the name "Davidia Jones" scrawled across the front.

Blood rushed to my head, and I could feel a sweat break out over my entire body—even though I felt extremely cold. I was like a block of ice unable to move for fear of cracking.

I made the connection for the very first time that this was what my books meant when they said that some character "broke into a cold sweat."

My heart stopped, then lurched, and then soared as I tore open that envelope, my fingers forming a forever memory as they pulled out the simple note card. It read, "You are cordially invited to Farrell Manor for The Best Party Ever." I smiled, because giving the party such a rah-rah title had to have been Tammy's idea, and I could just imagine James having to facilitate the argument between her and Veronica over it.

Below the announcement was a time and the Farrell Manor address, which I didn't need because I already knew how to get there by heart. And below that was a handwritten note:

*Hope to see you there. James.*

I read and reread that line about fifty times. I took note of the period behind "there," and was impressed because it was so much more laid back than an exclamation point. I also like the large, confident way he signed his name with a huge "J."

I loved him. I loved him so much that I didn't know how to express it anymore. It was beyond words at that point. All I could do was let my love for him fill me up from head to toe, until it was glowing out of me from every pore.

I put the invitation in my backpack and took the money jar out of my locker. I had taped a piece of paper on the side of it, which had served as an accounting ledger as I put money into it.

Right now the ledger read: $1,017.30. At the beginning of fall, I had barely broken six hundred dollars, but the classroom floors had been especially kind, plus there was all of the money that Congressman Farrell had given me.

I had thought to use the money for Rider University after I graduated, but as I read the number on the side of the jar, I could see something else in my future:

A dress.

A dress that would transform me from bottom-of-the-totem-pole-ugly to deserving-of-the-most-popular-guy-in-school. A dress like the ones that had transformed Molly Ringwald in *Pretty in Pink* and Ally Sheedy in *The Breakfast Club* . . . and Cinderella at the ball.


I USED TEN dollars on a jitney cab to The White People's mall.

The eyes of the woman at Caché followed me around the small store as I tried to find a dress to match how I felt inside. I didn't care. She was Mr. Greeley, except white and a woman and tall.

There was only one dress in the store that would do. It was bright yellow like the sun and James's soul. It was floor-length, with slightly darker sequins that started at the V of the waist.

It cost two hundred and sixty-five dollars.

I picked one up in my size and took it over to the counter. The white woman looked down at me.

"Yes, may I help you?"

I took out my jar and counted out three hundred dollars. As I placed the money on the counter her look went from frosty to confused.

"You want this dress?" she asked me.

I handed the dress to her and nodded.

"Don't you want to try it on?"

I shook my head.

"Okay . . ." she said. She picked up the dress and rang it up. All through the transaction she kept giving me guilty looks, like me buying a dress in her store meant that she was somehow taking advantage of me. I think she thought my muteness to be an indicator of bigger problems in my head. The kind of head problems that would send a nothing little black girl like me into a store to buy a three-hundred-dollar something-person dress.

Still, in the end, she handed me the dress in a long plastic bag. "Now you're sure you don't want to try this on? I don't mind if you do. I don't mind a bit."

She was being kind. It was a startling realization that I didn't quite know what to do with, since I wasn't used to kindness.

I shook my head, and I smiled at her. Smiling wasn't something I often did in regards to other people, but I figured I should start practicing for tonight with James.

She blinked and smiled back.

"Well . . . thank you. You enjoy that dress now."

I walked out of there, and for the first time that I can remember, I truly believed that the world was a good place.

I HAD EXPECTED Cora to be gone for the night. We had run out of alcohol at home, which usually meant that she hit the bar at four in anticipation of happy hour.

But when I opened the door with my dress over my arm, she was sitting on the couch, smoking.

She looked at me when I entered.

I didn't move my arm, hoping that if I walked in without calling attention to it, she wouldn't notice the dress.

Usually when we crossed paths, she didn't really look at me.

As it was, her eyes went back to the television.

"Get me a Vess," she said.

I wanted to ask her why she was still here. Why she hadn't gone out to the bar yet.

But of course I didn't. I put the dress down in the easy chair, and I went into the kitchen to get her a kiwi-strawberry Vess soda.

She was watching *Entertainment Tonight*, and it was 6:45, so maybe that meant she'd be gone in fifteen minutes.

If I could just act normal, I thought, she wouldn't even notice the dress.

But when I stepped back into the living room, she was standing next to the sofa chair, untying the plastic at the bottom of the bag.

She was dressed in her sequined bolero jacket and she had her purse over her arm, like she hadn't just asked me for something. This often happened with Cora. She'd send me to get her something right before she was fixing to leave, and I'd come back from fetching it only to find her already gone.

Ten minutes. If I had just gotten home ten minutes later, I would have missed her entirely.

"What this?" she asked me.

I didn't answer.

"Where'd you get this from?" She was pulling up the plastic now.

I didn't answer.

She looked at the price tag. "Where you get enough money to buy this shit?"

I didn't answer.

"You been stealin' from me?" She came over and looked me up and down, repatterning me in her head from servant-daughter to servant-thief.

Then she backhanded me.

It wasn't unexpected, but I must not have been prepared for it, because I flew. The can of soda also flew. We both hit the wall.

"You been stealing from me?" She screamed that question over and over again. She kicked me and she slapped me on the arms and shoulders and then my hands when I shielded my face from her.

It hurt, but as she hit me, I was glad of three things:

1. That she didn't hit me on the face again.
2. That she didn't find out that there was more money where that came from in my backpack.
3. That she didn't get soda on the dress.

Because sometime between getting hit and hitting the wall, I had calmly decided that if any of those things were to happen, I would grab the butcher knife out of the kitchen and stab her to death. I wrote out my self-defense argument in my mind while she beat me. I wondered if my court-appointed lawyer would be able to get testimonies from classmates and teachers, avowing that I was indeed crazy and did not talk, and yes, I was insane enough to kill my mama.

I was still thinking about this scenario when she stopped hitting me. She grabbed her purse and said, "You return that dress right now, and you gimme that money back. I'm going be home tonight, and you better have my money."

Her words came at me like bullets.

But they missed their mark, because as soon as the door closed behind her, I got to my feet.

I went to the bathroom and showered. Afterward, I used her Oil of Olay face wash and moisturizer. Then I went into her room and found a pair of white peep-toe high heels. It turned out that her feet were now about half a size smaller than mine, but I squeezed my big, wide feet into those shoes anyway because they were the only ones in her closet that matched the dress.

I went to her vanity, and I used her comb to pick out my hair the best I could. Then I dug a rubber band out of my backpack and put the whole mess into an Afro puff.

I used her makeup, too. Her blush, her eye shadow, and her lipstick. I tried to use her tweezers to shape my eyebrows the way Molly Ringwald did Ally Sheedy's eyebrows in *The Breakfast Club*, but my arms were still sore from the beating. They didn't want to stay up long enough to finish the job.

I went back to the living room and put on the dress. The fabric settled over my body like it belonged there, like it had been waiting for me. I had noticed that my body had been transforming for James. I used to be a skinny thing, all legs and arms, but after I met James, it seemed like my breasts went from handfuls to ample overnight and that there was more and more weight on my hips every day. My sixteenth birthday was two months away and I could see in the yellow dress that I now had more curves than Tanisha Harris, more proof that God and Molly Ringwald were on my side.

When I went back to the bedroom and looked at myself in the full-length mirror, it was somebody else standing there. Not Monkey Night, but a girl who wore makeup and dressed expensive and got invited to parties at Farrell Manor.

I could already see James and this new girl kissing over a cake with sixteen candles on it.

THE SHOES PINCHED my feet as I walked down Main Street, but I didn't care. I was happy and it was spring. In fact, I stopped near the town statue of Robert C. Glass, the man who used to own all of our ancestors, and I picked a daisy. I put it behind my ear, just like I had put a flower behind my ear before handing James my note. Not only did it match my new dress, but also my newfound happiness.

"You ain't supposed to be picking them flowers!"

I looked behind me and saw the three old men who kept up a continuing rotation of checkers games outside Mr. Greeley's store. Back in the day, this is what all men did when they retired in Glass: played checkers outside the mini-mart until they died. Now maybe they go places and travel like the rest of the country, but somehow I don't think so.

I don't know which one of them yelled out to me, but they looked noble, sitting out there with the moonlight illuminating all the history on their wrinkled faces.

I smiled and waved at them, because I was young and had my whole life in front of me.

Two of them waved back, but the other one just stared at me.

It occurred to me that all they saw was a vision in yellow picking daisies from underneath the feet of the former massah. They probably hadn't recognized me as the ugly and sad Monkey Night. And that made me smile as I walked away.


BY FAR MY favorite and most beloved scene in *Sixteen Candles* is when Molly Ringwald comes out of the church, and a couple of cars pull away to reveal dreamy Jake Ryan, standing in front of his red Porsche. I still remember how I felt the first time I watched that scene, watched Molly as she looked over her shoulder to make sure he wasn't there for somebody else.

As I walked up the dirt road toward the front of Farrell Manor, I imagined that scene with James and me in the lead roles. I rehearsed what I would say when James looked up and saw me for who I really was: the woman of his dreams.

I decided that I would start off with "Hello" because no one in our school ever said "Hello," just "Hey" and "Hi" and "What up, fool?" "Hello" would set me apart from all the other girls, just like him embodying everything that was good in the world set him apart from all the other guys.

I could see Farrell Manor in the distance now. I skirted a mud puddle left over from the spring rains earlier in the week. Then I looked back to the house, where a few people who I couldn't really see from so far away were milling around on the large front porch.

A car honked behind me and I got out of the way. As it drove past me, I saw it was Corey in his white Rabbit. He stared at me through the open window as he drove past, a confused look on his face.

I guess James hadn't told him that he had invited me. I wasn't surprised—I knew from all the eighties movies that men never talk to each other about stuff like girls.

By the time he pulled up to the front of the house and got out, I was close enough to see him point at me when Veronica and Tammy came out to greet him. I slowed a little.

Veronica and Tammy were both wearing bell-bottoms, which I knew from watching television had made a comeback, but I hadn't expected to see denim at this party. Then I noticed that Corey was also wearing jeans.

I looked down at the invitation. Maybe I had gotten the time wrong. Maybe they were still doing setup, and they hadn't changed into their party clothes yet.

But when I looked up from the invitation, I saw a lot of people on the porch. And they were all wearing jeans. And they were all staring and pointing at me.

That's when I realized a few things:

1. *Sixteen Candles* was about a pretty, rich white girl growing up in the suburbs of Chicago. And
2. I was an ugly, poor, black heifer from Mississippi who all the kids called Monkey Night. And
3. Of course, the invitation had been a trick.

I ran. I ran as fast as the skirt of that stupid dress would let me. Then I hiked up the skirt, so that I could run even faster. But Cora's shoes weren't really designed for running. The heel broke and I fell straight into the mud puddle that I had skirted just moments ago.

The laughter had gotten so loud back at Farrell Manor that I could still hear it, even though I was halfway up the road.

"Come back, Monkey Night!" I heard some boy yell behind me. "You look so nice in your pretty dress!"

I pushed myself up out of the mud, kicked off the shoes, and started running again.

MY FEET WERE bleeding by the time I got home. And my heart was so tired.

I went to the mirror and saw that I was myself again—but now I was wearing a muddy dress and makeup that was ten times too bright for me. Also, my mascara had run down my face, because of all the crying and running.

I didn't want to do anything but crawl onto my couch and sleep. I didn't think I even had enough energy to get out of the dress.

But Cora would be home with whatever man in a few hours, and I didn't have time for self-pity.

I took a shower first, and while I was in there, I mapped out a plan in my head.

I think the shower was what reinvigorated me. Or maybe it was just having any sort of plan at all, sketchy as mine was.

I dumped the schoolbooks out of my backpack and replaced them with *The Color Purple*, toiletries, and the yellow dress. Then I got Cora's plastic suitcase out of the closet and put in some more stuff. Clothes mostly and some of the money. I placed the rest of the bills from the jar at various places on my body, just like I'd seen a hooker do once in a movie, so that if she got robbed the thieves wouldn't get all her money. Seemed like a good strategy to me.

I looked around to make sure I wasn't forgetting anything, and my eyes landed on the scrapbook, which was still sitting on the couch. I had flipped through it before I had left for Farrell Manor, savoring the fantasy one last time before it became a reality.

But three hours ago seemed like a lifetime ago.

I didn't take the scrapbook or my Molly Ringwald VHS movies with me when I left. In fact, those were the things I made sure to leave behind.

# PART II

# IN BETWEEN
# THEN AND NOW

# EIGHT

WHEN I THINK BACK ON THE night of the Farrell Manor Incident, I feel a lot of things: shame, anger . . . but I also feel pride. Because at least I knew when to go.

As I walked west on the road out of town, I imagined all the kids at that party, standing on the steps of the school, waiting for me on Monday morning. I could see them laughing and talking about how funny it was: my dress and my makeup and my hair. I hear the less popular kids hanging on their every word as they recount me falling into the puddle. Maybe Perry even does an impression of me falling, his arms flailing and his eyes wide like mine.

But then the second period bell rings, and people who normally have class with me start to realize I'm not there. And that's sort of strange, because further discussion reveals the fact that I had never missed a day of school in my life. By lunchtime, the laughing has turned to confusion. Then people would start to figure that I've skipped school because I'm so embarrassed, which would be understandable.

I imagined that it would probably take weeks —maybe even a month— for them to realize I wasn't coming back.

That's what I thought about while I walked to the closest truck stop. I think it took me three hours to get there, but that was just a guesstimate.

I didn't have a watch, and I hadn't checked the time before I closed Cora's door behind me. But my feet hurt so bad by the time I arrived, I figured three hours sounded just about right.

I felt scared, but my heart lay silent in my chest. I wasn't going back. It was decided. And there was nothing that life could do or throw at me to make me change my mind about that.

So I went into the diner attached to the truck stop's gas station and gave the waitress two dollars of my money for a cup of coffee and a side of hash browns, pointing them out on the picture menu. Then I waited for someone to give my first words to.

I knew that it would be a woman.

Women were mean, and women said nasty things to you, and sometimes women even hit. Nine times out of ten, women who did this were women you knew—women who had some kind of context in your life. But in my experience, women were never mean to complete strangers. They didn't rape, mug, or slit the throats of people they did not know— especially if that person was another woman. So I knew that if I was going to get to where I was going, which was simply away from where I was for forever, it would be a woman that drove me.

So I waited. It took a long time for a woman without a boyfriend or husband to show up, but around five in the morning she came in, sat down at the lunch counter, and ordered a cup of coffee.

She was a large black woman in jeans and a T-shirt so billowy that it didn't even hug her large, low-hanging breasts. She wore a trucker's cap, and it didn't look like she had any hair under it. I had never, ever seen a black woman who dressed like a man and wore her hair cut short like a man's in my entire life—not even on television.

I just stared and stared.

She must have felt my eyes on her, because as the waitress was refilling her cup, she turned around on her cracked red leather stool and stared back at me.

"What you looking at?" she asked me. The question wasn't hostile. It was just a question and almost gentle in the asking.

"She don't talk," the waitress told her. "She been here since three A.M."

"You want some more coffee?" the big woman asked.

I shook my head.

Now both she and the waitress were staring at me. "What you want then?" she asked.

I swallowed and worked my throat a couple of times, so that I could make sure my voice came out clear when I spoke.

But I did it. I answered, "A ride."


HER NAME WAS Mama Jane. She was a truck driver of a certain age. And she was going to California, where she had a nephew named Nicky who was about to open a nightclub and would maybe be needing some help. Maybe I could wash dishes or something.

I found out her name in the diner after she came to sit down with me at my booth, and put out her big rough hand for a shake.

"Everybody call me Mama Jane. What they call you?"

I thought, *Monkey Night*, but answered, "Davidia Jones" since the monkey part of my life was over now.

"Davidia Jones," she repeated. Then she chewed on it for a second like she liked the taste of it. "Davidia Jones. Davidia Jones. That's some kind of handle. Black folks name they children the strangest things. You named after your daddy?"

"Kind of."

"Kind of, huh? Where he at now?"

"I don't know. I never knew him."

"Okay, that's a common story." She raised her coffee cup in a toast. "Where's your mama?"

"She's at home. She's an alcoholic. It's going to take her a while to figure out I'm gone. And when she does, she won't come looking for me."

Mama Jane went quiet. Took a few more sips of her coffee. Then she asked me, "You sure about that?"

I nodded. "She ain't that kind of mama."

Mama Jane finished her coffee but told me, "I need one more cup. I gotta have three to get started. You don't mind, do you?"

I didn't say anything, because it didn't seem like that was a question in need of a verbal answer.

The waitress came over and refilled her coffee cup. She looked from Mama Jane to me, then back at me and said, "You ain't seriously thinking about giving this child a ride?"

The waitress was white with thin tight lips. We both waited for Mama Jane's answer.

I FOUND OUT that she was a lesbian later that night in Dallas, Texas. Mama Jane pulled into a Motel 8 right off the highway and got us a room with one queen-sized bed.

While she was in the bathroom, I looked out the dusty hotel window and saw the rates printed outside on a big rotating sign. I sat down at the little plywood desk and did the math, splitting the rate in half and calculating the tax, assuming it would be about two cents more than the Mississippi sales tax. After all, Texas was a lot bigger. Then I pulled what I owed Mama Jane out of my bra.

I had the money waiting for her when she came out of the bathroom. I tried to hand it to her, but she pushed my hand aside. "My job got this. They got to put you up in a hotel if they got you hauling shit across the country."

I didn't answer. I put the money away in my backpack pocket. I felt awkward now. Truth be told, I wasn't used to people being nice to me and I didn't know what to do with my hands. I kept folding and unfolding them on top of the desk.

She looked down at me. She had taken off the T-shirt and was just in her bra and jeans now.

"How old are you?" The way she asked it sounded more like an accusation than a question. "You could pass for eighteen, but you sound like a kid when you open your mouth."

I looked down at the new body I had developed since first meeting James back in the fall. Did I really look eighteen now? I had felt like a woman when I had seen myself in that yellow dress for the first time. But after the Farrell Manor Incident, I saw a child playing dress-up when I looked at myself in the mirror again.

Maybe sometimes I looked like a woman and sometimes I looked like a child, depending on the circumstance.

And in this circumstance, Mama Jane was confirming what my health textbook had promised: My body had developed from girl to young woman. Unfortunately, that didn't erase the fact that I was still a minor.

I answered Mama Jane with book knowledge, being totally and utterly without street knowledge. "If the police pull you over, you're not going to want to know how old I am. I don't have any ID, so there's no way for them to tell, unless they find my birth certificate. But I've got that hidden real well."

Mama Jane kept on standing over me. "If the police pull me over?" she repeated. "I thought you said your mama wasn't going to look for you."

"She isn't. I'm talking hypothetically."

She looked at me. "You got some big words for a little girl I found in the boonies."

I got quiet then. I could feel her anger, hot like Cora's, coming off of her. But I didn't know what to do about it or what I had said to cause it. I wanted to become like the soft white girls on television. Wanted to whine, "Are you angry at me?" Wanted to gaze at her with beseeching eyes until she started being nice to me again. But I was loath to say anything else at this point. And my beseeching stare was hit or miss, considering that I hadn't spent a lot of time practicing it.

So I stared at my feet.

On the edges of my vision, I could see her go sit on the bed.

"I like women. You know what I mean when I say that?"

I nodded my head.

But that wasn't enough for her. "Say it then, so I know you understand it."

I thought of telling her about *The Color Purple*. How I knew all about the love that could happen between Southern black women, since I had read it about a thousand times. Instead I just said, "You're a lesbian."

"Yeah, I'm a lesbian." She was pulling off her shoes now. Dirty white New Balance tennis shoes that had seen better days. "And you cute, so that's going to make this trip a little harder for me. But I'm pretty sure you a minor. Plus, you don't need a lover right at this moment. You need a decent mama. So you and me ain't going to happen, okay?"

Later, when I looked back on this conversation, I would feel intense love for Mama Jane for not taking advantage of the position I was in. I liked men and until that point James exclusively, but if she had asked me for my body, I would have given it to her. And I would have thought that it was more than a fair trade for her facilitating my escape from Glass.

I wouldn't properly appreciate the danger I had put myself in by traveling across the country with a woman I didn't know until I grew up and really examined my life. Though my picking-a-woman logic had felt one hundred percent sound, the fact was I still could have been raped, mugged, or killed—my first sexual experience could have been completely commercial. Later, I would review those three days of my life and feel such profound relief and gratitude that I had survived them with my body and soul intact.

At the time, though, I didn't feel any of that.

I was only fifteen.

When Mama Jane said the last thing she would ever say to me about us possibly getting together, I wasn't relieved or grateful—I was shocked. And it took every ounce of my reserve not to say, "You think I'm cute?"

I went quiet, trying to figure out what kind of ugly Mama Jane had encountered in her life to make her say a thing like that.

The next day, Mama Jane got us a hotel room with two twin beds.

And the day after that, we arrived in Los Angeles.

I DIDN'T LOVE Los Angeles the first time I saw it. Driving in through downtown, the streets were dirty and there were homeless people. Actual homeless people.

I had seen such people in movies and read about them a time or two in books, but I had never actually clapped eyes on anything like Skid Row in Los Angeles.

As we lumbered down the streets toward the factory for the drop-off, Mama Jane kept on having to stop when a woman or a man would wander into the road.

Sometimes they were older people with fat bellies and sores. And sometimes they were younger people with dirty hair and sores and faces that looked like they used to be appealing before all the dirt.

"It's the drugs," Mama Jane told me as we drove down the street. "Some of them is crazy, but when you see them young like that, usually it mean some drug done got ahold of them. Meth maybe, but usually crack. The crack done hit real bad out here."

We had had crack in Glass back then, but not like this. Back in Glass, we were all spread apart, with neighbors you didn't have to see unless you sought them out. But the streets of downtown Los Angeles were close, with trash and people piled up on most corners and a constant stench that made me roll up my window and think maybe this was hell. Maybe the poets were right about hell on earth, and when you lived a bad life, you died and came back as one of these people wandering out in front of trucks that never hit you.

I thought about Cora then, wondered where she had been during the years between leaving me with my grandmama and coming back to do a less than half-assed job of raising me. Had she gone to a big city like this? Was that where she had learned to drink and make friends? Was that what I was going to have to learn in order to survive out here?

I must've shivered because Mama Jane said, "Don't worry. We ain't going to be down here long. I'm dropping this load off, then we'll head out to Nicky's."

## NINE

I HAD SEEN PICTURES OF SEEDY Hollywood on television and in the movies, but I never saw it close up until I climbed out of Mama Jane's truck and looked up at Nicky's. It was several blocks down from the old Cinerama Dome on Vine in a gray, two-story building that looked like it had seen better days. Maybe back in the fifties, it had been a nice place, but now the only thing new about it was a large neon sign that read "Nicky's."

Mama Jane came around the truck and took in the place with me. "He's been fixing it up. It's gonna be real nice when he finishes. Plus, he says that he talked to some people that were setting up a redevelopment fund for the area. So this part of town might be nice . . . someday. The point is, he's only twenty-five, and he's already done all this. We're real proud of him, no matter what happens with it."

Mama Jane did not sound optimistic about the chances of this club working out for her nephew, and I could see why. There was graffiti on every storefront as far as the eye could see. There were also dangerous-looking men in flannel shirts, and hookers, who upon second look turned out to also be men, on nearby corners. But I figured beggars can't be choosers, and desperate people like me shouldn't have any truck with pickiness, so I followed Mama Jane into the building.

I was surprised to see that it was actually very nice inside. There were hardwood floors, elegant black leather bar stools, and round mahogany tables that seemed suited for an upscale crowd.

"Wait here," Mama Jane said. Then she disappeared behind a dark wooden door with the word "Office" stenciled on the outside in faded, yellow lettering.

She closed the door behind her, but I could still hear it when a deep male voice yelled, "Are you crazy? You picked up some girl on the road?"

Nicky did not sound like the younger, male version of Mama Jane that I had been hoping for.

I couldn't hear anything else after that. Mama Jane was probably trying to further explain, but I guess it didn't work. The door slammed open, then Nicky came out and made a straight beeline for me.

"Your mama ain't looking for you? That's what you trying to tell me?"

He was dressed in a suit and a tie, but he was a very large man. Six-five at least with thick muscles and an extremely unsettling, unblinking stare.

I had to control the urge to flinch and take several steps back as he yelled at me. I found myself very scared of this loud man and his loud words, but still I said, "No, she isn't looking for me. I swear she isn't, sir." I told him like I told Mama Jane, "She's not that kind of mama."

Nicky's eyes bugged and he looked back over his shoulder at Mama Jane. "And she talk country, too? Now I know she got somebody looking for her. Her people probably worried sick because she out here with you."

He turned back to me. "Where are you from?"

Something in his voice told me it wouldn't be wise to deny him the answer to this question, or even to hesitate.

"Mississippi," I said.

"Mississippi," he repeated. "What part of Mississippi?"

I went quiet again. No, my mother wasn't looking for me. But if this man put in a phone call to the Glass Police, they might go out to Cora's house or stop by Glass High and find out that I hadn't been in school since last Friday. If just one of them got it into their heads to do the right thing, then there'd be APBs to worry about.

Mama Jane put a hand on Nicky's beefy arm. "Maybe she could wash dishes or sweep up around here. She smart and she work hard." She promised this, even though she barely knew me.

My heart swelled. I was already coming to love Mama Jane. Love her like the mama she had told me I needed back in the first hotel room.

But Nicky turned on her. "We got illegals for all that shit. Nobody with papers in L.A. is doing that work no more."

"Maybe she could be a waiter."

Nicky stared at her like she was one of those Skid Row bums on crack. "Okay, then ABC come up in here and then what?"

"ABC? Who's ABC? And what they got to do with it?" Mama Jane asked.

"Alcohol Beverage Control. They the ones that come up in here asking for IDs, then what happens when they find out this one's underage. They'd shut me down. Plus I already got all the waiters I need."

"Well, what else do you need?" Mama Jane put her hands on her hips and drew herself up to her full six feet. She glared at Nicky like this whole situation was all his fault.

But Nicky wasn't backing down, "I don't need nothing, Aunt Jane. I got everything I need except a singer, and I got girls coming in to audition for that tomorrow."

"I can sing."

Everybody, including me, looked surprised to hear those words. It even took me a second to realize that it had been me who had said them. And I only figured out it was me because I just narrowly stopped myself from adding that I used to be Tina Turner when I was six.

Mama Jane and Nicky both turned toward me now. Nicky, especially, looked me up and down, his eyes running over my thrift store T-shirt that said "Hattiesburg," and my stonewashed Wranglers.

"You can sing?"

I didn't blame him for looking incredulous because I didn't believe me—didn't even know why I had said that. But somebody else, somebody I can only describe as Me-But-Not-Me, answered, "Yes, I can sing."

Mama Jane, bless her heart, picked up the baton of my lie. "Just let her audition for you. If you don't like her, I'll take her to the shelter. They got good programs for runaways." She looked back at me. "You'll be okay."

It sounded like she was trying to reassure herself more than me, but I smiled back at her. Even though I had no idea how I'd survive in a shelter of runaways when I couldn't even survive high school.

Nicky glared at Mama Jane. "If I listen to her sing, there won't be any crying afterwards. No more begging me to give her ass a job? None of that?"

Mama Jane nodded. "I'll take her right on to the shelter, I promise."

My heart shuddered a bit. At that moment, I really, really wished I could sing.

NICKY SAT DOWN at a shiny black baby grand piano and pulled out a songbook.

"Who do you know?" he asked me.

Then, off my blank look, he reframed it, "Who do you know, song-wise. This here is going to be an old-fashioned nightclub, modeled after the ones from the thirties and forties. I want to attract a certain kind of clientele. Diverse, but with money. The kind of people who don't mind dressing up to eat. So I'm going to need a chanteuse."

I stared at him.

"Do you know what a chanteuse is?"

I did, but I didn't answer. I was too shocked about his vision for this club. Considering what I had seen outside, it did not seem practical.

As it was, Nicky got upset again. He twisted around on the bench and said to Mama Jane, "This ain't going to work—"

"I know what a chanteuse is," I rushed out.

And then I just started shoveling words into the situation, trying to prove to him that yes, I could talk and yes, this could work—even though I knew that it couldn't. "When I was a kid I used to pretend I was Tina

Turner. And I know she's rock and roll, but I've got all the words to every Nat King Cole song memorized, because my grandmama left behind all of his albums. And I'm a fast learner, so I could memorize some more songs by other people. I know I could."

I broke off with a little gasp and waited to see if any of that had worked.

Nicky rubbed a hand over his eyes, but he turned back to the piano. I was extremely grateful for that, until he actually started playing the opening of "Nature Boy."

"Do you know that one?" he asked me.

I nodded, and then said yes, because he wasn't looking at me, he was looking at the keys.

"Then sing." His voice was short and irritated. I knew I had better sing.

I stood there, my body a little leaned forward, my mind screaming, *SING! SING!* and my heart thumping in my chest so that you'd think it was about to bust.

But nothing came out.

Nicky repeated the opening. Once then twice. But I couldn't even open my mouth.

He stopped playing with a bang of the keys. "Okay, get her out of here," he said to Mama Jane.

Mama Jane came over to me. "Wait a minute, Nicky."

"No, I wasted enough time. I got shit to do, Aunt Jane."

Mama Jane glared at him. "I changed your stanky diapers for a year while your mama and daddy was finishing up grad school. You can wait a fuckin' minute."

There were two things about this statement that amazed me:

1. Nicky apparently had two parents. He had not, as I had previously assumed, been raised by loud and impatient wolves. And
2. Mama Jane's words actually worked. Nicky got sullen and

quiet, but he did not get up from that piano. In fact, he squirmed under Mama Jane's gaze until she let him go by turning to me.

"Listen, you can do this, baby," she said. And I felt bad, because that wasn't true. I had lied about being able to sing. I didn't have any training, and I had barely spoken, much less sung, since I was a six-year-old Tina Turner in my mama's vanity mirror.

Mama Jane rubbed my arms. "Yeah, you can do this. I know you can."

The touch combined with actual eye contact was too much. I felt overwhelmed, and tears welled up in my eyes. I knew it was all bullshit—that I had gotten here on bullshit—that my life was an infinitesimal piece of bullshit in a world full of bullshit, bullshit, bullshit. But all I could say was "Really? You think I can?"

She smiled and nodded. "C'mon baby," she said. Then she said it again when I didn't move. "C'mon, baby."

She was standing there, believing in me and looking at me and touching me and calling me "baby" like I was her child. And I was standing there trying not to cry, because I couldn't sing and I wasn't anybody's child, not really.

And only then, only when I was moments away from crumpling onto the ground in a ball of inability, did Me-But-Not-Me finally decide to step forward again.

She was the one that sang, *"There was a boy . . ."*

"Yes," Mama Jane said, like it was the most profound thing she had ever heard.

*"A very strange, enchanted boy."*

Mama Jane was nodding now. And as I kept on singing, I felt like I was explaining something to her. Telling her the story of my life. It started off with one of my first memories, which was my grandmama, putting on this record and singing along with it as she went about the house. I sang, and in my heart, I told Mama Jane about how later, after my grandmama had died and Cora had taken up residence in her room, I had come to think of the boy from this song as my brother. Someone who spent most of his days alone and valued love because he didn't have it.

Somehow I had forgotten about my grandmama. I had only been five when she passed, but when Me-But-Not-Me was singing, I remembered her.

When Nicky joined me on the piano after the first few lines, I watched Grandmama clean the house, and I heard her tinny voice joining in with Nat's. I felt her hand wrap around mine as we walked down Glass's Main Street. I missed her as I sang about the boy wandering very far over land and sea.

Mama Jane stepped back to look at me. And, to tell you the truth, so did I. I had to get a good look at me so I could see that Me-But-Not-Me was actually Me Then. She was Little Davidia, the girl that I had been before Cora knocked her out of me.

And man, could she sing.

I mean, she was killing this song. She was taking it home to its rightful maker and showing it off in heaven. She was letting people know that she had risen from the dead and that she was back.

Little Davidia finished the song on a long note—not because she was showing off, but because she did not want it to end.

The piano part finished. Nicky put his hands in his lap. Mama Jane was openly crying now. But I couldn't let it end, not till every last breath was gone from my body, and even then, I fell to my knees, holding it just a little longer.

I was wheezing by the time it was over. I could feel Little Davidia running her hands over me, comforting me like she used to comfort our grandmama when she had coughing fits.

The room was silent. I was wheezing. Mama Jane was weeping and Nicky was staring at me in a very loud way.

Which is why I was surprised by how quiet his voice was when he actually spoke. "How old are you?"

This time I didn't beat around the bush. "I'm fifteen," I said. Straight up.

"1969. Remember this year when ABC comes up in here. We going to get you some ID, but sometimes they ask you a follow-up."

He got up and walked over to me and took me by the chin. "Show me your teeth."

I had read that overseers used to do this when buying slaves, but I showed him my teeth anyway.

"They're straight and it don't look like you got any cavities. Good. But you better start flossing or you're going to have trouble with them gums down the line. How old are you?"

"Twenty-two," I answered automatically. I didn't even have to think about it.

He smiled down at me, showing off his own pearly whites.

"You a fast learner. Good." He let go of my chin and turned back to Mama Jane. "Davidia. That's ugly."

I flinched. I thought for a second he was saying I was ugly, just like the people back in Glass said all the time.

But then Mama Jane shrugged. "You can call her Davy," she said. And I understood it was my name, not my face, he had problems with.

Nicky nodded. "Yes, yes, I'm liking that shit. But with an 'ie'—like Billie Holiday and Stevie Nicks. Davie, what's your last name?"

"Jones."

Nicky laughed. "For real? Davie Jones? Like the Monkee?"

"And the pirate's locker."

He shook his head at me, smiling like he had finally gotten the joke. And it was a good one. "That's it," he said, pointing at me. "That's exactly it."

# TEN

TAKING MY CACHÉ DRESS WITH ME when I hightailed it out of Mississippi had been an impulse decision, but it turned out to be a good one for my destiny because Nicky refused to buy me a dress until I proved that I could do what I did in the audition in front of a crowd.

"I like you," he said. "But let's not go crazy. You going to have to come up with your own dress for opening week."

So we worked it out. I offered up my muddy yellow dress, and he agreed to pay for the dry cleaning.

I didn't know how much dry cleaning cost back then, but from the sour look on Nicky's face as he agreed to pay for it, I figured it must be a lot.

That was before I really got to know Nicky. I would figure out later that he just didn't like to spend money. He wore the same sucked-lemon look when handing out paychecks and forking over cash for his purchases at the grocery store.

And if that didn't make it clear enough, he barked at every Girl Scout, Salvation Army ringer, and homeless panhandler that dared approach him, "Move on bitch. You done asked the wrong brutha."

It was real embarrassing if you happened to be with him when he said it. Outside of my mother, I don't think I have ever met a less altruistic human being.

But at least Nicky gave me a chance to earn a living. There were worse things that I could be doing to get by than singing in a club owned by the cheapest man on earth. Much worse. I mean I passed by tranny prostitutes every day on my way in to work.

I was grateful for the opportunity, which is why I worked day and night the entire week between getting hired and the restaurant opening.

Nicky told me that he wanted me to sing ten songs four nights a week, and only three of them could be by Nat King Cole. And none of them could be by Tina Turner, which was the only other kind of song I had memorized.

So I borrowed four cassettes from Nicky's office music collection: *Billie Holiday Live*, *Peggy Lee All-Time Greatest Hits*, *The Best of Shirley Bassey*, and *Nina Simone in Concert/I Put a Spell on You*. Then, every night for five days, I transcribed as many of the songs as I could while everybody else in Mama Jane's Inglewood apartment complex was sleeping.

I had to push the rewind button a lot and usually my hand started cramping by the third or fourth song. I listened to cassette tapes on tinny earphones that I had picked up at the 99-cent store. That's what dollar stores were called in L.A.—99-cent stores. And the penny difference was truly shocking, because everything else in the city was way more expensive than the stuff in Glass.

Around four A.M. I'd fall asleep, then I'd wake up at about ten A.M. the next day and practice for a few hours before I took two buses to the club, where I performed a couple of songs for Nicky.

He never said hi when I got there, just asked if I had completed the task that he had assigned the day before. "You got 'Fever' memorized?" or "You been walking in the high heels like I told you?" or "You watch that jazz documentary?"

I always said yes, even if the answer was "I don't know" or even just plain old "No."

And he'd always respond, "That's what I'm talking about." Then he'd take out his clipboard and wait for me to get up onstage and sing a few of the songs that I had committed to memory the night before.

This clipboard seemed to be an extension of Nicky, because that's where he kept his multi-page to-do list, which he made up every morning on his electronic typewriter.

I once got a gander at it and found out that it included everything, I mean absolutely everything, that Nicky planned to do that day, including stuff like "Call Mama" and "Ask Leon the name of that one reggae band" and "Look at the calendar to see what day July 4th falls on this year." You think I'm kidding, but I'm not. The list was so extensive, I could only figure that Nicky must have gotten all kinds of joy and satisfaction from crossing things off it.

Though you'd never know that he actually enjoyed working on the list from the dead-eyed way he'd sit through my songs. It was like he was waiting for me to be done already. And the only thing he ever said after I was finished was "Sing 'Fever.'"

"Fever" was the closing song, and he wanted to make sure I got it right.

After that, he'd give me about two minutes of notes on how to improve my stage presence, then he'd bark another homework assignment at me and walk off without saying good-bye.

It felt just like high school to me, but with more studying and higher stakes.

Still, I was determined to become a match for my newly found-out-about singing voice, so I worked hard on transforming myself into Stage Davie.

I listened to the *Nina Simone in Concert* album and wrote audience asides in the same vein, without any of the political stuff. Then I copied her husky tones as I practiced my performance in front of the bathroom mirror. I would have preferred a full-length mirror, but Mama Jane didn't have one. She didn't make a habit of looking at herself in the mirror, which was yet another thing that set her apart from every Southern woman I had ever known.

I had to hope my hips were swinging the right way as I walked away from the mirror for a few steps, then made a dramatic turn back around to sing "Big Spender."

Two days before the big opening, I sang that and the other nine songs, including "Route 66" and "Fever," for Nicky and his best friend, Leon, a dreadlocked brother with sleepy eyes, who looked even bigger and stronger than Nicky. Nicky had introduced him to me as the club bouncer and general situation guy.

Then off my confused look, he explained that if anybody got physical with me or anything like that, Leon would handle it. Nicky put special emphasis on the words "handle it," which brought to mind images of back alley beatings. And I began to suspect that unlike Nicky, Leon might have acquired his muscles not in a gym, but in a prison.

Still, Leon was a very nice guy. At least he clapped after I was finished, unlike Nicky, who just said, "Better hope you do it that way on Friday. Because if you get up on that stage and you can't sell them like you sold me, then it's right on to the foster home. Remember that."

He pointed at me to seal the threat, then he went back to his office and closed the door behind him. As usual, he didn't bother with a good-bye.

"I think you did real good," Leon said.

My eyes stayed on Nicky's closed door. "Thanks."

MAMA JANE WASN'T able to be there on opening night. She was doing a big haul up to Seattle, but she called to wish me luck.

"Are you nervous?" she asked me.

"The nice thing is I'm so nervous, I've gone numb, which doesn't feel like anything at all. So I guess I've got that to be thankful for—as long as I don't pass out onstage or anything."

"Don't talk like that. You're going to be fine." Her tone was so motherly it was hard to believe this was the same woman who had come close to asking me to put out for her a few weeks ago.

I thanked her for her kind words, hung up, and went to work on myself.

I used her old, black-fist plastic pick to get all the knots out of my hair. Then I switched to her hard-thistle brush to gather it all up into a sophisticated-enough Afro puff.

Mama Jane didn't have any makeup, so I just had to let that part go. Still, when I pulled the yellow dress up over my shoulders, I thought I looked good. Real good. I could almost see what Mama Jane was talking about when she said I was cute.

But backstage at the club, Nicky looked me over and said, "What's up with your makeup?"

"I don't own any. I'm only—" He gave me a warning look, and I caught myself. "I'm only twenty-two."

"Most girls I know been wearing makeup since they were thirteen."

Same here. In fact, some of the girls at my school had started in with the lipstick and eye shadow when they were ten. But I wasn't going to tell him that.

"You need makeup," he said.

"Okay, I'll buy it after I get my first paycheck," I answered. It would have to be cheap makeup, I decided, since I still had to figure out an apartment. I only had two weeks until Mama Jane got back from her trip. And before she'd left, she had warned me that I probably wanted to find my own place before she returned and "things got funny."

"Un-uh. You need to do it after this show. This is L.A. Only hippies don't wear makeup here."

"But I can't really afford to spend money on makeup right now. I've got to find an apartment."

"You need a apartment? I got a empty apartment above the club."

"You do?"

Nicky pulled out his clipboard. "Yeah. Upstairs. It's a studio. But it got a stove. You smoke?"

"No. Like I said, I'm only twenty-two."

"A lot of teenagers smoke out here because all the actors do it." Nicky pushed the curtain-open button for a second to see if it worked. Then he checked that off his list. "Don't start smoking. It's stupid."

"I hadn't planned on—"

"We'll see how you do, and then we'll revisit the apartment rental.

Because if you fuck it up tonight . . ." He pushed the curtain-close button and made another check on the list. "Well, you know wards of the state don't need they own apartments, right?"

Then he walked away.

We didn't have foster care in Glass, but I figured it couldn't be a good thing if Nicky kept on threatening me with it.

I hid in my dressing room, which was really just a large converted closet, and stared at myself in the vanity mirror. Unlike Cora's vanity, this one had large lightbulbs all around the frame, so that every imperfection on my face was illuminated. The extra light made the small space hot, and I could feel the sweat around my temples and at the back of my neck.

I put wads of tissues under my pits, and squeezed my arms to my sides to make them stay. I looked ridiculous, but this dress had to last me a week.

It was hard not to feel small and alone at that moment. The optimism that had allowed me to truly believe that a guy like James Farrell could ever be interested in a girl like me had completely abandoned me. I wondered if life would always be out of control like this, if I would have to live in fear for the rest of my days, my heart in my throat, my body tensed and braced for what was to come. And most of all, I wondered if I'd always have to force myself to go against instinct and be brave.

The door opened, and I turned to see Leon standing there with his large hand on the knob. "You're on in five," he said.

I WALKED OUT onstage to the most sophisticated and diverse audience I had ever seen gathered in one room. There were white people and Latinos and blacks, all turned out in designer dresses and colorful suits. I had never seen anything like it. Even television didn't have the level of diversity that a California nightspot had back then.

I could see Nicky in the wings, waiting for his cue to press play on the backing machine. But I did not feel ready to sing. The Stage Davie I had been honing all week was nowhere to be found. And I didn't dare to open my mouth for fear that something nervous and awkward would come out.

If I were still in Glass, this would have been a good moment to shut my eyes against the rest of the world and pretend I was in a Molly Ringwald movie. But I had let her go—plus, Molly didn't sing—unless you counted that one lip-synching scene in *The Breakfast Club*—which I didn't.

Instead I closed my eyes and imagined that I, Davie Jones, was beautiful. Even more beautiful than Veronica Farrell. I said to myself, *How would Beautiful Davie, the most perfect woman in the whole wide world, handle this situation?*

I opened my eyes. "Hello, everyone. Thank you for coming," I said, in my polite but country accent. "I have a few songs for you to listen to. I hope you like them."

Then I cued Nicky.

The audience loved Stage Davie. They clapped after each song, and they gave her a standing ovation after "Fever."

Nicky even hugged her when she ran off stage. "Good job, baby girl," he said. "They loved that 'Fever' number, huh?"

Then he looked at my Afro puff and his good mood passed as quickly as it had come.

"But we still got to do something about that hair." He got on his walkie-talkie. "Leon, send Russell backstage."

Russell, a short, pudgy waiter with a row of hoop earrings going up the sides of each of his ears, appeared a few minutes later.

"You gay, right?" Nicky asked him.

"Yeah, why?" Russell frowned. "Wait, are you about to fire me because I'm gay, because that would just be so wrong."

"No, fool." Nicky got back out his clipboard. "She don't have a car, so I need you to take her someplace to get her hair done before the show tomorrow. And after that, take her to some sort of makeup counter."

Russell looked from me to Nicky. "I would be offended, but you do need to get your hair and makeup together, girl. You sing too fierce to be looking that tore down."

I could see the compliment in that, so I said, "Thank you."

"I got a cousin with a shop on Pico. I'll pick you up at nine thirty. Then I'll run you over to the Fashion Fair counter at the Beverly Center."

We exchanged information, while Nicky checked us off his list.

When Russell left, Nicky took me by the arm and said, "His gay ass is the only male friend you're allowed until you're eighteen. No dating till you're legal."

I was confused. "So I can't be friends with you?"

Nicky screwed up his face. "I'm your boss, Davie. I ain't your friend. Remember that shit." Then he pulled some money out of his wallet and handed it to me. "Have them give you a perm and put your hair in a bob with a straight bang. If your hair ain't at least down to your shoulders, then tell them to put some tracks in. But don't go crazy. I don't want weave all down your back."

I had no idea what he was talking about, but I took mental notes, figuring that the hairdresser would.

I HADN'T BEEN in a lot of cars before I climbed into Russell's '87 Toyota Corolla, but I could tell from minute one that he was a bad driver.

There was a bunch of tire screeching and cusswords emitting from other cars as we drove up Crenshaw toward Pico.

Russell, however, seemed more concerned with messing around with the radio than obeying the traffic laws. He flipped through stations until he found "My Name Is Not Susan" by Whitney Houston on some smooth groove R&B station. He sang along with it for a few bars, then he cut off, glancing over at me.

"What? You ain't going to sing? You got to sing if you driving with me."

So I sang with him, and I hummed on the parts I didn't know.

Russell's voice wasn't great and he couldn't hit any of the big notes on the chorus. But he was dramatic, and I liked the way he threw his whole upper body into singing along, even though it caused us to swerve into other people's lanes a few times.

He turned off the radio after the song was over. "So what's your story? You came out here to sing?"

"No, sir," I said. "I didn't know I could sing until I got here. That was a lucky surprise."

Without warning, Russell turned and reached into the backseat. He strained against his seat belt and completely blew a stop sign. Horns blared.

He finally got ahold of his small moleskin notebook and turned back around. "I'm going write that down just in case you get famous," he said.

Russell, like most people who want to be famous in Los Angeles, assumed that everybody else who came out here wanted to be famous, too. He was an aspiring screenwriter, and he figured I wanted to be some kind of big singer. But he was so excited about my quote that I didn't have the heart to tell him that for me, Nicky's was just a job.

In the back of my head, I was already thinking about the part of my life that would come after I turned eighteen and could legally do whatever I wanted.

I'd rather chew on lead paint than go back to high school, but the one dream of mine that hadn't been dashed back in Glass was going to college with sophisticated people who wanted to learn something and didn't make fun of you because you were dark.

And though I knew it was a little early in the process to start planning, I figured if I could hang on to this singing job at Nicky's for about two more years and save up some money, then I could take the GED and go to college. I could better myself, so that I'd be smart and people would take me seriously. Just like the Farrells.

But for now, I was taking it one step at a time, so I came back to the now. "Russell," I asked, "how do you figure a bob with a straight bang would look on me?"

# ELEVEN

RUSSELL'S SALON-OWNER COUSIN, SOPHIA, GREETED HIM with a
bear hug and sent me over to a woman with big hips and a skinny waist
named Pearl. She had a country accent like mine and she kept oohing and
aahing as she picked out my hair.

"Ooh, girl, you a virgin. No chemicals? No dyes? No perms ever?" I
shook my head, and she just about fainted. "I have never, ever met a black
virgin over the age of twelve . . . where was you raised?"

It was more a squealed demand than a question. It made me think that
maybe she was preparing to go to my home like Muslims go to Mecca.

But it was nice to be described as a lucky hair virgin, as opposed to
the child of neglect. "Mississippi."

"No, you ain't," she nearly screamed. "I'm from Columbus, Mississippi. I swear it's true. Where you from?"

"Glass."

"Glass," she said. "I ain't never heard of there."

I guessed a lot of people probably hadn't. Even folks in Glass had
thought our town was nowhere and small. "It's right next to Wills."

"Oh, I know Wills. Isn't that where the Farrell Fine Hair factory is?"

Veronica and Tammy laughing at me on the porch sprang into my
mind without warning. I could feel myself getting angry and embarrassed

all over again, like it was happening now, right in front of me, and not over two weeks ago in Mississippi.

Still, I managed to choke out, "No, the Farrell factory is in Glass."

Pearl kept running her hands over my Afro. It was a soft animal that she couldn't stop petting. "Actually, we only use Farrell products for our relaxers up in here. But I know you ain't wanting a relaxer. I know you don't want anything for all this beautiful hair but a trim."

Back then I didn't know how unnatural Los Angeles was, or I would have understood how rare it was to have a hairdresser pass up service and profit to make sure I didn't put any chemicals in my hair. If I had understood that me not having a weave and still having my original down-home accent made me special in Pearl's eyes, I wouldn't have hesitated about going against Nicky's orders. Not even for a second. But in the end, it was the Farrells that helped me decide it.

I'd be damned if I would spend Nicky's cash on any product that would put more money in the Farrells' pockets.

AS IT TURNED out, what they called "ugly" in the South was simply "ungroomed" in Los Angeles. And if there's one thing Los Angeles knows how to do for a child just off the bus, it's get them looking real good real fast.

Four hours later, I walked into my dressing room with a huge Afro and a fully made-up face (courtesy of the Fashion Fair cosmetics counter in the Beverly Center Macy's). I had grown up thinking of my hair as lumpy and unmanageable. But Pearl must have done some kind of magic on it because now it looked so thick and healthy that Russell said, "Damn, Pam Grier," when he came to pick me up.

I didn't have any trouble getting through the door or anything, but the Afro was definitely large and in-charge. I could feel my hair all the way out to my shoulders now.

"Do you think Nicky will be all right with it?" I asked. "He told me to get a perm."

"Girl, forget Nicky. You are ready for the spotlight." He grabbed my hand and led me back to the car. "Wait till we get some makeup on you."

It was funny, because I had given up on having a Molly Ringwald Ending, but here I was caught up in one of those eighties movie make-overs; and when I slipped on my yellow Caché dress a little while later, there was no refuting it.

"Davie Jones," I said to myself. I loved the taste of my new name in my mouth. "If James Farrell saw you now, he just might ask you to the prom."

That thought had sounded good in my head, but when I said it out loud it made me feel sad even though I was standing there in my beautiful dress, with my gorgeous hair. As long as I was feeling bad, it seemed like as good a time as any to break the new look to Nicky.

He hit the roof when I walked out of the dressing room with my hair still natural and now blown out into an even bigger Afro. "What did I tell you?" he said over and over again, like repeating it would turn the Afro into a perm. "Ain't nothing authentic about a 1940s-style singer with an Afro. What didn't you understand about that?" He stuck out his hand. "Give me back my money."

"I only have half of it now, because I got a trim and a blowout. But I'll pay you back the rest with my first check," I promised him.

"You'll pay me with—" He stopped to clench and unclench his out-stretched hand. "You ain't got a apartment. You ain't got a car. And you already spending a check you ain't got yet on a hairstyle that's about to get you fired?"

Well, when he put it that way, it did sound country simple. But I could not make the only offer that would get me out of this situation. I could not say, *Okay, Nicky. I'll take two buses back to that lady and I'll ask her to put Farrell product in my hair*—no, I couldn't do it. So I stood there, waiting to get fired just because Pearl had liked my natural hair and used the wrong kind of relaxers.

He took me by the chin, and looked over my hair like a scientist study-ing an ancient species. "I didn't even know hair salons were still doing blow-out Afros."

He let go of my chin, sucking on his teeth. "When I kick your ass out of here, you planning on becoming a revolutionary?" he asked.

I shrugged. "Maybe."

His eyes nearly came out his skull. "Maybe? Did you just say maybe?"

I answered him the only way I knew how, though I could tell it wasn't the smart thing to say even as it was coming out my mouth.

"Anything could happen."

Which is true. I mean, here I was thousands of miles away from home, singing in a nightclub, because some spoiled rich kids had played a trick on me. I was living the truth of that right there, so I said it again, straight-up: "Anything could happen."

Apparently that was funny, because Nicky started laughing. It was a surprisingly light sound coming out of his large, mountainous body. "Anything could happen," he said, shaking his head.

Then just like that, he let me off the hook. "Davie girl, go get ready for the show."

I guess the prize for me making him laugh was not getting fired.

I didn't question it. In fact, I turned and rushed toward my dressing room. But I didn't get so far so fast that I couldn't hear him say behind me:

"And don't fuck with me again."


WITH REGULAR SALON visits and trims, my Afro only got larger, which didn't please Nicky in the least. But other than that, I took him one hundred percent at his word and did not mess with him again after the Great Hair Battle, which meant I asked one of the darker-skinned waitresses to teach me how to put on the makeup I bought at the Fashion Fair counter. I let Nicky take my rent directly out of my paycheck before he gave it to me. And when one of the busboys caught me by the hand and said, "Hey, you want to go see a movie with me?" I answered no flat out, even though he was the first boy that had ever asked me out or even shown an interest in me in my whole life.

But I obeyed Nicky. Not just because I didn't want to get fired, but also because I was new to boy-girl relationships that existed outside of my head or off the movie screen. The busboy's straightforward come-on made me uncomfortable, like he was asking me to do something that would get me in trouble.

I ended up issuing noes to him and all the other guys who asked me out. But I couldn't explain to any of them about not dating until I was eighteen, since ABC and the rest of the world outside of Nicky and Mama Jane thought I was in my early twenties. So I just had to tell them, "I'm not interested." Blunt, all traces of Stage Davie gone.

"You know everybody think you a lesbian, right?" Russell told me soon after I turned down the busboy. Russell loved to share gossip, even if it was gossip about me.

He relayed how he had actually seen a waiter point out Mama Jane and tell the new hostess to always give her special treatment.

"He straight-up said she was Nicky's aunt, and you was her partner," Russell said. "He had like no doubts, girl."

I just shrugged. Considering everything Mama Jane had done for me, being mistaken for her girl was a downright honor. Plus, the plain truth was I didn't care what people at the club called me, as long as they didn't call me Monkey Night.

# TWELVE

AFTER YEARS OF "DO THIS" AND "don't do that," Nicky knocked on my dressing room door the night before I turned twenty-one. I should point out that it was a real dressing room now that I had been there five years and the club was solidly in the black. It had four walls, room enough to move around, a vanity, and even a wardrobe—I felt very blessed.

"Hey, what you got going on tomorrow night?"

"Russell and a few of the waiters been threatening to take me out for drinks, but so far, nothing concrete." I started putting on my foundation with a foam triangle.

"Okay, then," Nicky said. "I made us reservations at Matsuhisa."

"Seriously?" Matsuhisa was the most exclusive sushi place in Los Angeles—probably the most exclusive sushi place in America. I was always reading about movie stars eating there.

Nicky shrugged. "Yeah, I know a guy. He got us in."

He got out his clipboard. I could almost see the list item as he checked me off: "Inform Davie of Matsuhisa reservations." Then he left without saying good-bye. The club was fairly successful now, and we even had a few celebrities come through these days because of its retro appeal. But no matter how many Important People Nicky had to meet and greet, it never occurred to him to work on his manners.

I KNEW BY now that an evening dress was too fancy to wear even to a nice restaurant like Matsuhisa. But the thing was, having to dress so extravagant for work meant that I spent all my regular time almost exclusively in jeans and band T-shirts. Jeans, because they were comfortable, and band T-shirts, on account of Russell getting them for free at his side gig as a music freelancer for *So Gay L.A.,* an alternative weekly.

He always asked for a small and then passed them on to me, since according to him, "I'm too fine for T-shirts. But if you are so intent on being a fashion victim, the least you can do is promote some cool bands." If I had grown up with anyone other than my mother, Russell might have gotten on my nerves. But he had a great sense of humor, and I liked all the free T-shirts, so in the end I decided to keep him around, even past my eighteenth birthday when Nicky started allowing me to have other male friends.

I borrowed a green mini-dress for Matsuhisa from one of the waitresses who looked to be about my size.

Mini-dresses were in that year; however, I spent most of the time between putting it on and Nicky showing up at my door tugging at the skirt and wondering how I was going to sit down without showing the whole world my natural wonders.

But when we got to the restaurant, I fit right in. In fact, compared to some of the other women there, my hemline was on the long side.

Matsuhisa wasn't elegant in an icy way like I expected. It actually had a warm atmosphere with a decor that exuded easy ambience and made me feel at home, even though I was fairly sure that Courteney Cox and Jennifer Aniston were sitting a couple of tables over from me and Nicky.

"You never had sake before, right?" Nicky asked. He didn't wait for my answer before giving the waiter an order for nigori.

I don't know why he asked in the first place. He was the one who had handed me my first glass of red wine when I was sixteen and told me to always order just one glass and sip on it throughout the evening. He then told me if he ever caught or even heard about me drinking something other than wine, then it was off to foster home—yeah, Nicky rode that foster home threat until I turned eighteen, and sometimes I wondered if he missed it.

But the day I turned twenty-one, he opened up the menu and said, "This is hella better than the foster home, huh?"

"Sure is." I opened up my menu, too.

"I'll order for both of us," he said before I could even look it over.

Turning twenty-one meant I no longer had to do everything Nicky told me to for fear of losing my job. But I was used to it by now, so I closed my menu immediately.

And that turned out to be a good move because I loved everything he ordered. I had never had sushi before, and after my first bite of the spicy tuna roll, I said to him, "Everybody says the Japanese are smart, but now I believe it. Because who else would figure out how to make raw fish taste good?"

Nicky nodded. "The shit is kind of brilliant, ain't it?"

We ate and laughed over sake and club gossip. Then we came back to the club, and had dessert in Nicky's office along with a half bottle of port.

After that, Nicky walked me up to my apartment and asked if he could come in.

This was the first time we had ever hung out on a social level, and the sake and port had made the night so fuzzy and fun that I figured he wasn't ready for it to end yet, either.

"You want some tea?" I asked when we got inside.

"Sure." He was already giving the place a good once-over, probably checking for any damage that would allow him to keep my deposit if and when I ever decided to move out.

In the kitchen, I hummed as I filled up the kettle. My body felt warm from all the drinking, and I placed my hands against the cool gray metal of the pot for a second before putting it on the burner.

Suddenly Nicky was behind me.

I had not heard him come into the kitchen, but I sensed his presence now. The way he was standing there, so perfectly still, raised the hair on the back of my neck. Why was he hovering?

I turned on the burner, and after a series of clicks, blue flames appeared underneath the kettle.

Nicky moved closer, and I felt him against my back. Not just his muscles, but also his desire, unmistakable and resting against me.

That's when I realized that this whole night had been a date, that we were, in fact, still on a date, and that he was waiting for me to respond.

My heart filled with panic. I didn't quite know what to do. I had engaged in a couple of romantic fumblings before this, but they weren't quite what you'd call relationships. More like a few dates, sex once or twice, and then a fizzling out. It was hard to date when you couldn't be even halfway truthful about who you really were. I did not quite know what to do with this man who was ten years older than me. A stern, cranky man who I had thought I knew until he pressed himself against me, already hard and desirous.

I closed my eyes.

For a fleeting second, I thought of James Farrell. He had graduated from Princeton and was now working in the marketing department of Farrell Fine Hair. His father had stepped down as president, after getting elected to Congress, but that didn't mean that James couldn't step into the position with a few years of experience. . . .

Nicky put his hands on my shoulders.

Suddenly James was gone, and it was just Nicky and me and a big decision that had to be made right now. I asked myself, *What would the most beautiful woman in the world do at this moment?*

Then I switched off the burner and turned around.

TWO THINGS HAPPENED in September 2000:

Farrell Fine Hair sold itself to Gusteau International, a cosmetics conglomerate based in France, for three hundred and sixty-two million dollars. Since Farrell Fine Hair was still a privately held company, that meant big payouts for the Farrell family. But it also meant that James would never be president of Farrell Fine Hair. The position he had been groomed for his entire life was gone.

When I read about the sale online, I felt both sorry and happy for James. Sorry because he had spent just about his whole life preparing to be president of Farrell Fine Hair, and happy because at least he was free to do whatever he wanted now, and he had a lot of money with which to do it.

I had been with Nicky for three years, so I could afford to be somewhat generous with both my pity and my good wishes where James was concerned. Somewhat.

The other thing that happened was that Russell gave up his screenwriting dreams and decided to funnel his natural talents for both gossip and journalism into a staff position at *Celeb Weekly*, which meant he was finally making enough money writing to quit his waiter job at Nicky's.

Nicky hired a girl named Chloe Anderson to replace him. She was a pretty caramel-candy girl with big brown eyes and even bigger curls that stopped just above her shoulders, and she had actually come into the club inquiring about being a backup singer. But Nicky said no, because he had just taken on a three-piece band to accompany me, and he was waiting to see how that worked out.

Our section of Hollywood had steadily gentrified in the eight years since the club had opened, which meant more people with more money coming through the door. And now, right up the street, there was some high-end movie theater called ArcLight being built around the old Cinerama Dome. So maybe even more people would be coming in for a post-movie drink and show.

But Nicky didn't want to hedge his bets. So Chloe had to settle for replacing Russell. Nicky did tell her she could sub for me if I got sick or hurt, which Chloe actually took as an opportunity. She didn't know then that Nicky wasn't exactly the kind of guy you asked for sick days, even if he was your boyfriend. There wasn't a flu on this earth that would make putting up with Nicky's mouth worth it, so I always showed up for performances no matter how miserable I was feeling.

I HAVE NEVER respected that phrase, "I love hard." In my opinion, when a woman claimed to "love hard," it usually meant she was incapable of conducting a healthy relationship because she was stuck on the image of herself as a person who somehow loved more strongly and better than almost everybody else—which, when you think about it, is pretty dang arrogant. So when problems came up, and they almost always did, the woman who "loved hard" just couldn't see herself as anything other than the victim, the perfect lover who had been wronged by the man who didn't appreciate her.

Still, even I had to admit that Chloe loved hard. Two months after joining the staff, she fell for our next new hire, a twenty-three-year-old actor named Michael Barker who had moved here from the East Coast. This was a common story: Almost all the handsome actors in Los Angeles moved here from someplace else. They were the prettiest, most popular people in their classes, and when they arrived they slowly but surely found out that their backstory was so common, it was worse than boring—it was sad and embarrassing for them and everyone involved.

However, Michael "call me Mike" Barker was different from the rest of those pitiable actors. He had that certain thing about him—I could tell as soon as I clapped eyes on him—that glow that all celebrities seem to have even before they become celebrities.

I had just finished rehearsing with the band, and Chloe was setting up the tables with a couple of other waiters. We both looked up when he walked through the door. He was tall with a smooth complexion and perfectly straight teeth. He gave us a little smile and a wave as he made his way through the club and into Nicky's office. He reminded me of James in the school hallway when he did that.

As soon as she was done with her part of the setting up, Chloe came over to me. "Did you see that guy earlier?"

Her eyes were pinned to Nicky's door like she was afraid the guy would come out at any second, and she'd somehow miss him.

"Yeah, I saw him," I answered. "He was cute." Though in the back of my mind I was thinking, *Not as cute as James.*

"He's more than cute, he's fine. Really fine." She clasped her hands together. "Do you think he's interviewing for a job?"

"I think he's getting a job if he's been in there that long." Nicky wasn't the type to keep on talking if he wasn't fixing to hire you. Over the years, I had seen a lot of waitstaff applicants go into Nicky's office and come right back out thirty seconds later. Nicky didn't waste time.

Chloe leaned against the stage and kept her eyes on Nicky's door.

AFTER TWO WEEKS of dating, Chloe moved Mike Barker and his dreams into her small one-bedroom apartment in Koreatown.

"Do you really think that's wise?" I asked when she told me they were moving in. Even with my limited experience, I could see that this was a bad idea. "Maybe ya'll should do some more canoodling first. Kick the tires some more."

"I am sure," she said. "I have never been so excited about a person. He is so amazing in every way, you just don't know what he's capable of."

She was wrong. I so suspected what a guy like Mike Barker was capable of, and it all came to pass a few months later.

Chloe threw herself fully into their relationship, proving from the very start that she was willing to focus all her time and energy on Mike, which made them a good match, because Mike was also willing to focus all his time and energy on the very same person: Mike Barker. Pretty soon, Chloe was coming around to Nicky looking to pick up extra shifts, because Mike needed new headshots, or because Mike was wanting to take a highly recommended class with an eighties sitcom star, or because Mike had decided he wanted to rent a sporty convertible for an audition with an A-list director, or—

"Why can't he pick up extra shifts himself if he's the one that needs whatever?" Nicky would ask her every time. This was a rhetorical question, a game he played, so that he would have gossip for me when we came together at night. The truth was if anyone was going to get extra shifts, he preferred to give them to her. Chloe, being such a sincere doormat, turned out to be a very good waitress, whereas Mike spent too much time laughing and joking with the tourists, charming them out of bigger tips, instead of upselling them with more alcohol and desserts that they didn't need.

Chloe always replied to Nicky's questions with an impassioned defense. "You don't understand. It's hard for actors in this town. He's had a very hard life and now he's trying to make his dreams come true." Once she even said, "He's not lucky like you."

And, let me tell you, she only said that once, because it got Nicky so mad, he actually told his best waitress that no, she couldn't have her damn extra shift.

"Like me opening up a successful restaurant at the age of twenty-five was just something I walked into. Like shit got handed to me like she handing shit to that actor," he complained while I turned down the bed at his Baldwin Hills house. Then he stared out the window and breathed out through his nostrils for a while.

He didn't say, "Fuck that bitch." But I could tell he was thinking it.

Mike broke up with Chloe about seven months after he moved in with her. He said her "mommy act" wasn't sexy, and left her for a model with a luxury condo on the Westside. Some men were like that. They couldn't just leave you, they had to stomp all over your self-esteem on the way out.

Nicky was almost gleefully smug after it all went down. Every weekend he asked Chloe if she wanted extra shifts, even though I had told him that he needed to stop on several occasions. After he got tired of that, he started pointing out to Chloe that he was working for his money, not being given it, whenever he passed by her. He kept this up for a good three weeks, but then Chloe began dating Wade, the horn player in the trio that accompanied me on weekends.

She was wild about him, too. He had his own money, so she attached herself to him in other ways. The man couldn't sit down for a second without her fetching a drink for him from the bar. During our twice-a-week afternoon rehearsals, she brought him lunch. Lovely sandwiches with the crusts cut off and bursting with deli meat. At first it was cute. The other guys in the band laughed and said they were jealous. But when she kept on showing up in a new, pretty dress for every dang rehearsal, it got weird. Nobody laughed when she came in anymore. They just sat there, watching the exchange in silence, until she left, leaving a trail of cheap perfume behind her.

At one point, even I, in all my constructed, nonjudging cool, told her that she needed to calm the eff down.

"But I can't, Davie. Love makes me crazy. I'm actually okay with being alone in between. It's kind of fun. I go to the movies with my girlfriends. I take my voice lessons, and I think my life is pretty good. But then I see a guy, and my nose opens, and he's all I can think about. I dream about Wade every night, even the nights when he's lying right there beside me. When I'm in the post office line, I'm thinking about things I can do to make his life easier. I breathe that man. And I swear to you there is nothing I can do about it."

She explained this to me like a terminal cancer patient explains their condition for the thousandth time. As if this was the hard science of her life, which I was in no position to deny.

Wade got another gig at another club and then quietly broke up with her in the alley behind Nicky's about twenty minutes before we were set to open.

Nicky was furious. He hadn't minded Mike Barker quitting after he and Chloe split, but Wade was actually good at what he did.

"Don't date nobody else that work here," he commanded, when she came in from the alley, puffy-eyed and dumped. "In fact," he called out to the rest of the staff, "From now on, nobody is allowed to date nobody else working in this club."

He actually put the rule on the books, he was so mad, and whenever some bold staff member would ask him about me and him, he would answer, "Grandma clause, muthafucka. Now get back to work."

The rule worked with Chloe for a while, but then we got a new chef. A freelance writer from the *L.A. Weekly* came to do an article on him, and

Nicky told Chloe to show him around, since she was our best waitress, and real pretty to boot.

I was there. I saw when she came out of the kitchen to greet the tall writer, who looked like he had been born from dark brown storks.

I saw their eyes meet . . . and lock. And I thought, *It's like he's handing her an Invitation to Crazy.*

I myself had been crazy about James. I had stalked him and constructed fairy tales about us that went beyond the realm of imagination. But to my credit, I had never accepted another boy's Invitation to Crazy.

And watching Chloe at that moment, I vowed I never would.

# THIRTEEN

FIVE YEARS INTO MY RELATIONSHIP WITH Nicky, things came to an unsettling end. I nicked my thumb while cutting an apple in my apartment. I went downstairs to get a Band-Aid out of the supply closet. And that's where I found Nicky fucking a light-skinned cocktail waitress from behind, his pants down around his ankles.

"Damn it," Nicky said when he saw me standing there, sucking on my bleeding thumb.

"I ran out of Band-Aids." I wish I could have thought of something cooler than that to say, but my thumb hurt.

He and the cocktail waitress stared at me, and I walked out, closing the door behind me. This was the supply closet that used to be my dressing room before Nicky upgraded me, which struck me as kind of funny for a few seconds, but then the anger set in.

Except for getting a perm, I had done everything Nicky had ever asked me to do. For five years, I had gotten up early and made him breakfast, even though most days I didn't even have to be at work until six in the evening.

And you know what else? I had blown all my college savings back in 2001, because I had thought we'd be together for the long haul. Now the past five years lay behind me like a joke, a wasteful joke. How could

I have given up college for a guy who would cheat on me with a cocktail waitress?

I had thought my love for Nicky was the opposite of my love for James Farrell. Practical and, this time, not based on delusion. Nicky, for all his quirks, had not seemed like a man who made sudden and unexpected moves. But apparently I had been wrong about him.

As soon as I got into my apartment, I unplugged the thirty-six-inch television that Nicky had gotten me for my real twenty-fifth birthday and heaved it right out the window. The television landed in pieces outside the back entrance to the club, which gave me some satisfaction. But not nearly enough.

An image came to my mind: Nicky mesmerized by the television's broken pieces when he walked out to the parking lot that night. Then I saw myself jumping out of the shadows and stabbing his trifling ass with the same knife I had accidentally cut myself with earlier, the same one that had sent me down to the supply closet in the first place.

*I will never let a man hand me an Invitation to Crazy.*

The vow that I had made two years ago came floating back to me. And the knife plan faded just as quickly as it had come.

I sat down on my bed and breathed. And after about an hour or so of thinking on it, I figured out that I was less upset about Nicky cheating on me than I was about him doing it with someone who looked like my complete opposite. She was tall and yellow with a weave that hung to her butt. She looked like a poor man's Veronica Farrell—that is to say she was pretty, but common. She didn't make heads turn in L.A.

I had to go right back downstairs and ask him about it.

His pants were back up when I stormed in and demanded, "Why a light-skinned girl? Why did you get with the lightest girl in the club?"

"That's what you're going to get mad about?" he asked back when I asked him.

"Yes," I said. "I understand cheating, but if you loved me . . ."

"I love you," he insisted. "Me being stupid don't change that. If you took me back—"

I interrupted him before he could go into the sales pitch. I had semi-lived with Nicky for years, and I knew he had a way of making what he wanted sound like the completely logical conclusion. The man sold the forties to one of the most modern cities in the world, and I bet he could sell heaters in Glass during a Mississippi August. So I wasn't even going to let him get started down that road.

"Why her?" I repeated.

Nicky shook his head. "Let's talk about us." He reached across his desk for my hand, but I snatched it away before he could even touch it.

I wanted him to say that she was the first person that crossed his path after he decided to cheat and that it had had nothing to do with the cocktail waitress and me being at opposite ends of the black melanin spectrum. But as I sat there, I knew I wasn't going to get a straight answer from him now with our possible breakup hanging over the situation. Maybe not ever.

The next step in Nicky's sales pitch to get me back was to fire the waitress. It was 2002, but suing for sexual harassment still wasn't something black people did in large numbers, and almost nobody did it in Los Angeles. So Nicky could get away with firing her for sleeping with the boss, without her putting up too much of a fight. She walked in to start her shift, and walked out about five minutes later after a whispered conversation in the corner of the restaurant. Nicky did it quietly, but out in the open where he knew I could see him.

She looked at me, then back at him. Resigned and heavy-eyed, like she had already guessed this would be coming. Still, she glared at me as she walked out. This might be me projecting, but I don't think she could quite figure out being passed over for a dark-skinned woman with natural hair.

Nicky came over after she left. "I love you," he said. He kissed my cheek. "I'm sorry." Then he went back into his office. We had been together five years, and he still hadn't learned how to say a proper good-bye.

For about a week I thought and thought on whether to forgive Nicky. He had some stuff going for him, including giving me my first chance, my first apartment, and my first reciprocated love. But he also had some cons.

For one thing, he was always after me to get a perm. And after I had gotten sick of him asking me about it all the time and poured my heart out about my history with the Farrells, he had just said, "Farrell perms ain't the only ones out there. Get one of them other ones," which let me know that no matter how close we got, Nicky would never, ever fully get me—another con.

Also, he was still in the habit of telling me what to do all the time—a routine I was starting to get tired of now that I was twenty-six. And he had never been very supportive about me eventually going to college. I had gotten my GED back when I was eighteen, and over the years I had taken enough classes at Los Angeles Community College to apply to a four-year UC school. But Nicky hadn't exactly been behind me one hundred percent on this.

"I went to college so you wouldn't have to," he would say whenever I brought it up, "Trust me, the best way to learn how to run a business is to start it and then run it with all you got. Simple. There's your college degree right there."

"What if I don't want to study business?" I asked him the last time we had that argument.

Nicky looked confused, like he hadn't been aware that there were degrees you could get outside of business. "What else would you want to study? You already know how to sing, you don't have the right attitude to be a lawyer or doctor, and none of that liberal arts shit is useful." I had hated him a little bit after he said that, but I hadn't brought it up again.

The biggest con, though, was that Nicky had never asked me to marry him. I wasn't one to dream much since the Farrell Manor Incident, but I didn't know many other women who had been five years with a man without a peep out of him about marriage. Hell, I had gone to civil ceremonies for gay friends that were based on shorter courtships.

I had asked him about it once, and then it turned into an argument. A bad one. It lasted about a week. And at one point, he even yelled at me, "If you want to get married so bad, why don't you dump me and find somebody else?"

This question deeply unsettled me. Nicky had always taken care of me. Did he really think I'd rather be married to someone other than him? Had he somehow guessed that even though I tried my so very hardest not to ever think about James in that way anymore, sometimes I still found myself daydreaming that things went differently in high school? I imagined myself arriving at the Farrell party in jeans and a nice top and expertly applied makeup. Maybe James would have looked at me different then. Maybe we would have . . .

I let the marriage fight with Nicky blow away. I kissed him and then lay down on my back for fabulous make-up sex.

I guessed that was another check I could add in Nicky's pro column. He was great in bed. Surprisingly tender even, because he was so big.

He had also given me my first orgasm. And after that, he had diligently worked at it until he was able to make me climax no matter what position we were in.

I would have thought it romantic, but I suspected his determination was less based in love and more due to Nicky's intense need to be ridiculously beyond excellent at everything he put his mind to. Which was another check in his con column.

And, of course, there was the whole cheating thing. Not to mention that all I got were annoyed sighs and orders to "just come back," whenever I tried to question him about it.

But really what helped me decide to end things for good with Nicky was remembering how I felt after I threw that television out the window. As my heartbeat had slowed and my anger faded, an unexpected feeling had come sneaking in, while I sat on my bed.

Relief.

It had wriggled its way up from my true heart, and dissipated my rage faster than any rational thought ever could have. And as the weeks passed without Nicky, without anyone telling me what to do or making snide remarks about my hair, I found that all I missed about him was the intimacy, which I could get with just about anybody. And that made me sigh.

ABOUT TWO WEEKS after the Closet Catch, I walked into his office and threw down my application for UCLA, which had been sitting in my bottom desk drawer, all filled out, for about five months now. "We're not getting back together," I informed him.

"What's this?" he asked me.

"It's an application to UCLA," I said. "I need a recommendation—a good recommendation—from you. I also need you to start scheduling rehearsals around my class schedule. And you have to let me do three shows a week, instead of five."

Nicky read over the application. He wasn't just cheap—he was also a time miser, and the thought of me not working every day at the club probably bothered him. "So, that means I only got to pay you for three performances, and I'll have to get Chloe to sing for the other two."

"No, Nicky. This means you pay me the same shitty wage. I'm already going to have to take out a bunch of loans to make this work."

Before Nicky could even twist his mouth to protest, I leaned over the desk and added, "You need to pay me back for the cocktail waitress, Nicky. I was with you for five years. Four years for five. That's a good bargain."

I had figured that this was the only argument that would work with him. Nicky didn't understand doing things out of kindness or common decency, but he couldn't stand to be in debt—financial or emotional. Plus, he loved a good bargain.

So when he agreed to my terms it was because he felt like he was paying me back for hurting me. And in a way, that was true.

So for the first time in my entire life, and at the age of twenty-six, I was finally in charge of my own destiny and making the decisions based on what I wanted to do. Freedom was a very unfamiliar feeling and, to tell you the honest truth, all sorts of scary. But I loved every bit of it, and I promised myself I would never let go of it again.


OFTEN WAITERS WOULD start at the club with their high school diplomas and showbiz dreams, and I would overhear them saying stuff like,

"There isn't anything college can teach me." I would have to fight the temptation to ask them, "How would you know?"

Because college taught me a whole lot.

It seemed like the answer to every question I had ever had about my life and America and the world could be found in a class or a textbook. In fact, two years into my psychology major, I was not only able to let go of my beef with the Farrells, but also able to walk into Nicky's office and deliver new terms for our ongoing relationship.

Nicky, as usual, was on his computer doing work when I entered. If I ever came in and caught him playing solitaire or looking at online porn like most bosses behind closed doors, I think I'd likely drop dead of shock.

"What you want? I'm doing the payroll."

"You want some lunch or something?" I asked him.

"Leon'll bring something round from the kitchen in a little bit."

I half smiled. "No, I mean you want to go someplace and get something to eat."

"Why would I want to get something to eat when there's free food right here?"

I shrugged. "My treat."

Nicky took off his reading glasses and looked up at me. "Davie, how many times do I have to tell you not to spend your money on stupid shit? I don't pay you enough to beat around the bush with lunch offers. If you want to get back with me, just say so."

"Nicky, I don't want to get back with you. And by the way, if I did want to start going with you again, what you just said was so the opposite of romantic, it would have killed any desperate feelings I was having. You've got to work on that if you ever want a woman to stick around."

Nicky put his reading glasses back on and went back to clicking his mouse. "Then why are you here?"

I sat down in the IKEA folding chair in front of his desk. "Listen, Nicky, my life—I don't need any more crazy in it. I've already had enough crazy. I mean look at how all I grew up. I want to be in a boring relationship. A very boring relationship, with no Closet Catches, no surprises. Just me and a guy. Simple. That's what I deserve—no, that's what I need at this point. So understand, you and me are never going to happen again. And you need to stop bringing it up, because I've been thinking, and the thing is, what you told me when I first started working here was wrong."

I could see Nicky's muscles straining underneath the Loyola T-shirt he wore when he did the payroll, instead of his usual suit. It looked like he was physically restraining himself from throwing me out of his office. "What thing I told you?" he asked.

"You said we weren't friends. And I'm here to say that I think we are. In fact, I think we're best friends. So you're going to have to deal with that."

Nicky's brow knit so deep I was afraid his forehead might stay like that. "Okay, fine. You said what you had to say. Now get out. I got to finish up this payroll."

"So no lunch?" I don't know why I felt disappointed. It's not like I had ever known Nicky to have any friends outside of Leon.

"Not if you don't let me finish up this payroll," he said. "Give me half an hour, then we'll go to that new Kabuki sushi restaurant up the street. I ain't been yet. And after that maybe we can see that Denzel movie at the ArcLight. I heard okay things about it."

I was so stunned, it took me a moment to realize that he was not only saying yes to lunch, but agreeing to be my best friend.

"Okay," I said, trying to keep my voice light. "I'll be waiting outside."

And that's how Nicky and me got over the whole cheating thing.


AT FIRST, IT seemed like I was going to be awash in tests and papers for the rest of my life, but then one day college was over, just like that. Nicky, Mama Jane, Chloe, Russell and the band came out to cheer me on at graduation. UCLA handed me a diploma for a bachelor of arts in psychology, and suddenly I was right back where I started.

At the club.

Not that I didn't like the club. Actually that was part of the problem. As much as I had taken a real shine to learning, I really couldn't think of any career better than the one I already had.

Sure, I'd make more money if I put my degree to work, doing something like social work or maybe going into research. But other than better insurance, the appeal of a nine-to-five was lost on me. And to tell you the truth, I just didn't think I could go into an office every day.

Still, I needed something else. A second job or something on the side to keep up with the bills. I mean I could've straight bought a house back in Glass for what I had out in student loans. Sure it'd be a small house, maybe a shack like the one I used to share with Cora, but the point was, my debt situation was no joke.

I think Nicky's Spidey sense picked up that I was fixing to ask him for a raise now that I was back at full-time hours, because he's the one that came up with the Big Idea.

I was rehearsing with the band when Nicky stormed into the main room.

"Davie!" he yelled over the music. "I got an idea."

I waved at the band to stop playing.


HIS IDEA WAS Soul BunnyGrams, a business that sent me out in a bunny suit to deliver singing telegrams with soul. He would drum up the business, I would go out on the calls, and he would get a fifteen percent cut for all his labor on my behalf.

I immediately liked the idea because it meant I would be able to sing songs that were written after the fifties. But I'd learned a few things in the five years that I had dated Nicky, so I kept it cool and said, "Ten percent, Nicky. I'm already going to have to pay the government one hell of a commission, since it's 1099 work."

After a few days of hemming and hawing about ungrateful people and maybe needing to get some new blood onto the club stage, Nicky agreed to twelve percent. I said, "Deal," because Nicky was truly ornery. And though I knew he was proud of me for negotiating him down, I couldn't count on him not putting me out on the street if I didn't agree to his second offer. He loved me, sure. He probably loved me more than anybody in this world besides his parents and Mama Jane. Still, business is business, and Nicky was always about the money. No matter what.

Soul BunnyGrams quickly became the first thing black people in Los Angeles thought of when they wanted to send their loved ones singing telegrams. And then the second or third thing creative white people thought of when they wanted to do something unexpected for their friends. We had almost no Latino business. But that was okay, because Soul Bunny-Grams was better than huge. It was good enough, which meant that I had plenty of extra work to keep up with my student loan payments, but not so much that it ever seemed like a hassle.

All in all, I was happy. Even better, I was content, which is why what happened next in my life was so very, very fucked up.

PART III

NOW

# FOURTEEN

IT WAS 2007, BUT FOR WHATEVER reason, I could not get "California," Fatboy Slim's club hit from the nineties, out of my head as I drove down Alameda toward Disney Studios. And there were basically only two lines in the entire song, so it was starting to get annoying.

I started a line of vocal warm-ups, partly to get rid of that song, partly to get ready for my performance, and partly to mask the sound of the muffler on the '87 Toyota Corolla that Russell had sold me for eight hundred bucks six years ago after he had started getting gossip reporter paychecks and could afford to upgrade to a Lexus. It was actually pretty reliable for the price, but it consistently broke down every four months like clockwork, and my muffler was demanding some attention.

So I was grateful that Derrick Taylor's wife loved him and wanted to send him a Soul BunnyGram for his thirty-fifth birthday. Plus she had even been thoughtful enough to call ahead to his assistant to make sure that I got a drive-on pass, which meant I didn't have any problems getting through security and onto the lot. Though I did get a lot of funny looks, being dressed in a large brown bunny rabbit suit and all.

Further good signs that today's Soul BunnyGram would go well: Derrick Taylor had been at his job for over a year—I always advised my clients against sending a singing telegram to anyone who wasn't well established at his or her job. There was nothing on this earth less fun than singing to someone who was cringing the whole time and requesting that I keep my voice down, so as not to tip off their boss.

I walked down the hall and blotted the sweat off my face with a handkerchief. My bunny suit covered everything but my face, so it was basically like walking around in a big old furry body sweater, which was fine during the winter, but it was May now, so I had to wipe my face down before I entered the cubicled work area outside of Derrick Taylor's office.

When I arrived on the scene, there were already several people gathered outside his office. Mostly other executives and assistants, who could probably use a break from their usual boring routines.

I always shook my head when I saw a singing telegram being delivered solely to one person on television. It was my experience that even if you started off singing to one person, anybody within hearing range had come to stare by the time the song was over. And if people knew you were coming, a crowd usually gathered, just like today.

Feeding off their energy, I put my paw to my lips to signal for quiet. Then I hunched down and crept on tiptoe to the door. The place was silent as a tomb, and I could almost hear their wide eyes following me.

In fact, quite a few of them jumped when I threw the door open and shouted in my best Tina Turner voice, "Mr. Derrick Taylor, I hear it's your birthday!"

Inside the office, a shaven bald man in glasses looked up from his paperwork.

"What is this?" He was already smiling, paperwork totally forgotten.

I took my iPod portable speaker system out of my satchel and switched it on. The start-up melody and background vocals for "River Deep, Mountain High" flowed into the room, wrapping itself around the crowd.

"Your wife asked me to deliver this remote control to your brand-new LCD bathroom TV," I said.

His eyes lit up like a kid on Christmas when I handed him the remote control.

And then I used my best Nina Simone to tell him, "And she says there's a lot more waiting for you when you get home, baby, if you know what she means."

Mr. Taylor's smile got even bigger. "Oh snap, I'm going home right now!"

Everybody laughed, except for me, because I had to hit my cue a millisecond later. I tossed my head, just like Tina would've (if she was wearing a bunny suit), and started singing.

Everybody clapped when the song was over, Mr. Taylor loudest of all. "Do another one."

When he said that, I remembered the dreams I used to have of performing in the kindergarten talent show, and the memory made me smile.

I was about to hit an encore with "Simply the Best," when his assistant said, "I'm afraid you don't have time for that, Mr. Taylor. The gate called earlier. James Farrell is on his way up."

My heart froze. I barely heard him say, "No, don't stop. James is a buddy from college. Believe me, he's going to want to see this."

It felt like the world slowed down for a few terrible seconds, then snapped back, pushing me into fast forward.

"Sorry," I said, all traces of Stage Davie gone. "I've got another appointment. Happy birthday."

By the time I was done saying this, I had already put my portable player back in my satchel and was halfway out the door.

"How about your tip?" he called after me.

"Already taken care of," I called back.

It wasn't already taken care of. In fact, tips were a big part of the money I made at this, but I had to get out of there.

High School Davie was full-out screaming in my head, *Run, girl, run!* as if I were in a horror movie.

I can only blame my state of complete and total mind-numbing panic for what happened next.

I rounded the corner and hit somebody so hard that I flew back—I mean I actually had air before my cottontail hit the floor with a teeth-rattling thud. I could hear the contents of my satchel skittering across the carpet.

The sad thing is that the panic had me back on my feet and gathering up my things before I even had time to register what had happened or even the faint ache in my tailbone.

I found my wallet and my portable player and put them back in my satchel. I could hear faint voices all around me, cubicle people asking if I was all right.

I mumbled, "Fine, fine. I'm fine."

But then one voice came through my fog of panic, clear as a bell. "You sure?" he asked. "You went down awful hard."

I looked up.

Standing above me was James Farrell.

And I could see immediately why he hadn't gone down like I had. Fifteen years later, he was still ropy-but-strong. And though I could tell from his few words that he had ditched his Southern accent, he was just as beautiful as ever.

He wore his hair in one of those hip, urban Afros, and his skin shone out bright against the lightweight tan suit that he had on with a red T-shirt and very expensive-looking leather slip-ons.

How could he still be so incredibly beautiful? It made no sense. Absolutely no sense at all.

It is a surprising thing that my heart didn't just burst open right there. As it was, my head filled with static, and I couldn't hear anything but the sound of High School Davie whimpering and Little Davie saying over and over again, *I used to be Tina Turner.*

I froze, crouched over my satchel bag, and waited for him to recognize me. I doubted that he would call me Monkey Night in front of all these people. Still, I didn't know what I was going to do or how I was going to respond when he said, *Hey, didn't we go to high school together? Weren't you that sad little girl that gave me that sad little note?*

But he didn't say any of that; he just kept looking down at me with worry—but no recognition—in his eyes. And eventually I could hear him through the static saying, "Are you sure you're all right?"

He didn't recognize me. Probably because I was dressed in a large bunny suit, I realized, a little late in the game.

Well, I wasn't going to give him a chance to figure it out. I slung my satchel back over my shoulder, ran past him to the elevator, and thumbed the down button like my life depended on it.

And let me tell you, the immediate sound of the arrival ding was just about the sweetest, most wonderful thing I had ever heard.

I backed into the elevator, unable to stay, but equally unable to take my eyes off him. He was walking toward me with a look of concern on his face, but then the elevator doors closed. And he was gone.

I slumped against the elevator's back wall and covered my poor, abused heart with my hand. It felt like a bomb had gone off inside my chest.

"What the fuck?" I asked the empty elevator. "What the fuck?"

I HAVE NO idea how I got back to the club. I don't remember driving. I don't remember rehearsing with the band. It was all pretty much a daze, until Nicky came up to me and said we needed to switch Friday morning's rehearsal to Saturday morning.

A film was coming to shoot in the club, which Nicky encouraged over all else because not only did he get the rental fee from the production company for using the place, but free publicity, too. Over the years more than one tourist had wandered in, asking, "Is this the place from . . ."

"Hold on," I said. "Let me get my planner."

I walked over to my satchel, still thinking about James. What had he been doing there? Did he live in Los Angeles now? It had taken only a few psychology classes in college to gather that I was mentally unstable when it came to James and his sisters. After that I had forced myself to stop scouring magazines and the Internet for mentions of him.

The last I had read, he was living in New York, and he, Veronica, and Tammy Farrell had been relegated to acting as "the faces" of Farrell Hair. It was just Farrell Hair now. Gusteau had kept their family name for brand recognition, but had dropped the "Fine," which in my opinion was a good call, since it had seemed old-timey even back in the nineties.

So the Farrells no longer owned the company, but they did represent for it. Tall Tammy Farrell, with her girl-next-door looks, was the Farrell Hair spokesperson and the main model for the spin-off makeup line Farrell Cosmetics. I wasn't quite sure what James and Veronica did, but it seemed to consist of going to a bunch of red carpet events and society parties in order to promote the revitalized brand. James always had a game smile in all the pictures, though I never was sure if he had truly accepted his new position or if he was just acting like he did for the cameras.

I had also never been able to figure out if the Farrell family had been blindsided by Gusteau's offer, or if Mr. Farrell had seen the writing on the wall as black-owned companies sold out all around him and prepared himself, but not his family, for the sale by seeking out a career in politics.

I had a feeling it was the latter, and that made me feel bad for James, but not so bad that I could feel any less embarrassed about running him down in a bunny suit, of all things.

During the years before college, when I had occasionally allowed myself to dream about running into him again, that is so not how I saw things going down. My face burned hot all over, and I started to get all worked up again just thinking about him standing over me with pity on his face.

Then I realized that I had been rifling through my satchel for a while now, but still hadn't found my planner. So I focused and searched again. But it wasn't in my satchel. For the second time that day, my heart dropped into my stomach.

"Is Saturday cool or what?" Nicky asked from across the club.

"Hold on," I said. This could not be happening. I wrote every appointment down, and was religious about not agreeing to anything before I checked to see what I already had on the books. Taking a cue from Nicky, I scheduled everything, and I mean everything. I even wrote down when I would be washing and deep conditioning my huge Afro every week. I kept my entire life organized in neat handwriting *in that appointment book*. And because I prided myself on being responsible, I had never misplaced it. Not once. Until now.

I searched my car. I had weddings and singing appointments for the next six months in that planner. And all my contacts . . . But it wasn't in the Toyota.

Nicky and the band helped me search the club. I tried bargaining with the universe. "If you give me back my appointment book, Universe, I promise to keep an online calendar," I vowed. "You do not, I repeat, you do not have to teach me a lesson."

But it wasn't in the club. And it wasn't in my studio apartment. And it wasn't on the street outside the club. Now I was doing a lot of cursing.

Eventually, I broke down and called Derrick Taylor's office after telling myself over and over again that there was no way James would answer the phone.

"Derrick Taylor's office. This is Connie." Thank the Lord, it was the assistant that had gotten me the drive-on.

"Hey Connie, this is Davie."

"Davie? Girl, are you all right? I heard you slipped—"

"I'm fine," I said. "But I think I dropped my appointment book. Did anyone bring it by?" My voice went up on "anyone," because of course by "anyone," I meant James.

"No, we didn't get any appointment books, but let me check with the security desk."

She put me on hold, then came back a few minutes later to say that there was nothing in lost and found.

"But they said sometimes it takes people a while to turn stuff in. I told them to keep an eye out and call me if they find anything."

I thanked her and got off the phone. My heart, which had been on edge all day, now felt like a stone in my chest.

MY SHOW WAS a lot more sad than usual that night. I bluesed my way through most of my Peggy Lee song set. And when it finally came time to end the night with "Fever," you would have thought I was condemning passion, the way I sulked through the audience. It was less sexy and more like, "He gives me fever. Isn't that the saddest thing you've ever heard?"

However, I was a professional, and I did manage to turn it up a notch right toward the end. The last verse of the last song was always performed with me sitting in the lap of a patron. Nicky had been to Vegas one time too many and had started insisting I do this about three years ago.

Usually, I didn't mind. It gave me a chance to practice my flirting skills, which I had to keep honed, since they really did not come naturally.

I looked around for Leon. To minimize scenes, he always identified the guy who should receive the last song of the night. Nicky had given him explicit instructions (really, what other kind did Nicky give?) in order of preference: The guy should either be alone or with another guy. If that kind of guy wasn't in attendance, then Leon was supposed to find a guy with a date who was the complete opposite of me—somebody blond and stick thin. Under no circumstances was he to lead me to the lap of a married man—unless he was there alone. And if no one fit Nicky's criteria, then Leon would shake his head and I was allowed to sing the rest of the song onstage.

But it almost never came to that. Guys rarely came in alone, but gay guys were like fifty percent of my regular crowd, and even better, they were usually thrilled to get a lap song. And I was thrilled that they were thrilled, but wouldn't get any ideas.

I spotted Leon at a table near the bar. It looked like he had gotten lucky tonight. He had found a guy who was sitting alone. Nicky's number one choice.

I sang the chorus as I sauntered over to him, swinging my hips with practiced seduction inside my long, shimmering gown. I was giving my best Eartha Kitt, but my mind was already about forty minutes ahead of the moment, running a bath and trying to calm myself down enough to read some before bed.

I glanced at the man as I sat in his lap, but I didn't process him. It was dark and I don't think my brain was allowing me to register what I was doing.

I gave him my usual show-gal flirty "Hello, mister, how you doing?"

He smiled, his teeth so straight and white, you had to wonder if he had come out the womb with braces. "I'm good," he answered in the overly hospitable way of Southerners, even the ones that had lost their accents. "How are you?"

"Well . . ." I launched into the last verse of "Fever."

But then the spotlight adjusted and his face came into full view under light bright enough that my subconscious could not trick me into thinking it was not who I didn't want it to be.

That's when I saw that it was James. Yes, James Farrell. In my club and sitting beneath my butt.

# FIFTEEN

IT TOOK EVERY SINGLE OUNCE OF cool that I had constructed in the fifteen years since the Farrell Manor Incident not to throw up.

And nothing could prevent the static. It filled my ears as soon as I recognized him, and then I couldn't hear anything. Not even myself. Truly, I could only hope that I was on key for the last verse of "Fever" and keeping up with the music as I sang about Pocahontas and Captain John Smith.

What felt like hours passed before I got to the part where I declared that chicks were born to give men fever, and the spotlight led me out of James's lap and back up onto the stage.

"*What a lovely way to burn,*" I sang over and over again.

The farther I got from him, the more the static receded. But it never completely went away. And as I walked up the stage steps, I could feel his eyes on me. I thanked the band, the waitstaff, and everyone else for joining us, and I could see James clapping along with the rest of the audience, his expression droll and amused. Just like Andrew McCarthy in the record store in *Pretty in Pink*, when Molly Ringwald tells him that the Steve Lawrence album that he has jokingly picked out is "white hot."

I had to get out of there.

"Good night, darlins." I kissed the palm of my hand and threw it out to them in an arc of waggling fingers, just like I always did. And then I headed backstage before the lights were all the way down.


THE PLAN WAS to gather up all my stuff from my dressing room, and then run—not walk—up to my apartment.

But Nicky was waiting outside my dressing room door.

"You in love?" he asked.

I froze. "What?"

"You was barely looking at that guy and you were stiff. That's not how I taught you to do it. So I'm thinking you must be dating somebody else, and that's why you couldn't do your job tonight."

"Oh, you're complaining about my performance." I unfroze and continued into my dressing room. Nicky always came out to watch me sing "Fever." Most nights it felt fatherly, like he was watching over me. But sometimes he had notes, and then it got annoying.

He followed me into the dressing room. "Damn right I'm complaining about your performance. What the hell?"

"Nicky, I'm sorry. I'll be better tomorrow, I promise." I gathered up my makeup bag and purse and started to leave, but he got in front of me.

"Hey, I'm not paying you to phone shit in tonight and do it right tomorrow. You're supposed to be bringing your A-game every night."

Usually I didn't mind Nicky, but at that moment, I was truly afraid I might cut his fool ass if he didn't let me by.

"Okay, then, don't pay me." I tried to push past him.

But he stopped me with a hand to my chest. "Wait a minute, what did you say?"

"If you're so disappointed in my performance, then don't pay me for tonight."

Nicky crooked his head to the side. "Since when you ready to give up a paycheck? You don't got money like that." His eyes went from suspicious to worried in an instant. "Are you okay?"

"Nicky, I so appreciate that you've finally learned to be my friend first and my boss second. But right now, I do actually need you to let me go, before—"

A knock sounded on the door.

I am not a psychic. I couldn't necessarily know for sure who was on the other side of that door, but it had to be James, because my brain immediately went to static again. It was like I could smell his pheromones through the door.

"Hold on," Nicky called out. "We're talking about this later," he told me.

"No, Nicky don't—"

But it was too late. His hand was on the knob, and he opened the door to reveal Leon standing there with James right behind him. And James was smiling. At me.

It was still like staring into the sun. I know I've said that before, but I really cannot stress it enough. I was truly afraid that I'd come away from this encounter blinded and that he would see me for the ugly teenage girl he used to know.

In some dim corner of my mind, I noted that Leon was saying something, but I couldn't hear him over the static. I was in complete thrall.

That is, until James stepped around Leon. He held out my appointment book with one hand and placed his other hand on my arm.

Just like with the Note Incident, the static stopped the instant he touched me.

Suddenly the whole world got quiet, and I could hear him talking now. " . . . I wanted to make sure you got it. Your work address was in the front," he was saying.

I took the appointment book from him. "Thank you," I said. It was my regular country voice. I could barely form a sentence, much less give him the Stage Davie treatment.

"No problem," he answered. "I don't encounter hit-and-run bunny rabbits every day."

I waited for recognition to dawn in his eyes now that I was out of my bunny suit.

But he just stood there, studying me, with a little smile on his face, as if I was a strange new species at the zoo.

"No, I guess you don't get knocked down by somebody in a bunny suit every day. Sorry about that."

I didn't know what to say next. This waiting-for-him-to-recognize-me stuff made me feel very, very awkward. Like a soldier right after he's realized that he's stepped on a land mine—you know, right before he blows up.

But James had enough charm for the both of us. "So Leon tells me you've got next Tuesday off."

"Yes, yes, I do."

I had to concentrate on not looking him in his eyes for fear of getting lost in them.

"Well, I noticed you didn't have anything marked down for that night, so I made an appointment for you."

I opened up the planner to the last week of May. And sure enough, there were the words, "JAMES FARRELL, Café Stella, 8 P.M." And a number that I could only assume was his.

My brain shut down for a second, and when it started up again, he was asking questions.

"You live upstairs, right?"

"Yes," I answered.

"Would you like for me to send my driver to pick you up?"

"No," I answered. "I've got to go now."

"Okay," he said.

He took his hand off my arm, and the static did not start up again but I did feel a little fixed to faint when he smiled down at me with all those white teeth of his.

I wished I was tall like his sisters. I wished that I could hold my head up and look right back at him.

But only being five-four, I didn't even try to meet his gaze. "Bye," I said, my eyes on my feet.

He held up his large hand and spread his fingers wide, "Bye." And then he was gone.

I sagged sideways against the doorjamb. My heart was racing like I was fifteen again, but the rest of my body felt much older than my thirty-one years. Seeing James Farrell twice in one day was exhausting.

And I was just glad I had turned down his offer of a date and wouldn't have to go through that again. But wait a minute, had I turned him down?

I went over the conversation again in my mind. I had said, "No," but had he understood that meant no to the whole date, not just no to him sending a car over for me? I mean, would he have smiled at me like that before he left if he had understood I was saying that I never, ever wanted to see him again? An unpleasant, heavy feeling started to build in my stomach.

"Who was that?" Nicky demanded, nosy like the sister I had never had. I had forgotten that he was still in the room with me.

"James Farrell," I answered. My voice was so weary, you'd have thought I'd just run a marathon.

Nicky's mouth fell open, and for once he didn't have something smart to say.

"WHAT DO YOU mean he didn't recognize you," Mama Jane said. I had called her as soon as I was out of my gown and makeup to tell her about the Return of James Farrell.

"I mean he didn't recognize me," I repeated. "He must have forgotten me."

Mama Jane, bless her heart, sounded honest-to-God confused when she asked, "But how could he forget you?"

"I don't know, Mama Jane. Maybe he never really even saw me the first time." This whole conversation was making me high-school-level depressed. "Maybe that's why he asked me out, because he didn't recognize me as the same girl from high school who gave him that note."

"Well, are you going to tell him who you are on the date?"

"No, I can't tell him. And there's not going to be any date."

"Why can't you tell him? And why can't you go out with him?"

"Because . . ." I trailed off.

The truth was I had done some bad things In Between Then and Now. Not just bad, actually. Awful. So awful that I couldn't tell Mama Jane about them, even though I told her just about everything else. So awful that I didn't even dare to think about meeting James at Café Stella next Tuesday.

Even if he was James Farrell and still the finest boy on the planet.

So I told Mama Jane the sorta truth. "He's obviously slumming," I said. "And I don't want to be some rich kid's adventure."

"You don't know that," Mama Jane said. Even though she was a truck driver and really should have known better, Mama Jane was in the habit of assuming the best in everybody. "Just in case you haven't taken a good look at yourself lately, you're a real cute girl. Plus you're smart, and you're scrappy, and you're very talented. There ain't no reason to assume that boy don't want to go out with you for all the right reasons."

Before she could continue on with her self-esteem pep talk, I asked, "How's Akron? Did you ask that waitress out yet?"

Lucky for me, Mama Jane was very susceptible to a changed subject, especially when it involved her love life. "I can't tell if she's flirting with me or just being friendly."

Mama Jane was in her sixties now, but she still seemed to have trouble reading the women she liked.

So we talked about that, and I tried to stuff James back into the memory box I had kept him in for fifteen years now.

But it wasn't that easy. He lingered with me for the rest of the evening. And when I closed my eyes that night, I dreamed me and him were on the steps of Glass High, and that I took a diamond stud out of my ear and put it in his. Just like Molly Ringwald and Judd Nelson in *The Breakfast Club*.

"Goddamn it," I said to myself after I woke up from that dream, my heart all sped up. "James Farrell just handed me an Invitation to Crazy."

BUT I DIDN'T have to take him up on his invitation. I could obsess over it, and turn it over, and examine it from every angle under an electron microscope, but I did not have to take it.

At least that's what I told myself. Tuesday night finally came around, and at eight P.M., I began preparing to do something that High School Davie could never have imagined herself doing in a million years plus: stand up James Farrell.

I turned off my cell and put it in the far back corner of my closet, so that I wouldn't be tempted to check it every five minutes.

Then I turned off the AirPort wireless on my laptop, and put on *Tina Turner's Greatest Hits, Volume 1.*

After that, I ran a bath, and pulled my hair into a lopsided Afro puff at the side of my head, before climbing into the water with a book by a Pulitzer Prize winner from the nineties. The plot was so unromantic and outside my life experience that I was actually able to concentrate on it. I read the first few chapters, occasionally taking breaks to run hot water so that the bath didn't get cold.

Reading in the tub was nice. Like a yoga session in water. And I felt good when I got out, because not only had I managed to avoid James Farrell, but I had also had a very relaxing evening so far.

That is until the doorbell rang.

I rolled my eyes. Nicky, bless his little heart, had a real bad habit of dropping by unannounced on the club's dark nights. Truth be told, he really didn't know what to do with himself when free time was involved.

I opened the door. "You know, you need a hobby or something, Nicky," I said.

But it wasn't Nicky. It was James, standing there in checkered gray slacks, a short-sleeved blue shirt, and a white vest. He looked like a Ralph Lauren ad come to life and, if possible, even more classic and flawless than I remembered.

I stared at him, pretty dang agog. And he stared back, his eyes taking in my bathrobe and lopsided Afro puff.

"You weren't at the restaurant," he said, his voice dark and confused.

"Well, no. I wasn't," I answered. I was confused by the situation my own self. "I stood you up."

He blinked. "What?"

"I stood you up," I repeated.

"Why didn't you call me?" he asked. "Or answer your phone? I was scared something had happened to you."

"Because I was standing you up," I explained. "You don't call or answer the phone when you're standing somebody up. That's just how it works."

Something flashed in his eyes. "Can I come in?" he asked.

"Um, do you understand that I didn't show up at the restaurant because I didn't want to go on a date with you?"

Apparently he didn't, because the side of his mouth actually hitched up into a smile. "So you're saying I can't come in?"

"Yes, I'm saying that. And I'm also saying that this thing you're doing, showing up at my apartment and asking to be let in? It's creepy."

His face suddenly lit up. "Hey, you're from the South, aren't you? What part?"

"Mississippi," I answered. "That 'creepy' insult just went right over your head, didn't it?"

"No, but keep on trying. Something might stick and hurt my feelings. What part of Mississippi? I did a year of high school out there."

"I know. And your father's a congressman."

He folded his arms. "So you did your homework? What, did you Google me or something?"

I had already said too much. If James still didn't recognize me from high school, even though I wasn't wearing any makeup now, great. But I had no intention of getting into the particulars of just how much I knew about him and how I knew it.

"Thank you for stopping by, but I've got to get back to my book," I said.

I tried to close the door then, but he blocked it with his hand before I could get it shut.

"Can I ask what turned you off?"

The expression on his face still wasn't hurt or angry. He really seemed just honest-to-God curious about my motivations.

And it dawned on me that James didn't quite understand rejection. Didn't fathom it the way a normal person would because he was, well . . . a golden boy. And nobody ever turned down gold. Everybody liked gold.

So when a woman came along who said, "No, I don't want you," he didn't register disinterest. He didn't go away like any other normal guy would've. He reclassified. At first I was simple. And now I was a challenge.

And unfortunately, James was the kind of guy who liked a challenge. I could see that. Now.

My heart sank. I had been playing this all wrong. If I had known he was one of those guys that got all nose-wide-open when a woman didn't want him, maybe I would have handled the conversation differently.

"Look James, I can't be clever with you right now. That's not the way it works where you and me are concerned, so I'm just going to say straight up that we are in no way a match. And when I say no way, I mean that we're complete opposites. And when I say complete opposites, I mean we come from two extremely different worlds, and we have absolutely nothing in common. And just in case I'm still not making myself clear enough, let me add that you and me could never, ever work out. And that's why I stood you up."

"So I'm not your type," He stroked his square and clean-shaven chin. "That's an interesting argument. Let's talk about it some more. Over dinner."

I kind of started to hate James then. Because seriously, how charmed had this guy's life been that he didn't understand basic concepts like rejection and being stood up? How could there be someone in this world so untouched by all the nasty things that happened when women and men dealt with each other? And moreover, how could he occupy the same universe as me?

I could taste the rage in my mouth.

"You really want to go out with me?" I asked, my voice low and dangerous, just like his had been when I first answered the door.

James leaned forward, so that his face was only a couple of inches away from mine. "Obviously I want to go out with you."

Sigh. "Okay, fine. Give me a minute. Wait here."

Then I really did close the door in his face.

IT DIDN'T TAKE me long to get ready. I just put on a pair of black jeans, some high-top Converses, and a Strokes T-shirt, which was pretty much what I wore all the time. I had given Russell a tip so good that it had gotten him a promotion at *Celeb Weekly* a few years ago, and one of his thank-you gifts had been an entire box of about fifty Strokes T-shirts left over from a promotion the magazine had just finished up. So now, when I wasn't in evening gowns, I usually just threw on one of the T-shirts. I wasn't a huge fan of the band, but I liked the simplicity of just wearing the same thing all the time.

I usually put in some effort and wore something nicer for dates; however, this thing I was about to do with James wasn't so much a date as it was willfully throwing myself into a train wreck just to get it over with.

I really did not want to go back out there and face him, but given the conversation we had just had, it seemed like the only way to shake this little boy was to show him the difference between Stage Davie and Real Davie.

WHEN I OPENED the door again, I found James leaning against the landing rail and typing on his BlackBerry.

"Sorry," he said, not looking up. "I have to tell one of the publicists at my company that I won't be able to make it to an event I had scheduled for tonight."

"You can still go," I said, leaping at the chance to get out of this.

"Just two more words," he said, like he hadn't even heard me make the offer.

He finished and pushed send. Then he put the BlackBerry away and looked at me. His eyes barely registered that my outfit wasn't exactly hot-date material.

Nicky, who grew up in Los Angeles, used to give me a hard time if I even tried to go to the grocery store with him looking like this. When we had been together, he had considered me a reflection of him whenever we went out, and we had had more than one Wardrobe Choices argument. But James just took my hand and walked us toward the stairs. "What are you in the mood for? We could go back to Café Stella."

I took my hair out of the lopsided ball, and finger-combed it into a no-frills Afro. Not because it was more attractive out, but because having it tied up in an Afro puff was starting to give me a headache. Still, James watched as it came out.

"I like your hair," he said. "It's different. Big."

I took my hand back from him. It still tingled from the thrill of being in his. "I know a place where we can go eat," I said.

JUST AS I got to the last few steps coming down the stairs, I saw a classic 1984 red Porsche 944 sitting in the club's parking lot. Luckily I wasn't try-ing to be cool that night, because I sure enough tripped over the last two steps when I saw that car.

James caught me before I could eat the pavement, just like any movie hero would. "Are you okay?"

His arms wrapped around my waist to steady me and then lingered there. I picked up the cinnamon on his breath, and the musky amber scent of his cologne. He even smelled beautiful.

I stood up straight, pulling myself out of his embrace. "Is that your car?" I asked.

I already knew the answer, though. It was the same car that Jake Ryan had driven in *Sixteen Candles*. Of course it was his car.

"One of them. I have a thing for cars from the eighties." He walked ahead of me to unlock and open the passenger door. "No keyless entry, though. So I'm opening your door all evening."

My teenage heart gave a lurch. I could almost hear the opening strains of the Thompson Twins' "If You Were Here" playing as I got in.

"Thank you very much," I said. No matter how I was raised, I was still Southern, and my manners were automatic.

But I was determined. This thing with James had to end. Tonight.

# SIXTEEN

"YOU'VE NEVER BEEN TO HOUSE OF Pies, right?" I asked as we pulled out of the club's parking lot.

"Not yet," he said. "But I know where it is. I live right by there."

"In the Los Feliz Hills?"

"Yeah, good guess."

I shrugged. "That's where all the cool rich kids live these days."

He downshifted to make a right onto Sunset. "So you don't like me because I've got money." It was a statement, not a question. And he didn't look at me when he made the accusation.

"No, I've got plenty of reasons besides that."

James's hands tightened on the wheel. "Care to share them with me?"

I turned to stare out the window. "No need. You'll get bored soon enough and it won't even be an issue."

"You think I'll get bored?" There was a hint of bravado in his voice, like he thought I was double-dog daring him to find me interesting.

"James, I'm not who you think I am," I explained with more patience than I actually felt at that moment. "The bunny thing and the singing, that's just something I do for a paycheck. In real life, I read a lot, and I watch movies on my laptop. Sometimes I go for walks, but that's about as fun as I get."

"I like walks."

"I also have a psychology degree that I'm still paying for but don't use. And that's because I like my life just the way it is. You think I'm this intriguing mystery woman, but I'm so boring. I really am."

That was a huge speech, especially for me, and for a second James looked like he was taking my words under serious consideration. But then he said, "I want to believe you, I really do." He stepped on the clutch and went into first to stop at a red light. "But the thing is, you're already the least boring woman I've met in L.A., so I don't think I can trust you about that."

I stared. He would have the perfect comeback.

As analytical as I was, I could not understand this situation. It was like we were on two different dates. I was sick with dread and almost having to restrain myself from jumping out of his moving Jake Ryan car. But James seemed to be having the time of his life.

HERE'S THE THING about House of Pies. The pies there are fantastic, maybe the best in the West. But the food is almost inedible. I knew this, because in my early twenties I had actually tried everything on the menu in an attempt to see if anything, anything at all was palatable, and after much unappetizing research, I had come to the conclusion that nothing was.

But the pie was great, and every night House of Pies attracted a diverse crowd from all walks of life.

When we arrived, the place was almost filled to capacity with college kids, hipsters, and a black actor whose name I could not remember but who I recognized from a late-eighties sitcom.

We found a booth. I ordered coffee and pie and watched with a completely straight face as James ordered the chicken breast.

He looked around the place with his eyebrows raised.

"This is interesting," he said.

"Yeah," I agreed, looking around myself. "It's not a faux diner like most places in L.A."

"Faux diner?"

"Yeah, you know. Most diners in L.A. kind of look like movie sets. Retro, but clean and done up in great colors. This place keeps it real. Ugly fluorescent lighting. Ugly mint green booths. It's not faking the funk."

He grinned. "Faking the funk. I haven't heard that one in a while. What part of Mississippi are you from again?"

I smiled. "The bad part. The part that made me leave and come here." I said it in a tone of voice that I hoped let him know that I wasn't open to any more questions on this particular topic. "Why are you in Los Angeles anyway?" I asked, changing the subject.

He folded his hands on top of the table. "So you didn't do all your homework."

"Look, James, I know who you were. I used to keep up with the Farrell family back in the day, but I stopped Googling you guys over four years ago."

"What made you stop?"

I shrugged. "I went to college and I figured out that I had better things to do with my life than tracking the Farrells."

My coffee came just then, and I was grateful for it. Putting cream and sugar into it gave me something to do with my hands, which had taken to trembling underneath the table. Being this close to James and talking to him so candidly, my poor nerves didn't know what to do with themselves.

James watched me prepare my coffee. "My sister Tammy actually used to be the West Coast ambassador for the Farrell brand, but a few years ago, she went through a pretty bad breakup and wanted to move to New York. Farrell Cosmetics asked that either I or my other sister, Veronica, come out to Los Angeles to represent the brand at events. At the time I was engaged to an actress who had a series deal out here."

Erica London. I knew all about Erica London. She had happened before I got my mind right in college and stopped obsessively reading everything that had to do with the Farrells. "Yeah, I read about you two in *Celeb Weekly*. It didn't work out, right? "

James shook his head with a rueful smile. "No, we didn't work out. She called off the engagement."

I could see that it still pained him to admit that.

"But you came out here anyway?"

"I needed a change, and now that I've been here four years, I really like it. Great weather. Great job. Who could complain?"

Four years. I couldn't believe that James Farrell had been so close all of this time. Los Feliz wasn't even five miles from where I lived.

And I was also having a hard time believing the line that he was trying to feed me about his job. "So you like using your fancy Ivy League degree just to go to parties all the time?"

He shrugged. "Well, you have to admit, getting paid to attend events is a pretty sweet gig. Gusteau could have cut all ties with us after they bought the company, but they kept both my sisters and me on. I guess we got lucky."

I took a sip of my water. "I wouldn't call that lucky."

A shadow passed over his face. "What would you call it?"

"Um, I don't know. . . . Spin? Denial? I mean you were supposed to be the next president of Farrell Fine Hair. That's what you were groomed for, and at the last minute you guys decided to sell the company?"

"I was outvoted by my family on that one. So I made lemonade."

"Really?" I asked. "Because it sounds like you took what they gave you. And that ain't making lemonade, that's plain old giving up."

His eyes went hard, and he leaned forward. "Listen," he said in a low voice. "I can see that you weren't joking about Googling me a few times, but that doesn't mean you know anything about me or my family. Understand?"

I found his reaction intriguing and couldn't resist the urge to poke a little more. I mean this was the only date I would ever have with the James Farrell. When would I get another chance like this to probe his psyche? "I understand that your underwhelming career choice obviously makes you uncomfortable."

James sat back then. "I'm surprised that someone who claims to not be using her psych degree would be so judgmental."

I laughed a little at that comeback. "James, you're the one who doesn't know anything about me. Because if you did, you'd realize that I am already so much more than anyone ever expected me to be. I don't have anything to prove.

"You, on the other hand, are a very attractive, very rich, and very intelligent man. That's really nice for you, and I'm sure that there are a lot of women in L.A who would be creaming their panties if you asked them out. But you're not even trying to live up to your potential. And in my lowly opinion, that's just unattractive."

He gritted his teeth, but before he could respond the waitress came to the table with my pie and his chicken.

We ate in silence. From the start, he had a hard time getting his knife through his rubbery chicken, and I kind of felt bad about it. Contrary to tonight, I do not make a habit of being bitchy or of not warning the person I'm with about the food at the House of Pies. But I knew in my heart that this awful, awful awkward date was the best thing for James. Because it was the only way he would see that I wasn't mysterious or a challenge. Just a cold bitch that stood him up and then grilled him ruthlessly about his so-called job.

James gave up on his chicken after four bites, and by the time I finished my pie, he had already signaled the waitress for the bill.

It was strange, because High School Davie would have killed for this opportunity—was at this moment thrilled just to be sitting at the same table as James. But Real Davie was all the way at the other end of that crush spectrum. And I was relieved that I'd finally made him understand that an affair with me would not be fun.

HALFWAY THROUGH THE drive back across town to Hollywood, I started humming along with the radio, which he had turned on in lieu of conversation as soon as we got back in the car.

He let me go on for a while, before asking, "Are you happy now?"

"Yes, I am." I gave him a sassy country smile. "The pie was very good."

He didn't take the bait, just downshifted to turn left onto Vine.

I was trying to come up with the perfect exit line. Something other than "Bye-bye, baby," which is what Date Davie usually said—because really how else would a torch singer say good-bye on a first date?

But I definitely wasn't Date Davie tonight. And as we pulled into the club's parking lot, I settled on "See you around," even though I had killed any chance of that ever happening. Thank the Lord.

But before I could deliver my perfect exit line, he cut the engine and asked, "Answer this for me: If we're not a match, then why is my dick harder right now than it has ever been in my entire life?"

"UM . . ." I DIDN'T really know how to answer that. I was, quite frankly, shocked to hear words like that coming out of his Ivy League mouth. So I fell back on the psychology that I had learned in college. "James, I think you're looking at this as a rejection. And because you're not used to rejection, you're processing it as a challenge. And that's why you're . . . aroused."

His body was rigid and he was still staring straight ahead with his hands on the wheel. "The same thing happened when you ran into me in the bunny suit."

Oh. My. God. "Well, maybe you have a fetish. Maybe you should explore that with somebody. You know, like a therapist or something."

He finally turned his head to look at me. "Are you creaming your panties?"

I blinked. "What?"

"You said most girls would be creaming their panties if I asked them out. Are you turned on right now?"

Well, truth be told, I hadn't been up until this conversation. But when he had said the thing about him being turned on, I did feel an instant ping down there. And there was a certain item on my body that was definitely standing at attention right now.

But I tried to lie. "Um, no. Not really."

He continued to study me. His eyes seemed to glitter in the moonlight and he looked like something primitive and animal in the dark car.

I decided to put away Real Davie and bring back Stage Davie.

"Okay, well, I've got to go now." I pasted on my noncommittal stage smile and said with as much cheeriness as I could muster, "See you around."

At least I had managed to get out my exit line. I'd always have that, I thought, as I started to go for the door handle. But then he touched my hand.

Every nerve in my body froze. I could hear High School Davie screaming, *Oh my God! Oh my God! He's touching me!*

Then his other hand came up toward my face. I jerked back, banging my head against the window.

"I'm sorry," I said. Distantly, I could feel my head throbbing where I hit it, but I could not feel any pain. At least if you didn't count the pain of total embarrassment.

I had thought I'd gotten over reeling back every time someone unexpectedly raised their hand near my face. I had been working for years to control it. But I guess it was like a stutter: It came back when I got too nervous. "I'm sorry," I said again.

"Are you okay? You hit your head pretty hard."

"Did I hurt your window?"

"Did you hurt yourself?" His eyes were filled with concern.

"No, I'm fine." I wished he would stop looking at me like that. "I'm fine. But this is a really nice car. I hope I didn't crack your window."

I tried to turn around to see if I'd done any damage, but he brought his hand up again.

And this time, I held myself still. No jumping. Not even when he laid his palm against my cheek. "The window's fine. Even if it wasn't . . ." His eyes moved to my lips. "I don't care about the window."

I stopped breathing. I didn't know what to do. I felt naked. And very afraid.

Then he kissed me. He laid his big soft lips on mine and eased his tongue into my mouth. It was gentle at first, but the longer it went on, the more his mouth insisted that this kiss was leading somewhere.

I pulled away first. Which was hard, like separating a heavy-duty magnet connection. In fact, I had to put my hands on his chest and push him away to keep him from coming after me again.

We were both breathing hard. Panting, really. And I knew that there was no way I was getting out of this car without him.

"Okay," I said. My voice was so quiet that even I could barely hear me. "Let's go up to my apartment."

I WALKED UP the stairs in a trance. He was directly behind me, close enough that I could smell his cologne and feel his eyes on the back of my Strokes T-shirt.

One part of me felt removed from the entire situation, like I was standing somewhere else and watching Davie Jones lead James Farrell up to her apartment. Another part of me was back in Mississippi.

I was walking up to the Farrell Manor porch again. And I saw him there, talking with Corey. Had he known? Had he helped his sisters plan it?

High School Davie didn't believe her James could ever do something like that, but Real Davie knew better. She had seen some things, done some things, and now she was struggling to remember if he had pointed and laughed along with the other kids when she fell in the mud.

But I pushed those thoughts away. That night at Farrell Manor was done and gone. And this one was happening right now in real time.

I pulled my keys out of my satchel and tried to unlock my door, but it was hard to do with trembling hands; I couldn't get the key into the lock.

After four unsuccessful tries, James took the keys from me and unlocked the door himself. Then he pushed it open for me.

"Thank you," I said, walking in past him.

"You're welcome." He followed me in and closed the door behind us. There was a soft click. And then he suddenly wrapped me up in his arms from behind. His hands were everywhere. On my back, my breasts. Unfastening my jeans.

And then one hand went further. Inside my yellow cotton panties.

I came embarrassingly fast. There was no build-up, just three strokes from him and an "Oh God!" from me before the orgasm overtook me, causing me to bend forward, so that my butt was now against his hard-on.

That was it. I heard a foil package being ripped open. And I barely had time to kick off my jeans before he stood me up, turned me around, pressed me against my front door and was inside me.

I could feel his hot breath on my neck as he whispered, "Please! Please! Please!" between increasingly ragged breaths.

I wrapped one of my legs around his waist and just held on to him. I didn't know what else to do, and I could feel, against all odds, another orgasm coming.

I came again right before he did.

We collapsed to the floor. Me in my bra and T-shirt. Him with his checkered pants around his ankles.

I could hear him beside me still breathing hard, but I was too exhausted to turn and look at him. Plus I was afraid I would say, "I love you. I always have and I always will." Or something equally inappropriate.

But I didn't have to worry about that. My body was jelly and my mind was gone. I couldn't have formed words at that moment, even if I wanted to.

I closed my eyes, trying to figure out what to do next.

And when I opened them again, he was still there. But now he was breathing steadily with his mouth closed and the most peaceful look on his face. He was sleeping.

James Farrell was sleeping on my apartment floor.

This was a complete nightmare. I got up and turned off the lights. Then I crawled into my bed, praying that when I woke up in the morning James Farrell would not be there.

WHEN I WOKE up in the morning, James Farrell was no longer on my apartment floor.

He was lying in bed behind me with his hand resting on my thigh.

"Seriously, what does a girl have to do get rid of this guy? Am I going to have to call Ghostbusters?" I whispered to Mama Jane on the phone a few minutes later. I was sitting on the cold bathroom floor, leaning against the wall, but I still felt hot all over just thinking about what had happened with James last night.

"I thought you said the sex was good," Mama Jane said.

"It was good. One-night good. So why is he still here?"

"Why don't you just tell him to get out? I've had some women do that to me the morning after." Mama Jane sounded a little bitter when she said that.

"Saying go doesn't work with him. It just makes him think I'm playing hard to get. And he seems to like hard to get. A lot. I mean like way more than I ever would've figured."

Mama Jane started laughing.

"It's not funny," I whispered as loudly as I could without James hearing me. "I don't know what to do. This is so bad."

"Maybe if you told him about what happened in high school—"

"No," I said. I remembered how he had looked at me in the car the night before. All want and need. It had made me feel so sexy, so beautiful.

I didn't ever want to go on a date with James again, but I couldn't bear to see the hot way he looked at me morph into pity. What if he started looking at me like the nice kids at Glass High had looked at me when I was Monkey Night? Just imagining him feeling sorry for me made me feel sick to my stomach.

"No," I said again.

"Well, then, maybe you could just sneak out of there if he's still sleeping. I've done that a few times."

"That's the smartest thing I've ever heard. That's exactly what I'll do." I looked down at my Strokes T-shirt and the panties I had hastily pulled on before slipping into the bathroom with my cell phone. I wasn't exactly dressed for a big getaway, but my jeans were still lying crumpled near the door. I could put them on, quiet as a mouse, then run downstairs and wait in Nicky's office until James went away.

Suddenly a knock sounded on the door. "Davie?" came James's voice. My heart sank.

"That's him, isn't it?" Mama Jane said on the other side of the line.

"Just a minute," I called to him. Then I said to Mama Jane, "Yeah, it's him. I've got to go."

"Call me back," Mama Jane said. "This thing you got going on is way better than the audiobook I'm listening to right now."

I OPENED THE bathroom door to find James, standing there with my yellow top sheet wrapped around his waist.

His voice was tight and uncomfortable when he said, "There's someone here to see you. He, ah . . . just let himself in."

I looked over James's shoulder to see Nicky standing in the middle of my apartment.

His eyes went from me in my T-shirt and panties, to James in my yellow top sheet. "What the fuck is this?"

I think he was actually expecting me to answer that. But what do you say to the ex-boyfriend who barges in on you having a morning-after with the man you claimed had turned you off perms fifteen years ago?

The polite and Southern thing to do would have been to introduce them, despite the situation. Southern women excelled at being gracious at the most awkward times, and I did still have my accent. However, both my Southern background and my good manners refused to kick in. I just stood there with my mouth half open, trying to figure out how to handle this without it coming out that I was Monkey Night.

"I thought you weren't going to go down this road," Nicky said, brandishing his landlord key at James, like I had actually given him permission to use it.

"I wasn't, but he was real insistent."

"Are you guys talking about me?" James asked, looking between us.

Nicky glared at him. "Insistent like romantic insistent? Or insistent like I-need-to-kick-his-ass insistent?"

"Excuse me?" James didn't look so Ivy League when he took a step toward Nicky, one hand holding the sheet at his waist and the other clenching into a fist at his side.

I got in between them real quick. The last thing I needed was James Farrell and my ex-boyfriend breaking out into a fistfight in my studio apartment. "Nicky, everything's fine, but what have I told you about coming in here without permission?"

"I'm your landlord," Nicky reminded me. "I can come in here whenever I want."

"Nicky, you know that's not true. There are laws." I hoped.

But there must have been something on the books, because he backed down and admitted, "I thought you was gone. Ain't you supposed to be in Burbank singing right about now?"

I cursed. With James and all the whatnot, I had totally forgotten that I had a Soul BunnyGram appointment at 9:30 in Burbank. I looked at the clock. It was 9:10, which only made me curse again.

I scurried past Nicky to retrieve my jeans from where they were still lying right by the door. "I'll be on the road in five minutes."

"You need to be on the road now. Our client ain't paying for colored people's time."

James stepped to Nicky again, stoic, even though he had my butter yellow top sheet wrapped around his waist. "I'll make sure that she gets to her appointment on time."

And then he did what few dared to do with Nicky. He stared him down. He did this even though Nicky was taller and a lot more muscular than him.

Nicky stared back for a few seconds, but then he got tired of that game and looked at me.

I guess Nicky and me, being best friends, were on a whole new level of ESP, because somehow he understood that I really, really needed him to not say another goddamn word and go.

He gave James one last hard stare and left, though the dramatic manager in him made sure to slam the door on his way out.

As soon as he was gone, James's face went from hard to bemused. "Is that the same Nicky that owns the restaurant downstairs? The guy that was in your dressing room when I brought you your appointment book?"

I went to my closet. "Good memory." At least for recent events.

"So he's your landlord, too?"

I pulled my bunny suit out of the closet. "And my manager for the Soul BunnyGrams. And my best friend, technically."

James was also pulling on his clothes now, and he was fastening his pants when he asked, "And your ex-boyfriend, too?"

No way was I getting into a conversation with James Farrell about my complicated history with Nicky.

I started putting my bunny suit on. "You don't have to take me to my appointment," I said.

"I think I do. I promised your weirdly inappropriate boss-slash-landlord."

"No really. I've got a car. I can get myself there."

"Do you want me to zip you up?"

I had a hook that I kept in my kitchen drawer to do that job, but I was in a hurry, so I turned and let James zip me into the bunny suit.

"I'm afraid if I don't drive you, that you'll run," he said behind me.

"Even if you did drive me, I'd run." I was too late and flustered to lie to him. "I'd just run later."

"Well, luckily I'm only worried about now."

I grabbed a hair band and pulled my Afro into a low puff at my neck as fast as I could. "Listen, James, I'm just going to be straight up with you." *Sort of,* I added to myself.

I gathered up my iPod speaker box, my satchel, and the rest of what I would need to deliver the BunnyGram as I explained the situation to him.

"I have made a vow to myself never to accept a guy's Invitation to Crazy, and from the moment you showed up at my dressing room door, that's what I've felt like you've been trying to hand me. I don't think you're a terrible person necessarily, but I've had enough psycho moments in my past and I must protect myself. Which is why when we part, I have every intention of running away and not ever accepting another one of your calls or answering the door if you show up here again. I also plan to tell Leon not to let you back into the club. I hope you can understand that."

James stopped me mid-gather, by cupping his hands around my shoulders. "Invitation to Crazy. That's a good one. Last night I was trying to figure out why I was so attracted to you, even though you stood me up, told me to go away, and then tricked me into eating overcooked chicken." He pulled my bunny hood up over my ears. "But now I know why. You handed me an Invitation to Crazy. That's a perfect description for it."

"Only thing is," he said in my bunny ear, "I'm not hesitating to take it."

# SEVENTEEN

THE PRESIDENCY OF FARRELL FINE HAIR (now Farrell Cosmetics) notwithstanding, James was the type of guy who always got what he wanted, and what he wanted was to drive me to my gig. Five minutes later I found myself on the 101 freeway, once again in the passenger seat of his *Sixteen Candles* Porsche.

I couldn't help but notice how traffic parted for him as he sped down the highway. Every time I thought we would have to slow down because cars were backed up, all the cars in front of us would suddenly decide to move into another lane, just in time for James to speed through.

Watching this happening over and over again was a little awe-inspiring, and it made me think of that one Heart song from the seventies.

*Try, try, try to understand, he's a magic man.*


I GOT TO the appointment only a minute after my call time. It was just a simple cubicle birthday at a small shipping company. I sang "Let's Hear It for the Boy" for a portly payroll administrator. Then I gave him a balloon and posed for a couple of snapshots with him and the coworkers who had ordered the BunnyGram for him.

It all went so smoothly that I almost forgot that James was waiting for me in the parking lot. Almost. But not really.

He was on the phone when I came back out to the car, but he got off as soon as he saw me and reached across the passenger seat to unlock my door.

"Who were you talking to?" I asked after I got in.

"Work," he said. "They want me to go to this thing tonight. A store opening on Melrose." He started up the car. "How did it go?"

"Good. Simple. Ten-dollar tip."

James patted my knee like he could actually fathom being happy to get a ten-dollar tip. "Good job then."

Having finished with the chitchat, I began what I already knew would be the hard work of trying to convince James to just take me home now.

"Thanks for driving me," I said. "But I've really got to get out of this bunny costume and take a shower. If I get the suit musty, then I have to live with it, because I can only afford to dry clean it like once a month."

"Okay, then let's go back to my place. You can get out of your suit, and we can have some breakfast."

My stomach leaped at the word "breakfast." Singing first thing in the morning had made me hungry, but I tried to keep up my resolve.

"I've got rehearsal at the club at three P.M. And you've met my boss."

"I can get you back by three P.M."

I scrambled for another excuse, but all I could come up with was "I don't have anything to wear after I take off the suit."

He grinned. "Believe me, that won't be a problem."

He maneuvered the car into the right lane and headed toward the 5 South on-ramp.

I would've argued further, but I was hungry and hadn't had my coffee. Plus I was overwrought, and truth be told, I was getting tired of having to fight him every step of the way. "Okay, breakfast," I agreed. "But that's it."

James smirked in such a way that I knew he considered my last statement a line in the sand. A line that he fully intended to cross.

———

I HAD BEEN to Griffith Park before, but I had never been up into the nearby Los Feliz Hills. I had only seen aerial shots of the luxury homes, many of which were owned by younger and B-level stars, in magazines like *Celeb Weekly*.

The roads seemed to become both steeper and narrower as the car twisted its way through the hills. Although my bunny costume didn't give me much in the way of peripheral vision, I could see that the houses were also getting bigger. Then the large houses soon gave way to full-out mansions.

James drove with his hand resting on my furry knee. "You ever been up here before?" he asked.

"No." I noted that the mansions had now turned into spreads with separate guesthouses. "I've been to Baldwin Hills. That's where my boss lives. And I once delivered a BunnyGram to a record producer in Beverly Hills, but that's about it."

James turned left down a road with a "No Outlet" sign. "Well, I hope you like my place."

At the end of the road there was a gate, which slid open with quiet precision to admit us. James drove through, and the road twisted and turned a few more times before we finally stopped in front of a large two-story, Mission-style villa.

And if that setup didn't beat all, there was a butler—yes, an honest-to-God butler—standing at the top of the stone steps, which led to two humongous dark wood doors.

"Are you serious?" I asked James.

"What?"

"I expected ostentatious. But come on." I shook my head.

"Ostentatious," he repeated. "That's a big word."

I looked at him. "I may be country, but I'm not dumb."

He just chuckled. "Believe me, Davie. Nobody's accusing you of being dumb. Stubborn, yes. Dumb, no."

The butler opened my door for me and held out his hand to help me out of the car.

With considerable embarrassment, I gave him my paw and stepped out into the hot sun. Bless his heart, if he thought there was anything strange about his employer showing up with a girl in a bunny suit, he wasn't letting it show on his face.

"Thank you," I mumbled.

"You're welcome, ma'am," he said, revealing a faint Jamaican accent.

Now that he was closer, I recognized him as the same guy that I had once seen taking out the trash during one of my many sneak visits to Farrell Manor back in the day. In the early nineties, his hair had only been dotted with gray, but now the gray had taken over his entire head.

"Thanks, Paul," James said. He came around the car and tossed the Porsche's keys to Paul, who let go of my paw to catch them.

James wrapped his arm around my waist. "You wear a seven-eight, right?"

I nodded. "Paul, she'll need some clothes. Can you have something delivered?"

"Of course." Paul's eyes lingering on my bunny suit for just a second too long was the only indication he gave that this situation was kind of strange. "Have you eaten yet, sir?"

"No, but we're going to take a shower first." James started walking us up the stairs. "Can Mildred send up something in about half an hour?"

"Of course, sir," I heard Paul say behind us.

Then we were walking into a foyer with high ceilings and cork floors.

"*Mi casa*," James said with an offhand wave.

He led me toward the winding staircase, and I tried not to gape as we climbed the stairs to the second floor.

"I have a butler, too. But I gave him the night off," I joked.

James squeezed me against him. "Paul's not a butler. He's the house manager. He kind of does a little bit of everything, and he makes sure everything runs well. His wife, Mildred, cooks and takes care of all the housekeeping. It's a little more service than I really need, but they've been with the family since I was young. When my parents started spending more time in Washington, they thought Paul and Mildred might be happier out here with me."

"Are they happier with you?"

"I know they don't miss Mississippi. Same as you."

I highly doubted it was the same as me. Farrell Manor didn't even compare to the shack I grew up in, but it was a common story out here in California. Almost everybody liked here better than where they came from.

We stopped in front of a set of thin double doors, so intricately carved that I couldn't help but bring my paw up to trace them.

"They're Andalusian," James said. "My interior designer found them at an abandoned monastery in Spain."

"They're beautiful," I said.

He started tracing the patterns on the door, too. "Yes, beautiful. And complicated and mysterious. Like you."

I let my paw drop from the door. "James, please don't say things like that to me. I don't appreciate lines."

He moved closer to me. "The first thing I wanted to know was how Moorish doors ended up on a Catholic monastery. I asked my interior designer, and she said they were a gift from a converted Moor who became an artist after he found Jesus. Then I asked her to find out everything she could about that Moor, because the minute I saw these doors, I wanted them in my life and I wanted to know everything about them. That's how beautiful they are."

He leaned down, his cinnamon breath warm against my face. "It's not a line, Davie," he said. Then he stepped away and opened the doors to his bedroom.

My eyes widened. His bedroom alone was bigger than two, maybe three of my entire apartments put together. The room also had cork floors, though here it was accented by the mostly wood furniture and dark blue wallpaper.

I hoped James had shown his interior designer proper appreciation, because she had somehow managed to make his bedroom masculine, yet airy enough to be a beach bungalow. Two sets of electric bamboo fans spun overhead, making the room cool, but not cold, and two corner walls were composed entirely of floor-to-ceiling French windows, all of which were thrown open to reveal a stunning view of the Los Angeles skyline, including Griffith Observatory and the "Hollywood" sign.

I walked around the room with my mouth open, trying to take it all in.

"Everything about this bedroom is perfect," I told him. "If I were you, I would live here exclusively."

"I'm glad you like it." He came up behind me and unzipped the back of my bunny suit. "But if you were me, you would already be out of this costume."

A FEW MINUTES later we were standing naked in front of a large glass-encased room with rows of platinum fixtures that James claimed was his shower.

"Did you special-order it from NASA?" I asked.

He laughed.

"I'm not kidding," I said. "It looks like a spaceship. I'm afraid to get in there."

James slipped the hair band off my wrist, and used it to secure my Afro in a lopsided ball at the side of my head. "This is the way you like it, right?"

Inside the shower, James hit a few buttons on a touch screen panel, and warm water sprays hit us from three of the four walls. It was disconcerting at first, but soon I got used to it, especially when James grabbed a bar of black soap and started rubbing it over my body.

"What, we have to do this ourselves? Your shower doesn't soap us down, too, like a car wash?"

"There might be a function for that," he said. "But I like this better."

He kissed my neck and used his index fingers to get behind my ears, and he took extra care with my chest, lifting up each breast to get the creases underneath them. Then he handed the soap to me.

He seemed to enjoy having me give him the same treatment, but when I lingered too long on his penis, he removed my soapy hands and said, "I missed a spot on you, but I need a condom to get to it. Hold on."

He climbed out of the shower and was back a few moments later, sheathed and ready to go.

He pressed me against the fourth wall, the only one without fixtures on it, but then he went still.

"I need to see you tonight. I want you to promise me."

The haze of lust I had fallen into cleared a little bit. "You're blackmailing me with sex?"

"I'm communicating to you that it's going to be hard for me to enjoy this if I'm worried that I won't be able to see you again."

I glared at him. "I don't like being manipulated by you."

"Believe me, I'm not happy about this, either. It's bad for my self-esteem."

He cupped my breasts in his large hands and flicked his thumbs over my hard nipples. "But I do what I have to do to get the job done."

My mind told me to say no to his date-later-for-sex-now offer, seeing as how I was determined to end this. But then he pushed against me with his hard-on, and my body started insisting, *Yes, take the offer. Agree to anything that would end this conversation and get him inside of you.*

"Okay," I said.

He pushed against me again, and I was fixed to die it felt so good. "Okay, you'll meet me after your show tonight?"

"Yes, I'll drive over here after my show—"

He entered me before I could finish my promise. I suspected that I had given in too easily. But as the orgasm started to rush over me, I found it hard to care.

I DIDN'T REALIZE how hungry I was until I smelled the bacon as we came out of the bathroom. The still-unseen Mildred had left breakfast for us, all neat and prettily presented, on a maple table in the far corner of the bedroom.

There was also a full outfit set out for James and a robe for me with a handwritten note, saying that new clothes would be delivered for me within an hour.

"Where's my bunny suit?" I asked James, not seeing it anywhere in the large room.

"Paul sent it out for dry cleaning. It should be back around the same time as the clothes."

I did a mental check of my bank balance and realized that I only had about thirty bucks to last me until next Thursday. But I pulled a pen and my checkbook out of my satchel anyway. "Um, thanks. How much do I owe you?"

"Put your money away."

"Seriously, how much do I owe you?"

James shook his head. "I'm not sweating you for a few dollars."

"It costs like fifty dollars to dry clean that suit. More if you took it to a place that will have it back to you in an hour."

I started writing out the check, trying not to think about the overdraft fees I was about to incur.

"Look, it's hospitality. I feel bad for making you get your suit dirty—"

I lowered the checkbook. "James, are you really serious about pursuing this . . . this thing we've got going on?" I asked.

"Yes, I'm serious," he said. "You think I work this hard with every girl I meet?"

"Okay, then let me just emphasize my situation to you. I am poor. I am happy, but I am poor. I have college loans. I've got rent. I've got car repairs. I can't get used to your lifestyle. I cannot afford to get used to your lifestyle. Do you understand?"

James shook his head. "How long did you say you've been living in L.A? Because I have never had to have this conversation with another woman."

I started filling out the date area on the check. "And how much were the clothes that Paul ordered for me?"

He snatched the checkbook from me and tossed it back into my satchel. Suddenly I wasn't talking to gentle Andrew McCarthy James anymore. He was bad boy Judd Nelson James, and he looked real mad.

"I'm not going to take your money," he said with clenched teeth. Then he caught himself. He took a deep breath through his nose and said, "Davie, you've got your pride and I've got mine. You said you're poor, and I'm telling you that I can't take money from the poor."

I sucked on my teeth. "You mean, not unless there's a relaxer involved."

James's shoulders untensed, and the anger seeped out of his face. "An exchange of goods, yes."

"So if I wanted to pay you back for the Jheri curl juice . . ."

He laughed. "Hey, don't sleep. There are still people rocking those curls. Farrell Texturizer does brisk business in certain markets."

OVER BREAKFAST HE asked me, "Did you have a Jheri curl growing up?"

I knew he was joking, but it brought back the memory of the matted mess I used to wear on top of my head before I knew better. "No, I had a natural. Kind of like an Afro, but not picked out or anything."

Again, I found myself waiting for something to click inside his head, for him to connect what I was saying with the girl who handed him a quickly written note fifteen years ago with her heart beating in her throat.

But all he did was finish chewing, before saying, "Really? An Afro? Nobody our age had an Afro growing up."

I put my fork down. "Really? You never saw anybody at your high school who had an Afro? You never talked to anyone with an Afro?"

James actually thought about it, his eyes going to the ceiling like he was filing through his memory index. Then he said with such certainty that it chilled me to the bone, "No, every girl had braids or perms. No Afros."

My heart dropped, because at that moment I realized that James hadn't just forgotten who I was, he hadn't even registered my existence.

It had taken every ounce of courage I had to go up to him outside that locker room, and giving him that note had been one of the defining moments of my life. But it had meant nothing to James. It hadn't even made it into his High School Memory collection.

I knew then that he hadn't had anything to do with the Farrell Manor trick. I could see the scene clearly now. Him standing there, innocent as a lamb on the porch, greeting Corey and not even noticing me as I approached the house in my yellow dress. I could see him not registering the ruckus or the calls of "Monkey Night" as I ran away.

Just like it didn't occur to Andrew McCarthy that the rich girls were harassing Molly Ringwald before he met her in *Pretty in Pink*, it didn't occur to James that his sisters had gone out of their way to make my life miserable and then finally play that trick on me.

James Farrell had literally not known that Davidia Jones, aka Monkey Night, was alive.

That might actually be a good thing, I thought.

Him not realizing that I used to go to his high school, that there had been a sad little girl who had hung the moon on him, made me Angry with a capital "A."

And that Anger made any guilt that I might have had about the secrets I was keeping from James Farrell disappear. The Anger also made it easier to share breakfast with James Farrell. Made it easier to laugh with James Farrell like everything about us was new. And it made it easier to climb on top of James Farrell and finally fuck him in a bed.

It was as intense as the first time, and afterward he buried his face in my neck and asked, "Is it always like this for you?"

"No," I admitted. "It's never been like this."

His lips curved into a smile against my neck. "Good. It would be weird if it was just me."


PAUL DELIVERED ME to the club doors about ten minutes before three P.M. in another one of James's eighties cars. This one was a shiny black

Mercedes 300SD with a noisy old diesel engine that ran on vegetable oil and made my arrival more than obvious when we pulled into the club's parking lot. Paul cut off the engine and came around the car to open my door.

But I grabbed the Fred Segal bag, with my freshly laundered Strokes T-shirt and last night's panties inside of it, and opened the door myself.

I ended up nearly colliding with him when I got out. Then there was another awkward wrestle as we both attempted to close the door after me. In the end, I just let Paul do it.

After the Door Fight, I pasted on my Stage Davie face and said, "See you later, baby" before starting to walk away.

"Yes, at ten P.M., I believe."

I turned around. "You don't have to come back for me."

"Oh, I'm not coming back for you," Paul answered.

I let out my breath, glad that I had misunderstood.

But then he said, "I'm waiting here for you."

I looked from side to side, trying to understand what was going on here. "I have my own car."

"I've been told to stay," he said. I guess he didn't like me arguing with him, because his voice was quite a bit chillier now.

I walked back over to him, because by this time I could see Nicky hovering near the open club doors, and I didn't want him to overhear me arguing with James's manservant or whatever he was.

"Go," I said. "I'll call James and let him know I said it was okay."

He leaned in and answered, "Even if you tell him to tell me to go, he will tell me to stay. Mr. Farrell maybe feels you two are at a . . . tentative time in your courtship, yeah?"

"Okay, this is starting to piss me off. I don't have time to call James, I have rehearsal to get to."

"I don't mind waiting. I have a book." He pulled out a thin paperback and waved it at me.

"The point is that I can't have you waiting outside the club. People would start asking questions."

I looked back over my shoulder. Nicky was now full-on waiting for me outside the door with his arms folded. I had to end this conversation.

"Okay, tell James that if you're waiting for me when I come out of this club, there isn't going to be a tonight. Or any other night from here on out. Tell him he can be in my life. But he can't run it. That's for me to do." My voice was all Mississippi, and my face was just as serious.

I could tell my words hit home by the way Paul's lips tightened into a thin line. "I'll relay the message, ma'am."

"Thank you," I said, not even bothering to mask my exasperation. Then I turned around to face Nicky.


NICKY WAS ON me with questions as soon as I walked through the door.

"Who was that?" Then before I could answer: "And what the hell was that this morning?" Then before I could answer again: "James Farrell?"

"I'm sorry about this morning. That was weird, I know."

"So he recognized you from high school—" Nicky stopped, maybe taking a cue from the guilty look on my face. "You didn't tell him—"

"I've got to get to rehearsal. Can we talk about this later?"

"Are you kidding me? I own this place. We can talk about it now. I want to know what's going on." A beat. "He didn't recognize you from high school?"

I pulled him into the coat-check closet for some privacy. "Nicky, I just found out today that he literally did not know I existed in high school. It's crazy."

"You're damn right, it's crazy. When are you going to tell him?"

"Umm . . ."

"You're going to tell him, right?"

I shrugged. "I'm thinking about it. I'm not necessarily an honest person, you know. I've done some things, Nicky."

He let that one slide without comment, because he wasn't the kind of guy who held dishonesty against a human being. Him being a successful businessman and all. But still he must have found something distasteful about this whole situation because his next words were, "So, what? You're in some kind of relationship with him now? How'd that happen?"

"I don't know," I said. "I have been trying to dump this guy since he showed up at my door last night. But he's on some crazy eighties movie trip. . . ."

Nicky shook his head. "I don't understand what that means."

"He doesn't know how to take no for an answer, because nobody ever says no to him. It's weird. I don't know what to do."

"You want me to get rid of him for you?"

"No," I answered, not because I was above having somebody else do my dirty work for me—believe me I so wasn't. But because I honestly didn't think it would work.

Nicky held up his hands. "Wait a minute, what did you tell me the last time I suggested we get back together?"

"What? You've run out of cocktail waitresses?" I guessed.

Nicky didn't even crack a smile. "You said that you had already dealt with enough crazy for one lifetime, and that you needed—no wait, you said that you *deserved* a boring relationship. And I left you alone after that, because I figured you had a point. But this thing you're trying to do with James Farrell, that's a whole lot of crazy."

God, I felt like shit. Like hypocritical shit. "I know."

He looked me in the eye, father to a child. "Do you really know? Because you ain't acting like you know."

I gave him a helpless look. "It's James Farrell."

Nicky's jaw tightened. I didn't think he even wanted me in that way anymore, but it was the principle of the matter. I had told him so much about how the Farrell family had hurt me, he probably found it hard to believe, not to mention insulting, that I would prefer James to him.

But all he said when he opened his mouth again was "Nice dress."

I looked down at the Isabel Marant wrap dress that Mildred had delivered to the room along with Papinelle underwear and Louboutin heels about half an hour before I left James.

"Thanks," I said. Then I carefully edged past him out of the coatroom.

I had a sinking feeling in my stomach. I hoped this didn't hurt us. I hoped that Nicky wasn't my Duckie, and that he wouldn't stop talking to me or being my friend because Andrew McCarthy had come around.

I didn't even bother to also be scared that James would eventually reject me the way Andrew did Molly, because that was a given.

But I hoped to God that when this all went to shit, Nicky would still be my friend. I'd need somebody to help me pick up the pieces.

DESPITE THE SITUATION with James and despite the fight with Nicky, my set went really well that night. I wore my pink sequined gown and sang the hell out of four Shirley Bassey songs and six Peggy Lee standards. And after I finished "Fever" on the lap of a well-dressed man with frosted tips and hand-tooled Italian leather shoes, his equally well-dressed gay male friends came to their feet for a standing ovation.

All and all it was a good night. At least it was until I came into the dressing room to find a note taped to my door in Leon's caveman hand-writing. "Old Mercedes waiting outside for you."

I got out of my dress and put back on my laundered Strokes T-shirt and some old jeans that I kept in my dressing room just in case I had to do a quick change and didn't have time to go up to my apartment. Then I took off my stage makeup, all the while rehearsing the speech I would give Paul. *Tell your boss that nobody puts Davie Jones in a corner. Tell him that he's going to have to find some other girl to harass. Tell him I am my own damn grown woman.*

I had gotten in a real fine pissed-off mood by the time I came out of the club, and I no longer cared that he was James Farrell. If he couldn't respect my wishes, then he couldn't—

But James, not Paul, climbed out of the driver's side of the Mercedes. His sparkling smile filled up the night, and he caught me up in a huge bear hug before I could even process his presence.

What had I been saying?

"I told you not to come," I said, my face turned into his chest.

"You told Paul not to come," he corrected.

James was a clever boy.

He let me out of the hug and looked down at me. He didn't kiss me. Didn't try to convince me that he wasn't trying to crowd me. Just looked me straight in the eye and smiled, like there was no other place on earth that he'd rather be than here in this parking lot with me.

And I'm sorry, but I don't care how strong you are or what's happened in the past to prevent you from going down a certain road. When a boy looks at you like that, how can you resist?

Somewhere in the distant recesses of my mind, the opening strains of the *Sixteen Candles* song started up again. *Doo-doo doo-doo-doooo* . . .

"Hi," I said, because what else would a girl who had somehow found herself in a Molly Ringwald movie say at a moment like this?

"Hi," he said.

No doubt about it, James knew the script. He even bent down to kiss me at the perfect moment, right when I decided to give in and accept his Invitation to Crazy.

# EIGHTEEN

TWO NIGHTS LATER, I WALKED UP the stairs to my apartment to find James waiting outside my door.

"Hey," I said. We hadn't made plans, but somehow I wasn't surprised to see him here, looking like a runway model for some designer's summer collection in an unbuttoned gray vest and a turquoise shirt tucked into trousers.

"You always look so put together," I said, unlocking the door.

James followed me into my apartment. "Yeah, the company pays for a stylist." He fingered the vest. "This is all her."

I gave him my back. I had already taken off my fake eyelashes and makeup downstairs, but I was still in my evening gown and needed him to unzip me.

"Really? I thought only celebrities had stylists."

I could feel his thumb on my bare back as he pulled down the zipper on my dress. "Those are their high-profile clients. A lot of people who are seen a lot hire them, too, on the DL."

"Now I know."

He turned me around and kissed me. "Now you know."

I moved away from him to step out of the gown. "So what are you doing here?"

"I was at the ArcLight for the premiere of this movie that has Farrell

Cosmetics product placement in it. Thought I'd stop by, since I was in the neighborhood."

His voice was casual, but his eyes tracked me as I hung my evening gown up in the closet.

And when I turned back around to face him he was holding a small jewelry box.

"What's that?"

"Open it."

I stayed right where I was.

"C'mon," James said. He came closer and opened the box for me. There was a pair of large sapphire studs inside. "I was thinking these would look good with your Strokes T-shirt. Try them on."

I looked up at him. "Remember what I told you yesterday about not getting used to your lifestyle?"

"C'mon, they're a gift. You can't accept a gift?"

"No, I can't accept a gift. No presents. No fancy dinners. I don't want it. I don't need it. Especially from you."

James snapped the box close. "You're making me feel sleazy for trying to do something nice. That's a real problem."

"Oh, please stop whining. If that's your worst problem, then you've got it pretty good, rich boy."

My words hit the air between us with such force that even I was taken aback. And James now had such a dark look on his face that I opened my mouth to say, "Sorry" for saying out loud what I had only meant to think to myself.

But before I could cobble together an apology, he picked me up and tossed me onto my bed. I soon discovered that what had looked like anger on his face was actually unadulterated lust.

Afterward, I got out of bed and put on my robe. "Do you want something to drink?" I asked him. "I've got cheap wine."

"Sure," he said.

In the kitchen, I grabbed a bottle of Two-Buck Chuck and some crackers.

But when I came back out to the main room, James was in his black boxer briefs looking around confused.

"Where's the TV?" he asked.

I pulled a square blanket off my desk chair and spread it out on the floor. "I broke it about five years ago." I didn't add the part about throwing it out the window because I had found Nicky cheating. It was a little early in the relationship for all that.

His eyes went to the stacks of books lined up against my wall in horizontal columns. "So you just read? That's how you spend all your nights?" he asked.

I poured out the wine into two juice glasses. "No, I've got Netflix. Sometimes I watch stuff on my laptop."

While touring James's house a few days ago, I had seen that he had large flat-screen TVs in all the guest bedrooms and tiny ones in all the bathrooms. He even had a small twenty-seat theater, so I wasn't surprised by the look of horror on his face. "Come sit down. Have some wine."

He sat down across from me on the blanket, but he was still shaking his head. "You've got to let me buy you a television."

"No, James."

"It wouldn't be a gift. It'd be my TV, but I'd keep it at your apartment."

This time I laughed and gave him a soft peck on the lips, before saying again, "No, James."


"NO, JAMES" WAS something I found myself saying a lot over the next few months.

No, I couldn't go out to dinner with him at the hottest new restaurant in town. No, we couldn't fly to Cabo on my Monday–Tuesday weekend. No, I couldn't attend any event where there would be press.

The last one was the real issue, because he didn't understand what reason I'd possibly have for not going out to at least a few of these things with him, especially since it didn't cost us any money.

And I couldn't exactly tell him the truth, that I was dog-scared somebody would snap a picture of us, and one of his mean-ass sisters would see it.

Both Veronica and Tammy Farrell lived in New York now. From what I could understand, Veronica did the same ambassadorship, showing-up-places thing that James did, but on the East Coast. And Tammy—who was a model and went by Tam now, was the main face of Farrell Cosmetics.

Before they had sold the company, I had gotten used to seeing large billboards of her, peeping out at the world through a straight curtain of silky black hair for their hair products line, whenever I visited Mama Jane in Inglewood. But now that Gusteau had launched a makeup line under the Farrell brand, I saw her face everywhere. In magazines and winking at me in the makeup section at convenience stores. In these ads she was often with a round-eyed Asian model and a smoky Latina. They walked down city streets, hailed taxicabs, and laughed in the back of limousines. They always looked like they were having the time of their lives.

I was a MAC girl through and through, but I understood those ads now, because I was having the time of my life with James. And I didn't want to do anything that would endanger that. So I told him that I didn't have the funds to buy outfits for all of his events. He said he'd take care of it. Then I had to tell him again that I wouldn't accept gifts from him. But he insisted that it was a write-off, a business expense. Not a gift.

"I perform at parties, I don't go to them," I finally answered, shutting him down for real.

We had these kinds of conversations a lot. Afterward James would look hurt. And I would feel like the most unreasonable woman on the planet for basically refusing to be seen in public with the guy I was dating.

Still, I knew in my heart that no matter how it looked to him, I wasn't being unreasonable. I had my reasons. They were psycho reasons, yes, but they were mine.

THOSE WERE THE bad times. But for the most part, the summer of 2007 was good times for us.

I was thirty-one, and if I had thought my Bohemian lifestyle would turn James off, I was wrong. Against all odds, me not wanting to do expensive things actually made our relationship more interesting because we had to be creative.

We went on a lot of picnics and to free plays and black-and-white movies that were projected onto the sides of buildings.

Once we turned down the lights and turned up the music in James's den, which had a bar, then we danced until three in the morning, as wild as we wanted, since there were no paparazzi, bloggers, society page editors, or judgmental scenesters there to see us. Afterward as we stumbled, drunk, up his winding staircase, James declared, "That's the best nightclub I've ever been to."

We also took community figure drawing classes for five bucks in Silver Lake and practiced drawing each other nude. This was a lot more embarrassing for me than for James, seeing as how I actually had cellulite and a little tummy pooch and a few other things you didn't necessarily want your man to see in the bright, unforgiving light of a sunshine-soaked room. James, on the other hand, spent an hour working out every weekday, and was pretty much perfect. Not too thin, and not bulky. Just right. That's what James was.

Also, he was a lot better at drawing than me. My line drawings of him usually looked like disproportionate cartoons, whereas you could tell it was me in the ones he did. But his took a lot longer, because he usually called for a "nookie break" about halfway through—which, after the first session, actually killed my self-consciousness about lying there naked in front of him. That was the thing about James. He didn't just tell me that I was beautiful, he made me feel beautiful with the way he looked at me and held me and made love to me. And against all odds, after a few months of dating him, I actually began to believe I was beautiful enough to be with him—even if I wasn't good enough to make it last.


AS I HAD suspected, James had been to parties in the large modern mansions on the Venice Canals, but he'd never actually been to Venice Beach before. He was more of a Malibu/Pacific Palisades sort of guy. So I introduced him.

Like me, he loved the zaniness of Venice: the bizarre street acts, the kitschy art stands, the cheap sunglasses, and even the fat guys in Speedos. He took in the scene with appreciation and awe.

"It's like we live in two different L.A.'s," he said as we set our beach blanket on the sand so that we could watch people dance around the really bad drum circle that happened there every Sunday afternoon. "And I really like your L.A."

I watched a plane make its way overhead away from LAX. "Tell me about flying," I said. "I've always wanted to try it."

James peered at me over his sunglasses. "Seriously, you've never flown before? Not even coach?"

"No, I never had any reason to."

"How did you get here from Mississippi?"

Suddenly the conversation went from innocuous to dangerous. James knew that I had come out here by myself when I was a teenager and that I was estranged from my mother. But I had let him draw his own conclusions. He didn't know about me running away or about Mama Jane.

I tensed. "In a truck." I tried not to sound so guarded that he became suspicious. But I also didn't want to sound like I was open to more questions.

"Did your mother drive?"

"No, I came out here with a friend."

"A friend from high school?"

"No, I didn't have any friends in high school."

James shifted to face me. "I find it hard to believe that you didn't have any friends in high school."

"Trust me, I was a big ol' nerd. I would not have been allowed in your circle when I was in high school." I watched the plane get farther away from us. "You wouldn't have even known I was alive."

James shook his head. "I definitely would have noticed someone like you. Believe that."

Another rage spike. But I couldn't argue with him, couldn't tell him that was the most insanely untrue thing he had ever said. I had already let him in on more information than I had meant to give him. I turned my attention to the ocean. There was a mother standing right at the edge with her small son. I could tell they were from the Midwest, because she was wearing a full piece swimsuit with a ruffle skirt, and I don't think they even sell suits like that on the coasts anymore. She was trying to coax the little boy into the ocean.

But the kid was scared to go in. Their voices drifted up to us on the wind.

"C'mon, it's all right," she said.

"No, it's going to eat me!"

James chuckled. "Poor kid."

But then the little boy took a deep breath and walked into the ocean. Just walked right in, and started to doggie-paddle.

"Good job," James said beside me.

Without warning, I felt tears in my eyes. I didn't cry often, had never cried in front of James. But true bravery always moved me. When someone is scared shitless of something and they do it anyway, that got me every time.

I wished that I was half as brave as that kid.

THREE MONTHS INTO our relationship, the good times came to a screeching halt.

James and I were in his bedroom, reading Sunday's *New York Times* over the three-course brunch that Mildred had made for us, when I came to a page with a picture of Veronica Farrell, taken at a launch party for a new online magazine.

This wasn't unusual. I was always running across pictures of the Farrell siblings at parties, seeing how it was their job and all to get their pictures taken at parties. But James chose that moment to look up from the business section. "That's my sister."

"Yes, I know," I said. I had to seriously resist the urge to turn the page. Fifteen years later, I still found looking at Veronica deeply unsettling.

But then James said the thing that would start the countdown on the game-over clock for our relationship. "By the way, she wants to meet you."

Now, if it really had been an eighties movie, I probably would have spit out my orange juice or fallen out of my chair, or done something else that would have indicated my complete and utter upset. But since this was Real Life, I just sat there, as quiet and still as High School Davie. Which was not the right answer, because James kept on going.

"So maybe you can come with me when I go to New York for the Farrell Fierce Lipstick launch, next month."

"I can't." I answered so fast I knew it had to seem suspicious. "I've already used up all of my vacation days. And I can't afford the plane ticket."

He folded up the newspaper and laid it down on the table. "Look me straight in the eye and say that."

I'm not an honest person. Obviously, I'm not an honest person. But even I couldn't lie straight to this man's face.

"I can't afford the plane ticket," I whispered.

He continued to stare at me. "Okay, I'm going to ask you some questions right now, and I need you to answer them honestly."

I smiled and tried to inject a singsong lightness into my voice as I said, "Well, I'm not necessarily an honest person, James."

"I know you're not. Because I asked Nicky about letting you off next month as a surprise, and he said you were good for vacation days."

I looked down at the table. I didn't really have a response to that.

His next words came out slowly, like he had been thinking about the question for a while now. "Is Nicky your ex-boyfriend?" he asked me again.

This time I told him the truth. "Yes, we dated for five years. But that's so over. Now we're just best friends. Family, really. You don't have anything to worry about there."

"That's not what I'm worried about. I had already figured out that you guys had some history. Thank you, though, for at least being honest with me about that."

"You're welcome," I said, my voice as small as a mouse.

"What I really want to know is when you were with Nicky, did you let him pay for things?"

I thought about trying to lie. The rest of this doomed relationship would probably go a lot more easily if I could pull out Stage Davie and have her lie to his face. But I had loved him ever since I was fifteen, and I guess in the end, I just couldn't.

"He paid for everything, but I was younger back then. And we've always had this weird father-daughter dynamic. It's not the same."

Something went dark in James's eyes. "Have you let other guys take you out on dates? Buy you things since him? Have you gone places with them?"

"James . . ."

He slammed his hand on the table. "Have you?"

"Why are you so upset about this?" I asked, genuinely curious. "Most men in L.A. would be happy not to date a gold digger."

"Because I love you!" he yelled. "I love you so fucking much, I can barely function. And it feels like you're just playing with me."

He looked so angry, and stood up so abruptly when he said this, that I threw my hands up to shield myself against a blow.

Which led to a very awkward silence.

I lowered my arms to see James standing there and looking at me as if I had lost my mind.

"I just told you I loved you."

"I know. I'm sorry," I said. "It's me. It's me. I'm so sorry."

"Did Nicky used to hit you?" The way his body tensed when he said that told me he was prepared to go down to the club and confront all two-hundred-fifty, mostly-muscle pounds of Nicky if that was the case.

"No, it wasn't him," I said. "It doesn't matter who it was. I don't want to talk about it."

"You never want to talk about it. How can you be okay with me not knowing anything about you?"

Oh, I was more than okay with James never knowing that I used to be so ugly, so unremarkable, that he couldn't remember our one high school exchange, even though I used to dream of nothing else but having a Molly Ringwald Ending with him.

"James, I can't dwell on the past. I've told you before that my sanity is precious to me. I've got to stay out of that black hole."

I came around the table. "But the person you see standing before you; she's what counts."

For the first time ever during one of our arguments, I reached for him first. I laid my hands on his chest. "I love you, too. I promise that I love you, too."

I stood on tiptoe to kiss his mouth, his cheeks, his chin, and anything else I could reach.

He just stood there rigid with anger, even when I pushed his robe off over his shoulders and untied the string on his pajama bottoms.

He knew that I was trying to change the subject with sex, but he let me lead him over to the bed and lay him down on his back.

He didn't stop me when my lips moved down his chest to his stomach, and he was already hard by the time I took him in my mouth.

Eventually his hand came down to rest against the back of my neck and guide me further. A few moments later, I looked up at him. He was staring at me, his expression still pinched and angry. "You say you're trying to protect your sanity, but you're driving me crazy."

Then with a sharp intake of breath, his mouth dropped open and he came.

AFTER HE CAME down from his blow job, he decided to tell me the full story of Erica London, the light-skinned actress he had been engaged to until they had broken up under mysterious circumstances just two months before the wedding was supposed to take place. I already knew all about it. Russell had sent me three copies of the *Celeb Weekly* issue in which it was reported as one of the side-panel stories. But I stayed quiet as James explained what had happened from his end.

He said that he hadn't seen it coming at all. "We were supposed to go out to celebrate her getting a TV pilot, but a few hours before our date, she called me. She said that she needed to focus on her career. Alone. And she said that she couldn't marry me." He traced a finger down my bare arm. "To this day, I still can't figure out if she stopped loving me, or just never did."

He turned over to face me, his face half hidden by the down pillow. "That was five years ago. And you're the first person I've loved since her."

I folded my hand into his. "I understand that you're scared, because you don't want to get your heart broken again."

"She didn't break my heart. She just had me confused. I get that now. Because I look at you and it's like, 'Damn, this woman's got me twisted. She could *really* mess me up.'" He kissed me on the forehead. "I'm going to be a lot more upset if we end like that."

I let out a bitter laugh. "James, I would never just let you go like that. In fact, I can one hundred percent guarantee you that when we split up, it will be you who does the dumping."

"Well, I'm not going to dump you, so you can put that doomsday tone to sleep."

It was fascinating how confident he was when he said these things.

"Come with me to New York," he said, pulling me close.

And I said, "Okay. I'll tell Nicky that I need the time off tonight."

He rolled on top of me then, and we made slow, passionate love. And no matter how much I tried to fight it, that afternoon I ended up whispering, "I love you, I love you, I love you" every time I came.

AS SOON AS I got into my car after leaving James and promising him that I'd go to New York, I hit up Russell, who was now a staff editor at *Celeb Weekly*, on my cell.

"Please tell me you have something for me. It's slower than fucking death here, girl. The celebrities ain't doing nothing." This is how he answered the phone, in lieu of a greeting, even though it had been years since I had given him a story.

"I need a favor," I said.

"Does this favor come with a story?"

"Unfortunately, no." I considered Russell a good friend, but the last thing I needed was him reporting that the main Farrell scion was dating me, so I lied. "Nicky's trying to get me to do this jazz club owner convention in Vegas next month."

"In August? Ew, it's too hot then. It's like one hundred and twenty on a good day."

"Exactly, but he's got it into his mind that we should be making contacts out there, because he's thinking of opening another branch, off the Strip. And I agree that a Nicky's might work well out in Vegas, I just need him to wait until it cools off to send me out there. But you know Nicky never listens to me."

"Girl, who do he listen to? Don't worry, I got you. What weekend is the convention?"

Russell arranged everything within the hour. And that night I was able to call James and truthfully tell him that I tried to get the days off, but that *Celeb Weekly* had just told Nicky that they were sending around a reporter to do a "hotspot" review, so now I had to stay in Los Angeles that weekend.

James was disappointed, but being in marketing, he understood.

It also helped that when it came time for him to leave for New York, I kept him company in the backseat as Paul drove him to the airport. I promised him that I'd also come back with Paul to pick him up.

And I was glad that I did, because even though he was only gone four days, I missed him like a big dog.

When I had been with Nicky, I had never understood just how badly it felt to be away from someone you truly loved, because:

1. Nicky was a workaholic, so he never went anywhere. And
2. The few hours that I did manage to spend away from Nicky always seemed like little treasures of time for myself.

So with my limited experience, I wasn't prepared to miss James as I did. We called each other every day and talked for rushed minutes about nothing but loving and missing each other.

By the time four days had passed, and Paul had pulled up in front of the club to take me to LAX, I was wild for him. And though I knew back-seat sex was tacky, if James was feeling half as horny as I was, I didn't think we'd be able to make it all the way home to his house without clothes coming off.

Paul and I waited for him outside the baggage claim area, clustered together with all the family members and car service drivers anticipating the arrival of the 3:45 from New York.

James, having flown first-class, was one of the first passengers off the plane. And I don't know what came over me, but when I saw him walk off that escalator in a pair of jeans and a short-sleeved green polo, looking just like he used to in high school, I couldn't do anything less than run and throw myself into his arms. I even managed to negotiate the knee-length blue skirt that I was wearing with today's Strokes T-shirt so that I could wrap my legs around his waist.

I kissed him all over his face, saying, "I missed you, baby. I missed you!" over and over again while he laughed and held me tight and said, "I missed you, too."

I hugged him and rested my head on his shoulder, thinking there was truly no other place on the planet that I would rather be than in this poorly lit airport being held in this man's loving arms.

Then I opened my eyes.

And saw Veronica Farrell, looking beyond impeccable and perfect in a white pantsuit, standing there, right behind James, and staring straight at me.

IT WAS KIND of like in horror films, when something so terrible happens that all the sound gets sucked out of the room.

It felt that quiet in my head as Veronica Farrell stared at me, trying to process what she had just seen. She was even more beautiful than in her pictures, but her gray eyes had actually grown harder and icier with age.

I held my breath. But before I could even start to pray that she didn't recognize me, her eyes narrowed and she said, "What are you doing here, Monkey Night?"

On that day, I found out that no matter how evolved humans think they are, we still have the same flight-or-fight instincts of our caveman ancestors.

Without thought or reason I jumped down from James's arms and ran. Cut out, no joke, like I was trying out for the Olympics.

James probably called after me, but I'll never know for sure, because all I remember is running out of the sliding doors and jumping into the first thing I saw, which happened to be a yellow and black Parking Spot bus.

It pulled away from the curb, just as James came running out the arrival doors after me.

I could see him searching for me with a confused look on his face, and I don't think my heart started beating again until he and the airport were out of sight.

# NINETEEN

ABOUT AN HOUR LATER, NICKY'S ESCALADE pulled up to the curb outside the Parking Spot garage to pick me up.

I climbed into the passenger seat and pulled my satchel around, hugging it to my stomach. I felt like a little kid.

Nicky didn't speak until we were on Sepulveda and headed toward the 405.

"Your boy called me about three times."

I hugged my satchel closer and said nothing.

"But I didn't tell him where you was."

"Thank you." I didn't intend for that to come out as a croak, but it did. My voice was harsh with what had just happened.

"You don't got to thank me. You may have lost your damn mind, but I guess I still got your back."

For Nicky, that was the very height of sentimentality.

"It's over," I said. "He brought his sister home with him, and she recognized me."

Nicky nodded. "Of course she did. Women remember shit. Men ain't good with that kind of thing."

An electronic version of "Summertime," Nicky's ringtone, sounded. James's cell phone number flashed on the Escalade's Bluetooth display. "It's your boy again."

"Don't answer it—"

Nicky tapped the Bluetooth connector at his ear, before I could even finish my sentence. He loved me, but he loved seeing me squirm even more.

"Whassup James?" he asked, his voice deep and gravelly and seemingly bored. "No, I still ain't seen her. But I'll have her call you if I do. You want me to give her a message?" He listened, then said, "Okay."

He hung up without saying good-bye and grinned at me. "You want to know what he said?"

Of course I wanted to know what he said. But I answered no in the hardest voice possible, because I knew that Nicky would only relay the message if he thought I didn't want to hear it.

"He said . . ." Nicky put on an upper-crust accent that I guess was supposed to be James's Ivy League education, "Tell her we need to talk."

"Did he sound angry?"

"I ain't your girlfriend," Nicky said. "I'm not going to analyze how the boy sounded with you."

Fair enough. We didn't say anything else for the rest of the drive home.


I DIDN'T REALIZE that I had been both hoping and dreading that James would be waiting for us at the club, until we pulled into the parking lot and it was empty.

James wasn't there. And the phone calls came to an abrupt stop about thirty minutes later.

I didn't know whether to be sad or relieved that this thing with James ended before I thought it would. Our months together already seemed to be racing away, like the sweet memory of my grandmother. And I felt a certain sense of nostalgia as I chose a black evening gown for that night's show.

I got lucky. We had a Billie Holiday set scheduled. And the best gift that a torch singer can give her audience is a Billie Holiday set when she actually feels like singing the blues.

IT WASN'T A standing O night, but a few people were in tears by the time I was through.

As I came down the narrow hallway, I saw that the door to my dressing room was open, though I knew I had closed it before I went onstage. I always closed doors. It was a leftover instinct from when I slept on a couch and didn't have a door I could close. I was more than grateful for them now.

I slowed, just as Nicky fell in beside me with his clipboard folded into the crook of his arm. "How you going to switch out 'Sunny Side of the Street,' the one upbeat song in tonight's set, with 'Gloomy Sunday'? That just don't make any goddamn sense. How many times I got to tell you: Sad don't sell drinks."

My eyes stayed on my open dressing room door. "Did you let somebody into my dressing room?"

Nicky held up two large fingers. "Two things: I scheduled an extra rehearsal for you and the band tomorrow. Obviously, ya'll need to go over all them upbeat songs that sell drinks again."

We were getting closer to the open door. "Fine. But again, is there somebody in my dressing room?"

He scratched that off of his list. "Second thing, your boy showed up about halfway through your set, so I let him into your dressing room."

I didn't even bother to get annoyed. Of course Nicky had let James into my dressing room as a punishment for not sticking to the set list. What else would Nicky do?

I could see James through the door now. He was so tall and glorious that he made my dressing room look dimmer than I had thought it was before he entered it. He also made it seem shabbier, even though he was still only wearing jeans and a polo.

I didn't run this time. That only delayed the confrontation when it came to James, since he was obviously a big fan of hunting me down. But I did keep my eyes lowered as I walked into the dressing room. And though I was going for breezy, I sounded plenty sheepish when I said, "Hi, James."

He looked over my shoulder at Nicky. "Can we talk alone?"

Nicky shrugged. "Sure, but if you going to yell, take it upstairs. We ain't running no soap opera here backstage."

"Are we going to yell?" I asked James. "It's up to you."

"Davie—" James's teeth set, and he stopped himself from finishing that sentence. "Let's go upstairs."

AS SOON AS I closed my apartment door behind us, his eyes ran over me in such an angry, desperate way that I could tell he was trying hard to remember me.

"Veronica told you about me, right?"

His dark brown eyes ran over me again. "Yeah, she told me that you went to Glass High, and that you, her, and Tammy didn't get along." He continued to stare hard at me. "I don't remember you."

And there it was. The ultimate proof that my singular high school moment meant nothing to him.

"You don't remember me running away at your party? You weren't in on it?"

"No, I never would have let them do something like that to anybody if I had known about it. That's probably why they didn't tell me."

I hadn't thought he knew, but actually hearing him say it filled me with relief.

Still, I had to make sure. "You didn't see me fall in the mud when I ran?"

James seemed to search his memory, his eyes going up in the air and everything. But all he came back with was "I wasn't a saint in high school. Our parents were out of town and I was already drinking with a few of my teammates before people started showing up. I was probably too drunk to notice. I'm sorry."

"Wow," I said.

He shook his head, his eyes staying on mine. "I feel like shit. I can't believe that I don't remember you. And I'm really having a hard time with what my sisters did to you in high school. I called Tammy, too. And she said you ran away after . . ." He trailed off.

But I was still stuck on the Note Incident. "You seriously don't remember me giving you a note after you got kicked out of that football game?"

"No."

Well then. I shook my head, but I had to give it to James. At least he was always straight up with me, even when I couldn't—and wouldn't—be straight up with him.

"I'm glad you don't remember," I said. "I wouldn't want you to remember me like that. So it's okay."

"No, it's not okay." His face was more grim than I had ever seen it before. Even more grim than the first time he told me that he loved me.

I felt like a little girl, but I had to ask anyway. "You're not mad at me?"

His eyebrows raised. "I'm surprised you ran like that. But no, I'm not mad at you." He took a step closer to me. "Actually, this explains a lot."

To my surprise, I felt a laugh wanting to come up from beneath my scared heart. "Yeah, I guess it does."

He bent his head in the way that tall men do when they want to talk intimately with you. "Are you mad at me?"

"Yes," I admitted, even though I knew I was reversing my earlier "it's okay" line. "A little. I don't want you to remember me that way, but I'm still having trouble wrapping my head around you actually talking to me, then just forgetting me."

"I was a kid," he said. "Just a stupid kid,"


I THINK OF all the nights James and I spent together, that one was my favorite because it was the first time Davie and the guy she had a crush on in high school made love, which meant when James was inside me, he looked at me, and knew me for me.

Afterward I was more forthcoming about the crush. In fact I told him it was more than a crush. "I stalked the hell out of you," I confessed. "And you didn't even know I was alive."

"It was high school," he said, nesting his hand in my hair, as if that explained everything. Like most high schoolers went through almost an entire school year totally oblivious to the least popular and most made-fun-of girl in school.

We stayed up all night, alternating between talking about high school and making love. That's when I began to suspect that Veronica hadn't quite told James everything.

Though she had laid out my crush in excruciating and embarrassing detail, she had not said word one about his father and my mother.

I could just imagine her trying to explain to James, without bringing our parents into it, what an ugly waste of space I had been in high school and him totally not understanding. I could see now that he did not get the high school caste system in the way that only someone who had always effortlessly been at the very top of it could possibly not get it.

And I knew Veronica would have found his insistence on staying attracted to me baffling, if not full-on upsetting.

However, I hadn't guessed that it would bring her down to the club the next day.

I WAS AT the extra rehearsal that Nicky had called to punish me. And I had just finished the first verse of the previous night's abandoned "Sunny Side of the Street" when Veronica Farrell walked in, ignoring the club's closed doors and posted hours.

Just like in high school, every person in the room seemed to stare at her as she walked across the floor in stiletto sandals, paired with a high-waisted skirt and a print top that I could just tell cost more than what I made in a week . . . maybe even a month.

I stopped singing, the piano player missed a note, and all the waiters who had come in early to set up stopped putting down tablecloths and napkins.

Nicky was the sole person not affected by her entrance. He just barked, "We're closed!" from where he was taking inventory behind the bar.

I loved him even more at that moment, because, bless his heart, not even someone as outrageously beautiful as Veronica could stop him from telling an early bird customer what's what.

Veronica ignored him and walked right up to the stage. She lifted her Chanel sunglasses and perched them on top of her hair, which was pulled back in a classic ponytail. Her hair was blond now, I noticed, with highlights that were so professional that if she wasn't black and I hadn't known her before, I might have believed that this was her actual color.

"I said we're closed," Nicky yelled even louder behind her.

Veronica just raised her cool eyes to me and said, "We need to talk, Monkey Night."

For a split second, my mind went totally black with rage. When it cleared, I was almost impressed with the utter completeness of her fucking gall. Almost.

I scrolled through my characters and decided it was time to bring out Stage Davie. I wanted Hard Davie, the one I used in customer service situations when things weren't going my way—but looking into Veronica's stone-cold eyes, I knew I wasn't going to out-hard her.

"Okay, take ten," I told the band.

"Take ten?" Nicky had come around the bar now, and was walking across the floor toward us, saying to Veronica, "Who you? And what the hell you doing coming up in my club. Telling my singer you got to talk to her. You must have lost your damn mind."

Veronica actually turned to him then, with a withering look that had probably brought more powerful men than Nicky to their knees.

But Nicky just looked back at her, widening his eyes as if to say, *You heard me!*

"Nicky, it's okay. This is James's sister, Veronica Farrell."

I don't think her name had ever crossed my lips before then. I had always called her "James's sister" in all the stories that I had told Nicky about her. Now the name tasted kind of funny in my mouth, like fancy caviar that didn't belong there. But Nicky must have recognized her as my arch-villain, because he said, "You want me to call Leon?"

"Who?" Veronica asked.

"The security guard," Nicky said, his voice cold. The way he was eye-
ing her, you'd think she wasn't beautiful. Or even human.

Which just caused Veronica to glare even harder at him. "Most people
figure out not to mess with me pretty fast," she informed him. "You're
either recklessly brave or incredibly stupid."

Wow. Apparently she had not softened over the years. Like at all.

Nicky's nostrils flared and his eyes bugged out wider than I had ever
seen them. "Leon!" he yelled.

I stepped in between them.

"I can give her ten minutes," I said to Nicky. "We were about to take
our break anyway."

Nicky stared at the both of us for a long moment, then said, "Okay,
you all can take ten," like it had been his idea in the first place.

I turned and walked back toward my dressing room, trusting that
Veronica would follow. *I am Stage Davie. I am Stage Davie. I am Stage
Davie. The coolest woman in the world*, I repeated to myself over and over
again as we walked down the narrow hallway.

"So you talk now," she said behind me.

"A little habit I picked up along the way," I answered, Stage Davie in
full effect.

When we got into my dressing room, Veronica scanned and dismissed
it with one scathing glance.

"I see you've moved up in the world." She had retained just enough of
her Southern accent that sarcasm had a knifelike effect as it rolled off her
honeyed tongue.

"You have ten minutes," I reminded her. "If you've got something to
say, you should go on head and say it."

She studied me for a second, then pulled out a check and handed it
to me.

It was written out to Davidia Jones in the amount of fifty thousand
dollars. "What's this?" I asked her, even though I knew. Back in the eighties, this had been a common scenario in movies, to the point that actually
taking part in this conversation not only felt unreal, but also real cliché.

"I've discussed this with my family and our attorneys, and that's what we're prepared to give you to go away and leave James alone."

Leave James alone, she said. Like I was bothering him. The situation made me think of Erica London all of sudden. Had his family liked her? I wondered.

"James agreed to this?" There wasn't really anything else I could say to a proposition like that. It was so much money, it almost didn't seem real.

"James doesn't need to know that this conversation took place," she answered.

"Okay, then, it's time for you to leave." I tried to give her back the check.

But she didn't take it. "He won't marry you. You'll never stand to gain more money than this from your association with him."

"If, by association, you mean our relationship, then I guess I should let you know that I'm not with James for his money. I'm with him because he wants me to be, even after I told him it wouldn't be a good idea, he insisted. Now, I'm sorry if that upsets you, but seriously, that's the way it is. Fifty thousand dollars won't change his feelings. Or mine."

"Like I said. He won't marry you. You're just a phase he's going through," she said.

She really seemed stuck on this marriage thing.

"I'm not looking for marriage, Veronica."

"Then what are you looking for?" she asked. "Because I want this over. As a matter of fact, I can't believe it's gotten this far."

Veronica, like James, I could see, found it hard to fathom not getting her own way. She would talk me to death before she would let me just waltz away with her brother. And I didn't have the patience for all of that. So I made my position real simple for her.

I ripped up the check and threw the pieces at her feet. "It's time for me to get back to work."

Veronica watched the dramatic fall of the check, now in pieces, floating to the floor, but she did not look impressed.

In the following silence, my dressing room suddenly began to feel hot and sticky, and it seemed like Veronica was the only source of cold air in the space. It was like we were back in Mississippi again.

*But this is not Mississippi*, I reminded myself. *Los Angeles is warm and temperate and never humid. And Veronica Farrell no longer has any power over you.*

Still, I had to resist the urge to turn tail and run again when her gray eyes went from the check pieces back up to mine. She looked absolutely livid.

"That was stupid," she said. "Very stupid. I can't imagine what you thought would be gained by that."

I began to tremble, which was not a Stage Davie move. Accordingly, I ratcheted down my self-expectation from answering her with pithy one-liners and settled for just staying put. If I could just stay put underneath the icy stare of Veronica's scorn, then I was doing okay, I decided.

She didn't reach out and snake her fingers around my neck, but it felt like she did when she said in a low, feral voice, "I will make your life hell if you say anything to him about your mother and my father."

I had absolutely no plans to tell James anything else about our shared and super-sordid past. If I started revealing stuff on my own now, then everything could come out, and I wouldn't —and, moreover, couldn't— risk that. But letting Veronica know that I was technically on her side where this particular issue was concerned didn't seem right.

"Your ten minutes are up," I said. "I need to get back to rehearsal. But thanks for stopping by. You can let yourself out the back door."

Her face didn't change, but I could almost feel her go from cool to fuming in zero seconds flat. Now the whole room and everything in it was hot and sticky. Including Veronica.

I rushed out of there, before she could say anything else or offer me any more checks. As conditionally brave as I had learned to be over the years, I doubted that I could bring myself to tear up two fifty-thousand-dollar checks in one day.

I could feel her eyes on my back as I left the room.

My internal clock felt like I had just spent an eternity in that dressing room, but my watch told a different story. Only seven minutes had passed.

Once I had cleared the door, Stage Davie slipped away. Truth be told, she'd barely been hanging on. I ducked into Nicky's office and spent the next three minutes just trying to breathe.

Talking to Veronica again was like confronting every single fear that I had ever had in high school. Terrifying. She terrified me.

And the truth was, in my heart, I knew she was right. James was not meant to marry the girl that Veronica still called Monkey Night. I had just turned down fifty thousand dollars for something I knew could not possibly work out. And now I was in my boss's office hyperventilating about it.

God, I hated Veronica Farrell.

WHICH IS WHY I looked at James like he was telling me a very bad joke when he invited me to his house for dinner with Veronica and the rest of his family. In fact, I said it. Yes, I said it: "Have you lost your damn mind?" I asked him just like Nicky asked Veronica two days before.

We were spooning, having just had morning sex in my bed, and I had been in a good mood until he dropped the bomb that not only was his entire family in town but that they also wanted to have dinner with us the next night.

He pulled me deeper into his arms. "They're in town for a couple more nights. You're my girlfriend. You should meet them."

"They tried to pay me off," I reminded him. "That doesn't exactly scream dinner party."

"Yeah, that was more Veronica's idea. The rest of my family just went along with it because—well, because she's Veronica." He shook his head with a smile in his eyes as if Veronica was just an obstinate family pet. Like Marmaduke or something. Not a complete viper. "But I've talked to them, and they really want to meet you."

I sat up in bed. "James, are you just not getting that Veronica hates me?" Because frankly, I was beginning to wonder if maybe this oblivious thing of his had reached a new level. I mean, even Andrew McCarthy stopped taking Molly Ringwald around his friends after they treated her like shit at that one party in *Pretty in Pink*.

"Veronica will be on her best behavior," he said, sitting up in bed, too. He sounded so confident that I knew that he must have already had a conversation with her regarding this dinner. "And it's only going to make things worse if you don't come over for dinner."

"Worse how?" I asked.

He had looked tired when he showed up at my door earlier. Had his family put that weary look on his face? Were they saying the same thing as Veronica: that I wasn't good enough for him?

But James just shook his head. "Davie, this is not optional. I love you and I love them. And we've got to figure this out. One night. That's all I'm asking. Please."

He looked at me. I looked back at him. And suddenly I didn't want to be on the list of people giving James a hard time right now. In fact, I was sick and tired of being one of those people giving James a hard time.

"Okay," I said. "When and where?"

# TWENTY

EVEN THOUGH I WAS OFF FROM the club on Tuesdays, I had back-to-back Soul BunnyGrams on the Westside at four and five in the afternoon. The five P.M. asked for three encores, and rush hour traffic was terrible as usual; even though I got off the freeway and took surface streets, I didn't get back to my apartment until 6:30. And then I barely had time to exchange my bunny suit for the only sundress that I owned and spritz on some perfume before I had to get back in the car and fight more crosstown traffic to get over to James's place.

I was only fifteen minutes late, which, by L.A. dinner party rules, was actually a little early. But when Mildred guided me to the dining room, a section of the house that I had seen but never actually eaten in before, his whole family was already there and seated at a long ebony table. I guessed Southern dinner party rules applied here.

James and his father both stood up like good, old-fashioned gentlemen, but the other three sets of eyes went straight to my outfit. My sundress was bright yellow and a little wrinkled because I hadn't had time to run my evening gown steamer over it. But I had worn it anyway, because it seemed more appropriate than a Strokes T-shirt or an evening gown or the Isabel Marant dress that James had given me, which was lying balled up on my dressing room closet floor, waiting for me to get around to dry cleaning it. Though now I was beginning to wish that I had worn the Strokes T-shirt and jeans, since I seriously doubted that James's mother and Veronica could look any more disapproving than they did now.

Not for the first time in the last twenty-four hours, I wondered why I had agreed to this.

All three of the Farrell women were wearing well-tailored black dresses, which made them look like light-skinned Jackie O's. And I wondered if they had all decided together to dress like they were going to a funeral.

James and his father were both wearing light suits, so I guess they hadn't gotten the dress-in-black memo. I felt very out of place in my twenty-two-dollar H&M dress as James introduced me around the table.

First came his father, who greeted me with a warm smile and a kiss on the cheek. "So good to finally meet you."

At first I thought that he, like his son, didn't remember me. But then his eyes held mine for a moment too long, and I realized that he was just being a politician. Playing the role as he wanted to be perceived. I understood then why he had won his first campaign by a landslide.

He had aged well. His hairline was a little farther up his forehead, and maybe the beard he now sported covered up a few fine lines, but all in all, he was still the gorgeous man who used to alight upon Cora's doorstep every Saturday night.

Next came James's mother, who I had seen pictures of but had never met or even viewed in the flesh. Her beauty, which must have been jaw-dropping when she was younger, was still in effect. And she wore her jet black hair pulled back in a bun that highlighted her patrician features: a thin nose, passed down from whatever white slave owner had decided to take her ancestor to bed, and high cheekbones, just like her children. She was not warm, but she wasn't cold, either. I guess I'd characterize her as very, very Southern. She cupped my hand in both of hers, but seemed more polite than genuinely glad to meet me.

She might have been aware that her husband had hussies on the side, but I came to the conclusion that she didn't know that one of them used to be my mother. I don't care how well you were raised—nobody's that good at keeping her cool.

"And you remember Veronica and Tammy," James said. He put his hand on my lower back before saying this and kept it there, like he was bracing me for the introduction.

I had rehearsed this moment in my head and in the mirror several times that morning. I put on Cheery Davie, the fake-but-friendly version of myself that I used whenever I was forced to participate in small talk.

"Sure I do." I arced both my hands in a double wave as opposed to offering my hand for a shake. High school was a long time ago, but I still wasn't going to shake either of their hands. "How ya'll doing?"

They didn't hold out their hands for shakes, either. "Good!" Tammy answered, her eyes wide and her smile cheerleader bright.

"Good," Veronica also answered, but her tone was dryer, and the word almost seemed to have two syllables in her mouth, she enunciated the "D" so hard.

James pulled out my chair, which was at the far left corner of the table, diagonal from Veronica. It was also as far as I could be seated from her without putting me at the head of the table, a position which he gave to his father, who sat on one side of me, while James sat on the other, directly across from his sister. I couldn't help but notice the look of extreme warning that he gave her before he sat down himself.

Dread filled my stomach like a big old ball of lead.

Dinner was a catered five-course affair, served by Mildred and an additional person that they had hired for the night.

It was brought out on elegant silver platters and dished onto delicate china plates, but I couldn't appreciate the presentation. The food might have been delicious, but I didn't have any appetite, so I ended up pushing it around on my plate for most the night. To this day, I wouldn't be able to tell you what we had or what it had tasted like.

We flitted from one safe topic to the next. First comparing East Coast weather to California weather. Apparently the heat was relentless in New

York and Washington, D.C., right now, and his mother was surprised by how pleasant it was in California.

They talked a lot about people and incidents I didn't know. It wasn't rude, though, just the way of families. Nicky, Mama Jane, and I were the exact same way when we got together with people who didn't know all three of us.

James's family didn't ask me a lot of questions, which should have tipped me off to what would go down a few weeks later, but I didn't suspect then that the rich were more than just used to getting their way. They were dead set on it.

We talked about Mississippi: how terrible the summers were there, humid, sticky, and mosquito-ridden. And college. Both James and Veronica had gone to Princeton, but Tammy had actually come out here to USC, where she had been a cheerleader (of course). We joked about USC and UCLA being bitter rivals, but we didn't go into the underlying reason behind the tension. Private vs. public. Rich vs. poor.

Tammy, I would say, was the biggest surprise of the evening. She was open and friendly, and actually seemed to be going out of her way to make me feel comfortable, introducing topics that might interest me, and steering her family back to the present whenever they went too far down memory lane. If we had met after high school, under different circumstances, I realized, we could easily have become friends. But we didn't, so there you go.

Veronica, for the most part, didn't talk much. And when she did, she almost never addressed her comments to me, unless it was something like, "Please pass the salt," in the same imperious tones that she employed with Mildred and the other server. She asked me to pass things even if I was nowhere near them, which forced me to locate the item she wanted and then ask whoever was nearest to it to please pass it on to her.

And whenever I did pass something her way with a Cheery Davie smile and a "Here you go," she just accepted it with cold silence. If this was Veronica's best behavior, I was dying to see her act a fool.

The whole situation made me tired. I wished I were somebody different, somebody cooler and deserving of James. Somebody who didn't have to pretend to be Cheery Davie in order to get through dinner with these people.

The ball of dread just refused to let go of me, no matter how many pleasant conversational passes I made with the rest of her family. I couldn't relax, because I just knew Evil Veronica was hiding behind Somewhat Polite Veronica, waiting to jump out at me at any second.

And the moment I had been waiting for the entire meal came just after Mildred had served dessert.

Veronica landed her gray eyes on me and asked, "So how's your mama?" She asked this with a smile, and as if she had been talking pleasantly to me the entire time.

The other Farrells turned to look at us. I'm sure that James had pre-warned them that I was estranged from my mother. So everyone else seemed surprised by Veronica's direct question. Everyone except me.

I laid down my dessert fork. "I don't know. I haven't spoken to her in a very long time."

"If I remember right, she was some sort of hooker, wasn't she?"

Her mother gasped from the other end of the table. "Veronica Farrell," she said.

"I'm sorry." Veronica steepled her hands over her dessert plate. "I thought that was common knowledge. Or maybe I'm wrong. She wasn't a hooker. She just slept with a lot of people. So she was a whore but not a formal one, correct?"

Everything inside of me had curdled and gone cold. I should have known. I should have known that this was the weapon she would use against me. I hadn't seen Cora in over fifteen years, but she had still managed to follow me all the way to California.

It took me a second to work up the courage to look over at James to see how he was taking this. And when I did finally cut my eyes toward him, he was staring at Veronica angrily.

"What do you think you're doing?" he asked her, his voice calm but hard as steel. "You're embarrassing me and embarrassing yourself."

Veronica's eyes blazed with anger as she pointed to me. "She should be the one who's embarrassed. I can't believe that she had the nerve to come here."

Veronica's mother look horrified. Her hands fluttered about her face. "This has to stop," she said in a shaky voice. "Right now. Veronica, get ahold of yourself and act like a lady!"

"Why are you here?" Veronica asked me, pinning me with her gray gaze again.

There was so much hate in her eyes that any possible answer I might have given her froze in my throat on the spot.

"She's my girlfriend, Ronnie, and I invited her," James said.

"She's a liar. You want a liar for a girlfriend? You think she's appropriate for a Farrell?"

I looked over at the congressman and Tammy Farrell. They were both eating their dessert with such concentrated civility that I wondered if it was just me hearing the argument.

"I love her," James said, calm as a diplomat. "And you need to start respecting that."

"So you knew her mother was a slut? And an alcoholic?"

The question was so hard-hitting that everybody went absolutely quiet. Mrs. Farrell didn't try to protest, and Tammy and the congressman actually looked up from their pretend fascination with their dessert to look from me to Veronica to James, who just sat there, rigid with anger.

"Oh, she didn't tell you that, either," Veronica said.

I couldn't breathe. I couldn't speak. I couldn't look anywhere but at my own useless hands, as I waited for James to answer Veronica's question.

But then his hand wrapped around mine. And suddenly my hands weren't so useless anymore. I held on to him for dear life.

And when he stood up, I stood up, too.

"Tammy, Daddy, Mama, it was nice to see you again," he said. "Veronica, I will talk to you when you get some sense."

I didn't dare look at him or Veronica as he said this.

But Veronica really must have been surprised about being called out, because it took her a few sputtering starts before she returned with "I'm not the one that needs to get some sense."

"Are you ready to go?" he asked me, like she hadn't said anything.

"Um . . . sure," I managed. My voice was squeakier than I would have liked, but at that point and with my history, I was just happy that I was able to get any words out at all.

I let him pull me out of there. And when I looked back over my shoulder, everyone at the table was sitting there with their mouths open as they watched James storm out of his own house.

Apparently this was a Farrell Family First.


PAUL FOLLOWED US outside, but James waved him off. "We're going to take a little drive."

Something in the way he said "little drive" let me know that we were about to get into another fight. And walking to the garage where he kept all six of his classic eighties luxury cars felt like a death march. The silence was so heavy that I couldn't take it anymore by the time we got into his Jake Ryan Porsche. I stopped him with a hand on his wrist when he tried to put the key in the ignition.

"My mother did—maybe still does—have a big problem with alcohol and men," I said. "Obviously, it's not something I'm proud of. And she was the one who used to hit me. I'm sorry I didn't tell you before. And I'm sorry that I embarrassed you in front of your family."

James lowered his keys, but didn't say anything. He let the silence fill up the car again.

I had just decided to get out and ask Paul for my keys so that I could go when he spoke.

"You know," he said, "I'm aware that I am blessed and privileged. I mean, I know that I didn't scrape together my own career or put myself through college, and I know my job is basically bullshit." His voice was quiet, almost weak. Not like James at all.

It took me a moment to process that he was actually giving me a list of his negatives. And another few seconds to realize that all his negatives were actually my positives. It had never occurred to me that James, in all his worldliness, could feel that he lacked some quality that I had in spades. Before I could respond, though, he turned to me and asked, "But damn, are there any other secrets that you're keeping from me?"

I blinked. "Yes, of course there are." It was maybe the most truthful thing I had ever voluntarily said to James.

And then we both laughed.

I WOULDN'T SAY that Nicky came to like James after I told him the dinner party story, but the tension between them did seem to disappear. Nicky now shook hands with him when he came into the club, and on occasion, he would give James his first drink free—which for Nicky was damn near saying, "You and me is brothers from another mother."

Nicky liked that James was willing to stand up for me and he also respected the innate qualities it must have taken to grow up your own man with a sister like Veronica. Not that James ever brought up Veronica. He talked about his parents and Tammy, but Veronica, no. I felt bad, because it was almost like she was dead to him, and all because of something that happened so many years ago between our parents, something that James wasn't even aware of.

Plus I knew that it wasn't over for me and Veronica. She hadn't tried to contact me again since coming into Nicky's with the check, but I knew she was plotting something. And though Real Davie was happier than she'd ever been, High School Davie was definitely scared shitless of whatever Veronica was planning.

# TWENTY-ONE

THE SECOND WEEKEND OF SEPTEMBER, I woke to the digital version of J. Holiday's "Bed," which was the ringtone that I had chosen especially for James's calls.

I looked at the clock on my nightstand. It was eight, much earlier than either of us usually called each other on a Saturday morning.

Still, I answered the phone with a smile. "Happy birthday. You're up early."

"I'm looking forward to our weekend together."

I had taken off from the club for the whole weekend, and I had told James that we could do whatever he wanted. As long as it was free. "Me too. Do you want me to come over now?"

"No, I want you to open the door."

Oh, he was outside my door. "Okay, I'm coming."

I got out of bed, not bothering to put a robe on over the cotton panties I usually wore to bed. I figured a little morning delight was the perfect way to kick off his birthday weekend.

Then I opened the door and saw Paul standing there with a rolling suitcase.

I screamed and dropped the phone. The last thing I saw before I slammed the door was Paul's eyes bugging.

When I picked up the phone again, James was laughing.

"That wasn't you at the door," I said.

"No, but I'm downstairs, and I saw everything. Just like Paul." Another wave of laughter. I peeked out the window, and saw James standing next to his Mercedes, cracking up.

"I wish you had warned me that it was Paul out there."

"If I had known you were going to answer the door buck naked . . . well, I probably would have done the exact same thing. That was hilarious." More laughter.

"I'm glad you're amused," I said between clenched teeth. "Why is Paul at my door?"

"I sent him up to give you one of my rolling suitcases. We're taking a little trip. You'll need to pack two days' worth of clothes, some flats for walking around, and maybe a dress for dinner."

"That doesn't sound free—"

My call waiting beeped. I looked and saw Russell's name in the ID window. If he was calling this early in the morning, it probably meant that he wanted to have brunch. Russell was the king of asking people to hang out at the last minute. I pushed the ignore button. I'd call him later, after I figured out what James was up to.

"That doesn't sound free," I said again.

"It's all free. Trust me. I'm playing by the rules."

"I don't know, James. A trip? Where are we going?"

"Whose birthday is it again?"

He had a point. "Yours," I said.

"And how much do you love me?"

"Tons and tons. Universes and universes." I sighed. "Okay, give me thirty minutes."


I HADN'T BEEN on a vacation for years. Nicky hadn't been the vacationing type, and I had never had enough money to go anywhere special by myself.

Of course I had gone to Tijuana a couple of times with my college friends, but as anyone who grew up in California can tell you, Tijuana isn't really a vacation. It's more like a blurry rite of passage that leaves you with a bad hangover, and a lifelong revulsion for cheap tequila.

"You need to ask your boss for a raise," I said to Paul, once I was settled into the backseat of the diesel Mercedes with James.

"No, it is I who should be paying him," Paul said without missing a beat. His smiling eyes met mine in the rearview mirror. And James fell over laughing again.

I shook my head at him. "You're lucky it's your birthday."

"I think it's Paul's birthday, too," James said. That one cracked both him and Paul up.


TWO HOURS AND a lot of teasing later we arrived in Solvang, a town that's most popular for being the wine country backdrop in the movie *Sideways*.

I had heard of postcard towns, but I had never seen one until we drove down Solvang's storybook streets with their brick sidewalks, tasting rooms, quaint hobby shops, and Danish architecture. There were tourists everywhere.

"I figured you'd like it because it's less of a scene than Napa," James said.

"If it's not a scene, how did you find out about it, Trust Fund?" I asked with a smile.

"Actually, I've never been to Solvang," he admitted. "But friends of mine have used the fact that it's not a scene as an excuse for not going."

By "friends of mine," I'm sure he meant former girlfriends. Most of the time, I wondered what James saw in me. But when he told me stories like that, I kind of got it.


I'M NOT UNAWARE that being poor has had its perks for me. The elimination of material desire has been a higher calling for thousands of years, and the fact that I was nearer to it than a lot of other people did give me a certain sense of superiority.

For the most part, I had everything I needed. Sure, I wouldn't mind a more dependable car, one that didn't break down every four months. But other than that, I was usually fine with being poor, because I had a make-shift family, a fun job, a good education, and a rent-controlled apartment. Really, how could a person who grew up like me ask for anything more?

I found out the answer to that question when we went to Solvang. James hadn't been forthcoming when he said everything on our trip would be free. What he meant was that everything on our trip would be comped, which is the rich version of free, and unlike anything I had ever experienced.

First of all, our room was so big it looked like something out of a movie. And it came with a view of the wine valleys, which I joined James on the balcony to appreciate. "If this isn't good enough for L.A. folks, I can't imagine Napa."

James shrugged. "It's like this but with more young people . . . and nicer hotels."

Wow.


I DON'T REMEMBER *Sideways* that well, but I didn't have to because every restaurant, wine bar, tasting room, and pastry shop that had been featured even as an exterior in that film announced the fact in brightly colored chalk on blackboard signs at their entrances.

The town seemed to assume that everything everyone knew about wine was from the movie *Sideways*—which in my case was true, so that made me feel a little better about not really knowing anything about vino beyond Two-Buck Chuck.

After we walked around for a while, Paul drove us out to the Firestone Winery's tasting room, a large stone and dark wood affair with framed photos of past Republican presidents and Norwegian royalty on the walls. It was all so elegant, but "Do you think the owners feel weird that there's also a tire called Firestone? I mean that's what I think of when I hear that name."

James took me by the elbow and led me to a quiet corner where he proceeded to give me a five-minute rundown on one of the richest families in the United States.

Then I had to pretend like I had already known who the Firestones were when a dark-haired female Firestone cousin of a guy that James had roomed with at Princeton came out to say hello and give James a case of their renowned Riesling, on the house.

"Don't feel bad," he said after she left and we were carrying the case back to the Mercedes.

"I'm trying not to," I said. "But I don't exactly feel like I fit in here."

"I wouldn't worry about that. The Firestone family actually just sold the brand to a bigger wine company, so technically it's not really theirs anymore."

"They sold it? Like you guys sold Farrell Fine Hair."

James adjusted the case of wine in his arms. "Not exactly. They still have their brewery and Curtis, one of their brands."

"You sound kind of wistful about it."

"What do you mean?"

"I don't know, maybe you wish you guys had kept something for yourselves when you sold Farrell."

James snorted. "Like what? The Jheri curl division?"

But I didn't laugh. "You know, I noticed that there are a lot of men like you in L.A."

"Men like me?"

"You know, guys who spend a lot of time keeping themselves up. The hair, the skin, the nails, all that."

"You're talking about metrosexuals." James's voice held a hint of amusement, like he was bracing himself for an insult.

"No, I'm talking about black men who would probably appreciate their own line of products. I know Nicky would definitely buy something like that."

Before James could say anything, though, Paul came running over to us. "Why didn't you call me? I would have come in to get this."

Paul was funny like that. He actually seemed to get insulted when James did stuff for himself like regular folks. Usually James had to come up with practical excuses for carrying his own bags into the house or getting his own car washed, so that Paul's feelings wouldn't be hurt. It was a seriously strange dynamic. But today he didn't answer Paul's question. He just let Paul take the case from him, his mind obviously elsewhere.

"He wanted to stretch his legs some more before we sat down for the wine tasting," I replied to Paul's now worried look. "It's been a lot of sitting today."

Paul smiled. "Yes it has, now. You two should walk around the estate. It looks very nice here."

I took James's hand and led him away. "That sounds like a good idea."

After twenty minutes of walking the grounds in a pensive silence, James said, "You know what? I think you have a point. I'm going to pitch a Farrell Men line to the product development department when I get back."

"I think that's a real good idea."

I smiled up at him. And he smiled back down at me. "You know what else?" he asked, pulling me into his arms.

"You love me," I guessed, laughing.

But his face was dead serious when he answered, "Yeah, I love you." He tipped my chin up with his finger. "The first time I saw you, even though you were in that bunny suit, you had me thinking, *Yeah, that's a girl I could fall in love with*. I just knew. Have you ever just known?"

"Once," I confessed, now as serious as him. "When I first saw you."

He scanned my face. "You're not joking," he said. "You really loved me. Even way back then?"

I nodded.

And he finally smiled. "Well, obviously you were smarter than I was in high school."

I laughed. "Obviously."

He started to kiss me, but I pulled away. "Wait, I have something for you."

I reached into the pocket of my H&M trapeze jacket and handed him one of the red cocktail napkins from Nicky's.

"What's this?" he asked.

"Your birthday present."

I had written on the napkin:

> *Tonight, Davie Jones will do this to James Farrell:*
> *1.*
> *2.*
> *3.*

James eyes darkened with lust as he read the napkin. "This is my birthday present?"

I nodded. "You can fill in those three blanks with whatever freaky thing you want."

His face went from amused to what I can only describe as full-on challenge. "Anything I want?" He pulled out his Montblanc pen and started writing on the napkin, against the wall.

I tried to read over his shoulder, but he shielded the napkin with his hand. "Un-uh. You'll find out what's on there tonight. Believe that."


NICKY HAD A strict "no comp" policy at the club. It didn't matter if you were Brad Pitt, he wasn't giving you a table or anything on our menu for free, because he said once you started that mess, you'd be giving freebies to celebrities forever. He had explained this to me in the same tone of voice that most people reserved for talking about termite problems.

But apparently not everyone felt this way, because James got a lot of stuff for free that weekend. Not just the hotel room and the Firestone wine, but also massages at a local spa and a picnic lunch from some other old-money winery.

I had always known that James was kinda-sorta famous for being that token rich black guy whose picture often got taken at the hottest parties. But I realized that weekend that he was also very well liked in a certain circles. And I could see why.

He had the easy charm of a Will Smith. Was effusive in his thanks, jokey in his manner, and when he talked to people, he somehow seemed completely engaged in what they were saying and always followed up their statements with a dead-on and pithy comment. Rich people loved his ass.

"You're still the most popular kid in school," I told him over dinner at the Brothers' Restaurant at Mattei's Tavern that night. The Brothers' Restaurant was an old stagecoach stop that had been converted into a swanky restaurant, but had still managed to retain its nineteenth-century charm by holding on to embellishments like the fireplaces and a cozy, but simple, decor. A friend of James's had once had an engagement party there and knew the owners personally, so voilà, yet another comp. I realized he must have spent a lot of time planning this trip around my parameters, which made me feel guilty. After logging on to my bank's Web site and seeing that I only had fifty bucks left to get me through to the next paycheck, I had decided on the napkin trick. And that had been that. Obviously James had put a whole lot more effort into his birthday than I had.

"I'm still the most popular kid in school," James repeated. "Then what does that make you?"

I picked up my pint of Firestone pale ale and tipped it toward him in a slight toast. "The luckiest girl in school."

His eyes grew serious and he said, "I hope you really mean that."

The next thing I knew, there was a violinist at the table, a reed-thin man with graying temples dressed in a full tux. And he started playing "Fever."

My first, almost Pavlovian, instinct was to get up and sing along, but this wasn't that kind of situation.

I realized that when James pulled out a leather box and flipped it open to reveal what had to be at least a three-carat diamond engagement ring inside.

"JAMES, CAN WE talk? Can we just talk about this in private?"

A little less than an hour later, I watched Paul tuck my suitcase, which he had also hastily packed at James's angry request, into the back of the Mercedes.

James ignored me. "Paul, I'm riding in the front with you."

I got in front of him before he could open the passenger side door. "It wasn't a forever no. It was just a no-for-now, because there are some things standing in the way for me."

James finally looked at me, but only to say, "That doesn't make any goddamn sense."

I tried to take him in my arms, but he stepped back before I could reach him. "No, don't touch me. Sex isn't going to solve this."

"I'm not trying to use sex," I said, though truthfully that solution had been in the back of my mind when I reached for him. "I just want to talk to you."

He spread his arms wide. "Then say it. Tell me why you turned me down in front of a restaurant full of people. Because I'd be really interested to hear you explain your way out of that one."

"I'm sorry you didn't get what you wanted," I yelled back. "I know that it's hard for somebody as spoiled as you not to get every single goddamn thing you ask for, exactly when you want it."

It was so unfair. I knew that, even as I was saying it. But I couldn't stop myself. It was like I was in full panic mode and my mouth had just gone on "say something crazy" autopilot. "Get in the car," he said.

"James . . ."

"No, I'm done talking to you. Get in the car."

He was standing there, his body held in one rigid line with his fists clenched at the sides. And he wouldn't look at me. His eyes darted from the car to Paul to the sky to the parking lot pavement, but he wouldn't meet my pleading gaze.

I got in the car.

I think that drive was the most uncomfortable situation that I have ever been in my entire life, and yes, I am counting that time when I found myself outside Farrell Manor in a yellow evening gown, and I am also counting that time when Cora beat me so bad that I stopped talking. Because neither of those uncomfortable moments lasted two and a half hours, which is how long it takes to get from Solvang to Los Angeles on a Saturday night.

James sat in the front passenger seat as promised. His continued silence hung over the car like an arctic blanket as we drove out of Solvang. There was a moment of activity when we got on to the 101 South. He called Mildred on his BlackBerry and told her to box up anything of mine that was in the house and mail it to my apartment first thing the next morning.

After he hung up, he hit the glove box with the palm of one hand and covered his eyes with the other. I was afraid he might be crying. Like that one time in the high school locker room.

"Please don't cry," I said in the backseat. "I'm not worth crying over."

"Shut up," James whispered. "Please, just shut the fuck up."

It was the meanest thing he had ever said to me, and at that moment I thought of Elmer, sitting in Cora's living room long after she had rejected him and gone out for the night to find another man to have sex with. I had never thought I'd be able to do to another human being what Cora had done to Elmer. Apparently I had been wrong.

Elmer had only come around a few more times after that, but as I sat in that car behind James, Elmer's words the night Cora rejected him, suddenly came back to me.

"She don't love me. She don't care if you got a daddy or not," he had said. "She don't think about nobody but herself."

The memory sent a little lightning bolt through my mind. What had he meant by, "She don't care if you got a daddy or not"? Was Elmer, not the supposed "David," my real father? And had I not realized it back then, the way I hadn't realized that Cora was my mother for the first few months after she came to live with me?

The possibility froze me where I sat. Was I just like Cora?

There had to be something of Cora in me. Something so mean and evil that I would rather have James Farrell believe that I didn't love him enough to marry him than actually tell him the straight truth.

ONE WOULD THINK that my hugest regret in this entire situation would be what I did in the past, before I met James again. But it's not. I absolutely don't think there was anything else I could have done, given who I was and my history. No, the thing I truly regret is being too chickenshit to say anything on that ride home.

I regret opening my mouth several times to say it and then closing it before any words could actually come out. That's what ate me up at night for months afterward.

My phone rang several times on the trip back. First it was Chloe, then Nicky, then Russell again. I didn't answer any of their calls, just checked the caller ID.

If I couldn't talk to James at that moment, I doubted I could get through a conversation with Chloe about the show or Nicky about the club or Russell about his latest breakup—which he must be going through, if he was calling me twice in one day. I switched the phone off.

It seemed for a while like the trip and the indecision would never end, but then we were driving up James's gated driveway and pulling up in front of his house.

I was so despondent that it took me a second to realize that there was something on the steps that shouldn't have been there.

It was Veronica Farrell, standing at James's door, dressed in black city shorts and a sleeveless black cowl-neck shirt that highlighted her toned arms to perfection. I caught myself wondering if she had a personal trainer, before I remembered to wonder what the hell she was doing here. The last I had heard, she had flown back to New York right after the Dinner Party Debacle and hadn't spoken to James since.

But now she was running over to the car and yanking open James's door before it had even come to a complete stop.

I heard the words "private investigator" and "Erica London" and "Corey Mays" and "your psycho girlfriend." And then I knew exactly why she was there.

Truth be told, there were a few things that I did not include in the "In Between Then and Now" section.

# PART IV
# IN BETWEEN THEN AND NOW
## (The Amendment)

# TWENTY-TWO

IT'S FUNNY THAT WHEN I THINK back on the five years I was with Nicky, I always feel shame for being so very passive and for not ever really standing up for myself. I think of myself as keeping my head down all the way until Nicky proved that he wasn't worth all that submission.

But that's not entirely true. I had my moments. To be specific, three aggressive moments, the first of which happened in January 2001 and involved Mike Barker, the actor who broke Chloe's heart.

According to his *E! True Hollywood Story*, Mike Barker had grown up in the roughest part of Pittsburgh, in the East Liberty projects, a place where white people only went to collect the rent. The child of a single mother with two jobs, an escalating crack habit, and little time to monitor him, Mike got caught up in the drug game early on. He started as a runner at age eight and worked his way up through the ranks, until at age sixteen, he was, by his own estimation, the number one high school dealer in all of Pittsburgh, with a client list that ranged from early onset crack users to suburban weedheads and the rural OxyContin kids.

He maintained good grades throughout high school in order to stay close to his client base. Then he surprised the higher-ups in his gang by not only graduating at the top of his class, but disappearing the day after he gave the valedictorian speech. He had secretly applied for and gotten a full scholarship to attend Amherst, a prestigious private college in western Massachusetts that was so far away in nature from the projects of East Liberty, the school might as well have been on the opposite side of the globe.

His former colleagues had no idea what had happened to him. Many assumed that he had been killed and his body disposed of by a rival gang.

That is, until Mike started appearing on movie screens, first in charming black romantic comedies, where his rock-hard abs, engaging dimples, and solid acting skills carried him through a lot of bad writing. His first reviews were often "everything buts." As in, "everything but Mike Barker was awful in this movie."

Then he graduated up to being the cocky black sidekick in a bunch of action films, in which he consistently stole all the scenes from his overpaid white headliners, until the powers-that-be finally took a chance and put him at the helm of a thirteen-million-dollar action throwaway, which was expected to be a Memorial Day weekend trifle, called *Dark Matter*. But thanks to Mike's ad-libbing and an otherwise lackluster box office season, *Dark Matter* ended up being the sleeper hit of the summer.

Better scripts flooded his agent's desk. And Mike kept on doing bigger and better movies, bringing in the box office every Memorial Day. And by the time he was twenty-nine, *Celeb Weekly* had taken to calling him the Memorial Day Rainmaker.

But here's the thing that the *E! True Hollywood Story* didn't cover, much to Nicky's irritation. The first and only legitimate non-acting job that Mike ever held down was as a waiter at Nicky's, which is where he had met and dated Chloe for several months.

Like I said before, I could see he would go far the first time I laid eyes on him—not just because of his good looks, his acting talent, or his full-on possession of "it," but also because, simply put, Mike had a real talent for bullshit.

After meeting Mike once, people often came away feeling that he was just like them. And that's what impressed me most about him. He basically did the same thing that I did with Stage Davie, but he did it better. He was a true chameleon, and it was extremely hard to see through the seams of his act unless you watched him very closely.

Luckily, I have always been good at watching people very closely.

I began to notice that there was one time a month when the person that I suspected was the real Mike Barker came out to play. Literally.

Nicky hosted a poker night at his home in Baldwin Hills every third Tuesday save in November and December. When Nicky and I were dating, I would usually read a book in another room during this event, but after Mike joined the game, I started hovering near the door and watching, simply because I had never seen this side of him. When he was betting, he was focused and calculating and razor-sharp with his instincts. He rarely folded, and when he did, it usually turned out to be a ploy to put the other players at an ease they shouldn't have felt, because every time he came to Nicky's poker table, he went home with the majority of the pot.

A loose plan began to form in my head. I had been dating Nicky for almost three years, lived in a rent-controlled apartment, and had not yet accrued college loan debt, so I had actually managed to set some money aside for my college dream. Not a lot, but maybe just enough to attract Mike Barker.

"You've always been a cool kid, haven't you?" I said to him, the fourth night that he came over to play. I had just taken his coat, and Nicky was in the kitchen while Leon and the rest of the guys were setting up in the dining room. Stage Davie was in full effect.

"Not as cool as you, I'm positive," he said, matching my husky tones exactly. He didn't realize that he was mirroring my mirror of Nina Simone. He also didn't realize that I had never been cool, only played the part for my stage show.

"You know," I said, "it's not just Chloe. All the waitresses are in love with you. Some of the waiters, too."

He let his eyes go intense. "But you're not, right? Nicky's still a much luckier man than I am."

Mike Barker was the worst kind of flirt. The kind who said things with such absolute sincerity that you actually believed him. But I saw right through him, and used that to my advantage.

I leaned in close to him and whispered, "You know what, if you kept this up, you could definitely convince me to cheat on Nicky, baby."

His eyes hooded with satisfaction, and he backed off. The thrill of knowing he could have me, if he wanted me, was better for him than actually hooking up with me. He was so simple to read, I almost felt like it was too easy as I laid down the words that would set my trap. "You could probably get any woman you wanted, I mean not Tam Farrell or anything, but definitely any regular woman."

Tammy Farrell had just started appearing in the new Farrell Cosmetics commercials and billboards at this point, and black people were buzzing about her in Los Angeles because she had just relocated here.

"You don't think I could get Tam Farrell?" Mike said it as if it was a joke, but I could hear a hard challenge underneath his tone.

I actually pretended to think about it. "I don't know. You're good, but you're not *that* good. I mean, she's a model and an heiress—she's out of your league."

His face went from affable to serious in a millisecond. "You want to bet?"

I snorted. "Baby, I have three thousand dollars in my bank account that I would love to double if you were crazy enough to bet me on something like that." For effect, I cut my eyes sideways at him before saying, "Plus, you're with Chloe. Remember?"

Now it was his turn to pretend to think about it. "Things change. I just might take you up on that bet," he said.

He held out his hand for the shake, and I had to force myself to pretend to think about it, before taking his hand and nodding. "Bet."

After that bet was placed, Mike continued on with Chloe, but apparently he also did his due diligence with Tammy Farrell on the side. He not only managed to meet her, but date her and after a few months got invited to move into her penthouse condo on the Westside.

I knew about this before Chloe did, because Mike showed up at my dressing room door the night before he broke the news to her. "You owe me three thousand dollars, baby," he said, with a happy smirk.

I did not hesitate to write him a check. And though I felt bad for Chloe, her getting dumped and all, I did not let that stop me from anticipating the inevitable. If Mike could be this callous with Chloe, I had no doubt that his breakup with Tammy would be even more fun (for me) and horrible (for Tammy).

Even though it had taken my life savings, I got my wish a little over a year later. This is how it went down, according to *Celeb Weekly*: After a year of dating model Tam Farrell, who had once called him "her soul mate" during an interview, Mike Barker had dumped her for a much more famous A-list actress. And apparently he had delivered the news over the phone, while on a private jet headed to Las Vegas, and while sitting next to the A-list actress who was now replacing Tammy the way that Tammy had replaced Chloe.

The youngest Farrell sibling was devastated. One source called her "inconsolable."

I drank the story in, unable to believe that something that I had planned had actually come to fruition. It was a heady feeling of power that inspired me to sing an unprecedented bent of upbeat standards for a whole week straight. Nicky was thrilled.

And though I did not deliberately plan Veronica's heartbreak, there was a niggling thought in the back of my head: *I wonder if I could do this again.*

IN AUGUST 2002, two months after the Tammy Farrell Heartbreak, Corey Mays walked into the club for a dinner meeting with his agent. I saw him as soon as he came in, and I wondered if God wasn't perhaps on my side, because here is what had happened to my old chemistry partner since I had run away from Glass:

He went on to Florida State University and played Gator Ball. He was the seventeenth-round draft pick for the New Jersey Jaguars. And thanks to his happy-go-lucky nature and an obvious tendency toward kindness—

which most of his fellow teammates did not possess—he ended up being a bigger hit with the fans than anyone would have ever expected. This led to major brand endorsements, which put enough money in his bank account for Corey to set his mama up for life and to finally pursue Veronica Farrell in the manner she was accustomed to. Eight years after he had first clapped eyes on her in high school, he proposed. And she said yes.

From what I could see, it wasn't a great match. He was warm, and she was cold. He was one of the most beloved sports figures in the United States, and she seemed like she was doing him a favor by deigning to live in his mansion and wear his many-carat engagement ring.

So when he walked into my club, it seemed like fate.

Unlike James, he had the good grace to recognize me, and even asked Leon to come get me after my set.

Leon near about lost it. "You know Corey Mays?" he said, when I answered his knock on my dressing room door. I had to promise to get him an autograph before he'd even let me go say hi.

I put on my Stage Davie persona and sauntered over to his table in my evening gown. It was not lost on me that the last time he had seen me I had also been wearing an evening gown.

"Corey Mays. It is good to see you again." My voice was dripping with Southern charm and sincerity.

Corey, who had stood up as soon as he saw me approaching, now enveloped me in a warm hug. He was much larger than he used to be in high school, and his hug felt a little like getting crushed. "It's good to see you, girl. You look good. Real good. I can't believe it's you."

Like me he still had his accent, and that made me smile even wider. "You better start believing, then, because I'm standing right in front of you."

To both our embarrassment, he started crying.

"I ain't never heard her talk before tonight," he said in way of explanation to his agent, his voice cracking.

Nicky's wasn't exactly a paparazzi hangout, but in the age of cell phone cameras, I thought it wise to hustle him out of there. "I'm going to take him somewhere private," I said to his agent.

"Yes, yes, hurry." His agent was already looking around for people with camera phones.

I took Corey into Nicky's office, and as soon as we were behind closed doors, he started in with a rushed explanation, the words near about falling over themselves to get out of his mouth. "You gave us a real scare when you ran off like that. I didn't know where you could've got off to. I was scared you'd be dead or having to turn tricks someplace because of us."

I handed him a Kleenex. "But I'm here. You can see that now. I'm okay." I forced my voice to stay light and casual, even though I could feel the old anger rumbling around in my tummy now. "So you knew?"

Corey nodded his head. "Veronica and Tammy told me and a few other people about it. I didn't like it, but I thought you'd be able to take it since everybody was forever making fun of you anyway, and you always just went about your business. But when I saw you in that dress, I knew she had gone too far. If I'd known how it would turn out, I never would have let Veronica do it."

His eyes were still a little red from crying earlier. I tried to concentrate on that and not on the mounting rage, which was demanding that I scratch his eyes out for coming in here with such pitiful excuses. I couldn't follow the rage. The only thing that separated me from Cora was that I didn't let that rage consume me and guide my actions—even when I most wanted it to.

"I'm just glad to see you here and prospering," he was now saying.

I perched on the side of the desk, and concentrated all my willpower on keeping my voice even as I said, "Don't worry about it, Corey. Seriously, it's all in the past."

So he had known about the trick that Veronica and Tammy were about to play on me. He sat by me in chemistry the day of the party, knowing what was in store for me but not telling me, because even though he was a nice guy, his nose had been too wide open for Veronica.

The rage suddenly disappeared, leaving behind cold calculation in its place. This was a good thing, I decided. It would be easier to do what I had started planning to do as soon as I had seen him in my audience.

Back in the early nineties, when I was first learning how to speak to people, I had read a book on overcoming shyness that said to try and figure out what the person you were conversing with needed most, and then see if you could be of any help to them in getting it. That way you had a mission to focus on as opposed to just thinking about how uncomfortable you were.

I had found this method to be wildly successful, especially in Los Angeles, where people rarely seemed to focus on anyone other than themselves. And I brought it back out for my first two-sided conversation with Corey ever.

We talked in Nicky's office, much like we used to in chemistry class, with him going on and on, and me listening quietly. And by the time he was finished telling me about all his career pressures and how much he wanted Veronica to see that he was worthy of her, I had figured out what he needed.

I told him that he should ditch his agent for the night and come out with me and my friend for a drink.

As soon as he left to get rid of his agent, I called Chloe on Nicky's office phone. This is probably the part I feel worst about, because she had been in a good place at that moment, just getting over the reporter who had left her for a fashion assistant.

But Corey needed her, so really it didn't even feel like I was making a choice as I dialed her number. "Girl, I know it's your night off, but I need you to come out with me and Corey Mays."

"*The* Corey Mays," she repeated. "Are you kidding me?" I think she was falling in love with him before I had even hung up the phone.

I used the key that Nicky had given me for emergency use only to unlock his bottom filing cabinet and pulled out his new digital camera. Nicky had shown it off to me like a new mother preening over a child. It was a professional-grade camera, the kind a photojournalist would use, and it included what was, at the time, a new concept on digital cameras: a feature that let you take pictures at night without a flash.

MUCH LIKE TAMMY Farrell, Chloe had a delicateness of feature that drew men to her. She also had the curves of a woman but the nature of a child. That is, she had a way of looking at a man from underneath her bouncy black curls, like maybe he had hung the moon in a past life and just didn't know about it.

The downside of Chloe's MO was that most guys eventually came to hate so much idolization. Admiration is like candy: It tastes good at first, but too much of it, and you get sick.

That night, though, it was her and Corey's first time meeting, and he ate her up from go as she asked him question after precious question. How do you stay in such great shape during the off-season? How do you manage to stay so calm on the field? Do you have nightmares before games?

The only thing she didn't ask him about was his fiancée.

I found it all a little ridiculous, but Corey answered her questions with consideration and bemusement. After a while, neither of them seemed to notice that I was still there or the fact that I was making sure that both of their wineglasses stayed full.

Corey and Chloe. The situation was almost too cute to be true.

THANKS TO THE wine and Chloe living in a ground floor apartment with a bedroom window and me being in criminal possession of a camera that pretty much did everything itself to take a good picture, I got some quality images.

I called Russell the next morning. At that point, he had yet to break a cover story, so he was more than grateful for the tip. He asked me to e-mail him the pictures right away and downloaded them while I was on the phone with him. "Oh my God," he said as the first picture came through. Then: "Oh, now I know Miss Veronica would never let him do that to her. Girl, this is money. Both literally and figuratively. Do you know what the photo fee is for pictures like this? You are about to receive a nice check."

That made me feel a little bad. Humiliating Veronica Farrell was one thing, but profiting from it was another. "I don't need any money, just anonymity."

"Company policy. We got to pay you, and you got to sign a waiver saying we own these bad boys. I'll courier over the paperwork right now."

That night, I took a frantic call from Chloe. Russell had called her for a quote in the story. Luckily, she had never met him or she might have put two and two together.

She told me that she had been calling Corey all day, but that he hadn't picked up or answered any of her messages.

"I think he thinks I set him up," she wailed.

I had to create a new character for the occasion. Shocked Davie. This one was self-righteous and couldn't believe we lived in a day and age when paparazzi would follow somebody home from a bar.

Shocked Davie assured her that if Corey called me, I would let him know that Chloe was a good person who would never ever make a deal with the paparazzi. This was an easy promise to make: Corey did not have my number. And I seriously doubted that he would want to look me up, since our short time together was now tainted by scandal.

Still, I soothed Chloe as much as I could, then hung up and again waited for the inevitable. I could not be sure that Veronica Farrell would dump a perfectly rich man for cheating on her, but I knew she wouldn't hesitate to dump him for humiliating her in public.

And I was right. She announced the dissolution of their romance to one of the *New York Post*'s Page Six editors three days after the "Corey Caught Cheating" issue of *Celeb Weekly* hit the newsstands.

Then she moved to London, a place where they didn't care about American football, for about three months until the firestorm died down. From what I gleaned during the fallout, James also severed all ties with his old friend.

It was funny I had been terrified that James would recognize Chloe the few times that she was on shift while he was at the club. There had been an especially bone-chilling time when she served him. But he never figured it out. He had let the affair end his friendship with Corey, but he couldn't even pick the woman that Corey had slept with out in a crowd.

I DON'T KNOW when my unhealthy love for James turned into an equally unhealthy hate, but the switch is common in stalkers. And relationship sabotage is a classic psycho's move. I learned that in one of my psych classes my sophomore year of college. Unfortunately, I decided to sabotage James's relationship with Erica London in April 2003 during my freshman year of college, so that information came a little late for me.

Breaking James's heart required a lot more effort on my part than my other two triumphs. The humiliation of Tammy and Veronica had been as much luck as anything. But James's heart didn't break quite so easy.

For one thing, it took James a while to fall in love. He went from one carefree relationship to the next. The women were always outrageously attractive and usually possessed big, gorgeous smiles and an overabundance of long glossy hair. They seemed perfectly happy to be dating James. And when he ended these relationships—it was always he who ended them—there was never any scandal attached. Just a good-natured "time to move on" effect. In fact, I had seen many pictures of him kissing girls he had dumped on the cheek at later events.

Somehow he always managed to leave the women he dated sad—not mad.

But Erica London changed all of that. She was an up-and-coming actress who had arrived in Los Angeles with a degree from NYU, a flawless, caramel complexion, and a knack for landing cute-girlfriend roles in commercials.

She actually made her living rolling her eyes at the antics of her boyfriend in a Ford commercial or walking hand-in-hand down an urban street with her boyfriend in a "Come to New Orleans" commercial or getting a salad while her boyfriend got a big, juicy burger in a McDonald's commercial, and so on.

Then she met James Farrell while he was in town for the Farrell Cosmetics launch. His inheritance had been sold to Gusteau, and for once his life wasn't going exactly as had been planned. Maybe he was feeling vulnerable, but after six months of dating, he decided that he was ready to spend his life with someone, and that someone was Erica. Then two months before their June wedding she landed a role as the cute girlfriend of the school's star jock in a hot high school drama.

Basically, her future was so bright she had to wear Dolce and Gabbana shades.

I wouldn't say I was jealous of Erica. At that point, James was more like a distant concept than a person I could ever fathom meeting, let alone having an actual relationship with.

In fact, I tutted at the news because the only piece of dating advice that Nicky had ever given me before he and I hooked up was this: "Don't date no actor. Don't EVER date no actor. If there's a nuclear war and everybody in America is destroyed except for you and one actor, figure out how to get your ass to Canada. Because even then, you don't want to be dating no actor."

It didn't feel like jealousy to me as I plotted how to destroy James's relationship with Erica. It was more like I was doing him a favor.

"ERICA WHO?" RUSSELL said when I called him about her. I could hear the click-clack of his keyboard on the other side of the line. Russell was busier than ever now that he had moved up from reporter to a staff writer position at *Celeb Weekly*. And if you weren't A-list, he always continued typing when he was on the phone with you.

"Erica London," I repeated.

"Davie, baby, I don't want to sound rushed and annoyed with you, but I am rushed and annoyed with you. I've got a million deadlines and no time to hunt down dirt on this Erica Landry."

"London." I switched the cell phone to my other ear and lowered my voice, so that no one outside my dressing room door could hear me. "Listen, Russell, how about if I give you a big fish? Then would you get me the Erica London dirt?"

The typing stopped. "An A-list fish?"

That's how I ended up giving him Mike Barker. Mike's image was squeaky clean back then, and everybody liked him, which in Hollywood means that you're ripe to be knocked off your pedestal. I promised Russell that if he dug, he'd find out that Mike had a pretty significant gambling addiction. And I even offered to be the "source" that knew him before he was famous. The one that claimed that Mike would bet on *anything*.

Not only did Russell find proof of the gambling addiction, he also discovered that Mike was in so much debt to certain casinos that he had started doing paycheck movies, or as Russell had indignantly put it in his piece, "cheating his fans, so that he could feed his addiction."

It was another cover story, and another big check, this time accompanied by what I needed to bring Erica London down.

I NEVER TOLD Erica my name or why I was doing what I was doing. I just showed up at her Los Feliz condo two months before her wedding in large sunglasses and a hoodie sweatshirt that covered my Afro.

I handed her the mock-up of the article that Russell planned to do and let her read about how up-and-coming actress Erica London had actually slept with her high school principal and then blackmailed him into forcing the theater coach to give her the lead in two school plays, which would be the catalyst for her getting into NYU.

It was the kind of gossip that could only kill a career at its beginnings. The TV execs might get spooked that middle America would not want to watch a program about high schoolers that starred a real-life Lolita. I told her that I had the authority to not only make sure the story never ran, but also to replace it with a puff piece about her being an actress to watch in the upcoming fall season.

The two big conditions were that she had to dump James within the week, and that she couldn't tell him the real reason she was calling off the wedding.

Then I walked away, ignoring all the alternative bargains of money and favors that she was yelling at my back.

The plan was shaky at best, because three things that I believed to be true had to indeed be true in order for it to work:

1. Erica, at twenty-two, had to be too young to be able to see the big picture of her life. She had to honestly believe that wildly handsome and rich men came along with proposals all the time.
2. She had to love her career more than she loved James. And
3. She had to come to the conclusion that playing along would be better for her than calling the authorities on me, since what I was doing was very illegal.

As it turned out, I was right on all counts. Russell ended up running a story on how Erica London, the next big thing, had just called off her engagement to "a millionaire hair company heir," and she actually managed to come out looking kind in it. She told Russell that she could not give only fifty percent of herself to any endeavor, and that she was afraid she would be cheating James out of a focused and committed wife if she married him.

James was devastated. Russell told me that he refused to comment for the story. And for a couple of months afterward, I couldn't find any event photos of James, which meant that he wasn't attending any functions. And in his world, total seclusion equaled heartbreak.

When I finished reading the article in *Celeb Weekly*, I smiled. James was now suffering over Erica the way I had suffered over him back in high school, and I discovered it was true what they said about revenge: It was very, very sweet.

# PART V

# BACK TO NOW

# TWENTY-THREE

AT LEAST REVENGE HAD SEEMED VERY sweet back then. But now that I was standing there in James's driveway, I could suddenly see something very clearly. Contrary to my now sixteen-year-old belief, he was not—and had never actually been—a movie character. He was a real man with real feelings.

And I had now broken his heart not once but twice.

"Is this true?" he asked me.

Both he and Veronica were staring at me with twin sucked-lemon expressions on their faces.

I wished I was back in Mississippi. I wished I was still traumatized and known as the girl that didn't talk. Also, I wished I was still the kid that took time to think up perfect replies, and then never, ever said them out loud.

But I wasn't that person anymore. So the first thing out of my mouth was "Of course it's true."

Then I said, "And I'm not sorry I did it. I truly believe in my heart that you guys deserved it."

That didn't come out right. I should have said "truly *believed* in my heart" that they deserved it. I could have explained that this was before I got my college learning and realized that what I had done was neither healthy nor rational.

When I looked back on this conversation later, I wished that I had explained, that even though I was thirty-one years old now, my love life had been severely stunted due to being a social pariah in high school and a fake over-twenty-one-year-old for most of my teenage years. Therefore, I only had the experience of maybe a twenty-two-year-old when it came to matters of the heart. So I had been little more than a child when I had done those things to the Farrells, a child stuck on something that had happened in high school. Maybe he would've understood and forgiven me if I had explained it that way.

Instead, I stood there in his driveway, with hot tears welling in my eyes, and said the least helpful thing that could possibly be said after your boyfriend finds out that you manipulated not only his heartbreak, but also that of his two sisters.

I said, "Fuck you, Veronica. You're a fucking bitch. I've always wanted to tell you that."

Veronica's expression went from repulsed to incredulous. "I'm a fucking bitch? Well, you're a fucking psycho."

What could I say to that? It was the perfect comeback.

Because while what I had said about her being a bitch was true, what she had just said about me being crazy was even truer. Especially at that moment.

James stared at me. "I wanted to spend the rest of my life with you," he said.

Of course, I had thought about the possibility of James finding out what I had done before this point. I had imagined him getting angry and dumping me, so that it would hurt less when our breakup happened. But somehow him saying that he wanted to spend the rest of his life with me, and then just standing there, looking like a kicked dog, was much worse than anything I had ever imagined.

*Damn it.* . . . A wave of humiliation, larger even than the one outside of Farrell Manor fifteen years ago, washed over me.

"I'm sorry," I said. "But I told you from the start that us getting together was not a good idea. Now you understand why I—"

Veronica interrupted. "Come inside." She put her arm around James's shoulders. "You're not supposed to engage psychos. They can turn violent."

Anger rose inside me, and I realized she was right, because as she walked away with James, I wanted to tear her to pieces for exposing me. I could see myself jumping on her back and yanking out her perfect blond highlights. The rage was so powerful it immobilized me.

Obviously Veronica thought she could just leave me here in the driveway, that I was some bug that could easily be swatted with a private detective and a late-night confrontation.

And for a second, I figured she was right about that, because my limbs felt heavy as stone and incapable of running after them as they turned their backs on me and walked toward the house. But then I realized . . .

My mouth still worked.

"So you're not planning on telling him all my secrets, Veronica? All our secrets."

Veronica started walking faster, tugging James along with her. I could hear her saying, "Ignore her."

At that point, another eighties movie came to mind, one that didn't have anything whatsoever to do with Molly Ringwald. *Fatal Attraction*. And I even thought to myself, *I will not be ignored.*

"You're not going to tell him about your daddy and my mama?"

James turned around, and now Veronica looked desperate. "Just ignore her."

"What did you just say?" he asked, walking back toward me.

Veronica had gone from all-powerful to pleading. "Please James, she's crazy. She'll say anything to keep you."

"Oh, I'm not trying to keep you," I said to James. "I promise you that right now. But I am trying to enlighten you some more, since your sister seems to think it's so very important that you know everything."

"Shut up. Just shut up, you bitch," Veronica screeched. Then she bit her lip like a pouty little girl and said, "You promised."

For once I had the truth on my side. "I never promised you anything,"

I reminded her. Then I turned back to James and said it straight-out before I could lose my nerve for like the millionth time that night. "Your father and my mother slept together. They had a short affair. And that's why your sister hates me."

James stared at me just the same as if I had hit him, then he looked at Veronica, who refused to meet his gaze. That's when he knew I was speaking truth.

He shook his head, his body almost humming with the anger of somebody who had been kept in the dark so long and about so many things.

But in the end, he really was the gentleman I had believed him to be from the beginning. He didn't scream at me. He didn't advance on me and beat me into the ground like my mother would have.

He just said, "Paul, take her home." Then he turned back around and walked away.

Veronica ran after him, teetering a little in her high heels.

And that was it. My time with the Farrells, I realized then, my almost-Molly-Ringwald-Ending sequel, was now over.

I didn't call after him again. I mean, what could I say, really? It was all just so fucked up.

I turned to Paul. A few moments ago his head had been swiveling back and forth among us like he was watching a nighttime soap.

But his face was expressionless now. "I will take you home."

Pride is something that I can take or leave most days. I let most of it go during my high school and Nicky years, but every once in a while it flared up, demanding that I do the heroic thing even if it meant putting my entire secondary education on hold and hitching a ride across the country to a state that I had only ever read about and seen in movies.

And right now my pride was telling me to leave James's suitcase and toiletries behind, and to just walk away with nothing but the eight dollars in my purse to get me back home to Hollywood.

But then I looked at James's retreating back again, and I felt so tired.

I got in the car.

We drove home in silence, except for my whispered "thank you" when he pulled up in front of the club. Paul didn't answer, just popped the trunk. That's when it occurred to me. Paul had known. He had known all along, because he had chauffeured Congressman Farrell to his Saturday night dates with my mother, so that Mr. Farrell wouldn't have to risk somebody seeing his nice car in Cora's driveway.

But I didn't have any more confrontation left in me. I didn't ask Paul about this, I just got out of the car and pulled my suitcase out of the trunk.

Chloe was outside the club, smoking a cigarette four feet away from the building as California law (and, more importantly, Nicky) required. Chloe was one of those people who only smoked when she was upset. So I knew she was angry even before I got within hearing distance.

Her sweet face hardened when she saw me. "I've been trying to call you all night. This private investigator stopped by here earlier today and he was asking me and Nicky some questions. Then he told us some things . . ."

I didn't hear the rest because I kept on walking past her without even pausing, I was already most of the way up the stairs by the time she dropped the private investigator bomb. And I let the landing door close on the rest of her words before she could tell me anything else.

NICKY WAS KNOCKING on my door not even ten minutes later, but by then I was in bed, curled up in the fetal position, and I had no intention of getting up. High School Davie was back in charge. And the absolute silence she demanded slipped over me like a welcome friend.

"C'mon, Davie girl, I know you're in there," he said from outside my door. "Your ass better let me in."

Then when those nice words didn't work, he said, "Don't make me go all the way back to my house to get my spare keys."

Baldwin Hills was about sixteen miles south of Hollywood. It was late at night, so the traffic wouldn't be too bad, but it would be inconvenient, and Nicky couldn't abide being inconvenienced. Still, I couldn't bring myself to get up out of bed and answer the door.

"I know you're sad or whatever, but if you make my ass go all the way to Baldwin Hills to get them keys, then you fired."

It was a good sally as far as threats went, but I felt exhausted and hopeless throughout every bone of my body, and I didn't have the strength to move, much less walk across the floor and face Nicky's angry questions, and much, much less fight High School Davie's desire to just not talk anymore or ever again.

After five more minutes of threats and knocking, he went away, only to let himself in with his landlord key about forty-five minutes later.

"This is some bullshit," he said, standing above me. Then: "You hungry?"

I didn't answer. Whatever desperate magic had transformed me from an ugly mute fifteen years ago was gone. I was once again High School Davie. Without words, and the kind of girl a boy like James could easily not know existed.

Nicky made me some soup anyway. I didn't eat it, didn't even respond to the spoon being thrust in my face.

"This is some bullshit," he said again.

Then he took away the soup, turned off all the lights, and got into bed with me, wrapping me up in his large arms.

He was taller and broader than James. I had known that technically before, but I understood it physically now that I had lain with both of them.

I didn't fight off his embrace, but I didn't come out of the fetal position, either.

And the next morning, Nicky woke up to find me still curled up in a little ball, still staring at the wall, still not talking, and still not eating.

He made a call, and twelve hours later Mama Jane came through the door.

I COULD FEEL her large hand stroking my hair as Nicky explained to her what happened.

This is when I found out that my accepting money for those pictures was what had led Veronica's investigator to what all I'd done. He had somehow gotten ahold of my bank statements and had taken interest in the two large sums of money that I deposited into my account in August 2002 and April 2003.

From there, all he had to do was track down Russell, who kept my name out of it but couldn't hide that he had broken two of the most scandalous Farrell stories of all time. Then he had gone to Erica London, who never did quite live up to all the potential that she had thought she had at the time I had blackmailed her. Despite a lot of hype, her television show had bombed after three episodes. And though she was still very pretty, she was now making a lesser living playing no-nonsense wives and mothers in commercials for practical things like disinfectants and life insurance.

She had been forthcoming, as had Corey Mays, who had been blaming his weakness and Chloe's duplicitous nature for his broken engagement all these years. Now he, like everyone else, was aware that it had all been me.

On a hunch, the PI had then gone to Mike Barker, who had told him about my bet. Then, after visiting Chloe and Nicky, he presented my solved case to Veronica Farrell as a neat little package the very same day. She had flown out from New York, shown James the evidence in his driveway, and that was that.

Mama Jane tutted during every dramatic twist and turn of the story, and when Nicky finally finished she patted me on the shoulder and said, "I didn't know you had in you, Davidia Jones. That is some story."

"It ain't funny," Nicky said. "These rich bitches could sue her ass. They got lawyers, and what Davie did was off-the-hook."

Mama Jane harrumphed. "They ain't suing nobody. And if they try, send them to Mama Jane. I'll run them over with my truck."

High School Davie, who had never had a defender, was startled into laughter. The image of Mama Jane running over the Farrell family with her eighteen-wheeler was so hilarious that the laughter didn't even seem to be a choice. It just came hiccupping out of me.

Then the sound of my own voice broke me, and I started crying.

Mama Jane sat me up and pulled my head to her shoulder. "That's the stuff, baby. Let it out."

And that's how it went. I was catatonic High School Davie for one day, and then I was myself again, crying off and on for about three days straight. Mama Jane stayed with me the entire time, making me soup and sandwiches for lunch and dinner, and then sleeping on a pallet on the floor until I was ready for a bowl of cereal the next morning.

ON THE FOURTH day of my recovery from the Driveway Confrontation, Mama Jane and I were sitting on my couch, eating cereal. She had a big haul that she was leaving for that afternoon, so it would be our last breakfast together for a while.

"I don't know why I did it," I told her. "I guess I felt like if I couldn't have my Molly Ringwald Ending, then none of them should get to be happy and in love."

"What's a Molly Ringwald Ending?" Mama Jane asked. She was dressed in her usual off-duty uniform of boxer shorts and a tank top. Probably the least attractive thing a graying, butch, and overweight black lesbian could wear, but it wouldn't be Mama Jane if she showed up to dispense advice in anything but the least fashionable attire.

"It's a perfect ending. It's when somehow, against all odds, people manage to surmount all issues of class, status, and personality to get together at the end of a story." I thought about that definition, and then realized for the first time: "It's basically impossible. I've never seen that kind of ending happen in real life. I mean not ever."

Mama Jane patted my hand. "I never met this little boy, and I ain't condoning what you did to him and his. That shit was funny, but it ain't right."

She waited for my contrite nod of agreement before continuing on.

"But don't you think you're giving somebody who didn't even know you was alive till very recently a lot of power over your life?"

It was such a profound statement that the tears threatened to overtake me again, but this time I kept them at bay with a hard sniff. "I think I'll go back to work tonight. I feel ready to sing again."

Mama Jane smiled and gave me another pat on the hand. She didn't approve or disapprove of my decision, just said, "Drink your coffee, baby."

## TWENTY-FOUR

I FOUND OUT WHAT MAMA JANE already knew when I went downstairs for rehearsal.

Chloe was there, doing warm-up exercises while the band set up.

I stopped walking when I saw her, trying to figure out why she was there for rehearsal. Then I realized that Nicky must have retained her as my replacement until I came back to work, which was awkward, because after the Corey Mays Reveal, I didn't want to be the one to tell her that she wouldn't be needed for rehearsal or tonight's performance.

So I slunk through the shadows at the back of the club to Nicky's office. I figured he could let her know about the change of schedule after we talked.

"Good news: I'm ready to come back," I announced as I walked into his office. "Bad news: You're going to have to tell Chloe that."

Nicky was writing out checks for club vendor bills, and he had that pinched look on his face that he always got when he had to pay anybody money for anything.

Yet he took the time to paste a smile on his face and ask, "How are you, Davie?"

My stomach dropped, because Nicky never exchanged pleasantries. I mean ever.

I had expected the first words out of his mouth to be, "You look like shit." Which was true. My skin was broken out from three days of intense grief, my Afro was in serious need of a pick, and I had lost weight in a not good way. My breasts felt saggy and my hips felt bony, like they had never known a curve.

But Nicky hadn't mentioned any of this yet. Which was bad. And to add to my discomfort, I didn't know how to deal with this pleasant Nicky, since I had never met him before.

"I'm fine," I answered carefully. "I'm ready to sing now."

He took off his reading glasses and rubbed his temple as if he had a sudden headache. Then he brought out his clipboard. "You know I love you, Davie, but I told your ass I would fire you if you didn't open that door. And you didn't open the door."

I blinked. "Are you kidding me?"

"No, I'm not kidding. These past few days have gotten me to thinking about us."

"About how we're best friends?" I asked, giving him a not-so-subtle reminder.

"No, about how we're family now. I love you like you're family, and since you were fifteen, I took care of you like you were family."

"You've slept with members of your family?"

Nicky continued on like I hadn't made that remark. "But the thing is, I don't live with my parents anymore. After college I got my own apartment and moved out. And I think I might have done you a disservice by not making you do the same thing when you graduated."

He was serious, I realized then. He would never talk this much and this kindly if he weren't anything but completely serious. I sank down into the plastic folding chair.

"But I love this job," I said. And moreover, "Where will I go?"

Nicky shook his head. "Well, you still got the apartment. Mostly because I can't legally kick you out of it under California's current rental laws. But you're either going to have to give up the Soul BunnyGram business or do it yourself."

I thought about the day I mowed James down in my bunny suit, and I said, "I don't ever want to do another Soul BunnyGram again."

Nicky shrugged. "Then use your degree. What's it in again?"

"Psychology," I said.

Then we both got quiet, because really the irony of that was almost a little too much.

"Nicky, this is the worst possible time for you to do this. I don't under-stand."

Nicky leaned back in his seat. "One day you'll thank me."

"You always say that, and I have never thanked you for any of the things you made me do. Not once," I hissed. I had gone from hurt to full of rage in a split second.

"I know. You've never thanked me. That's why I'm firing you. Because even I gave my parents a goddamn thanks every now and then."

I wanted to yell that he wasn't my real father, but we both knew that wasn't true. In every way that counted Nicky had guided me through the last fifteen years, and he was right: I had never thanked him for his extraordinary kindness. But still, the Cora in me made me say, "If I let you fuck me, would you still be my daddy? And could I keep my job?"

Nicky checked something off on his clipboard. Probably "Fire Davie." He then got up and opened his office door for me. "I'll see you when rent's due next month."

I wanted to scream. I wanted to hit him. But mostly I wanted my father back.

I stood up and walked past him, out of his office. Sullen as all get-out.


MAMA JANE WAS waiting for me upstairs. Her eyes followed me as I walked in without a word and got back into bed.

"The trip I'm about to go on is taking me through Glass," she said behind me. "You could come with me."

I thought of not answering her, but she had already coaxed me out of one catatonic state, and it seemed unfair to make her do it again. "I have to get a job."

"It'll only take a week round trip."

"Mama Jane . . ." I turned over to say no. But she looked so dear and worried in her boxer shorts and tank top. And I no longer had a job. "Okay, I'll go with you."

Mama Jane smiled, and for the first time in five days, I suddenly felt a little good. Good enough to get out of bed on my own and say, "Let me pack my bag."

THE SOMEWHAT GOOD feeling evaporated three days later, though, about an hour outside of Columbus. That's when it occurred to me that I didn't quite know why I had come back to Mississippi.

"I'd think you'd want to visit your mama," Mama Jane said to me, after I suggested she drop me off at a coffee shop in Columbus, then pick me up when she finished dropping off whatever she was dropping off; I hadn't asked about the details of her trip.

I didn't want to visit Cora. I had just learned the hard way that life was not a movie. So now that I had hit bottom, I did not want to confront my mother or face my demons or do any of that stuff that made eighties movies so cliché and predictable.

"I haven't spoken to her since I ran away," I said. "I don't even know if she's living in the same place."

"But you don't know she ain't living there, either. You should at least go by and check. And if she ain't there, you can ask the people that live there now where she moved to."

I had never heard an idea more repugnant than actually seeking Cora out. "I really don't want to see her," I told Mama Jane flat-out.

"You really didn't want to lose your job at Nicky's, either. Sometimes it ain't all about what you want."

I folded my arms and pouted. "It's never about what I want."

Mama Jane just laughed. "You always so quick to tell me what to do when I'm nosing around some new woman, but the minute I try to get you to do anything, you get all upset."

We went back and forth like this for the next hour and a half. But I couldn't stop Mama Jane from dropping me off in Glass. Believe me, I tried. At one point, I even brought out the rarely resorted to Screaming Child Davie. But in the end, the eighteen-wheeler pulled into Glass and I climbed out in my black jeans and Strokes T-shirt.

Mama Jane took off as soon as my red Converses hit the pavement.

I looked around. It still looked like Glass, but with a modern overlay. Johnson's Gas was now a BP, and I could see that Greeley's Mini-Mart was now a 7-Eleven. Old Mr. Greeley was probably dead by now. Hunh.

My feet seemed to carry me down Main Street of their own accord, past a Starbucks that hadn't been there in the early nineties, and then down several tree-lined roads, until I was standing outside my old house.

The grass was a little too high, and the windows could use a washing, but other than that, the little gray house was pretty well maintained. I couldn't remember which one of Cora's friends used to tend to all the mechanics of the house for her. I could see his face, dark and sweaty. And I could see the flashlight he always carried with him, because he only came around at night. But I couldn't remember his name. Was he still doing maintenance work for her under the cover of night? Or was this some-one else's house now? Someone who would look at me strangely when I knocked on the door and who would not be able to tell me where Cora got off to. She wasn't exactly the type to leave behind a forwarding address.

I knocked on the door. And waited. Then I waited some more.

Mama Jane wasn't due back to pick me up for another two hours still, and like I said, I'm a very patient girl.

Several minutes after my first and only knock, a small woman opened the door.

"What you want?" she asked me through the screen door.

I couldn't see her face against the dark shadows of the house, but I knew it was Cora from the harsh, cigarette-hardened sound of her voice. "It's me. Davidia—"

"I know who you is. What you want?"

"May I come in?"

Hesitation. Then she pushed open the screen door and moved out the way so I could come in.

The first thing that hit me when I walked in was the smell. The air had the heavy stench of cigarette smoke, which I hadn't experienced in quite a while. California had strict indoor smoking policies for businesses, and even the artists I knew who smoked did not do so inside their own apartments and with closed windows. They weren't hard-core like Cora.

The aggressive smell of the place made my mother seem like a throwback. Had it smelled like this when I lived here? Had Mama Jane been taken aback that a teenager could so reek of cigarettes when I climbed into her cab that first time?

The second thing that hit me was that Cora had grown older. She wore a wig now. And her heart-shaped beauty was gone, replaced with the creases of hard living, heavy drinking, and her two-pack-a-day habit. She had also shrunk some, so now even though I was only five-four, it felt like I was towering over her.

"Why you come here?" she asked, picking up her pack of cigarettes— still Virginia Slims, I noticed.

I kept on looking around the room: at the mirror that I had stared at myself in before I left forever; at the connecting kitchen, where I had made myself a fresh batch of Hamburger Helper every Sunday and Wednesday, which I then ate as leftovers during the days in between. I now couldn't abide the taste or even the smell of Hamburger Helper. Even during my tightest months, I couldn't bring myself to eat it.

I doubted she would respond well to *Why are you such a mean, hateful bitch?* or *Why couldn't you have shown me even a speck of compassion growing up?* So I asked her the only question I had that she might answer.

"Is Elmer my father?"

Cora let her Virginia Slim dangle in her mouth. "You ain't got no right coming around here asking me questions like that."

"I ain't got no right?" My voice just about crackled with anger. "You don't have no right. How are you going to just stand there after all these years and still refuse to tell me where I came from?"

"You don't come from no place." Cora started coughing then, but she kept on talking around her smoker's hacks. "You ain't shit. I found you under a rock. A shitty rock. And I took you home cuz nobody else wanted your ugly, dark ass."

I turned my back on her. How could she actually be worse than I remembered? It didn't seem possible. "Okay, I'll go ask him myself."

"He dead," she said.

I turned back to face her. "I don't believe you."

Cora smiled around her cigarette. "You don't got to believe me. That bitch still in the ground, even if you don't believe me."

She wasn't lying. She was too happy to be giving me this terrible news to be lying.

He was dead. I had just now realized that he might be my father and it was already too late. I willed myself not to cry in front of her. I even pressed my fists against my eyes, trying to hold back the tears. But it wasn't any use. Despite having cried more these last few days than I ever had in my entire life, I couldn't control my tears now.

"Stop crying," Cora said. Like I was still a little kid and embarrassing her. "He ain't your daddy."

I shook my head. I really wished that she would just stop talking. It was like she had trained herself to only say the things that would be the least amount of help to anyone.

"Here, sit down," Cora said. She put her hand on my shoulder and kind of pushed me down onto the red pleather love seat that had replaced the couch that I used to sleep on. It was the first time she had touched me since beating me right before the Farrell party.

I sat down on the ridiculous piece of furniture and started wiping away my tears with the bottom of my Strokes T-shirt. I heard her walk out, and a few minutes later she returned with a box, which she plunked down beside me.

"Listen," she said. "This is all the stuff you left. You going to have to take it with you, because I ain't got room to be storing your shit for you."

My eyes widened when I saw the rainbow-covered scrapbook sitting on top of everything else in the box. I pulled it out. My James Farrell scrapbook. I couldn't believe that she had kept it all these years. I opened it and found all the articles I had clipped and the Polaroid I had stolen. I touched two fingers to the smooth film. He looked so young and carefree, with his hair cut in a box-top fade. Nothing like the man I had known in L.A. It was hard to believe that this was the same James that I had initially fallen head over heels for. My very first love.

I closed the scrapbook and went back to the box. There were several VHS tapes, including *Pretty in Pink, The Breakfast Club,* and of course, *Sixteen Candles.* But there was also *Say Anything* and *Some Kind of Wonderful,* and, bizarrely enough, *Labyrinth.* I had forgotten that I had also liked those films.

Underneath the VHS tapes, I found a framed photograph of my grandparents. I blinked, because I hadn't seen this picture of my grandmama and my grandfather, who had died of a heart attack before I was born, in years.

They looked different somehow. My grandmama's lighter face was not quite as kind as I remembered it. And my grandfather seemed even more unfamiliar, even though he was dark like me.

Dark like me . . .

A thought occurred to me then—a thought I started to dismiss at first because my grandfather's name was Arnold, not David. But then I remembered it wasn't just Arnold. It was Arnold D. Jones. I had seen that once on the deed to the house.

I turned around and asked Cora, "What was my grandfather's middle name?"

Cora went completely still.

And quite suddenly I knew that we were in dangerous territory here. What had just been a thought a few seconds ago was now transforming into a real and devastating possibility. "Was it David?" I asked. "Was I named after him?"

There was a second where nothing happened, in which Cora just looked at me. Then she whispered, "Get out!"

"Mama," I said then, because I finally understood why she was the way she was.

Her transformation to enraged was instantaneous. She threw the scrapbook and tapes in the box and pushed it into my chest. "Get out," she said again.

"Mama, we can talk about this. I didn't know—"

She screamed, "Get out my house! Get the hell out my house!"

Her hands were on my body, pushing me, shoving me. And then suddenly, I was out on the steps.

"So my grandfather is also my real father," I said, outside the door.

She slapped me. Hard. Then she slammed the door in my face.

I rubbed my cheek.

But I was smiling by the time I turned around and walked down the steps.

Somehow it made me feel better to know that I wasn't just a psycho. Like all sorts of European royalty in the history books, I was an inbred psycho. And that explained a whole hell of a lot.

As I walked back to town, I was all of sudden hit with a forgotten memory.

As ugly as I had been considered when I was nine, not all of Cora's friends had thought so. And one had not exited the house according to plan after he had pulled up his pants and left her sleeping in bed.

I remembered waking in the middle of the night to see him. He stood, still as a shadow in the middle of the living room. And he had the unsettling quality of a specter.

For a moment I had wondered if my sleep-filled mind was playing tricks on me. I had thought maybe he was a coat rack that I was just making out to be a man.

But then he had stepped forward into the moonlight, his index finger on his lips.

He must not have been from Glass, or else he would've known that asking me to be quiet was totally unnecessary.

"I'm not going to hurt you," he whispered.

Then he pulled down my blanket and looked at me in the same hungry way that I had seen men look at Cora.

I was more fascinated than scared at this point, and I just watched his fingers as they lifted up my T-shirt.

"Raise your arms," he said.

So I did.

Then suddenly Cora was on his back. Her red nails scratched his face from behind and sent him reeling into a wall. She jumped off his back and pushed his face into the wall, slamming it again and again.

I turned on the light beside the couch just as she finally stopped. He was stumbling around in a small circle now, his face bloody and his eyes dull with pain. Then Cora opened the door and shoved him out of the house.

It was the quietest fight I have ever witnessed.

After he was gone, she had slapped me. "Don't let nobody touch you, you stupid bitch. Don't you ever let any of them men touch you, you hear me?"

I nodded, expecting her to hit me again, but she just shook her head, looking disgusted, and returned to her bedroom.

Back on the road, I remembered all of this and realized Cora might not have loved me, but she did protect me.

She did protect me.

I was humming a half an hour later when Mama Jane pulled into the BP.

There were a few moments of hesitation, but then I dumped the box of my high school things in a close-by trash bin before climbing into the truck, quick like I was ripping off a Band-Aid. Lord knew I already had enough baggage.

"How was your visit?" she asked, after I had settled into the passenger seat.

"Good," I said. "Informative. We talked, and I decided to forgive her."

Which was pretty much the truth when it came down to it.

"Is that right?" Mama Jane released her air brakes, and they gave a satisfying whoosh as we pulled out of the BP parking lot and left Glass, Mississippi, behind.


TWO DAYS LATER, we drove into Los Angeles via downtown, just like the first time I had come into the city with Mama Jane. Except now I recognized the signs of drug addiction and mental illness among the people who wandered in front of the truck.

After we dropped off Mama Jane's load, she took me back to my apartment. And as we drove down Sunset, we saw two guys putting the finishing touches on a billboard for a new Keira Knightley movie called *Atonement*.

"Atonement," I said, tasting the word on the tip of my tongue. "That's a good word."

Mama Jane shot me a worried look. "Are you sure you're ready to go home?" she asked. "You can come out with me on another job. I appreciate the company."

It was a tempting offer. I wouldn't mind forgetting about my real life for another week or so and going on another road adventure. Then I thought about the billboard and decided. "Thank you, but no. I've got work to do."


A LITTLE OVER an hour later, I was sitting in Nicky's office, telling him that I was sorry for everything I had said the last time we talked and how truly grateful I was for every single thing that he had ever done for me, including keeping me away from drugs, drinks, and actors.

My extreme sincerity alarmed him. He asked me straight out if this was a ploy to get back my job, because he had already made a verbal agreement with Chloe.

I assured him it wasn't. Then I confessed that I had never really, truly valued the job. It was fun, and I liked what I did, but I didn't love it and had never wanted to go further with it. I told him I was now grateful he had fired me, because I would have stayed in the same holding pattern forever if he hadn't forced me to do something new.

But the words "holding pattern" and "something new" only furthered his suspicions. His eyes narrowed. "You about to ask for a loan, ain't you?"

"No, but if you haven't filled Chloe's waitress position yet, I could use the job while I do my atonement."

"Your a-what-ment?"

"I need a job while I make things right with everyone I hurt."

Nicky sucked on his teeth. "I see you on that New Age shit. I should've known. You going to start wearing muumuus and carrying around crystals, too?"

I felt my newfound appreciation for Nicky rapidly disintegrating. "Can I have the job or not?"

Nicky finally smiled. There was truly nothing he loved more than pushing people to the limits of their patience. "Sure," he said, picking up his clipboard and checking "Fill Chloe's position" off his list. He grinned. "All you had to do was ask."

## TWENTY-FIVE

MY ATONEMENT LIST HAD ENOUGH NAMES on it that I had to write them all down on the back of an envelope to keep track. And I felt pretty bad when I put my pen down.

First up was Corey Mays. I tracked down his private cell phone number through another waiter, who knew an assistant in the sports division at William Morris. As it turned out, Corey had recently retired from football with a bad knee at the age of thirty-four and was now living in Los Angeles, where he had gotten a gig with FOX Sports as a commentator. Was everybody from high school going to eventually end up in Los Angeles, I wondered, or was this God's way of letting me know I was on the right path?

When he picked up the phone, I said, "Corey Mays, this is Davie Jones. I need ten minutes. And before you hang up, please remember that you wouldn't have made it through chemistry without me."

"You abandoned me right before finals. I only ended up with a C," Corey said. But he didn't hang up, which was a start. "How'd you get this number?"

"Same way I got those pictures. Through scheming and determination."

Corey chuckled. "I guess you good at that now, huh?"

"I was good at it back then, too, I just didn't talk about it."

"No, you sure didn't. It's still real freaky to hear you talking now, to tell you the truth." There was a silence on the line for a bit. Then: "Okay, say what you got to say."

"What I did was heinous and wrong. And I know how it is to want a Farrell more than anything, but, Corey, Veronica was a bad match for you. You weren't happy, and I probably saved you from a divorce later on down the line. Surely this must have occurred to you in the years after ya'll broke up, or you wouldn't even be talking to me now."

"So you think you did me a favor?" Corey asked. I could hear anger at the edge of his voice.

"No, I definitely don't think I did you a favor. My actions were dirty and down low, I'm not arguing that. But, Corey, Chloe had nothing to do with it. She's just as much a victim as you in all this. And I would like to believe that you wouldn't have cheated on Veronica if you hadn't liked Chloe an awful lot. So if you're not with somebody else right now, I'm just asking you to maybe consider calling Chloe. You seriously could not do any better as far as finding a girl with a good heart is concerned. She is the exact opposite of Veronica Farrell. And most importantly, I think she's the kind of woman that you need in your life."

The silence stretched on so long this time, I checked my cell's call timer to make sure he hadn't hung up. When I saw it was still ticking away, I said, "Hello?"

"Yeah, I'm here. I'm just wondering how I got to a place in my love life where I'm seriously considering letting the girl who tricked me into cheating on my ex-fiancée set me up on a date."

Well, when he put it that way I was a little stunned that he was considering it, too. But that didn't stop me from sealing the deal and promising to get back to him with Chloe's contact info.

As soon as I hung up, I ran downstairs to find Chloe. It had been cold business between me and her since my return from Mississippi. Betrayal is a hard obstacle to surmount friendship-wise—even if she did get a pretty sweet singing gig out of the whole ordeal—so the reception was chilly when I walked into what used to be my dressing room without knocking.

But that all ended as soon as I told her that I had talked to Corey, and that he was fixing to call her, probably in the next day or so. She immediately started freaking out. Fell all over me with hugs and kisses, thanking me as if I hadn't been the death knell in their short-lived relationship in the first place. Unfortunately, Chloe had grown so used to friends and lovers taking advantage of her that it honestly took her by surprise that someone would do anything nice for her. That was something we were going to have to work on before Corey called her.

"You know you deserve this, right?" I said, pulling out of her embrace.

She just laughed and started thanking me again.

But I wasn't letting her get away with being humble anymore. Los Angeles was a funny place. There are Takers here without talent or decency, people who truly believe that they deserve the earth. Then there are ridiculously kind Givers, like Chloe, who give and give without thinking to reserve something for themselves.

I cupped her shoulders in my hands and said, "You deserve my job. You deserve to be happy. And you deserve Corey Mays. That's a given. But the real question is does he deserve you? For the first three months of the relationship, I want you to look hard for reasons not to date him. Do not cut him any slack. If he trips, let him go. You've got to promise me that, or I'm not going to give him your phone number."

The forgiving smile suddenly dropped off her face. "Are you crazy?"

"Yes," I said. "Yes, I am. That's pretty much been proven already. But I think you're a little off, too, which is why I cannot watch you kill another relationship with kindness." I semi-quoted from a book I had once read about supposedly kind people in a supposedly kind relationship who still ended up crashing and burning into a love wreck. "Killing with kindness is still murder."

"I don't understand," she said. And she honestly looked hurt. "Why would you come in here and say that Corey wanted to see me again, but then tell me I have to be mean to him?"

"I'm not telling you to be mean. I'm telling you that you need to adopt some effing standards already." I took her by the hand and pulled her out of the dressing room. "C'mon."

"I still have to put on my dress and makeup," she said. Ever the good girl, she tried to pull back into the dressing room. But I just dragged her with me on into Nicky's office.

"Nicky," I said, coming through the door with her. "Do you think Chloe's nice?"

Nicky looked up from the meeting he was having with his alcohol vendor, a long gray-haired guy with tattoo sleeves on both arms. "Yeah, she nice," Nicky answered like he didn't have company. "Too fucking nice. That's why she always crying over some man. I got business here. Do you mind?"

"One more question. Have you ever wished that Chloe would find a guy who was as nice to her as she is to him?"

For once Nicky didn't have anything mean to say. He just answered, "Yes, I have," so emphatically that Chloe was struck silent for a good minute.

"What's going on?" Nicky asked me.

"I'm trying to convince Chloe to stop letting these little boys walk all over her."

"Oh, I'll cosign that check," Nicky said. "Chloe, start acting like you got some sense when it comes to these dudes. That's an order."

Chloe had never been one to go in the face of a direct order. And maybe she was a little touched that somebody as gruff as Nicky would actually care enough to weigh in on her love life.

"Okay," she said to me. "Okay, this time I'll be different."

AND THAT WAS that. I called Corey back with Chloe's number and they started dating. And it was all sweetness.

Though something did happen a few months later.

We were in her dressing room, both admiring her new haircut in the mirror.

It was that modern twist on the bob, which was called the Posh or the Victoria Beckham if you were white, and the Rihanna if you were black.

Chloe, who had been wearing her hair in simple shoulder-length curls ever since I met her, had gotten it done in homage to her new perspective on life.

Trying to find a reason to dump Corey had taken so much going against nature on Chloe's part that she hadn't had the energy to smother him with love. And that had resulted in the first healthy relationship she had ever been in.

"Things are going so well with Corey," she said. "I was like, I should try something new with my hair, too. Do you like it?"

"I love it," I said. "What did Nicky say?"

"He wasn't happy about the little blond streak in the front," she admitted. "But he said at least it was a lot more authentic than an Afro."

Chloe wasn't as good of a singer as I was. She had a little too much training, and it always felt like she was holding something back from the audience. Apart from that, Nicky was over the moon at having a docile singer who also looked the part.

"Firing you was the best decision I ever made," he often said straight to my face. I would have been hurt, but it was Nicky, so I just ignored him.

"Have you shown it to Corey yet? What'd he say?"

"I just got it done a few hours ago, but we've got our big two-month-anniversary date after the show, so he'll see it then."

"Two-month-anniversary date?" I asked, suspicious that she was doing her ridiculous Chloe thing again.

"It was his idea, not mine," she said, reading my tone. "Corey is really, really sweet. And so romantic."

Since I had forbidden Chloe to tell Corey how much she liked him to his face, she often ended up gushing about him to me behind his back. It was not fun, but I considered sitting through her syrupy accolades part of my atonement.

The chirping crickets of her ringtone interrupted her before she could really get started, though. She pulled her pink RAZR out of her bag and checked the caller ID. "It's Corey," she said, and a smile split her face. "When am I allowed to give him his own ringtone again?"

"When he gives you your own ringtone or in six months, whichever comes first," I answered. Again. They'd only been dating two months, but somehow Chloe and me had already managed to have this conversation about a hundred times.

"But how am I suppose to know if he's given me my own ringtone if I can't ask him if he's given me my own ringtone? That doesn't make any sense. Hold on."

She answered the phone. "Hi, Corey. How are you?"

She listened. Then she frowned. "Can you hold on?"

She muted the RAZR, pressing it to the front of her chest. "He says that he needs to cancel our big dinner."

"Why?" I asked.

"Because he's worried that he's going to have bags under his eyes if he stays up late. The game he's hosting tomorrow is in HD."

"You have a show tomorrow. Are you afraid that you won't be able to sing if you stay out late?" Then before she could answer that, I added, "More importantly, would you cancel a date two hours before it was supposed to happen?"

Chloe looked torn, but then she brought the phone back to her ear and said, "Corey, I bought a new dress and got a new haircut for tonight's date, which you asked me on. I was really looking forward to it. But canceling at the last minute with an excuse like that is just disrespectful. Obviously you don't value my time the way I value yours." The next words seemed harder for her to squeeze out, but she did it: "And if that's the case, you should just lose my number. Good-bye."

Then she hung up. "Oh my God," she gasped.

"Lose my number?"

"I saw it in a movie once." She sat down and clutched her chest. "I can't believe I did that. He's Corey Mays."

I was so proud of her, I didn't know what to do. I was also relieved that I wouldn't have to do anything nefarious to sabotage the relationship, which was my plan B if I saw that Chloe was letting herself be taken advantage of again. Obviously I was pretty good at 86ing relationships, and I figured I might as well use my questionable talent to teach Chloe again and again until she learned.

But luckily it hadn't come down to that.

"Yes, he's Corey Mays. And you're Chloe Anderson, one of the best people I've ever known. He needs to recognize. So put on your makeup and get dressed. You've got a show in thirty minutes."

She turned back to the mirror and perked up a little when she saw her new haircut again. "Yes, I'm Chloe Anderson," she said with conviction. Then she picked up a foam triangle, put on her brave face, and started applying her foundation.

"WHAT IF HE doesn't ever call me again," she all but wailed an hour later during the set break. She had turned off her phone before going onstage, but checked it as soon as the first half of the set had ended and found no messages from Corey. Then she came to find me, hunting me down at the bar as I rushed to fill drink orders during the break.

"You don't want the kind of guy who won't call you after you make a perfectly reasonable demand. If Corey shows his ass like that, then he's doing you a favor by not calling," I said.

Chloe just stared at me. "Tell me again why I should take your advice? You're still single. And you're crazy."

She made such a good point that I immediately switched to underhanded tactics. I let my face go soft and sad. "Please don't remind me that I'm single, because I lost James."

That brought Chloe out of her crisis. The one thing she still couldn't resist was lending a helping hand, when she saw that one was needed.

"I'm sorry, I was just being mean. You'll find somebody else, girl," she assured me, drawing me into her arms.

But I didn't want anybody else. Just James. It had always been Just James, even when I was with other people.

However, even I could tell that wasn't a healthy thought, so I didn't say it out loud.

I just let her hold me—even though I could feel Nicky's eyes boring a hole in my back because I wasn't serving drinks and taking more orders.

Corey showed up a few minutes before her set was over, with an armful of flowers and a chagrined look on his face.

After that near breakup, Corey started referring to Chloe as his girlfriend. And about a month later, he asked her to move in with him.

I was thrilled that my first atonement was such a success, but in the back of my mind I did note that Chloe and Corey would probably be the easiest names to cross off my list. Now the real hard work began.

## TWENTY-SIX

THE WEEK AFTER COREY STARTED CALLING Chloe his girlfriend, I
showed up unannounced outside of Mike Barker's Beverly Hills mansion.

He answered the gate buzzer himself, his voice coming out of the
little speaker box, loud and clear. "Is that you, Davie Jones?" he asked. He
sounded like he had been drinking. "What are you doing here?"

"May I come in?" I asked.

"What are you doing here?" he asked again.

"I need to talk to you," I answered. "About what all I did."

"That was fucked up what you did. Ratting me out to *Celeb Weekly.*"

"I know. Can I come in? I want to apologize."

"You want to apologize?" he slurred through the box. "Yeah, you're
right. You need to apologize to me."

The ornate black steel gates swung open for me and my beat-up car.

MIKE HAD MANAGED to hang on to his mansion, but all the furnishings
that I had seen in the *Architectural Digest* spread during the height of his
fame were now gone. As were all but one of his sports cars. He had hung
on for a few years after the article that I had sourced came out, but eventually the casinos had seen the writing on the wall re his falling star and
called in his millions of dollars of debt.

"You ruined my life," he informed me, standing in the middle of his empty foyer, with a nearly empty bottle of Jack Daniel's clutched tightly in his right fist.

Apparently the only reason Mike had allowed me into his now empty home was to tell me this.

He was dressed in a beautiful smoking jacket and trousers, but he had gained at least thirty pounds since I last saw him. He smelled aggressively tart, like he hadn't bathed in a few days. A definite sign of depression, I noted. The hair on top of his head was a hot mess, wild and matted, like he hadn't run a pick through it in weeks—maybe months. He had also grown what Nicky referred to as a "jail beard." Mike now reminded me of High School Davie, and that about broke my heart.

Still, I let him know: "You're the one who ruined your life, not me." I pasted a distasteful look on my face and surveyed his bare walls and the empty sitting room beyond the foyer, as if I actually had the right to look down on his living space. "Now do you want to take the next few steps to the bottom, or do you want to stop this and get your shit back?"

Mike's eyes flashed with desperate anger. "I thought you came here to apologize."

I felt bad for him. He had probably liked having me to blame for his downfall after Veronica's PI visited and let him know everything. I hated to bust his bubble like that, but it had to be done. I asked again in the hardest voice possible: "Do you want to hit bottom or do you want your shit back, little boy? You've got to answer me now, because I don't have all day."

Pure bluff. I had sworn to give as much time as it took to do right by everyone that I had wronged. But he didn't know that. And something must have clicked in that addict brain of his, because he said, "I want my shit back," in a voice so gruff and quiet, I had to depend on the echo of his empty mansion to carry his words to me.

I resisted the urge to smile and said, "I don't like you. I've never liked you. I've always thought you were incredibly fake and insecure and I pegged you as a gambling addict from the door."

Mike looked stricken, which confirmed my suspicions that his priorities were still in the wrong place. "But me not liking you is a good thing," I said. I took the bottle out of his hand. "Now go take a shower."

MIKE'S SECRET TO becoming one of the most beloved actors in Hollywood was simple. He never talked about himself. Every conversation that he had with anyone in the business was always about the other person, and this had been surprisingly effective in a town known for its vanities.

So it took a couple of hours and several awkward false starts for him to really start telling me his life story. It didn't come out as one neat package, but in spurts and fits over the next three days as we did everything together.

I had done my research on him before showing up, but still there were a lot of surprising details that *E! True Hollywood Story* and Google hadn't been able to give me.

When he was growing up, his crackhead mother had a nasty habit of getting high at night and telling him that his father had left them because of him. She would say it over and over again until Mike had been reduced to tears and apologies.

Also, because his mother had been consistent only in spending her entire paycheck on rocks as opposed to, say, food for her child, Mike had learned from an early age to depend on the kindness of strangers. As he got older and less cute, he had happened upon tricks like laying the attention on thick with others in order to keep food in his stomach and clothes on his back.

This template had worked out well for him, until the first time he played poker at Amherst. From what I could tell, the rush of taking money off of rich kids who had gotten everything handed to them their entire lives had been the first authentic emotion that Mike had felt since the fear and desperation of his early years. And he had been pursuing that feeling ever since. Even after he stopped winning. Even when they came for his cars and his furniture and finally his career after he had missed one too many call times in Hollywood because he was at a blackjack table in Las Vegas.

Near the end of our first night of talking, I said, "I'm going to move in with you for a few months. Do you have an air mattress?"

I guess it must have been real lonely on top of Mike's mountain of debt, because he didn't offer up a word of protest except "I don't have an air mattress, but there's still a bed in one of the guest rooms."

"No," I said, "I need an air mattress. I've got one at my place."

So Mike drove me back to my apartment in his Bentley convertible.

"You're coming in, too," I said, when he tried to remain behind in the idling car.

Again, he didn't question me, just turned off the engine and came up to my apartment with me.

Once inside, I went to the closet and took out the rolling suitcase that James had given me. A sharp pang hit me when I touched it. For a moment I was overcome with the memory of his hands on my body, touching me everywhere. I wondered what he was doing now. Did he even miss me? Or had he already moved on—it had been over three months now.

I wanted to be silent again. For a few moments, I wanted that so bad I could feel my voice leaving me. But I had work to do. I shook off the temptation, and pressed on, unzipping the suitcase and throwing a few pairs of jeans and Strokes T-shirts into it. "Make yourself useful and grab my toiletries off the sink," I said to Mike.

He immediately did as I said. "Toothpaste, too?" he asked inside the bathroom.

"No, I'll just use yours. Can you grab my tampons though? They're beside the toilet."

When he came back with an armful of toiletries and a precariously balanced box of Tampax Pearls on top of it all, my suspicions were confirmed. At the bottom of all of this, Mike needed a mama. Someone to tell him what to do and how to do it, not because she had romantic feelings for him, but because she felt responsible for him.

And though I had never had a child, I knew exactly how that felt. I decided then and there that I would be responsible for Mike from now on. Not just because I owed him atonement, but also because I was thankful to Nicky for doing the same thing for me, and this felt like a good way to pay it forward. I went back to the closet and dug out my air mattress.

MIKE WAS SURPRISED when I set up the air mattress outside his door. "Why are you sleeping here?" he asked.

"Because you're a low-down addict," I answered. "And I don't trust you not to sneak out of here and try to get your gamble on."

"You don't have to do that," he said. "I won't go anywhere."

He tried to hold my gaze as he said this, but his eyes dropped after only a few seconds.

I pointed to his room. "Go to bed."

BEFORE I LAY down, however, I surveyed the entire house and was pleased to see that he hadn't gotten rid of the gym equipment in his personal fitness room. I could just hear his addict mind reasoning that he'd be using it again, just as soon as he started winning. He had probably been promising himself for years now that he'd lose the extra weight.

The next morning, I woke him up at eight in the morning and made him run on the treadmill at seven miles an hour. I stopped him after forty-five minutes.

"I can do more," he said, panting.

I gave him what I hoped was an appropriately stern look and said, "Forty-five minutes of exercise a day. That's it. Your life from now on is about moderation. Now go stretch out and take a shower."

Mike's eyes went to the readout on the treadmill's monitor. He looked like he wanted to up the speed and ignore me, but in the end he did what I said.

———————

MIKE'S REFRIGERATOR WAS also empty, so I went out to get groceries.

When I returned, he was waiting at the door in a towel, his love handles hanging out for the world to see. "I thought you had left."

He didn't have to add "for good." His panicked eyes told me that. I added "abandonment" to the list of issues I was compiling for my informal psych evaluation.

"No, I just went to get some groceries. There's more in the car. Put on some jeans and a shirt and go get them. We don't want any paparazzi taking a picture of you in your towel."

"I don't have any paparazzi anymore," he said. He sounded glum about it.

"Don't be so sure. Get back in the house unless you want to end up in somebody's 'Look Who's Gotten Fat' feature."

Mike looked skeptical, but he went back in the house and put some clothes on.

AFTER MIKE HELPED me unload the groceries in his large kitchen, I set him up with three egg whites, turkey sausage, and a whole-wheat English muffin. It was basically a smaller version of what I used to make Nicky for breakfast when we had been together.

He looked at the food distastefully, but ate it anyway. Later that afternoon, I made him an open-face patty melt from a *Cooking Light* recipe that I had found online, and he ate that, too.

Then we talked some more until it was time for me to go to work.

I told Mike about how I had gotten used to Paul driving me into work from James's house, and that I missed having a driver, then I told him to get the keys to his car.

Nicky was surprised to see Mike Barker come through the door with me, and even more surprised when I installed him at the bar and told him to wait.

"No comps," Nicky said, when I asked if he could send the chicken piccata over for Mike. "What are you doing with him, anyway? Is this part of that atonement mess?"

"Yes. I'm allowed to eat one meal for free as a waitress, right? Can I just give it to Mike for a few nights?"

Nicky screwed up his face in that familiar way. "How many nights?"

"I don't know. Twenty, maybe more, depending on how my shifts and his therapy sessions work out."

"You're giving Mike Barker therapy?"

"Yes, Nicky. Movie stars need mental help, too. More than the rest of us sometimes."

Nicky shook his head. "It's like just when I think you can't get no crazier, you bring Mike Barker up in my restaurant, talking about therapy and asking me to feed his ass."

"Nicky, please. Mike needs this. I need this—"

Nicky cut me off. "Stop begging. I taught you better than that. I'll send over the chicken piccata, but only because it's a slow night, and this shit is sort of amusing. Does Chloe know he's here?"

"Davie!" Chloe said behind us.

I turned around to see Chloe standing there in her evening gown, her hands bunched up like she was fixing to hit somebody.

"What is he doing here?" she demanded.

"Atonement. Same as you," I told her straight up.

Chloe wrinkled her pretty little forehead, she was so angry. "He got everything he deserved."

"No, he didn't, Chloe, and you know it. But he does owe you an apology. So come on, Mike."

Mike blinked, surprised. "You want me to apologize?"

"No, I want you to start taking responsibility for your actions. I hurt you. I'm sorry about that. And you hurt Chloe, so tell her."

"But I only hurt her because you bet me."

I shook my head. "C'mon, little boy. You can't possibly believe that."

Mike's mouth opened and closed a few times, but finally he hung his head and said, "Chloe, I'm sorry, okay?"

Nicky and I looked at Chloe for her answer.

"Does he even know what he's apologizing for?" Chloe asked.

"Sure he does," I said. "Mike, tell her you're sorry for using her, because you know that was wrong. And don't act. Tell her for real."

Mike drummed his fingers on the bar and rocked back and forth a few times before saying, "Chloe, listen. I'm a user. I've always been a user. And I'm sorry I used you, okay?"

Chloe pursed her lips. "Apology not accepted."

She then flounced away. To tell you the truth, I was real proud of both of them. I didn't think Mike had it in him to give an actual heartfelt apology, and I definitely didn't think Chloe had it in her to throw it back in his face.

Nicky cackled and waved down a passing waiter. "Get this man a chicken piccata on the house," he said to the waiter. He pointed to Mike. "You real entertaining."


SO THAT'S HOW it went with Mike and me. We developed a nice little routine that first week, with me getting him up to exercise for forty-five minutes every morning, then making him breakfast and eventually lunch, with a lot of talking in between.

On the eighth day, I asked him for his phone.

"What do you need my phone for?" he asked as he handed me his BlackBerry.

I scrolled through his contacts until I came to a name that didn't look like it belonged to an actor. "Who's Gerald Epstein?"

"He's my agent."

I pushed the button wheel and raised the BlackBerry to my ear.

Mike's eyes widened. "Are you calling my agent?"

"Gerald Epstein's office," said a chirpy woman's voice on the other end of the phone. She sounded blond.

"Why are you calling my agent?" Mike asked.

I held up a finger for quiet. "Hello," I said to the assistant. "This is Mike Barker's mama, calling on behalf of Mike. May I speak to Mr. Epstein."

"Oh, I'm sorry, Mrs. Barker. Mr. Epstein isn't available."

I waited for her to offer to take a message. But that seemed to be all she had to say on the matter.

Which made it much easier for me to say, "Well, could you pass on a message, then? Please tell him that Mike will no longer be needing his services, and he's fired."

"What?" The assistant's voice faltered. She now sounded confused.

"Thank you," I said, and hung up.

Mike looked fixed to have a heart attack. "You just fired my agent," he nearly yelled. Like many actors with good training, he overenunciated when he got angry. "You can't do that."

"When's the last time Gerald called you?"

Mike's eyes went skyward in an effort to remember.

"If it was that long ago, you need new representation," I said.

Then I scrolled down the list for the next business-sounding name.

It only took me about twenty minutes to fire his accountant, his manager, his personal trainer, and his lawyer. I also told the C-list TV actress he was seeing that Mike was taking a sabbatical from dating.

"Really?" she said. "But I just booked *Dancing with the Stars,* and I told them that Mike Barker would be in the audience. The producers are going to be so mad."

The sad thing was that she was dead serious. "Sorry," I said. "Doctor's orders."

"Well, tell Mikey to call me after he gets done with his sabbatical or whatever. Hopefully I won't be eliminated yet."

"I'm doing you a whole bunch of favors," I said when I got off the phone with her.

By the time I was done, Mike was pacing back and forth, his face twisted up in worry and frustration. I wasn't sure if he completely understood why I was doing what I was doing, but he never once tried to grab the phone from me. I think it might have given him a moment of pause to realize that none of these people called me out on who I said I was, even though Mike's mother had died eleven years ago.

———————

OVER THE NEXT week, we began replacing all the people he had fired. I let Mike do his bullshit mirroring and attention thing—it was almost an asset at this point—because it allowed the potential team members we talked with to self-identify as the same kind of people who would take advantage of Mike's insecurities and see him as a reflection of themselves, as opposed to the man who was paying their salary.

For both his new agent and manager, I told him to choose the mean-ass bulldogs, the ones that talked cold hard money and career comeback in between the usual compliments—because that's what he needed at this point. Also, I wanted to make sure that his next manager would be the kind of guy who would hunt Mike down in Vegas, tie him up, and put his gambling-addict ass on a plane, if it meant getting his fifteen percent.

I am proud to say that by the end of the first week of meetings, I stopped having to guide Mike's decisions. His new personal trainer, accountant, and lawyer were all business, all the time. And they all knew that his mama was dead.

# TWENTY-SEVEN

RUSSELL CALLED ME TWO WEEKS AFTER we replaced Mike's entire team.

"Here's what I want to know, did you really think I wasn't going to find out?"

I was confused. It didn't sound like Russell was joking, but I didn't know why else he would come at me this way, right off the bat.

"Find out what?" I asked.

"About your mother and Congressman Farrell. You know, the father of your ex-boyfriend."

My heart seized, just like it had in high school when I had seen Veronica Farrell standing outside our window. I went straight to begging. "Russell, please don't. You have no idea how many people this would hurt. I need you to do me this favor."

"No more favors, Davie. I've done a lot for you already and you wasn't forthcoming, so no more favors."

I couldn't believe him. The nerve. "You're acting like I'm all obligated to leak the worst details of my life."

"And you've always acted like I'm here to leak whatever you want."

I wanted to say that wasn't true, but of course it was.

I had thought I had felt the worst I could ever feel about my heartbreak campaign during the Driveway Dump, but now on the phone with Russell, I couldn't have regretted my actions more. My tongue felt like metal in my mouth as the repercussions of my spree of dirty deeds kept on sending out wave after wave of consequences.

"What do you care about Congressman Farrell, anyway?" I asked. "He's not exactly Britney Spears."

"Politicians are big game this season. That 'wide-stance' senator in Idaho, trolling for gay sex in the bathroom, moved a bunch of copy, so now we're doing a big exposé on shady politicians from all over, and your congressman is a sidebar. You know, your mother wasn't the first or the last. Apparently he was getting it on with his campaign manager, too, and she's talking to us. He dumped her when she started asking about a ring. Women scorned—half our sources."

"Did you get a quote from Cora, too?"

"No. I called, but she just cussed me out. Your mom's mean."

Understatement, but I tried again. "If it's just a sidebar, then why print it at all?"

"Because it's the perfect sidebar for the news cycle, and sometimes perfect is just as good as big." A few beats. "Okay, that's not exactly true. Big is still better than perfect. So unless you've got something big I can swap out . . ." He trailed off to let me pick up what he was putting down.

But I had no idea what he was talking about. "Big like what?" I asked.

"Well, I heard a rumor that you were living with Mike Barker now and that his mother just fired his entire team—only thing is, Mike's mother is dead. And the last time I talked to you, you were all tore up over James Farrell."

Wow. So I guess this is where he had been going with this from the get-go. Threaten to publish the Congressman Farrell story, and then offer to kill it in exchange for another Mike Barker leak.

"So you're saying that you won't publish the Congressman Farrell story if I source another Mike Barker story?"

Russell let a few seconds of premeditated silence pass. Then came back with "Yeah, I guess I could do that. If the Mike Barker story is big enough, I can kill the other thing—I mean, since we go so far back and all."

The thing was, I had caught Mike trying to step over my sleeping body two nights ago. When I woke up and caught him, he had begged me to let him go to the Hustler Casino, which was only a half-hour drive at that time of night.

"I just need a game. I just need to get my head straight—"

I slapped him hard across the face, like I was Cora. "If you have to gamble every time you get to feeling a little bad, then you're not ever going to get your shit back."

He cupped his cheek and pushed past me. "Bitch, don't you ever hit me again."

"Yes, Mike," I said. "Get angry. Call me names. I don't care. That's healthier than walking out that door."

He kept on going until I yelled, "I won't be here when you get back. Even if you win tonight you'll lose the only person who truly cares whether you live or die right now."

Mike stopped. Seconds ticked by as he just stood there at the top of the stairs. Then he turned around and headed back to his room. "Don't hit me again," he warned, glaring as he passed by me.

"I'll definitely hit you again. I'll do whatever it takes," I said.

He slammed the door behind him.

Really close call. And a smear article now would send him right over the edge.

But James was already so mad at me. What would he think of me after an article came out with Russell's byline? He wasn't a stickler for details, as we all know by now, but I was more than sure that Veronica would point out to him that this was same guy who had broken the Corey Mays, Mike Barker, and Erica London stories under my direction. She was real helpful like that.

Well, dang. Rock and a hard place didn't even half describe this situation.

Russell and I would no longer be friends after this. I knew that. And I think he did, too.

But this wasn't the Russell I used to know, anyway. He was no longer the kind, pudgy waiter with screenwriter dreams and a penchant for alternative bands that I had never heard of. That Russell had been replaced by a gossip writer who would do anything to get the story.

I fingered my Strokes T-Shirt and took a moment to grieve the boy I used to know, before giving him my decision.

AFTER I GOT off the phone with Russell, I went to find Mike in the TV room, where he was watching one of his old movies. A large residual check had come in a few days ago, and Mike had gotten a new flat-screen TV after paying down a lot of his debt. It was a tremendous first step, because the old Mike had been using his residual checks to feed his gambling habit for a while now.

"What's up?" he said, when I came into the room. "I'm just watching the movie that bought this TV."

"Nice," I said, sitting on the couch beside him. "I need you to pause it though."

Mike's face immediately went into worried mode. "Are you still mad at me about the other night? Are you leaving?"

"No," I said. "As long as you stay away from the tables, I'm not leaving until you don't need me anymore. I promise you that."

Mike smiled, more grateful than a grown man should be for that vow. At times like this, I found it hard to believe that he had dumped Tammy Farrell so callously. Then again, she loved him, so he dumped her before she could dump him. It had probably seemed perfectly logical in his traumatized mind back then. It probably still did, which was why I was going to advise Mike to take at least a year before he got involved in another serious relationship—even if that last girlfriend of his wanted him to make a cameo on *Dancing with the Stars*.

"But, Mike, I've got to talk with you about something. . . ."

I told him what was going on with the Congressman Farrell story, and also about Russell hitting me with his horrible-ass ultimatum.

After I finished, he nodded, like he completely understood the situation. "Davie, you've more than made up for selling me out to *Celeb Weekly*. Don't worry about it."

I shook my head. "See, this is why we still have a lot of work to do. I chose you, Mike."

I don't think he could have been more surprised if I up and slapped him again. "What? Why?"

"Because you may have done some wrong things and you may have made some bad decisions, but you're a good man. You are. And you deserve my loyalty."

Mike didn't say anything, just sniffed. And then he started crying. I drew him into my arms and wondered if I just had a talent for making grown men cry.

A WEEK LATER, Mike started spending the nights I was at work sitting at Nicky's bar and "gambling on good scripts"—which was our inside joke for choosing a comeback project.

Now that we had gotten the right team in place, and the word had gotten out about his "radical rehab," scripts and calls had begun trickling in. Also, I hadn't had to talk him out of a Vegas trip ever since the Big Decision, which meant I was sleeping better on the air mattress outside his room.

Times were suddenly good again. But I think I was most grateful because helping Mike un-fuck-up his life kept me 24/7 busy. I only had time to be sad about James at night before I went to sleep and in the morning. The disappointment of waking up without James was crushing at times, but this terrible emptiness couldn't last forever. I had to keep on living. And I had to make things up to Mike. That's how I convinced myself to get out of bed most mornings.

I WAS MAKING Mike breakfast a couple of weeks after the Big Decision when he came into the kitchen, talking on his BlackBerry.

"Yeah," he said, "yeah, you know I totally agree on that point, but you should probably talk with her about that."

He extended the phone toward me.

"Who is it?" I whispered.

"Hugh Phillips's assistant."

"Hugh Phillips? You mean *the* Hugh Phillips?"

Now the last time I checked, Hugh Phillips was the guy who had directed Mike in a string of blockbuster summer action flicks, back when Mike was still bringing his A-game to even the dimmest material.

From what Mike had told me, they had been good friends, until Mike started taking unsanctioned time off from filming because he couldn't leave the tables in Vegas.

Hugh had ended up having to replace him in the last movie they tried to do together, but the chemistry hadn't been the same and the movie had pretty much flopped.

I had encouraged Mike to reach out to Hugh and apologize, which he had done a few days ago, but . . .

"Why does Hugh Phillips's assistant want to talk with me?" I asked.

"Just talk to her," he said, extending the BlackBerry again.

"I'm cooking." I pointed my wooden spatula at his tomato, goat cheese, spinach, and egg-white scramble.

"I got this." He pressed the phone into my hand, then nudged me aside and took the spatula from me, so that he could finish his own eggs.

Now I had never seen Mike volunteer to make his own food. During one of our sessions, he said with some pride in his voice that even when he didn't have a dime to his name, he had successfully begged for meals, not groceries.

So seeing him scrambling those eggs got me convinced that this must be important.

I put his fancy cell phone to my ear. "Hi, this is Davie," I said.

"Hello, Davie, this is Martha," said a woman with a crisp and efficient English accent. "I'm calling on behalf of Hugh Phillips."

"Yes, so I've been told. What's up?"

"Well, Hugh wishes to employ your services."

"My services? Um, I don't do the Soul BunnyGrams anymore."

"I'm not quite sure what that is," she said. "But Mr. Phillips would like to use you in the same capacity as Mike Barker."

"Oh, you mean he wants me to un-fuck-up his life?"

A pause. Then: "Yes, I suppose you could express it that way. Apparently Mike has been singing your praises and says that you're best guru he's ever had. Hugh is intrigued."

I looked at Mike, who was transferring his scramble onto a plate next to the turkey sausage I had already made. He just grinned at me.

"Oh, I see. Well, I think Mike might have really exaggerated my status. I'm not a real guru or life coach or anything."

"I understand that your services are discreet and exclusive," Martha said. "Please let us know what would need to be done to get Hugh on your calendar."

"Um, seriously, I'm not a real therapist. I don't even have a master's."

"Yes, I understand, full disclosure," she said. She was disturbingly okay with my lack of credentials. "When is your next availability?"

"Well, I think I have about one more month to go with Mike, then I guess I could, um, meet with Mr. Phillips."

"Please call him Hugh. And how much do you charge for the initial meeting?"

Mike held up two fingers. "Two?" I said, confused. He really expected me to charge two hundred dollars, just for meeting with a guy? Was he out of his mind?

"Two thousand it is. I'll call in a month to schedule the meeting, and I'll have a check along with a nondisclosure contract for you to sign when you come up to the house."

I stood there frozen. Did she say two thousand dollars?

"Hello? Hello? Have we lost the connection?"

"No," I somehow managed to croak out. "I look forward to setting up the meeting next month."

"Yes, I'll talk to you then. Thank you."

Martha hung up.

I stood there, frozen, unable to form words. Two thousand was almost what I made in a month at Nicky's.

Mike sat me down on one of the kitchen island's bar stools.

He then took his BlackBerry out of my hand and replaced it with a glass of water. "So I guess I got to stay serious about getting over this gambling problem," he said, "because you're already getting booked up, girl."

BUT OF COURSE, all these glad tidings couldn't last forever. The *Celeb Weekly* with the Congressman Farrell article hit the newsstands the following Wednesday.

I know it was Wednesday, not because I went out and bought the issue, but because Veronica Farrell showed up at the club that very same night and tried to kill me.

# TWENTY-EIGHT

IT WAS JUST BEFORE OPENING ON the second Wednesday of January 2008, and I was hanging out with Chloe in her dressing room, as I usually did before my shift started. I'll never forget it, because Chloe was putting on her makeup in front of the large vanity, and we were talking about whether she could cut her hair even shorter and more pixieish without Nicky having a heart attack. Then suddenly there were three faces in the mirror: mine, Chloe's, and Veronica Farrell's.

Now, I have heard guys refer to being tipped off about a beautiful woman's mental instability by something they called "the crazy eyes." I had always believed this notion to be somewhat fictional. Kind of like the male concept of "PMSing"—which I personally thought could be better identified as "the one time of the month when women saw shit clearly."

But seeing Veronica in that mirror, I believed—clearly and avowedly for the first time—that there was such a thing as "the crazy eyes."

In fact, after that I would forever call them Veronica Farrell in the Mirror Eyes—but only Chloe would get the joke.

And it took her a very long time after what happened next to be able to laugh at the reference.

"Hi, Veronica. What are you doing here?" The reason I got that far in my greeting is because it took me a while to fully register that she was grabbing me by my hair and pulling me out of my chair.

Even when Chloe screamed, "Oh my God!" I wasn't fully getting it. It just seemed so out of the character from the Veronica that I knew. Veronica Farrell didn't show up in my old dressing room, unannounced, with crazy eyes. Veronica Farrell wouldn't lower herself to snatch a girl by her Afro. Veronica Farrell was certainly above throwing me to the ground and climbing on top of me.

Even when I saw her fist coming toward my eye with the sharp end of a metal nail file winking from inside of it, I still found it all just very hard to process.

Fortunately that didn't stop me from catching her wrist about an inch from my eye and asking, "Are you serious?"

As it turned out, she was. She redoubled her efforts and pressed the nail file closer and closer to my eye.

Now, I should probably tell you that I had been chewing on the problem of Veronica Farrell, for a couple of months at that point. I still hadn't been able to devise a scenario in which I could atone to Veronica for what I had done to her re the Chloe and Corey Incident. I had been trying to determine what Veronica might need, which was a tricky business with regular people, but even worse with Veronica because she was rich and beautiful and, from what I could tell, actually liked being mean. There didn't seem to be anything that she needed, much less anything that I could give her as an act of atonement.

But while I was keeping that metal file out of my eye, the answer to what I had previously thought might be an impossible question shone inside the room pretty damn clear and bright: what Veronica Farrell *needed* was a fucking beat-down.

"I'm getting Nicky!" Chloe ran out to get help, but that wasn't necessary. Veronica might have the crazy eyes, but I was crazy and poor. And in a street fight, poor and crazy beats down rich and crazy every time. Believe that.

I knocked Veronica's hand away from my eye and began pushing her off me. She was so caught off guard by my actually fighting back that she dropped the nail file and it went skittering across the floor. I took advantage of her surprise, bucked up, and flipped us over, so that now it was me crouched on top of her.

Then I raised myself up and put my ugly fist in her pretty face. And when I drew my fist back up, her face was bloody. I have never felt as satisfied to my very gut as I did then. I could feel the delicious rage that I had been keeping in check for so long course through my veins as I brought my fist down again and again.

But then there were hands biting into my arms and pulling me up. So I used my feet. I kicked out in angry arcs and I even managed to get Veronica in the ribs a couple of times before Leon's voice broke through my rage-induced haze.

"C'mon, girl, stop it," he said.

He held me back and Nicky bent down over Veronica. "Goddamn it, it looks like you broke her nose. Now I'm going to have to take her to the hospital. Leon, get Davie outta here."

The rage had drained away, and I was left mesmerized by the sight of Veronica on the floor. Blood was streaming out of her nose and running down her face. And her eyes were dazed and unfocused.

"No," I said, "I want to stay."

But Nicky wasn't having it. "Leon," he barked. "Take her up to her apartment and keep her there. I'll take this one out the back door."

Leon pulled me out of the dressing room before I could protest again. The last thing I saw was Chloe puking into a waste basket before Nicky kicked the door closed.


LEON ENDED UP depositing me in my apartment, which smelled a little stale from disuse, since I had been staying at Mike's for over a month now. "What do you want me to tell the Puppy?" he asked.

The Puppy is what everyone at the restaurant had taken to calling Mike, because he followed me around everywhere.

"Tell him I won't be working tonight, and I need a ride back to his house. I'll meet him down in front of the club, so that we don't run into Nicky taking Veronica out."

Leon hesitated, torn between following Nicky's command to the letter and knowing that he still had a security detail to get back to downstairs at the club. Babysitting me was definitely outside his job parameters.

After some more reasonable arguing on my part, he caved and called down to the head waiter, Tyrone, who went and got Mike at the bar. But before we left the apartment to meet Mike in the parking lot, Leon made me put a jacket on over my waiter's uniform. That's when I realized that there was now blood all over my white shirt.

NICKY CALLED, SOUNDING tired, just as Mike and I were walking in the door.

"So you broke her nose and bruised her ribs."

"I'm sorry," I said.

"Yeah, well . . ." he answered. "It could have been worse. You could have killed her, and you would've maybe gotten away with it, too, since according to Chloe you messed her up in self-defense. Plus I got her on trespassing for sure. Do you know that bitch actually broke the lock on the back door to the club? I'm going to have to replace it."

That made me smile. "Nicky, you sound a whole lot more upset about having to spend money on a new lock than about me nearly losing my eye," I said.

Sadly, I don't think he was joking when he answered, "Them locks ain't cheap."

"You should make Veronica pay for it then."

"Trust me, that's exactly what I'm going to make Miss Priss do—as soon as she get done with the nose doctor."

AFTER I HUNG up with Nicky, I changed out of my uniform into a Strokes T-shirt and jeans. Then I came back downstairs and asked Mike if he had gotten a chance to eat at the club.

"I was almost finished when Tyrone came to get me," Mike answered. "I'm pretty full."

"Good," I said. "Because I need to go out for a while. But I'll be back later tonight." I leveled him with my best mama stare. "I'm going to trust you here alone, because I know that you're stronger than your addiction."

Mike nodded. For once he didn't look stricken when I said I was going to have to leave him for a little bit.

TWENTY MINUTES LATER, I was idling outside of James's gate in my Toyota.

My arm felt heavy as I reached out to push the intercom button. Mostly because I had no idea how he was reacting to our current run in *Celeb Weekly*. For all I knew, he, too, would try to stab my eye out with a nail file upon seeing me. Maybe I just had that effect on the Farrells.

I pushed the intercom button anyway.

The voice that answered sounded raspy and mucus-filled at the same time, like Mildred or Paul had a cold. "Hello?"

"Hi, this is . . . Davie," I said into the speaker. "I know this is bad, me coming here, especially after the *Celeb Weekly* article, but I've got some important information about James's sister."

I waited. But no answer came. "It's about Veronica. I didn't want to tell him over the phone," I said.

Still no answer, but then a long electronic buzz cleared the silence and the two gates swung open.

I drove my old car through the gate and put it in park in front of the house. But as I walked up to the door, all the words that I had composed in my head on the way over to explain why I had put his sister in the hospital flew out of my head. I decided to concentrate instead on not passing out on his front steps from pure dread.

I could hear footsteps on the other side of the door, and I braced myself for either Paul or Mildred to answer it.

But it was Tammy Farrell who opened the door. "Tammy?"

"What's wrong with my sister?" She sniffled. Her nose was red, and it sounded like she had a cold. I realized that she must have been the one who had answered the intercom and let me in.

"Where's James?" I asked.

"He . . . left." She said this in such a way that I didn't think she was talking about him going out to a party.

"Do you know when he'll be back?"

"No." Tammy clamped, then unclamped her lips. "He moved to New York. And he took Mildred and Paul with him."

"So now both he and Veronica are going to represent the Farrell brand in New York?"

"No," Tammy said again. Her voice was clipped, like she was trying to figure out how much she wanted to tell me. "He presented a new line of men's products to the company. It got approved, and now he's launching the line from New York. Veronica and I moved in here, and he took over our apartment in SoHo. In fact, I got this cold on the plane coming here from New York."

She sniffled. I could tell that Tammy was still trying to wrap her head around me being here and asking her these questions. But I couldn't help the fierce pride that swelled in me when she told me about James getting his own line approved. "Good for him," I said, my voice soft.

Tammy sneezed. Then more time passed and I knew that I had to tell her about Veronica.

I thought to ask to come in, but I didn't want to prolong it anymore. So I just said, "Veronica came down to the club, and she tried to stab my eye out with a nail file. We ended up fighting and now she's in the hospital. With a broken nose."

Tammy's mouth dropped open. "Oh my God, I was afraid she might do something like this. You broke her nose? Are they going to be able to fix it without plastic surgery?"

"Wait a minute." I held up my hand. "You knew she was thinking about stabbing me?"

"She was really angry after she read that *Celeb Weekly* article. She loves Daddy so much. And she said some things." Tammy stopped and sneezed four times in a row. Then she held up a well-manicured hand. "Wait here while I get my purse."

But I followed her back into the house. "She said some things? Why didn't you warn me?"

"Because I didn't think that she'd actually do it. That would be psy—"

She broke off and looked away from me, guiltily.

"Psycho," I finished for her. "That would prove that she was just as big of a psycho as me, right?"

Tammy's eyes went all simpery. "You have to understand . . ."

"No, Tammy, I don't have to understand anything. She tried to stab me in the eye."

Tammy picked up her purse off a side table and took out some Kleenex, which she held to her dripping nose with a miserable look on her face. She was half a foot taller than me, but at that moment she looked like a little girl. "You shouldn't have given that reporter the story about our dad. That was wrong."

"Tammy, I didn't give him anything. He targeted your dad as part of the larger exposé on his own. I tried to get him not to run it, but I couldn't convince him. Now believe it or not, I'm real sorry that you and your mom had to find out this way, but that doesn't mean Veronica can come up to me where I work and try to stab out my eye. You get that, right?"

Tammy sniffled again. "You're not going to sue, are you?"

I wanted to say, *Yes! Yes, I am going to sue your bitch of a sister, just to prove that I'm not the only crazy person in this story.*

But then I remembered that Tammy's name was still not crossed off on my atonement list. "Okay," I said. "If I don't sue your sister, can you and me call it even on the Mike Barker thing?"

Tammy was nodding before I even finished the question. "Yes, we're even. Just please don't make this any uglier than it already is."

I tried not to calculate just how much money I was giving up by not suing Veronica Farrell and said, "Fine" through gritted teeth.

Tammy was suddenly all smiles again, back to her usual sunny cheerleader. "Also, could you drive me to the hospital? I'm all hopped up on cough medicine. We can take my car."

She pressed her keys, which had a BMW fob on the ring, into my hand. I hadn't even seen her take them out of her purse. Before I could say no, though, she was already headed toward the door.

Son of a . . .

I HADN'T BEEN to a hospital in a while. The insurance that I had at Nicky's came with such a high emergency room co-pay that I wouldn't have ever gone to the ER for myself unless one of my limbs was already halfway off. And my friends must be pretty healthy and lucky, because a trip with flowers and trembling smiles hadn't been required of me yet.

So I couldn't be sure if hospitals had changed from the cold antiseptic affairs that I was used to seeing on shows like *ER*, or if the rich just get taken to a lot nicer digs. But if there hadn't been several signs, assuring me that the tall and sprawling structure was a hospital, and not a resort, I might have passed it right up.

"Wow," I said as we pulled into the parking structure. "This is like the nicest hospital I've ever seen."

"Do you know what room number she's in?" Tammy asked.

"No, but you can ask at the front desk, or do they call it a concierge in places like this?"

Tammy pulled out her Farrell Girl compact and started brushing light powder over her red nose. "No, it's a front desk."

I watched her trying to mask the red on her poor abused nose. "You've got a cold, and Veronica's in the hospital. Do you really think she's going to care if your skin doesn't look flawless?"

Tammy answered with a thin, embarrassed smile and kept on buffing her nose down with powder. "You don't know Veronica."

NICKY AND VERONICA were sitting next to each other on the edge of the bed when we walked in, and I don't think it unfair to say that she looked like shit.

Her eyes weren't exactly black, but there was ugly purple bruising around one, and the other was swollen shut.

Her top lip was also swollen, and her nose was packed with gauze. She looked so bad, Tammy whispered, "Jesus," beside me.

I had one terrible second of pride that I, Davie Jones, had managed to mess up the face of the most beautiful woman I had ever seen. Then I shoved it down into the darkest corner of my heart where it belonged and said, "I'm sorry."

Her one unswollen eye glinted amid the purple bruise, but other than that she didn't respond.

That's when I noticed something that I should've spotted from the second I walked in. She was holding Nicky's hand in her lap. No, not just holding it. Squeezing it.

# TWENTY-NINE

I FOUND OUT WHAT WENT DOWN later while driving back to the club with Nicky.

Apparently it had all started while he and Veronica had been waiting for the nose doctor, Nicky standing near the window, she sitting straight-backed on the bed.

It had not occurred to Nicky to offer to call her family to wait with her. He wasn't that kind of thoughtful. And she had just tried to put out his best friend's eye.

Really, he had more been wanting to talk with her about the money for the lock than actually waiting with her. And as was his habit when he could see that somebody was at their lowest point, he made a deeply unhelpful observation, "I thought Davie was crazy, but you is a straight mess, ain't you?"

Veronica ignored him, but Nicky kept on, "Look at you. You went in to poke out her eye, and now you the one in the hospital."

Veronica continued to ignore him. "You're kind of like Davie," Nicky said at this point. "She like to pretend she don't hear shit when it's the truth, too."

An unfair comparison, I think, since Veronica actively ignored Nicky because she didn't like what he was saying, while I actively ignored Nicky because letting his cutting remarks slide over me was paramount to the maintenance of our friendship.

But back to Veronica. Nicky couldn't stop there, of course. Because he was Nicky, he had to keep on talking. "All this crazy shit over something neither of you have control over. It ain't Davie's fault your daddy dicked around with her mama. And it ain't your fault, either."

Apparently this was the moment Veronica stopped ignoring him, because when Nicky looked from the window to her, he said her face was all screwed up, like she had swallowed something nasty. At first Nicky thought her nose was hurting her, but then he realized . . .

She was trying not to cry.

He walked over to the bed and told her it straight again. "It wasn't nobody's fault but your old man's. He acted on his own, you didn't have nothing to do with it."

Nicky said she started wheezing then. And he said, "You'd really rather hyperventilate than cry? Really?"

And she said, "I'd rather die than . . ." But she couldn't finish the sentence, because the tears start spilling out, even though her eyes were squeezed shut against them.

She went after them with such vicious swipes of her palms that Nicky told me, "I had to hold her hands down to keep her from hurting herself. Then the doctor came in, and he was acting like he seen girls crying all the time. Just kept saying that the break wasn't that bad, and she'd feel better after he reset it and the swelling went down.

"Then he put her nose back where it used to be, and there was this squishing, cracking sound. You ain't never heard nothing like it, Davie. It looked like it hurt like hell. But I couldn't tell, because she was steady weeping over that stuff with her old man. Then he stuffed her nose with gauze, and asked her if she needed anything else. Let me tell you, he was nicer than any doctor I've ever encountered, I guess because she's rich or whatever. But she just said, 'Get out.' So he left and we sat there, and she kept on crying."

According to Nicky, she didn't get herself together until about ten minutes before Tammy and me came in. And somewhere in the middle of all that crying, he told her that she had to go out to dinner with him to pay him back for the lock she had broken.

I was most surprised about that last detail. Until that point, I had never known that Nicky had so much romance in him.

I THOUGHT THEIR thing would fizzle out soon enough. He had caught Veronica after her father had been exposed as a serial cheater and after she tried to stab my eye out with a nail file—obviously she was in a very vulnerable state. One date and that would be it, I figured.

But that wasn't how it worked out. They had one date, then two, then suddenly Veronica started showing up at the club all the time. She was real good at ignoring me, but she always had a smile and a hello for Nicky. Then the next thing I knew, months had passed, and he was calling her his woman in conversations. It went downhill that fast.

Over time, I could see the logic of it, though. They were cut from the same cloth: mean as the day was long, insensitive as hell, fiercely protective of those that they loved. I had never imagined losing my Duckie to the meanest girl in school, but at the end of the day, they made each other happy.

Plus, knowing what I did about the both of them, I wouldn't have wished those two on anybody but each other.

NICKY AND VERONICA'S developing romance mostly just made me miss James even more. The end of a relationship is a sort of grief for the dead, I suppose, and over the next few months, I often found myself close to tears at inconvenient and unexpected times. Like when I was walking Venice Beach Promenade with Chloe. The uneven display of talent that is the Sunday drum circle drifted up from the beach to the stand where we had stopped to look at some cheap sunglasses.

"What's wrong?" Chloe asked when I froze while trying on a pair of oversized green shades.

"I don't think I like this color," I said. That was a lie. I loved the lime green of the frames, but I still hadn't gotten to a place where I could talk about my problems getting over James. So I lied to Chloe and put the sunglasses back.

Another time was when I was at Trader Joe's. The checkout clerk looked nothing like James, but it was James I was reminded of when he said, "Have a nice day," and it sounded sincere.

Toward the middle of our relationship, James had taken to kissing me on top of my head whenever we parted in the mornings and demanding that I "have a nice day" before he let me go. Then the next time we would meet, usually later that night, the first thing he would ask me was "Well, did you have a nice day?"

Back during the time that I was actually with James, when I had imagined losing him, I had always thought it would be the intimacy that I would miss the most. I thought my body would burn for him at night, and that I would long for the feel of his arms wrapped around me. To be sure, those things were a problem.

But what I hadn't counted on was how much remembering our good times together would hurt. That's the thing people never warn you about with breakups. It's the good times that really get you. In fact, they hurt worse than the bad times.

Sometimes I woke up from dreams in which James and me were still together, and cried when I remembered that we had broken up under the worst of circumstances. After those dreams I was always glad that James had moved to New York. If he hadn't, I just know I would've driven over to Los Feliz and begged him to take me back. His moving allowed me to hang on to my last scrap of dignity where he was concerned, and for that I was grateful.

Most of the time.


IN LATE JUNE, I was taking a drink order from a table of Japanese businessmen when Nicky tapped me on the shoulder and said, "Watch this."

That's all the warning I got before he climbed up onstage and took the mic. Chloe and the rest of the band were on break, so the stage was empty, but the mic was still live.

"I need your attention up here," he said to the audience. "I'm about to do something I never thought I'd do in a million years."

"This man who?" asked the Japanese businessman closest to me.

"He's the owner of this place," I said, handing him his Midori sour.

"Veronica Farrell, are you listening? Because this is about you."

Everybody in the club looked around for this "Veronica Farrell," including me. I knew she had to be here somewhere. Against all indication of her personality, over the past six months she had proven herself to be a serious nester. She'd show up at the club every evening like clockwork and eat dinner with Nicky, before heading out to whatever event she had to represent Farrell Cosmetics at. Then she'd come right back to the club and go home with Nicky.

I don't think either of them felt comfortable with Nicky spending the night at James's house yet. In my higher self-esteem moments, I liked to believe it was because they could still feel the residual energy from James's and my relationship inside the house. Our short time together had been that powerful. But it was probably just because Tammy was living there, too.

Anyway, I spotted Veronica at a table toward the middle of the room. I couldn't really see her face, but then Nicky pointed at her and said, "Can we get some light on that woman right there?"

A spotlight turned on her, and I could see from her expression that she was just as confused as the rest of us. "What's this about?" she asked with that hard maple syrup tone of hers. Her voice was muffled, since unlike Nicky, she didn't have a mic.

"What do you think it's about?" Nicky asked like she should already know. "I'm asking you to marry me."

My mouth dropped open. Five years. I had been with Nicky for five years. I had thought that he didn't want to get married to anybody, ever. But apparently he just hadn't wanted to get married to me. Well, damn. I was kind of happy that I was still contending with the pain of losing James, or this whole scene would have hurt me a lot more than it did.

As it was, every waiter stopped serving, and everybody in the room turned to see what Veronica would say to Nicky's proposal.

She stood up. "You're asking me, Veronica Farrell of *the* Farrells, to marry you, Nicky Connell, nobody?" She shook her head like she couldn't quite fathom what had made Nicky decide to do this.

But he just shrugged and said, "Yeah. I got a ring, too." He brought out a box and flipped open the lid with his thumb to reveal a simple vintage engagement ring.

Veronica walked up to the edge of the stage. "You know what. You're really presumptuous, Nicky. Really presumptuous."

They stared each other down. Him above her onstage, and her below him on the ground. Everything was beyond quiet. Nicky and Veronica weren't moving. And neither was anybody else in the restaurant. We were all waiting to see who would win the staring contest.

But in the end, Nicky was the first to blink. "Fine. I'll sign a prenup," he said.

"My terms?" Veronica pressed.

"Fine," Nicky agreed, his jaw tight. "But only if the next and only word out of your mouth is 'yes.'"

Veronica's face lit up with a smile so big and wide, for a second I wondered if she hadn't been bodysnatched. I had never seen Veronica Farrell truly smile, especially not like that.

"Yes!" she said. And can you believe she actually had the gall to sound all excited—like she hadn't just made the man agree in public to a prenup before she gave her answer?

But Nicky didn't care about that. He pulled her up onstage into his thick tree-trunk arms, and they kissed while everybody else applauded.

Chloe took the stage about ten minutes later. "I'm sorry," she said to the audience. "I'm not going be able to put on a show as good as the one you just got. But I'll try my best."

I SUPPOSE THAT I should have been insulted that Veronica's family took to Nicky in a way that they had never taken to me. But in all fairness, he had never lied to Veronica about attending high school with her. Plus, with the club and all the rental property he had bought in Inglewood back during the housing slump after the Los Angeles riots, he was pretty well off. Not Farrell millions or anything, but he was definitely doing better than most. And a self-made man was pretty hard to resist.

And if his "tell it like it is" accent was a little off-putting, at least they had the comfort of knowing it was also put-on. Contrary to the way he talked at the club, Veronica had probably found out, like I had, that his parents were actually both college professors. And the few times we had visited with them, Nicky had spoken English like he was straight off an Ivy League campus, with dulcet tones that I wasn't even aware he was capable of—though I had a feeling that voice would make a repeat performance at the wedding.

Anyway, Nicky's being rich enough, successful, and well-educated, plus the unexpected wonder of seeing Veronica in love (I think in their secret heart of hearts they had given up on that ever happening) was enough to make them welcome Nicky to the family with open arms.

I was mighty tempted to ask him if Veronica had sicced a detective on him the way she had on me, but Nicky was happy, so I kept my thoughts on his fiancée to myself.

I was checking my mail a few weeks later, after Veronica said yes, and found an invitation to their engagement party.

Opening the envelope reminded me of the last invitation I had received from Veronica all those years ago in high school. And for a hysterical moment, I wondered if this one was a fake, too. Maybe I would arrive at the downtown Standard Hotel where they were throwing the party, only to find Veronica and her friends on the colonial porch, laughing at me.

But those were just crazy thoughts. The Standard didn't have a colonial porch. And unlike the Farrell party invite, this was one invitation that I didn't plan to accept.

A few minutes later, I hand-delivered my RSVP card to Nicky in his office.

He didn't argue when I dropped it on his desk, with the "I'm sorry, I won't be able to attend" box marked with a firm "X."

"I understand you got conflicts, so you don't got to come to the engagement party," he said. "But you got to be a bridesmaid."

I laughed, because I was sure that he was joking. Then I remembered that Nicky didn't joke. In fact, he often said that a sense of humor was overrated, and always ignored me when I asked him, "How would you know?"

The laugh died in my mouth. "Now I know Veronica didn't agree to that."

"Veronica understands that I'm not walking down the aisle if you ain't there. Plus I'm letting James be one of my groomsmen."

I sat down. This could not be happening.

"You've got to do it, Davie," he said with a determined look on his face. "By the time the wedding rolls around, it'll be over a year since you two broke up. You was only dating four months. How long you planning on carrying that?"

Had it only been four months? It felt like it had been so much longer. "All right, I guess so," I said. "As long as I don't have to walk down the aisle with him or anything."

Nicky shrugged apologetically. "Thing is, Veronica don't have any real friends, so she only has two people to stand up for her. And Tammy got to walk with Leon."

"Why?" I asked.

He frowned at me. "Because Tammy's the maid of honor and Leon's my best man, fool."

I couldn't think of anything that I'd rather do less than walk down the aisle with a man who haunted my every unengaged, waking thought even though I could never have him again.

Still, Nicky had been a surrogate father to me. So I guessed I owed him one. Or several. And that's why I ended up agreeing not only to be a bridesmaid in the wedding of my worst enemy and my best friend, but also to go and try on bridesmaid dresses with Veronica and Tammy. Seriously, go figure.

# THIRTY

THREE WEEKS LATER I FOUND MYSELF waiting outside my clients' house for a field trip that had "excruciating disaster" written all over it.

At this point, my side business had turned into a full-blown career. After finishing up with Mike, I had helped his director friend, Hugh Phillips, with what turned out to be a minor bout of career ennui. After a week of living with him, I prescribed long walks and switching genres. That had led to a fevered adaptation of a German novel about a May-December couple on the verge of divorce. Hugh was so happy with how it all turned out that he recommended me to the writer who outlined the film for him.

I helped the writer get back in shape and finally stand up to his blue-collar father, who had a habit of calling him a sissy for making his money with the written word. Then the writer recommended me to a few of his friends. A couple of former power listers later, I was now living with a husband-and-wife team whose marriage and joint film-editing career were falling apart.

As it turned out, Hollywooders were totally cool with being guided by an admitted recovering psycho with no license. Who knew. And at two thousand dollars for the initial session and two thousand a week after that, business was booming. I acquired a used hybrid and put enough money into the bank to quit my job at the club. There are a lot of used-to-be-somebodies in Los Angeles, and I had a waiting list of would-be clients that could hypothetically keep me busy until 2011 if I decided to offer all of them what I was now calling my Career Therapy Services.

I had been forced to turn some celebrities down. There were a few initial sessions with people who weren't quite ready to listen or work as hard as they would need to in order to be happy. But for the most part, I was finding plenty of crazy rich people to tell what to do and how to either get over their various mental problems or use them to their advantage. And can I tell you what else? I absolutely loved my job.

Which was why I was already resenting having to take a whole afternoon off from my editor clients when the Farrell sisters pulled up in Veronica's Hummer. I got into the backseat and immediately felt out of place in my Strokes T-shirt and Bermuda shorts.

Veronica didn't say a word for the entire trip to some high-end bridal shop in Beverly Hills. But Tammy talked enough for both of them, chattering on and on about how exciting this was, and how they had found the perfect church in Glendale. And did I know that Vera Wang was designing Veronica's gown? They were so excited about that.

I glanced over at Veronica's cold, unchanging face after Tammy told me that, and wondered if she hadn't misjudged her sister's enthusiasm for all these details.

But out loud I said, "Oh my God, I can't believe that. Vera Wang, really?"

Yes, I was much more authentic these days, but I had always had a soft spot for people who dare to make conversation in the face of great tension. And it seemed too mean to ignore Tammy like Veronica was doing, though I was tempted, because Lord knew I did not want to be in this car with them. But I shook off all the negative thoughts, and smiled for Tammy. Today, I tried to convince myself, was actually a good day. Dreading this outing had meant that for once, I hadn't woken up thinking about James. So maybe that boded well for the rest of my participation in this wedding.

All I had to do was get through this dress nonsense, and the rest of the preparations, and maybe, just maybe, I wouldn't fall apart as soon as I saw James at the wedding rehearsal. Maybe.

But Veronica wasn't making it easy. Tammy and I must have tried on twenty different dresses at her fancy store, and she still hadn't found one that she liked on both of us.

"She just wants it to be perfect," Tammy said in the dressing room, as she zipped me into a dark silver Jordan Couture.

I was impressed that Tammy had enough innocence where Veronica was concerned to actually believe that the reason her sister had forced us to try on so many dresses was because she was just a stickler for perfection.

We walked out of the dressing room and posed in front of Veronica. She was sitting in a white overstuffed chair, her legs crossed at the ankle, like a princess on her throne. And the two shop attendants, hovering behind her, made the royal picture complete.

Veronica looked us over. "I like it on you, Tammy," she decided, then cut her eyes toward my dress, "But not on you."

At this point, she had already said this about all the other dresses, and I could feel that old familiar rage creeping up on me again. "Okay, I'm never going to look as good as Tammy in any of these dresses. She's a freaking model."

I would say a hush fell over the room, but it was already pretty quiet, since the shop was by-appointment-only, and we were the only ones there.

Still, the two attendants exchanged furtive glances over Veronica's head. They looked scared.

Veronica just folded her hands and told them, "These dresses aren't working. Do you have another designer for them?"

"Veronica," I tried again. "There's no such thing as a dress that will look good on both Tammy and me. If she looks like a swan in something, guaranteed it's going to make me look like a sausage roll."

"I'm sure you're wrong about that," Veronica answered. She dismissed the attendants with a nod, and they went scurrying out to the store floor to do her bidding.

I shook my head. "Okay, I'm done here. Tammy, could you unzip me?"

Tammy didn't move. "Just a few more dresses, Davie. We'll find something, I promise."

"Tammy," I said, trying to hide the fact that I was resisting the urge to punch Veronica. Again. "You're really nice, and I dig that about you. But could you please stop pretending that this is about dresses, and just unzip me so I can get out of here?"

I turned my back to her, offering her the dress zipper.

"Tammy, go ahead and unzip her," Veronica said. Then she asked me, "So what exactly do you think this is about?"

"You don't want the daughter of the woman your daddy used to keep on the side to be in your wedding. And quite frankly, I agree with you. Nicky has no business making you do this. But we're not in high school. I'm a grown-ass woman, and I can't let you torture me anymore."

Behind me, Tammy finished undoing the long zipper and I was released from the too-tight dress. "Thank you," I said, holding up the front with my lower arm. I went back to the inner dressing room to put my clothes back on.

When I came out, Tammy and Veronica were in the midst of a quiet argument—which cut off sharply as soon as they saw me.

"Don't go, Davie," Tammy pleaded. "I know Veronica can be difficult, but—"

"Stop making excuses for me," Veronica said, cutting her off. "I'm standing right here." Her gray eyes landed on me, flickering and flinty. Like a snake.

"Tammy is trying to convince me to apologize to you."

"Veronica, I don't need an apology." At that point, all I wanted or needed was to go home to my editors.

"And I've told her that no apology from me would ever be adequate. But it occurs to me that you may be confused about some things." Her next words sounded monotone, like she was reading from a piece of paper. "What I did to you in high school was wrong, and I shouldn't have done it. I've always been jealous of you, because you are better than me."

What? Come again? Did she say "better than" her? Was she kidding? "I'm not—"

Veronica took my hand, which shocked me into silence, because the only other time she had ever touched me was when she was trying to stab my eye out with a nail file. "You are better than me," she whispered, her voice harsh and accusing. "In every way. You're noble, and you're kind against the greatest odds. Nicky has told me a lot about you. I wasn't aware before that your mother was . . ." She searched and finally settled for ". . . abusive."

"Veronica . . ."

"Or that you came out here with so few resources. You should know that I respect and admire you, and if I could take back what happened in high school, I would. I should have told you this earlier, but I've been too embarrassed to address it. However, I am truly sorry. I hope you believe that."

For several moments, I simply did not know what to say, but then I had to ask, "How about trying to stab me in the eye? Are you sorry about that, too?"

Veronica burst out laughing. "Yes, of course! I was out of my mind. I don't know why I . . ." She trailed off. "Well, I guess I do know why. It was because I've always wanted to actually be the perfect family we presented to the world. And then I found out about your mother. And then you tried to take my brother. And just when I thought I had it all under control, the one secret I had tried to keep quiet comes to light, courtesy of your little friend. I felt like you had destroyed my family."

"I had nothing to do with that story."

"I know. Nicky told me that, too. So did Tammy."

"Veronica . . ." I said again.

Sixteen years. I had hated this woman for sixteen years. And now look at what she had done. Gone and apologized.

I didn't realize the truth of my next words until they were tumbling out of my mouth. "I'm glad you did it. And I actually appreciate you for making me run away from Mississippi. Because that was the bravest thing I've ever done. I was strong before I met you, but you taught me how to be brave, Veronica Farrell. Even when I didn't want to be. You forced me to be better than I was. And I'm grateful for that, because being brave and strong is what's gotten me to where I am now."

Before I could fully finish, Veronica did something that I had never in my wildest imaginings thought she would ever do. She hugged me. Yes, she did. She hugged me right there in that fancy Beverly Hills dressing room. Then Tammy hugged both of us, her cheeks wet with tears. "This is so nice," she cried. "It's just like an episode of *Oprah*."

ABOUT A MONTH later, Mike Barker called for his weekly check-in. Now that he had graduated to living on his own, I made him call me every week for a little chat.

"Hey, darlin', how's the East Coast?" I asked when I picked up his call.

"Cold as hell. It's supposed to be fall, but I'm walking around in a snow coat. "

"Are you wearing a hat? Hugh will not be happy if you up and get sick."

Hugh had decided to set his adaptation of the German novel in the academic town of Northampton, Massachusetts, and he had hired Mike to play the struggling couple's therapist, who also happened to be having an affair with the young wife. It was a stretch in the right direction on the comeback road for Mike, and both he and Hugh were getting huge buzz for going outside their comfort zones.

"Yeah, I got a hat," he said. "I had to buy it myself. This movie has like no budget."

"Be grateful." Part of my job now was to remind Mike that he didn't deserve any of this and that comebacks weren't ordained, but a privilege.

"I'm grateful. I'm being grateful all over the place. But I'm going to regain that weight I think. My food service don't deliver out here."

I made a mental note to check in with Mrs. Murphy, the maternal, middle-aged personal assistant that Mike had acquired after I moved out of his house. Between the two of us, we should be able to find another diet food program that would be willing to FedEx him healthier food.

"Other than weight gain, what else is going on?" I asked.

"I'm going to the New York premiere of that new LaTrell Green movie this weekend."

Mike was the second person to say something about that new movie by hot playwright-turned-writer-director LaTrell Green. Tammy had mentioned in passing that Farrell Men had bought product placement in the film, and that all the male characters would be using Farrell products prominently at various points in the movie.

An idea popped into my head. "Really? New York, you say. Do you have a date?"

"Not yet. But I'm working on a few things. There's a cute little PA who's still wearing mini-skirts, even though it's arctic-level cold out. I think she's trying to impress me. And it's working."

"She sounds very classy, Mike, but would you mind taking Erica London if I paid for her hotel and air?"

"Erica London? Really?" I could almost see Mike frowning on the other side of the line. "Is this another atonement project?"

"Yeah. She hasn't exactly been open to me trying to make things up to her."

That was actually an understatement. Not only had she hung up on me every time I tried to get her on the phone, but when I showed up at her apartment, she had called me a "creepy-ass freak" and threatened to file a restraining order if I ever came near her again.

But like I said, I am a very patient girl, and I had known that if I just laid low long enough, an opportunity for atonement would present itself. Maybe being seen with Mike would give her star a much-needed boost. Plus I knew that James would definitely be at the premiere, too.

"Sure, I can do that for you," Mike said. "Call Mrs. Murphy, she'll set it up. And don't worry about the hotel and whatever. I got it."

Now that Mike had kicked his hundred-grand-a-month gambling habit, he could afford to be generous.

Still, I gave him a bunch of thanks for his help before getting off the phone. Erica might be able to ignore me, but it was pretty much physically impossible for a D-list actress to turn down an invitation from an A-list actor. There was no way she'd refuse to go out to New York for the premiere, even if she knew I was involved.

I pulled out the MacBook Air laptop that I had purchased a couple of months ago to drag around with me on my home stays. Then I typed the following letter:

*Dear Erica,*

*I know that what I did was unforgivable, but I hope this trip starts to make up for it. As you've probably figured out by now, giving up James was a huge mistake on your part. I hope with age that you've come to see that his love is worth more than a TV series. In fact, I'm sure that you see that now.*

*I've arranged for you to attend a movie premiere with Mike Barker. James will also be attending this premiere, and I hope that you take this next piece of advice as far as dealing with him goes. DO NOT PLAY GAMES. Do not wait for him to come to you. Seek him out and say this: "James, I am very sorry about breaking off our engagement. It was a terrible thing to do, and I will never ever lie to you again."*

*And then from that moment forward, be honest with him in everything you do.*

*Per your stated wish, this is the last that you will ever hear from me. Good luck.*

*Respectfully,*
*Davie Jones*

I pushed the save icon on the Word doc and titled it "Letter for Erica London." Then I attached it to an e-mail to Mrs. Murphy and asked that she set up the trip and also that she overnight the tickets to Erica along with a physical copy of my letter.

Maybe Erica would actually open it if it looked like the letter was from Mike. And maybe after she read it, she'd take my advice. Letting James go notwithstanding, Erica was a smart enough girl. She might just listen to me.

That thought—the thought of this plan actually working—made me sick to my stomach. My mouse pointer hovered for several seconds over the send button on the e-mail to Mrs. Murphy. Then I reminded myself that Erica was my second-to-last atonement.

I swallowed my nausea and clicked send.

# THIRTY-ONE

A FEW MONTHS AFTER THE ERICA London Atonement, Veronica switched our Girls' Night from James's old place to Nicky's house. This was a night that she, Tammy, and me were supposed to spend drinking martinis and collating the specially designed, one-of-a-kind invitations for her wedding, so I was immediately suspicious. Up until this point, she had been militant about not letting Nicky see any of the stuff we were doing for the wedding. Not because she wanted to surprise him or anything, but because Nicky always had an opinion about everything, and they both had such strong personalities that there was a real chance they wouldn't make it to the altar if Nicky decided to weigh in too heavily.

They didn't fight that much, but when they did, from what Tammy had told me, it was a nasty piece of business; they both had that habit of going from tropical breeze to arctic winter in zero seconds flat.

I often wondered who was on top when they had sex, but so far, I hadn't gotten up the courage to ask. In fact, I still wasn't comfortable enough in my and Veronica's unexpected friendship to ask her much of anything, which is why I waited until she went to make us a second round of martinis before I questioned Tammy about the Girls' Night location switch.

"So why did Veronica want to meet all the way over here? I don't know if we're going to get done before Nicky comes home from the club. Plus,

I'm closer to your side of town now." I was living with a once-famous musician in Atwater, which was right next door to Los Feliz.

Tammy lowered her eyes. "Well, um . . ." She took a deep breath. "No offense, but . . . James is back in town."

I was so glad I was dark-skinned at that moment, because I'm sure I would have visibly paled if I had been any other shade. "Really?" I said. "I thought he was going to stay in New York for a while."

"Um, he was, but Gusteau wants to test market some new Farrell Men products in Los Angeles, so he's back out here to oversee that."

I was confused. Why all the secrecy? "So he's just visiting for a few weeks?"

"It's a whole line, so it's going to take a while. He'll probably be here all the way up to the wedding. In fact, he might stay on indefinitely after that since he can work out of either office. He's not sure yet."

I could hear in the hesitant way Tammy was talking that there was something more she wasn't saying. "Were you planning on telling me this? Like ever?"

Tammy set down the invitation she was putting together. "Yeah, I wanted to tell you, but Veronica didn't think we needed to say anything, because she didn't want things to get awkward. He's, um . . . seeing that actress again."

My heart dropped with a sick thud. "Erica London?"

"Yeah." Tammy was wringing her hands and looking everywhere but at me now. "I didn't really like her the first time around, but she seems a lot better now. They got back together at the New York premiere of that LaTrell Green movie. James says he's giving her another chance, because this time she promised to be honest with him."

Now it was my turn to give up on putting together the heavy vellum invitations. "Wow."

Tammy reached across the dining room table and put a sympathetic hand on top of mine. "Be happy for him. He seems better these days. More at peace. If you had seen him after you two broke up, you'd be happy for him now."

I took my hand away from hers and got up from the table, nearly colliding with Veronica, who was coming back into the dining room with a tray of martinis.

"What's going on?" she asked, when she saw the look on my face.

"I have to go," I said.

Veronica turned on Tammy. "Did you tell her?"

"She asked," Tammy answered. "What did you want me to do? Lie?"

"It's okay," I said to both of them. "I just need to . . . go."

"I can't believe you told her." Veronica threw her sister a baleful look. Then she said to me, "No, Davie, you're staying here. We've still got a lot of work to do on the invitations. You're my bridesmaid. This is your duty."

I no longer had the mental energy to engage in an argument with Veronica. I just grabbed my purse from where I had deposited it on the table and rushed out the door, not stopping to retrieve my coat from the closet where Veronica had hung it.

I wasn't suffocating, but I had to work on breathing. In fact, something inside of me wanted to hold my breath until it hurt, wanted to hold my breath until James dating Erica London again was no longer true.

I got in my car and drove back to my apartment. I couldn't let the Atwater musician I was staying with now see me like this. I was supposed to be the professional in our relationship, and I didn't want him to see me this upset over a guy I had only dated for four months, a guy who had dumped me over a year ago.

But I had loved James for almost forever. Even before I knew him, I waited for him and I loved him. And now he was back in Los Angeles, and he was dating a woman who had chosen a TV series and a puff piece in *Celeb Weekly* over him. And now he would probably marry her. And I would never ever have my Molly Ringwald Ending.

I pulled into the club parking lot and got out of the car, but I didn't go up to my apartment. Instead, my thoughts chased me out to the busy sidewalk, and the next thing I knew, I was walking up Vine in short angry strides, my arms folded around me. The night air was nippy and I was only wearing a yellow vest over my usual Strokes T-shirt.

But I didn't go back for a jacket. I kept on walking. It occurred to me for the first time in years: Life is hard. Even when it looks easy, it's hard. And you know what? The problem with knowing you're insane is that you can no longer do anything truly crazy, because you can see your imagined actions for what they are: psycho.

But my heart was screaming for me to go to James. *Go to him now and get him to take you back.*

My brain also wanted to see him, but for different reasons. On some perverse level, it wanted to see him happy with Erica London so that I could stop carrying around this constant guilt over what I had done to him. My brain wanted me to stop longing for him before I went to sleep at night. It wanted me to stop thinking about him every time I heard some Muzak eighties song in an elevator or at the grocery store. It was time for the obsession with James to stop once and for all. That would be the best thing for me, my brain insisted.

My brain and my heart warred until I was in front of the Metrolink station. Then a crystal-clear idea formed: a note. I would go to his house and leave him a note like the one I had given him in high school.

THE COOL OCTOBER night air bit into my skin, when I emerged from the Metrolink station on Vermont. And as I hiked up the commercial street toward the Los Feliz Hills, I couldn't help but dwell on the fact that I had been replaced by the woman who plays the smiling black wife in antacid commercials. A woman who was all unblemished light skin, glossy weave, and artificially whitened teeth. A woman who was not me.

Tears sprang to my eyes again, and I kept my head down as I walked past Figaro, a French restaurant with outdoor seating. I could hear people laughing and talking. And I could feel the heat lamps, radiating the fake warmth over the entire scene.

I stopped near the empty hostess stand. I was determined to make it all the way up to James's house, but my teeth were chattering, and I needed a moment to get warm again. I stared into the traffic on the bustling street, trying to compose the perfect note that would fix everything with James, a note that:

1. Would not be creepy.
2. Would not move James to take out a restraining order against me. And
3. Would make James want to take me back.

Did the words that could fit all three of those criteria actually exist? I wondered. Was there any such thing or was it like a Molly Ringwald Ending—a complete myth?

"Excuse me! We need some more sparkling water."

I froze. I recognized the voice immediately, could still remember it yelling over her condo's intercom that it could and would call the police if I ever showed up at her building again.

"Excuse me," she repeated. "Did you hear me? We need more water."

I turned around. *God*, I thought. *If you love me, love me in any way whatsoever, please do not let James be sitting with this little girl at that table.*

God did not love me.

"Davie?" James said, when I turned around. "You work here?"

"No," I said. My voice felt tremulous and very far away, like it was coming from somewhere else completely. "I don't work here. I was just standing here, trying to get warm."

They both stared at me, and even I could see how bad, how stalkerish it looked for me to just happen to show up at the same place where they were having dinner, especially since I didn't actually live in this neighborhood.

Erica cut her eyes toward James. "We should go . . ."

She hadn't fully taken my advice, I realized, because though she had promised to be honest with him, she obviously hadn't told him about me arranging for her to be at the premiere and counseling her on handling James.

Her eyes were darting from me to James like she was scared, which was frustrating because I'm sure she was actually more frightened of me telling James what I had done for her than of me going crazy on them. But it was coming off to James like she was scared of me, because I was a psycho stalker.

I hadn't expected—or gotten—a thank-you note from Erica, but I also hadn't expected her to deliberately mislead James about my role in their reunion.

James pulled out his wallet. "We have a movie to catch," he said.

He was careful not to say which movie, I noticed. Was he scared that I'd follow them there, too? This was a fucking nightmare.

The note that I had been trying to compose slipped away like a day-dream on a cloud of what-ifs.

"James, I'm not stalking you . . ." I cleared my throat. " . . . again. You won't see me until the rehearsal dinner, I promise. I mean unless we run into each other at the ArcLight. I always run into people at the ArcLight." I stopped myself before my babbling went too far. "The point is that you don't have to worry about me bothering you."

James unstiffened, but just a little. "I get it, Davie. It's okay. We have to get used to seeing each other. Occasionally."

"Because of Veronica and Nicky."

He relaxed a little more and shook his head. "I never saw that one coming, huh?"

I laughed. "Me either. But now it kind of makes sense. They're really happy together."

He nodded in agreement. "Yeah, I've never seen Ronnie this happy. They're lucky they found each other."

Erica took ahold of his arm. "We have to go, or we're going to miss the previews."

James looked like he was caught between politeness and duty. He might have lost his accent, but he was still a Southern gentleman through and through. He always, I realized, had been a very nice boy.

"Go," I said. "The previews are the best part."

He gave me a grateful half smile. Then he tossed a few bills on the table and started to walk away with Erica.

But someone who I can only describe as Me-But-Better-Than-Me called out, "James."

He turned around. I could see a list of all the things I had done to him, said to him, and kept from him hanging between us, written in red on the air.

"I just wanted you to know that I didn't do the stuff I did because you deserved it. I know that's what I said, but it's not true." I stated this part more emphatically than I meant to. "I did what I did because I never deserved you. You're a good guy, and I hope you have a great life."

"Um . . . thanks."

He looked somewhat taken aback by my fierce tone, but for once I wasn't flooded with embarrassment. It had been the right thing to say. I knew that. For the first time in my life I had said exactly the right thing. Out loud.

And as I watched him turn back around and walk away with Erica, I realized that they were a good couple. They were the same kind of attractive, they liked to do the same things, and they occupied the same universe. They belonged together.

My stomach clenched, but for the first time since we had broken up, I didn't feel the driving need to go to him, be with him. From the beginning, when I had fallen in love with him at the age of fifteen, I had always been consumed with what I had wanted. He had just been a player in the story. I had never really cared about what James wanted, what he needed.

But now I could see him clearly. And I knew what he needed.

He needed for me to let him go.

And so I did.

This was my last atonement. He would move on with his life, and I would move on with mine. I would start dating again and eventually marry and start a family of my own. And in time he would become a bittersweet memory. Like my mother. Tucked away with all the other lessons that life had taught me.

The sadness that had been dogging me for the last year lifted, and I was finally warm again. In fact, I had never felt so clean.

I took the Metrolink back to Vine, and I stopped by the Borders near my place to purchase my very own DVD copy of *Sixteen Candles*. I hadn't been able to bring myself to watch it or any other Molly Ringwald movie since I had run away from Mississippi. But I could feel new strength running through me as I got back in my car and returned to Nicky's house in Baldwin Hills.

When Veronica opened the door to Nicky's house, I held up the movie and said, "This is my favorite movie of all time, and I haven't seen it in many, many years. Can we watch it while we finish up your invitations?"

Veronica took the movie out of my hand. "*Sixteen Candles*. Sure, I like that movie, too. We can move the invitations into the front room and watch it." Then she regarded me with actual concern. "Are you okay?"

"I'm better than okay," I answered as I stepped past her into the house. "I'm happy."

Veronica arched her eyebrow. "Then why does it look like you're about to cry?"

"Because I'm happy," I said. "And I always cry at happy endings."

"Me too," said Tammy, coming into the front room. Her eyes widened when she saw the DVD in my hands. "Ooh, is that *Sixteen Candles*? I love that movie."

## THIRTY-TWO

ON CHRISTMAS MORNING, I WOKE UP in the guest room of a condo owned by a former black child star who had gotten out of rehab for the third time last July and was ready to get her career back.

It was raining outside. Hard with thunder and everything. That would have been okay, except it was also the day of Nicky and Veronica's wedding. So I called Veronica, because I knew she would be freaking out.

"It's raining," she said in a clipped voice when she answered the phone.

"Yes, I know. But it's going to be okay."

"Yesterday the weather report claimed that it was going to be sunny. But now they're saying that it's actually going to be raining off and on all day. Idiots."

You know how they say, "It never rains in Southern California"? Well, that's a straight-up lie. It often rains in the winter here. Even on Christmas.

"Yes, but your wedding's all inside. You've just got to get from the limo to the church. I'll hold the umbrella for you."

"How am I supposed to get from the limo to inside the church in ballet slippers and a full train without getting wet?"

Good question, which I didn't exactly know the answer to, but I said, "We'll figure it out." Which is a line that had served me well in my new career when my clients asked me things like, "How am I going to get that director whose wife I slept with when I was high on ecstasy to take me off his blacklist?"

Suddenly Veronica's voice went from angry to vulnerable. "I know I said you didn't have to be here until one, but could you come now?"

I looked at the clock. It was eight A.M., which meant that Veronica wanted me to hold her hand for like five more hours than originally planned.

"Well, I have my hair appointment," I said.

"Tammy's on the phone with your stylist now. She says that she'd be more than happy to come here to do your hair."

I blinked. "Really, Pearl agreed to that? Even though it's Christmas?"

"We made it worth her while," Veronica assured me, back to her cold voice. "Can I expect you soon?"

"Well, I have to shower," I tried again.

"We have showers here, too. I'm sure you're aware of that."

Fine, if she was going to say it like that, I guess I had to just tell her the true reason I was stalling.

"Um . . . is James there yet?"

So far, I had been lucky. I hadn't run into him again in the months leading up to the wedding. And three days ago, James had gotten called away to a product development meeting at Gusteau's Paris headquarters. Apparently Farrell Men was doing so well in the USA that they wanted to discuss a worldwide product launch. It was a huge deal for James's line, but it meant that he had to miss all the planned festivities leading up to the wedding, including the bachelor party and the rehearsal dinner. Although I was mostly at peace after letting James go, I couldn't say that I minded not having to see him until we walked down the aisle.

But on the other end of the line, Veronica didn't sound too happy with my hedging. "Does it matter?" she asked. "Does your coming right now or not depend on it?"

"Of course not," I lied quickly. Yes, I was trying to be more authentic, but old habits die hard.

"Then, no, he's not here yet. His plane doesn't land until two P.M."

I didn't say what I was thinking—that two P.M. was cutting it awfully close for a four P.M. wedding. I'm sure Veronica was already well aware of that and that it was probably one of the reasons for her current worse-than-usual mood.

And I knew her mother wouldn't be much help. Veronica's parents were still officially together, but Mrs. Farrell was currently residing at Farrell Manor while Congressman Farrell stayed at their home in Washington, D.C.

After the cheating story broke, he just barely managed to get reelected, but much like her daughter, Mrs. Farrell couldn't bear being humiliated. Other than hosting a small bridal shower in Mississippi, she had opted out of most of the wedding festivities and at last night's rehearsal dinner had announced that she would meet us at the church.

It made me sad for both her and Veronica that her own disillusionment left her unable to enjoy Veronica's special day.

"I'll be there in like twenty," I said, just deciding to give in.

"Yes, we'll see you then," Veronica said in such a brusque way that you'd think she hadn't just totally manipulated me into coming early.

Then she hung up. I looked at my now dead cell phone. If I hadn't grown to honestly like Veronica, I could have easily kept the hate alive. I threw back the covers and got out of bed.

I ARRIVED AT the Los Feliz house and immediately had to start putting out so many fires that I actually forgot about James's impending arrival.

First I came out of the shower to find Veronica chastising Pearl for being late, which, in the world of black hairstylists, is the equivalent of chastising the ocean for being wet.

"Bitch, it's Christmas," Pearl yelled back. "I could be at home in Mississippi right now with my family. But I'm not flying out until tonight, because of you."

"Yes, and we're compensating you extremely well for it. So get to work, before I decide to start docking your pay."

Pearl was not a celebrity hairdresser, so she wasn't exactly used to catering to folks. She stared at Veronica for an angry, hot second, then she said, "*You* are crazy. I'm leaving."

She started gathering up her things from on top of Tammy's dresser where we had set up an impromptu station for her to do my hair.

"Pearl, please don't go," I said.

"If you leave," Veronica added in such imperious tones that you could have mistaken her for the Queen of England easy, "I will sue you for breach of contract. Get to work now."

Pearl really started throwing things back into her backpack after Veronica made that threat. "Sue me," she said with wide, daring eyes. "I don't make that much money. Good luck trying to get shit from me."

"Whoa, Pearl." I got in front of her and spread my arms to bar her exit.

"Pearl, you're right. Veronica is literally crazy in a maybe-should-be-institutionalized sort of way." Then I said, "Shut up, Veronica," when the older Farrell sister opened her mouth to protest.

I pleaded with Pearl. "She should be pitied, not taken seriously. But you know it is physically impossible for me to get all of this hair pressed straight and into a bun without you. And you know how much I appreciate you delaying your trip. So if you stay, we'll reimburse you for your plane ticket home, okay?"

Pearl hesitated. On top of what she was charging for doing my hair on a holiday and the extra money she was getting for coming to us in Los Feliz, a plane ticket was hard to turn down. "Is she really crazy?"

"Yes," I assured Pearl. "But she's also extremely rich, so she doesn't know that she's crazy."

"I don't have to listen to this," Veronica said. "It's my wedding day."

Then she huffed out of the room.

Thereby fully proving my point.

"Girl, how did you get roped into this shit?" Pearl asked. She went back to the makeshift station, and started pulling out her hair tools again.

"Girl," I answered truthfully, "I still don't know."

It took Pearl longer than it should have to do my hair, because right before she was fixing to pin my newly straightened hair into a bun, Tammy came running into the room, crying.

"I hate her. I hate her so much!"

I gathered Tammy into my arms. "What's wrong?"

"She yelled at me for taking my hem up too high. It's only three inches, and now she's threatening to not let me walk down the aisle."

"Tammy, I'm sure she doesn't mean it."

I would've soothed her further, but then I saw the wedding coordinator run past the door and down the hallway in tears, so I had to leave Tammy and run that poor woman down to tell her what I had told Pearl about Veronica being crazy.

The wedding coordinator was a former actress who had parlayed her entertainment contacts into a very successful wedding and event planning service, but "I have never dealt with a client that is as verbally abusive as this one. She told me that I was the worst service person she had ever encountered and then she said since I wasn't good at my current job and I couldn't even make it as an actress did I really have any reason to live?"

Repeating that question set her off on a fresh wave of tears. Only Veronica could push a person into a full-on existential crisis with just one question. It took me more than thirty minutes to talk the wedding coordinator out of quitting.

Seriously, if I had known Veronica would go this buck-wild bridezilla before her wedding, I would have charged her my hourly rate.

But somehow I managed to shore Tammy up, get my hair and makeup done, and put on the strapless, gray, floor-length bridesmaid dress that had somehow managed to look good on both Tammy and me.

We were finally about to head out the door at 3:30 P.M. with Veronica looking like the iciest, most beautiful vision that had ever walked down a wedding aisle. Then Tammy wrinkled her cute little nose and asked, "Wasn't James supposed to be here by now?"

THE RAIN HAD paused briefly, and as we shuffled Veronica into the limo, she yelled at Tammy for not saying anything earlier.

"I didn't think about it earlier," Tammy wailed back, as if Veronica was actually still a human being who was capable of being reasoned with at this point.

I let them argue, while I hit up Paul on my cell phone.

"I don't know what could have happened to him, ma'am," Paul said. "His flight from France was delayed, but when it finally landed he was not on the plane. I am checking into it now."

"Okay, just call me as soon as you know." By now Veronica was going apeshit on Tammy, screaming so loudly that I was sure Paul could hear her. "Veronica's anxious."

"Yes, I understand. I'll call you as soon as I know something."

I hung up with Paul in time to stop Veronica from hyperventilating. I wrapped one hand around both of her thin wrists and I used my other hand to rub her back.

"It'll be all right and he'll be here soon," I said over and over again like a chant until her breathing returned to normal.

AS IT TURNED out, I lied. We got to the church at four P.M. on the d.o.t. Then another hour and a half passed, before Paul delivered the bad news. When James had discovered that his scheduled flight from Paris was delayed, he had opted for another flight but then had missed his connection. He had managed to find another plane headed to L.A. and was able to book a seat in coach—Paul paused after relaying that bit of information, like it hurt him to think of his young employer actually having to fly international with the common people—but the plane was only now just landing at LAX. There was no way he'd get to Glendale in anything less than an hour.

I relayed this information to Veronica in the same tone of voice that military commanders use to deliver bad news to the family of a fallen soldier.

"What!" Veronica screamed.

I was sure the entire church could hear her.

Then she let out a string of curses, so loud and so long that Leon showed up at the door to the back room where we were waiting.

"Is everything okay?" he asked, with a worried look on his face.

Veronica broke off cursing, and stared at him with cold, brittle eyes. "No, everything is not okay, you undereducated, ape ex-con. My brother is not here yet, and I want to cry, but I can't, because there's no one here to reapply my makeup."

Leon looked both hurt and confused.

"Um, could you tell Congressman Farrell to get in position, and also grab one of Nicky's male friends from the audience?" I said. "Anyone who's wearing a plain black tux, with no colors, and tell him to come back here?"

Veronica was already shaking her head as he left. "No, we can't do this without my brother."

I pulled her to her feet and started adjusting her veil. "We're going to have to. These people have already been waiting for an hour and a half. That's a long time, even for a black wedding."

"But it won't be perfect without him." Veronica's voice sounded small now, like the little girl she had probably never allowed herself to be.

"Sure it will," I answered with a gentle smile.

Veronica's mouth starting wobbling. It looked like she was trying to decide whether to cry or bare her teeth in anger.

While she was busy with that, I told Tammy to get in position with Leon, who had just returned with Pete, a small, skinny guy I recognized as one of Nicky's cousins. He still sported an eighties-era high-top fade, and he was a couple of inches shorter than me, but hey, at least he was family—and wearing a straightforward tuxedo.

I nodded to the wedding coordinator, who had been cowering outside the open church doors beside Veronica's waiting father this entire time. Seeing my cue, she waved to the violin quintet, who started playing the bridal processional.

I sent Tammy and Leon down the aisle and told her father to get into position at the top of the aisle.

"No, no, no!" Veronica kept whispering behind me as I gave out orders. She had the Veronica Farrell in the Mirror Eyes again.

I turned and took her hand, tugging her over to just beyond the church doors where the audience couldn't see us. "You have to," I said in a firm voice.

"Whatever." She snatched her hand out of mine. "You're just jealous. You're glad my wedding to your ex-boyfriend has been ruined, because you're still mad I exposed you to James."

Again, she was so loud that the entire church could hear her.

I smiled and let out a huge sigh of relief. "Oh God, girl, I was hoping you'd say something completely off-the-hook bitchy like that, because I wasn't sure if I could do it."

Her eyes narrowed. Veronica's confused, angry, and suspicious looks were pretty much all the same, so I couldn't tell which emotion she was feeling right now.

"Do what?" she demanded.

I shoved her ass through the church doors and sent her stumbling into the arms of her waiting father.

Seeing her, the violinists abruptly stopped and switched to the wedding march.

Everybody stood, and Veronica had no choice but to go forward.

And, bless her little heart, she untangled herself from her father and started walking as if this had been exactly what she had intended to do all along.

But halfway down the aisle, she turned to look back to where I was now standing in the church doorway, and she arched her eyebrow at me. I hoped this meant that she understood and forgave me for pushing her.

"Are we supposed to go, too?" Nicky's cousin asked beside me. His voice was squeaky, and pitched unnaturally high for a guy.

"No," I answered. I watched Veronica take Nicky's hand and turn to the preacher. "We're just fine right here."

THE CEREMONY LASTED about sixty minutes. And even though it was raining again, I gathered with the rest of the crowd to throw black magic rose petals as Veronica and Nicky came out of the church.

Veronica was laughing now, and she squeezed my hand when she and Nicky ran past me to the limousine.

She didn't even wait for me to open an umbrella for her. She ran with Nicky to the limo, her train dragging behind her in the rain puddles.

That's when I knew that she and Nicky would make it. As crazy, mean, and cynical as they both were, they were so in love.

After the limo pulled away, I started to go down the stairs toward where Mama Jane had parked her Dodge pickup on the street. She was driving me over to the reception since I had come over in the limo with Veronica.

But then I realized that I didn't have my clutch and figured that I must have left it in the church's back room.

"I forgot my purse inside," I said to Mama Jane. "I'll meet you at the truck."

"All right, baby," she said, already loosening up the bow tie she wore with her tuxedo. I had never seen Mama Jane outside of the most casual wear, and I knew that this black-tie wedding with its dressing-up business couldn't be fun for her.

I went back inside and found my clutch on the table, where I could now remember tossing it, after I had gotten off the phone with Paul. At that moment I had only been concerned about breaking the bad news to Veronica.

But all's well that ends well.

I bumped into Nicky's cousin putting the programs into a box outside in the foyer. "It was a beautiful wedding," he said, in that weird helium voice of his.

"Yes, it was," I answered.

And as I walked outside, I saw that the day had now become beautiful, too.

It was like as soon as Veronica had agreed to get her dress wet, the sun had decided to come out and shine down on us.

Down the street, I could see Mama Jane, smoking a cigarette while she waited for me by her truck.

And in front of me, the last of the wedding guests were pulling out of street parking and driving toward Beverly Hills for the reception.

But as the last car pulled away, I noticed that there was one guy, staying put, dressed in a well-cut tuxedo and leaning against the door of his car. He kind of looked like James.

Then the last car pulled away, and I realized that it actually was James, leaning against his Jake Ryan Porsche.

He was looking straight at me. In fact, he lifted his hand and gave me a hesitant wave.

I looked over my shoulder to see if there was maybe someone standing behind me, somebody that James Farrell would actually want to wave at.

But there was nobody there. I turned back. There had to be some mistake. "Me?" I asked, pointing at myself with my bouquet.

He laughed and mouthed back, "Yeah, you," as he made his way across the street.

I was not sixteen. Let me repeat this: I was not sixteen. And I was deeply aware that my last birthday cake had thirty-two candles, not sixteen on it. But still . . .

I came down the steps to meet him. We both stopped short about two feet away from each other on the sidewalk.

"Hi," we both started to say at the same time and cut off.

Then I tried again. "Hi," I said.

He smiled and answered, "Hi."

"Um, what are you doing here?" I asked. "The reception's in Beverly Hills."

"Yeah, but . . ." He looked down at his shoes, then back up at me. "Tammy told me you were still here."

I stared at him, completely stunned. "You came here for me?" I asked.

"Yeah," James said, holding my gaze. "Is that okay?"

I can't say tears didn't fill my eyes right then, but I will always give myself credit for keeping it together enough to say my next line. "Yeah," I whispered. "It's okay."

"So, do you have a ride to the reception?"

"Yes," I said. "I mean, no. I mean . . ." I couldn't look him in the eye as I said this next thing. "Where's Erica?"

"We broke up," he answered. "A month ago. Tammy didn't tell you?"

"No, we don't really talk about . . . you."

James shrugged. "Well, Erica and I were a little different than I remembered. It didn't work out. Plus . . ." He pulled a red napkin out of his pocket and placed it in my hand. "I never got my birthday gift."

I looked down at the napkin. It read:

Tonight, Davie Jones will do this to James Farrell:
1. Give him the best blow job ever.
2. Say yes to spending the rest of her life with him.
3. Tell him all of her secrets.

# Acknowledgments

SO many people to thank:

Thanks to my sister and first reader, Elizabeth Carter.

Thanks to my first editor, Karin Gutman.

Thanks to Emily Farrell. So far you've shown me the attic at Tyler House, put me up for two weeks while I searched for a summer sublet in L.A., and copyedited my first novel. You are in every way that counts such a good friend.

Thanks to Jessica Sinsheimer for picking me out of the slush pile.

Thanks to Sarah Jane Freymann for being such a wonderful agent and also for taking me out for the best lunch I've ever had in New York City.

Thanks to Maya Ziv for coaching me through all the details.

Thanks to Dawn Davis for being the editor of my dreams and so easy to talk to!

Thanks to my father for always proudly quoting the limerick I wrote in third grade every time I see him.

Thanks to my extended family for being there after my mother could not.

Thanks to Marilyn Friedman and the many good folks at Writing Pad in L.A. for encouraging me through my first rewrite.

Thanks to Gudrun Cram-Drach for reading everything I send her, asking the right questions, and always inspiring me to write some more.

Thanks to my mother-in-law, Mary Zimmerman, for taking care of Betty during my negotiations with the muse and also for making coffee whenever I say I'm too tired to write.

Thanks to Monique M. King-Viehland for being the best friend in the history of ever and for always jumping up and down with me whenever I get good news, even though we are both grown and live thousands of miles apart. You remain the most amazing woman I know.

Most of all, thanks to my husband, Christian Hibbard. It's your love that makes me believe in true romance and it's your support that makes me brave.

Also, thank YOU so very much for reading this story. I hope you liked it.

100% Love,
etc

# About the Author

Ernessa T. Carter has worked as an ESL teacher in Japan, a music journalist in Pittsburgh, a payroll administrator in Burbank, and a radio writer for *American Top 40 with Ryan Seacrest* in Hollywood. She is also a retired member of the L.A. Derby Dolls roller derby league. She graduated from Smith College and from Carnegie Mellon University's MFA program. *32 Candles* is her first novel. Find out more about the book and read her blog at www.32candles.com.

# A Reading Group Guide for *32 Candles*

1. Davie's high school experiences affect her for the rest of her life. How influential were your high school years on your adult life?

2. Davie doesn't speak for the first third of the book. How does her chosen muteness serve her? How does it continue to affect her personality after she starts speaking again?

3. Is Davie a trustworthy narrator? Why or why not?

4. Davie ends up becoming best friends with her ex-boyfriend. Do you think that exes can really be friends?

5. Many of Davie's worst qualities are also her best qualities. Do you have any experience with vices actually proving to be talents?

6. Davie isn't able to move on with her own life until she confronts the pain of her past, including her relationship with her mother. Is it necessary to face the people who have hurt you most in order to live a full life? What may—or may not—happen if we don't?

7. Do you think that Davie's mother loved her? Do you think that Davie loves her mother? Why is it difficult for people to sometimes show love? What holds them back?

8. At one point Davie insists that she couldn't have acted in any other way because of who she is and the life that she has lived. What does she mean by this? Is our history the most important influence on our future? Can we "will" ourselves into a future markedly different from our pasts?

9.  Davie talks a lot about passionate love being an "Invitation to Crazy." Do you agree with her? Have you ever been handed an Invitation to Crazy?

10. Davie loves her deceased grandmother very much and mentions her throughout the book. What do you think about her grandmother? Do your feelings change by the end of the book? How do your feelings toward Davie's grandmother change?

11. The author portrays several substitute-family relationships in this book. Discuss these and explore their dynamics. Is it human nature to form these kinds of relationships when real parent-child ones fail?

12. What do you believe the future holds for Davie and James?

13. Veronica is a complicated bully. Did your feelings toward her change throughout the book?

14. Davie's circumstances change a great deal from the beginning of the story until the end, but one might argue that she herself does not. Discuss.

15. Davie sometimes compares herself to her mother. Is she anything like her mother? How?

16. Davie falls so in love with the movie *Sixteen Candles* that it literally changes her life. Has a movie—or other art form such as a play or novel—ever changed your life in this way? How?

17. Davie mentions her love for the novel *The Color Purple* because its hero, Celie, is dark-skinned and manages to achieve a happy ending. Does Davie achieve her own happy ending? Are we too caught up in the idea of happiness? How can we appreciate happiness if we don't experience sadness or loss? Have any literary characters inspired you in this way?